SAVING SOUTH

A ROCKER ROMANCE

AMY J. HEART

For Joanne

as South would say

she knows why

COPYRIGHT

1

MIA

Mad Wolf

N o one grows up planning to become a stalker. It happens quite by accident. How do I know this? Because I am one. An accidental stalker. Let me back up a little and explain.

The first time I saw South, I spilled coffee over my favorite dress. It was lunchtime, and I'd just parked my butt down at a cafe near work, flipped over a music magazine, and *boom* there he was on the cover. One tiny glimpse of him and along with my glittery eighties frock, I was ruined.

The coffee spillage was a sign. A warning to look away.

Run fast.

Scream loudly.

And did I?

Nope.

Why not? Because it was love at first sight just from gazing at two photos of the guy.

The article inside the magazine featured a small black and white picture of South onstage, his bee-stung lips making out with the microphone. On the cover was a close up of his face framed by golden hair, his azure eyes gazing into the camera lens like he was about to declare undying love to it.

Being a photographer myself, I appreciated the artistic lighting, the details of the composition. But as a single girl, I salivated over the sharp cheekbones, the square jaw, and fluorescent glow of his eyes. Poetry in motion, South as a complete package shook me to the core, and in all of three seconds I was a goner.

In.

Love.

Forever.

The article that I rabidly devoured revealed Up Void was a local band on the rise, and from that moment on, my enthusiasm for hot, sweaty gigs increased. I attended as many of their shows as possible, swaying in the front row with all the other girls who went along to make desperate eyes at the singer.

Sometimes, while his hips rocked to the pounding of the drums, our gazes would lock for a few magical seconds. I'd suffer a blast of that intense frown, and then his eyes would drift away.

It took a grand total of four gigs before I faced the sad fact that no matter how seductively I smiled, I couldn't hold his attention for longer than a few heartbeats. Platinum blonds with quirky long pigtails obviously weren't his type.

"What are you staring at, Mia?" asks my friend Ivy, startling me back to the present moment.

The crowded art exhibition opening that I'm plonked in the middle of comes into focus. Ivy's stunning artworks, our friends' happy faces, people dressed in flashy, crazy clothes, and loud chatter fill the gallery where we both work.

I clutch my champagne flute tighter. "Oh, just that amazing painting of yours." I point across Mad Wolf Gallery to the opposite wall.

She turns her smirk toward it. "You mean the painting of Nico that South's currently standing under?"

"Yep," I squeak, flushing a guilty shade of red.

She huffs. "Quick, silly, look away before he calls the police. As I've been telling you for the last few months, you need to stop being so obvious."

She's right, because here I am once again—accidentally stalking South. Thankfully, I'm not at all dangerous. I'm more of a friendly neighborhood stalker. Kindly and opportunistic, rather than sinister and devious. But still, I never in my wildest dreams imagined I'd be so obsessed with a guy. A guy who's a friend. Well, sort of.

See, not that long ago, Ivy met Nico—another hot rocker —and that event caused my love life to go from crap to tragic. She's ten years older than Nico and he had to work hard to wear down her *anti-cougar* resistance. Now they're together, madly in love, and I couldn't be happier for them.

The problem is, Nico happens to be great buddies with South.

So now that South and I attend the same parties, my comfortable crush has evolved into a raging case of unrequited love. It's not my fault he's a tall, tatted, entitled alpha male with a Southern drawl hot enough to melt the boulder holders off a grandma. I want him. I've sworn that I'll have him.

Just once.

One long, steamy session between the sheets is all I want. ASAP. And why not? Okay, so he's super intense and something dangerous brims within those brilliant blue eyes. He's obviously damaged and doesn't do girlfriends. Oh, yeah, and have I mentioned I'm not his favorite person?

"Mia? Mia!"

Whoops. I must've zoned out again.

"Sorry, Ivy, I got distracted."

Frowning, she flips her wavy, red locks over her shoulder. "Yes, I can see that. Move on, girl. He's not interested. You deserve to be adored, not ignored."

"I know." My palms smooth over my velvet cocktail dress. It's red—South's favorite color. "You're absolutely right, but you can't reason with a pining heart. Believe me, I've tried."

"Maybe you should skip the Up Void gig next weekend. Let yourself go through withdrawal. Tonight, you've followed him around nonstop, and it's too much. Have a break for a couple of weeks and see if it reduces the lust. You'll feel better."

"We'll see," I say, avoiding her gray eyes.

4

I fully intend to go next Saturday because, at a gig, I can stare at him all I want. Everyone else will be doing the same thing, so I won't look like a crazy stalker-girl.

Anyway, as if I'd miss an opportunity to see him on stage. It's thrilling, the pull of his emotional agony, the effect it has on the crowd. And when his eyes meet mine, it's like I've been plugged into a hazardous power source that, at any moment, might spark into flames and burn the venue down.

But no matter what Ivy says, I'm determined to hook up with him soon, and she needn't worry about the fallout, because I won't allow myself to get hurt. Growing up with wealthy parents who were too busy to take care of me themselves means I'm quite used to being ignored. As long as I get what I want, I can handle it.

And what I want is South. Only for temporary sexual purposes, of course.

I'll never let myself be a man's pawn, shuffled about and discarded when I'm no longer useful. No way. Like a master chess player, I'll make bold moves and stomp across the board until I've gotten back power.

Still, bedding South won't be easy because, unfortunately, he dislikes me. Well, at least I think he does. Why else does he run in the opposite direction whenever he sees me?

Sighing, I place my empty glass on the table beside us. "I'm going to head out, Ivy. It's been quite a week. Massive love and congrats on your awesome opening. You've sold every single piece!"

"No one's more surprised about that than me." She laughs and kisses my cheek. "Over the last five days, you've photographed two pet weddings as well as worked tirelessly to help organize tonight and didn't miss one day of work. No wonder you're beat. I'll call you tomorrow. Sleep well, honey."

As I duck through the crowd, the string quartet in the corner of the room shifts from a Beethoven piece to the breakout hit single from Up Void's debut E.P., *Lined Black*, and the crowd laughs. Everyone knows the song.

I can't help noticing South laugh too as he slides his hands into the pockets of faded black jeans. Then he looks up and, from only two meters away, glowing blue eyes stare into mine. Scorching me.

Time slows to a crawl. Sound warps. My heart beats faster.

I stare, too. But this time, I look away first.

2

SOUTH

Gig

"Zave, go harder!" I yell at our drummer. The rage burning through me needs feeding, requires more heat and speed.

Sticks flying, Zave responds by pounding the kit as if he hates the damn thing. Perfect.

Spinning back to the mic, I scream until the veins in my neck almost rupture.

The crowd charges forward like soldiers, battle cries spewing from their lips. They've all been waiting for this song—the one I saved for the encore just to fuck with them.

Panting, I lean into the mic. "This is *Lined Black.*"

They go nuts, their roar of approval surging like a rogue wave through the room.

I smash my fingers against my strings and laugh at our lead guitarist, Nate, as he trips on leads and bends his torso deep into the distorted riff.

The sound swirls like a hurricane and—me—I'm the eye of the storm, feet planted, hips pulsing and spine flexing beyond my control.

"Dirt. Black. Huh. Yeah, grind me clean."

The audience moshes hard, bouncing together and writhing like an almighty beast that grows bigger every second, taking over the room.

"The sea's my midnight. Water chokes. Black shine. Yeah, shine."

A sudden flash of silver in the mosh, illuminated by a roving spotlight, catches my eye. Mia's shimmering pigtails.

She's leaving already?

Whenever we play a local club, Mia comes, stays until the end. Comes backstage with my buddy Nico and his girl, Ivy. Always smiling. Always staring at me with those big golden eyes.

With the music shuddering through my bones, I watch her push her way to the bar, and I miss the cue for the chorus, coming in three seconds late. Shit.

"Black black blood is rain. Black black I ain't insane. Ain't insane." Actually, I feel pretty fucking crazy as I let loose another blood-curdling yell, stretch my guitar high, and then slam it down hard into my hip.

I'll regret that tomorrow.

Sweat drips into my eyes, and I swipe my face against my t-shirt sleeve to clear my vision.

Mia.

Mia.

Sweet Mia.

At least five guys scope her out as she waits in line to be served, their sleazy gazes tracking over her legs. Her sweet ass.

Fuckers.

I lean in to sing the chorus three more times, laughing as I try to shout louder than Nate.

Once.

Twice.

Then the last line, *"Black blood makes dirty rain. I ain't. Ain't insane."*

The drums crash three, two, one, then disappear. Feedback screeches. And screeches some more.

Wild applause and screams rain down on me while I stare into the abyss, hypnotized by the lights. Then seek out those white pigtails once more. I'll look away after five beats. I swear it.

Five.

Four.

Three.

Two.

One.

I'm still looking.

Then Nate says, "Night, y'all. Thanks for being awesome. We'll catch ya real soon."

People yell and whistle and chant the usual shit.

More. More. More.

Up Void. Up Void. Up Void.

South. Fucking. South.

I'm miles away. Planets out.

"Take your guitar off, dickhead."

"What?"

Nate stands in front of me, scowling and dripping sweat. "What are you doing hovering there like your brain's shorted out, man?"

Before I summon the sense to look elsewhere, he follows my line of sight to the bar and laughs.

"Right. You idiot." He shakes his rockabilly quiff at me and bumps my shoulder. "Just bone her already, will ya?"

Easy for him to say.

"Come on, man. You look fucking crazy. Get your ass off stage."

I shrug out of my guitar strap and hand my '72 over to a roadie. He throws me a towel.

Crew members slap my back and *hey-great-show* me all the way to the dressing room. Toweling off, I push through the door and check out the scene. The room is packed with booking agency and String Power Records staff and, worse, the label's managing director, Vince.

Shit.

The guy's a certified lunatic. Barely sleeps, drinks like a fish and constantly shoves powders and pills in all the wrong places. He's tall and lanky with a wild mane of frizzy hair, and he's a real pain in the ass. Luckily, he's also hilarious. I kinda like him.

The second he sees me enter the room, he darts over, rubbing his hands together like a mad scientist. "Amazing show, South. Amazing. Got me so fired up I'm not gonna bother sleeping tonight. You coming out? We're gonna hit that weird bar that's hidden behind a bookcase in that fake store downtown."

Yep, there's no way he'll get any sleep tonight. He's in constant vibrating motion. Eyes bouncing like pinballs. Legs juddering. Not so relaxing to stand next to.

"Do you know if Ivy's friend Mia is going?" I ask.

Vince nods. "Yep, that whole crew's coming."

Which means I'll decline.

I squeeze his shoulder and show him a face of fake regret. "Nah, not tonight. I'm heading home. Need some sleep."

Ben, our bass player, sidles up fussing with his man-bun. He loves to look pretty, and with his half-Japanese super-symmetrical features, he nearly always does.

"What's that you're saying?" Ben asks. Just like a thirteen-year-old girl, the dude cannot stand to miss one word of gossip.

"I *said*, I'm outta here."

"Why's that? Taking a chick home?"

"Nope. I'm beat."

His eyes bug out like I announced I've got a terminal illness.

The door bangs open, and a blast of shock erupts in my chest as Mia walks through it with Zave, laughing at him juggling drumsticks like a clown and then threading one through his long, wavy locks like a hairpin.

Our eyes meet, and she gives me a sunny smile. Same as always, my gut clenches, so I chin tip her, then quickly glance away. Lost for words, l look from Vince to Ben.

Yeah, it's the same old Mia effect. Fuck knows why it happens.

The buzz in the room gets noisier, increasing the claustrophobic feeling. Fifty sets of eyes penetrate my skin like a million needles... prick, prick, fucking prick. These people are getting ready to swoop down on me. Talk my ear off. Entertain me. Become my newest close buddies.

And Mia—she's getting ready, too, glancing over here every few seconds thinking I don't notice.

I notice.

I've gotta get out of here before I do something stupid.

To *her*.

Speaking to as few folk as possible, I work my way to the opposite corner and grab my duffel bag. Only takes twenty minutes. Finally, with a sigh of relief, I turn toward the exit to make my escape.

And bang. There she is standing right in front of me. Big smile. Platinum hair. Golden eyes. Hot body dressed in the kind of edgy clothes you'd expect an artist to wear, revealing just the right amount of skin.

She leans close. "Great show, South."

"Hey, Mia. Thanks." I try not to breathe so I don't get fucked up on her scent. It's like roses on a hot summer's day. Sexy.

She keeps smiling, silently offering up the usual bounty. Kindness. Laughter. Friendship. A sweet fuck. All the shit I'm not interested in. Well, that's a lie—I want the fuck.

Oh, man, do I want the fuck. But I don't want it sweet. Or fun.

I like it savage. Dirty, merciless, and completely unemotional.

I try to smile, dig my hands into my pockets. "Been well?"

"Yeah, I have." She squeezes my arm, and a bolt of lightning shoots straight to my favorite organ. "Oh, South, I went to the funniest cat wedding last week—"

"Yeah, right. Sounds great." I grip her shoulders and move her off to the side. Shit, I really don't like it when she tells me her pet wedding stories. They make me feel weird. Lighter. *Interested.* Ignoring the blast of heat radiating through me from touching her, I say, "So, yeah, I've gotta go. I'll see you around sometime."

Her smile drops away. "Oh."

As I slide past her, I give her a crooked smile and a wink. *Fuck.* I hate winking. I hate *winkers* even more.

"Guess I'll see you tomorrow at Nate's party," she calls to my back.

Double fuck. I forgot about that.

Without looking, I fling a thumbs up in her direction.

Why the heck did Nate have to organize such a stupid-ass thing? And it's funny how Mia calls it *Nate's party,* knowing full well the event at our house has nothing to do with me.

Even though Nate's mom, Abbie, practically raised me up

and he's more brother than best buddy, sometimes I wish I didn't live with the guy.

I keep walking.

As I wind through backstage passageways, insanely loud rock music vibrates out of the club's sound system, thumping through my chest so hard it feels like a near-death experience. I fucking love it.

What I don't love is the idea of Mia at my house tomorrow and so close to my bedroom. It's dangerous.

I bang through the metal door at the backstage exit and out into a beautiful crisp night. I take a minute to suck fresh air into my lungs, then head down an alley and onto the main drag, all the way feeling eyes on my back, like someone's standing in the shadows, watching, staring. I look around but see no one. That's weird.

The smell of meat sizzling from the souvlaki van parked under the bridge makes my stomach rumble. Groups of drunks roam, laughing and yelling like losers. The street vibe is festive—a bit like a Friday, not a Wednesday night.

I need a cab.

Scanning the road, I consider how best to avoid tomorrow's party. To get out of it, I'll need to do something drastic, like poison myself so I get carted off to hospital. Sometimes I like the idea of flirting with death but I'm pretty sure I won't be in the mood for it tomorrow.

Anyway, there'll be so many people at Nate's dumb shindig that I probably won't even have to speak to her.

Yeah, right. Who am I kidding? Ever since I met her through my friend Nico, she's been following me around like a bad smell that, come to think of it, actually smells pretty darn good. Like I said before—hot summer roses.

Truth is—Mia is supremely fuckable.

And totally untouchable.

She's too good for me. I don't sleep with friends. I don't sleep with friends of friends. I don't fuck nice girls or ones who look like they might break too easily. End of story.

So, yeah, even though I'm horny as hell, there's no way I'll touch Mia. *Ever*. I'll continue to keep my distance.

Even if it kills me.

The queue at the taxi stand is ten people deep. Sighing, I look right, then left. Hey, it must be my lucky night. A car full of hipsters approaches, crawling along the road in the right direction. I stick my thumb out, and they pull over.

Whenever I hitchhike, people always stop for me. Don't really know why. *I* wouldn't stop for me.

I stroll toward the beat-up sedan, lean on the roof and pop my head through the open window. Two guys and a girl stare back at me. They look wired.

"Hey. You lot heading east?" I ask.

The driver tucks jet black hair behind her ears and says, "We're going anywhere you want, gorgeous."

"Cool." I climb in and thank fuck that she's not sitting in the back seat. She's not my type.

Sadly, I like blonds with golden eyes, husky laughs, and great big massive hearts.

Damn it.

3

MIA

Nate's Party

To my great shock, it turns out that South and Nate live in a nice, big house—the kind of place that has a plant-filled courtyard where you can fry up steaks on a barbecue and host a cool party. I can't stop gaping at all the people packed into it.

"Close your mouth," says Ivy. "You've been here almost three hours. It's time to stop looking so amazed."

"But it's gorgeous out here. And inside as well. How did those two manage to get it all Mexican-fiesta themed?"

Ivy pats down her wavy mane and grins at me. "It's Nate's girlfriend's doing, of course. What? Don't tell me you thought dear South spent his Saturday stringing candy onto streamers and painting lanterns?"

I laugh at the idea. "No, I really can't see him doing that."

"Do you think maybe he's into guys?" she asks.

I choke on my corn chip. "South? No! I don't think so. What makes you ask that?"

"Well, when have you seen him getting it on with a chick? And he wasn't into any of the girls thrusting themselves at him backstage last night. No, apparently, he was *tired* and had to go home and get some *sleep*. More like watch some kind of alien porn. Maybe that's what he's into—a niche fetish." Ivy winks and heads over to Nico, her very own gorgeous rock boy who's sitting around the fire.

I shouldn't be relieved that South didn't take anyone home last night, but I am. How dumb. He's a rocker, not a monk. But I need to be realistic because a party is a perfect setting for a hookup, so he'll probably get with one of the String Power girls tonight. Enough of them simper around him, just waiting to be selected. Frankly, I'd rather sit through a twenty-four-hour Tom Cruise marathon than have to watch him flirt the night away. Which, so far tonight, he hasn't done. He's mainly hung out with his bandmates.

I pull my cell out of my bag and check the time. Shit. Nearly midnight already. Before I have to watch South make his inevitable move on someone who isn't me, I think I'll try one last time to snag his attention.

Nerves flutter deep in my belly, and I remind myself I'm only interested in his body; surely he can surrender that for one measly night and then release me from his spell?

When I arrived a few hours ago, he'd given me a chin lift and a huge smile that made my heart crash into my ribs. He'd looked happy. And friendly. Because that's what he is, right? A friend. Lucky me.

The word from Nico is that he doesn't sleep with girls who he knows. Well, tonight, my aim is to change that. And what could be the harm in having sex with South? My heart is strong and well-fortified. I just want to run my hands through that wild hair. Kiss those bee-stung lips. Stare into brilliant turquoise eyes. Have him moan into my mouth.

Just once.

Then we can go back to being friends of friends or whatever it is that we are.

I detour past the bar to collect two fresh margaritas and then look around for my target.

Tall, tatted, and built like a god, he's easy to spot standing over by a low garden wall talking to two girls and a guy I've never seen before. Maybe right now he's liking the look of one of those girls. And maybe I don't care.

Before I can change my mind, I stroll over and stand behind him, then gently kick his boot.

Eyes wide, he whips around.

"Sorry! I'd have preferred to tap your shoulder, but my hands are full." I lift the frosted glasses up.

Those incredible eyes of his narrow, but he seems too stunned by my arrival to speak.

"I brought you a drink."

He stares for a second too long then finds his voice. "Hey, thanks," he says as he takes a glass. "You having fun?"

"Yep. You live in a very cool house. It's not what I was expecting, to be honest."

He laughs. "That's what happens when you get a decent record advance. The living quarters improve."

"So, do just you and Nate live here?"

"Zave does, too. And Nate's girlfriend, Suze, spends a hell of a lot of time here."

"And what about *your* girlfriend. Does she stay here a lot?" I'm well aware he doesn't have one, but I want to hear his thoughts on the subject.

In a distracting move, he sucks on the corner of his full lip.

"I don't do those."

"Girlfriends?"

"Uh-huh," he says, stepping closer, and fixing me with a piercing gaze that makes me stumble backward into a metal garden table.

He takes hold of my upper arm and steadies me. Something is off about him tonight. His energy is too intense. Almost predatory. I like it a lot.

"Why not, South? Aren't you into girls?" Might as well find out what he *is* into, force him to tell me to my face that he's not attracted to me. Then I can move on.

He steps even closer, eyes scanning the short, blue skirt I'm wearing, my stripy punk-girl stockings. A lemony-coconut scent mixed with something earthy envelops me. Is it aftershave or deodorant? Either way, it's so yummy it weakens my limbs. As does the fact that, for the first time, he's touching me of his own accord and doesn't seem to want to let go in a hurry. I work to make my expression look normal. Inside, I'm dying a thousand deaths.

I look down at his big hand gripping my arm. God. This is a bizarre turn of events. He must be drunk.

"I like girls plenty, Mia, and—"

"Hey, South, man," says a deep voice behind me.

South and I jump apart and stare at Nico.

He laughs, then continues speaking. "Guess what Linc's doing? He's trying to move your couch out onto the porch. What an asshole."

South seems at a loss for words and only gives a vague nod.

Frowning, Nico pushes long, tawny hair off his face and bites his lip ring. "Did you hear me? Aren't ya worried? You know what an animal he is."

Linc is the lead guitarist for Nico's band, Burntbad, and if you search for the word *trouble* online, you're guaranteed to see a few photos of him.

"Why does he want to move it?" South asks.

"Apparently, he needs more space to break dance."

"Whatever. Let him give it a go. It's so fucking heavy, man, I doubt he'll be able to get it far."

"Okay. I'll tell Ivy she can release him from the choke hold she's got him in." Nico slaps South's back and disappears inside.

"Fucking Linc." South says to me.

"Yes, he's definitely a worry," I agree.

We stare at each other, and I can't look away. I'm shocked that he's even speaking to me. Usually, he runs in the opposite direction. So, this feels like a dream—South's body close, his eyes as hot as blue flames.

Well, I suppose I shouldn't waste this rare chance to get to know the guy.

"So, you're from the South originally?"

"Yeah. Tennessee. Nate and I grew up together."

"That's right. Nico said Nate's family raised you. What happened to your parents?"

Wearing a frown, he takes a big breath, blows it out, and stares off into the party crowd. "You don't want to know. Believe me."

Right.

"Why not try me?"

"How about I don't?" Arm muscles bunching and stretching the sleeves of his Sunnydale High t-shirt, he tosses back the rest of his drink. The fact that he's a *Buffy* fan makes me love him just that little bit more. I mean *like*—like him more.

Silent, he folds his arms and keeps scowling at me.

Family is obviously a sore point. So, if I want to improve my chances of landing in his bed tonight, I'd better change the subject fast.

I sip my drink and twirl a lock of hair around my finger. "So, are you into any one here tonight?" I ask.

"What?" He flashes a crooked smile. "That's an interesting question."

"Well, you did say you like girls. So, who are you gonna hit on tonight?" I wave my hand around at all the scantily clad options.

"No one."

"No way! Well, then I don't believe you *are* into girls, South. You just can't be."

His smile grows. "I can be. And I definitely *am* into girls."

"Then what's your type?"

He bites his grin and trails his gaze over my body. "Well, I really like girls with dyed platinum hair who wear kooky clothes. They seem to get my motor running real hot."

My breath catches in my throat. What. The. Living. Hell? Did he just flirt with me for real? No way I'm letting that comment dissolve into the night.

"Oh? So, a bit like me, then."

He just stares, doesn't say a word as his chest rises and falls a little faster than before.

I close the distance between us until our bodies are only a couple of inches apart and gaze up at him. I try a seductive smile. "And *I'm* turned on by blond guys with sexy tats and eyes as blue as a summer sky."

A strange expression passes over his face. It's a bit like indecision. Or worry.

Then he looks over his shoulder at the group gathered around the fire. "Hey, good to talk to you. Vince wants me to meet a festival promoter, so I'll see ya soon. Have fun." And then he's gone.

How bizarre.

I stand there for a while and watch the Up Void boys clown about as they speak to Vince and a smooth-looking guy wearing a paisley waistcoat and a strange hat. As the man tells a story, South smiles and crosses his arms over his chest. He's so beautiful that it hurts to look at him.

I badly need to drink another margarita and contemplate his strange behavior. One minute he's flirting, leading me on, and then the next he's running away like usual. I'm confused. Does he want me to chase him or leave him be?

Well, there's only one way to find out. He sleeps here after all, doesn't he? So, it's simple, then. I'll kick back and enjoy the party until it's time to take action.

His bedroom can't be too hard to find. The house isn't *that* big.

4

SOUTH

Escape

"**T**he nineties was the hey day for outdoor festivals. The Femmes, Nirvana, Iggy Pop, the fucking Ramones, Patti Smith!" Marco flings his arm out, his drink splashing my boot. At the rate he's speaking, our A&R guy is breaking freakin' speed records.

"Was it true that the sound could be pretty shit though?" I ask, shuffling backward as Marco and his thick mop of bouncing black hair follow.

"Yeah. Yeah. Usually caused by the wind swirling everything around." Nodding in Mia's direction, he says, "*Jesus*, would you look at all the fucking skulls on that girl's tights? Not sure they go with the stripes."

I *had* looked. Way too many times already. I must be developing some kind of sick hosiery fixation. Why else am I drooling to get my hands on her legs? And what about my dumbass mouth? Telling her I get turned on by girls who look exactly like her. I'm a fuckwit.

Man, my brain is shot tonight. I don't know what's wrong with me, but I think I need to go to bed and sleep off whatever it is as soon as possible.

Like a chickenshit, I spent all day at the studio trying to think up a believable excuse for ditching the party tonight. Finally, I thought, fuck it, I just won't go home. I planned to call Ben halfway through the night because he's the one who'd give the least fucks about my non-attendance and tell him I got wasted somewhere. He wouldn't care, and he'd most likely forget to tell Nate, too, which would work in my favor. That was my bright idea, anyway.

But, while slurping my lunch noodles in the control room, I made the mistake of wondering what Mia might wear to a party and how much skin she was likely to display. Then I got to thinking about all the party guys who might see that skin without me there to watch them do it. Whatever the fuck that means.

"Weird dress sense that chick has," says Marco, shocking me back to the party with his loud voice. "Always cute, though, don't ya think?"

"Um..." I gulp my drink down and once again study Mia's blue skirt. Those legs. I'd hoped to see tits spilling out of a low-cut dress, but it turns out they're well covered. That's disappointing. Still, her curves are worth applauding. "Sure. Yeah, she's real cute."

"Are you trying out the new song in tomorrow's set? South? Hey!"

"Huh? What was that?"

"Maybe you should try looking at me instead of her—at least then you can lip read." Marco smirks over at Mia and slaps my back. "Enjoy yourself." Then he rambles toward Vince who's holding court around the fire, yelling like always at our manager, Lane.

For kicks I look around the party, testing how long I can keep my eyes off her. Exactly four seconds. *Shit.*

Wanting a moment of solitude, I make my way to the low garden wall and slouch over it. Closing my eyes, I huff out a breath. I really need to get laid. Tonight. Then my brain might function again.

For some dumb reason, I didn't take up any of the after-gig offers last night. When I contemplated fucking those girls, all I saw in my head was Mia's bright smile.

Mia.

It would be the worst idea in the world to fuck her and then have to avoid her at gigs and shit like Nico's kids' birthday parties for the rest of our lives.

Man, that was shocking news. I nearly choked on my mouthful of potato salad when he told me earlier tonight that he and Ivy are trying to get pregnant. What the fuck is wrong with him? That's my worst nightmare right there in a nutshell. A kid. Christ.

"So, we'd like to know if you think two of anything is

always a better option than one?" comes a giggling voice above my head.

"What?" I look up into the rabid-eyed gazes of a pair of smoking babes. Then I blink at them. The redhead laughs, leans in and whispers something filthy in my ear.

Extracting myself from her ample cleavage, I say, "Uh, no thanks. That's okay." Then I wonder what the shit is wrong with me. *Again.*

They smile and preen.

"I'm a bit, uh. I'm feeling a little..." *Shit,* is it too much to hope for to get one complete sentence out? "Uh. Ill?"

Yep, apparently, it is.

The brunette wobbles on her heels. "Are you *sure?*"

Nodding at them, I laugh. The wrong girl, or girls, are offering to scratch the fast-becoming-unbearable itch.

"We were at the gig last night," she says in a breathy voice. "You were incredible. So hot. Whatever you're into, we'd do it."

My smile vanishes. "Ah. Right. Thanks." I look toward the back door just in time to see Mia disappear inside the house.

"Pass your phone over, and we'll put our numbers in." The redhead reaches for my back pocket.

"I don't have it," I say, pushing her hand away before she can make a liar of me.

"Well, if you change your mind, sexy, come find us." And off they totter, giggling and looking back over their shoulders.

Ben flops beside me. "Am I hallucinating or did you just knock that back?"

I laugh. What else can I do? I must be losing my mind.

"*What* is *wrong* with you, man?"

"I don't know. Maybe I'm getting sick or something." I get to my feet and scratch the stubble on my jaw. "I'm going to bed."

"What? By yourself? It's not even that late."

"Yeah, by myself. What's wrong with that? Don't do anything stupid, okay?" To piss him off, I reach over and muss his man-bun, then prepare to battle my way through all the wasted people to my room. Thank fuck there's a long hallway and a few doors to close between my bedroom and the party action.

Speaking of action, I hope I don't run into Mia on the way there. Who knows what I might do? I'm hornier than a two-dicked billy goat, and I'm dead tired of trying do the right thing by that girl.

But, still, no matter how many times I've dreamed of fucking her, to actually do it for real wouldn't be worth the fallout. I know this. I believe this. Just gotta keep reminding myself.

Over and over.

5

SOUTH

Caught

An arm flung over my eyes, I lay on my back, listening to the party—yelling and off-key singing, glasses shattering—it sounds like a riot. What a fucking mess the place is gonna be tomorrow.

The worst thing is, I'll be the only one bothered by it because everyone else will be too hungover to give a shit.

I roll onto my side and start to squash the pillow around my ears just as two hard raps shake the door.

What the hell?

If that's wasted-Ben come to keep me awake all night talking crap, I'm gonna slap him.

I flick the lamp on and yell, "What?"

The door swings open and Mia strolls through it. I'm so shocked I shoot up like I'm spring loaded, banging my skull against the headboard.

She shuts the door and walks forward. "I've often wondered what your room would be like, and now I finally know. It's big. And very messy."

"What are you doing here?" Dumb question.

Uninvited, she sits on the edge of my bed. Too close. Then gives me one of her sweet smiles.

"I heard a rumor that you went to bed alone."

I can't deny it. So I nod and sit there with the sheet around my waist, wishing I could draw it up to my neck. Or say something. Anything.

She stares at my stomach, and then her gaze slowly rises to meet mine. "I heard another rumor, too. Is it true that you haven't had sex in a while?"

"*What?*" My pulse goes double time. "Who the fuck told you that?"

"Ben."

Fucking Ben. He'd better start running.

She needs to leave. Right now, before I do something we'll both regret.

"Look, Mia, you're great. And damn hot, too." Her smile gets bigger. "But I don't fu... sleep with girls I like. It kinda ruins the friendship."

She laughs. "But we're not friends, South. Our *friends* just happen to be in love with each other. That has nothing to do with us."

"That's where you're wrong. It does, and it makes it

worse. We'll have to see each other at their shit all the time. For years. And it'll be weird."

"Why will it? What are you so afraid of?"

That comment makes me clench my fists. It's what *she* used to call me when I was a kid—a coward, a sissy. It wasn't true then, and it's not true now. "Hey, I'm not *afraid*—"

"You're not? Well, I just don't get it. You look like that…" She points at my body, then my face. "But you apparently don't get laid much. You must be hanging out for someone to touch you. In fact, I bet you're dying for me to kiss you right now."

She caresses the sheet next to my thigh, and I swallow hard, trying to focus on what it would be like going for drinks at Nico and Ivy's apartment after I'd fucked Mia. I'd have to put up with her mooning around and hassling me for some kind of date. Guilt tripping me.

"Kissing is so much fun, isn't it, South? The way your brain spins when it's done right. The feel. The taste."

My head starts nodding of its own accord, my mouth gapes open. Fists clenched tight so I don't reach out and touch her, I take in every inch of her amazing body. Creamy skin. Perfect curves. Doe eyes. Lips that probably taste like honey.

Do not fuck Mia. Do not fuck Mia.

Slowly, she brings her hand up and presses it into my chest, leaning close. Against my lips she whispers, "I bet you're hard as stone right now."

I swallow again.

She's right. I fucking am. The energy required to stop

myself from claiming her raises a sweat on the back of my neck. Her lips are so close, if I just leaned forward a fraction, I'd have her. Mia would be mine.

She makes a soft sigh against my skin, then stands up and walks to the foot of the bed.

"Come here, South. I've got an idea."

"What are you talking about?" My voice sounds gravelly, like I've spent the last hour chain smoking.

"Come and sit on the end of your bed, and then I'll tell you."

"Will you be leaving after I hear about this thing?"

"We'll see. Get moving."

I crawl over the bed like a silverback gorilla, my dick doing its best to bust out of my boxers. I want to roar. I want to leap on her and take her down to the floor. The way her eyes move over me like that makes me feel angry. Insane. My dick throbs so hard it hurts.

I can't fuck this girl. I can't. I have this terrible feeling, a strange premonition, that once wouldn't be enough. And *that* would lead to all sorts of trouble. Trouble I don't want.

As I sit in front of her, her breathing gets heavy. Stepping close, she puts a soft hand on my shoulder, strokes up my neck, and then sifts through strands of my hair. No one touches me like this. Not ever. I don't allow it, and this is why —it feels strange, but also amazing. I push down a groan.

She bites her lip. "Okay. So, this is my idea… I don't think blowjobs count as having sex with your friend, and I'd really like to give you one. So, what are your thoughts on that?"

My eyebrows practically leap off my face. I don't trust

myself to speak because what I want to say is *fucking great idea, Mia. Yeah. Good thinking.*

Her hand wraps around the base of my throat, thumb stroking over my skin. "Blowjobs aren't really that intimate. They're more about the heat and getting off, less about soft, gooey feelings. Don't you think?"

Think? Right now, I can't even arrange two words together in the right order. She's just blown my freaking mind. All I see are mental images of Mia's lips wrapped around my cock. And, to be honest, I may have pictured something very close to this scenario once or twice before. Alright, maybe eighty times. And, okay, each time, I most definitely had my dick in my hand.

She waits for me to speak while I give her one of my icy stares and battle with myself internally.

I should say *no thank you please leave now*, but the trouble is I want what she's offering so badly I wish she'd just put her mouth on me and I didn't have to say a word to make it happen. Then it will be her fault. In the future, every single time I feel bad about it, I can blame her. And, yeah, I know that's gutless.

"Do you like blowjobs, South?"

Shit. That's like asking if the sky is blue. The answer, of course, is *fuck yes!* And I wish she'd stop saying my name—I like the sound of it on her lips way too much.

Trying my damnedest to look chill, I nod.

She smiles.

Then in slow motion, she drops to her knees between my

legs, warm palms resting on my thighs. Oh, man. Am I awake? This has to be a dream.

But, wait, I should tell her to stop before it's too late. Yep. It's now or never…

I don't say a word.

She strokes my thighs, and a trippy power chord progression starts up in my head. It's cool.

"I'm guessing it's been a while since someone's done this for you."

Probably not as long as she thinks, but the last girl who tried to suck a new bend in my river only got me this revved up at the end—when I was about to come. Mia could probably make me blow with one single, soft touch of her lips.

Watching the muscles twitch in my stomach, she grips my hard-on through my black boxers.

This time I can't keep the groan inside. "Mia. What are you doing?"

She smiles, her expression dripping fake innocence. "I'm getting to work on a long overdue job."

I try to laugh, but it comes out like another groan.

Locking eyes with me, she trails fingernails over my fast pumping chest and down my abs.

"You're so beautiful. I've always wanted to touch you like this."

No. She is. *She's* beautiful. I want to tell her. The words are on the tip of my tongue, but as my lips part, she peels her top off and my braincells dissolve as I get a good look at her nipples through the transparent bra. It's black and lacy and scorching hot.

She clears her throat to get my eyes back on hers, and then frees my dick, her fingers wrapping around the base. She strokes up and flicks her thumb over the head, spreading pre-cum around. I make a weird half-laugh sound and close my eyes for two beats. Then I stare at her mouth. I don't want to miss a second of this, and there's no way in hell I'm stopping her now.

"Sh-*it*," I say when she cups my balls and uses her other hand to massage my shaft in a perfect rhythm.

The chord progression in my head changes to a messed-up hymn, soupy and thick—a real brain fuck—and if I don't concentrate, I'll shoot my load before her lips even touch me.

Man, I want to grip her waist, throw her on the bed and take her like a caveman. Do it hard. Make it nothing but painful, animal rutting.

She pumps. I huff out a rough breath. Then another. And another.

Okay, I really need to make her stop now. And I also need to lighten the atmosphere so she'll keep on doing it forever. "That... *fuu*... that sure is fine work you're doing there, Mia."

She gives me one of her sunny-day smiles, dips her head and presses a soft kiss on the tip of my dick. Shit.

"Yep, damn good wor—*Jesus*," I say as her tongue flicks out and she slowly licks her way up and down my length.

"Mmm. You taste as yummy as you look, South."

There she goes again saying my name in her husky voice. It must disconnect any remaining sensible connections between my brain and my mouth, because next I say, "And you're the finest damn thing I've ever seen."

Her eyes widen. "Really? If you keep talking sweet like that, I might have to kiss you."

With Mia on her knees, my dick in her hand, her perfect mouth about to take me in, I've officially passed the point of no return. I'm definitely fucking her tonight. Consequences be damned.

She has no idea what's coming next. This girl is mine.

"I might just let you do that," I say, making her huff out a laugh. Yeah. *No.* I probably won't.

Then she sucks me down deep, her tongue swirling, head bobbing just right. My hips buck at the soft rake of teeth, the awesome suction. "*Christ* don't stop that. It's perfect."

Lifting her head, she smiles. "I won't."

"You just did!"

She gives me a sassy smile and then works me how I like best. Slow and wet. Then faster to make me shake.

How does she know how great that feels?

Don't come. Don't fucking come.

I really don't want to touch her. I'm not into stroking and whispering and any of that gentle shit. But before I even know I'm doing it, my thumb skims over her throat. I run my fingers through her hair. It's sensory overload. The feel. Her harsh breathing. "Fuck, Mia. Jesus fuck."

When she lifts her head, every single muscle I possess tightens. Please don't let this be over yet.

"Relax." She stands and unhooks her bra, then flings it over her shoulder. Next, she wriggles out of her blue skirt, the stripy stockings, then her black panties.

Watching her undress, I'm in heaven. Couldn't be happier.

Her smooth skin glows in the lamp light, the ends of those crazy pigtails touching her tits. Shit, her hair must be real long when it's flowing free.

I reach and tug. "Take these out."

She raises an eyebrow and does as she's told. When she shakes her hair out, the silver locks curl to her waist. She looks like a fantasy game avatar come to life. A sexy pixie.

She climbs over my lap. I grip her hips tightly. Okay. This is really getting out of control now but, hell, naked Mia is in my arms—a silver goddess raised above my pulsing dick. I can feel her shake. Smell how turned on she is.

Those power chords looping through my brain turn into pure distortion, dissonant, soft, then loud. Fucking wild.

Her fingers link behind my neck, her breath panting over my lips. I could easily kiss her. She could kiss *me*. It would be so simple. So good. Neither of us move.

"South?"

"Yeah?"

"I think you should take your boxers off. And, also, get a condom." Her lips go to my ear, and she whispers, "Now."

"I shouldn't."

"But you will."

Yep, I will.

I lift and deposit her next to me. Then I stand, getting out of my boxers in record time.

I watch her wiggle up the bed, weight braced on her elbows. Naked. Mia's jiggling tits. Mia's wet pussy.

I need to get a handle on the situation or at least pretend

to be in control. "Your turn now, is it?" I ask. "You think I'm gonna come and put my hands on you? My mouth?"

Shoulders shaking, she laughs and nods.

"Well, I ain't. So, you'd better be ready, because ah'm not gonna be wasting any time here, Mia."

Ah, damn, I sound like a real hick. That means I've officially lost it. But, that's okay, because right now, I don't care about anything except getting inside her. The anticipation prickling over my skin reminds me of being out on the water, draped over my surfboard, waiting for the perfect wave to hit.

I fish out a condom from the nightstand, and she watches me roll it on. Then I crawl over her and fist a hand in her hair, grip my dick and slide inside her body. So slowly.

Oh, man.

Our gazes catch and burn, chests heaving like bellows. Seated deep inside her heat, I feel like I've died and been reborn in the space of one long shuddering breath.

Eyes glazed, I force myself to grin at her and make light of the situation. Truth be told, the last thing I want to do is diminish it, because this is Mia I'm wedged inside. I can't believe it.

Mia.

I. Am. Fucking. Mia.

Even so, I force smartass words out of my mouth. "Jesus, that was easy entry. And I haven't even touched you yet."

"Well, strictly speaking, you *are* touching me. In quite a substantial way actually and—"

"Or kissed you."

"I thought kissing was far too *intimate* for you, South, and too—"

"Did you?" I interrupt, giving her a smirk as I drag my hips back, and then plunge in. Pull back. Plunge forward.

And then I make a big mistake—on top of all the other ones I've made tonight. She's staring at my mouth. I'm staring at hers. The logical thing to do is to lean down and take those pretty lips.

So I do.

My lips brush hers, and when she sighs into my mouth, my breathing gets all messed up. I grip her face tightly, angle her head, and deepen the kiss. My head spins, my gut tightens, and in the space of a fractured second everything changes. Suddenly, I don't feel like an animal. I don't want pain and *just fucking*. I want something else. Something that scares the hell out of me.

I kiss her, my tongue moving in sync with each slow thrust of my hips. My hands do all the things I don't want them to do. They stroke. They mold around hot curves. Slick softly over wet folds. Grip. Cling.

I don't do gentle. But I can't stop these caresses, and it feels reverent. Important. Amazing.

What am I doing?

This needs to change.

I amp up the speed. "Fuck," I say, driving into her in a punishing rhythm, wanting to be mindless like I usually am during sex. All red-hot flames and nothing else. Yeah. That's what I want. Just that.

But instead of turning numb, I think, "This. This." And

the blank page I'm trying to hold in my mind is filling up with crazy lyrics about silver sirens and broken shipwrecks. And I'm all vibrating sensations, every cell focused on Mia, because she's gripping my arms tightly and saying my name. Over and over. And moaning, she's moaning too.

Then her voice changes. "Oh, South. Oh, South," she chants, strangely deep, and then falsetto high and not at all like how she usually sounds. But—hang on. That's not Mia. It's that loser Ben.

"Fuck off, Ben!" I growl in the direction of my bedroom door.

"Oh, God… I actually thought that was me for a second." Mia giggles.

I waste a moment laughing, and then get back to kissing her, deep and wet, the pace of my hips no longer smooth. My arms tremble, and my breathing is so loud and harsh it's almost funny. But I don't care. I'm so close. Ready to blow any second.

Ah, fuck, Mia.

Ben's machine gun laugh fades into the night as the front door slams shut. He sounds shit-faced.

Against her mouth, I say, "I'm gonna kill him."

"Just don't stop, South. Whatever you do. Don't stop."

"Okay. Okay. Shit, that's so… goddamn… good." I bite down on my lip, one hand gripping her waist and the other clamped around her neck like I'm worried she'll run away. "Hold tight, I think I'm gonna—"

"No! South, wait please—"

"I don't…can't…" Oh, shit. I try to distract myself with

thoughts of our manager, Lane—his slick silver hair, the Hawaiian shirts he always wears—and keep plunging into her, my pace uneven. My eyes roll back in my head. It's not working. Then I think of Zave at a dive bar last weekend doing the robot and how it cleared the dance floor. That was funny. But Mia's eyes are hot. They're huge pools of liquid gold, melting into mine.

Fuck.

In four hard strokes I let out a deep groan and, with my chest shuddering, I come like a broken fire hydrant, then collapse on top of her.

"Jesus Christ. Am I dead? That felt like a bullet to the chest," I say through sawing breaths. "Why haven't other girls ever wrecked me like that?" Oh, man, what the shit am I saying?

She smacks my chest. "Don't mention other girls while you've still got me skewered here. That's not nice."

"Sorry."

I scan her face. "You didn't come?"

"*No*, that pain-in-the-butt Ben put me off."

"Not for long." Easing out of her, I jostle her into a suitable position, close my teeth around her nipple and plunge my fingers inside her pussy. She's so wet my dick starts to wake up again. Unbelievable.

I find the spot that makes her pant and circle her hips, and then I work it good. In about ten seconds noisy moans fill the room as I push her over into oblivion.

When she recovers, she tucks hair behind my ear and says, "Wow! You're pretty good at that."

I give her an *of-course-I-am* smile. "That shithead Ben really got to you, huh? If he's got any sense he'll stay scarce for a while. Didn't bother me, though. I don't think anything could put me off while I'm doing you, Mia."

"*South*, yuck! Don't say *doing you*. It sounds terrible!"

"Okay." I smirk. "Would you prefer I said fucking you? Or maybe making *love* to you?" Internally, I shake my head at myself. Why? Why am I talking like this?

"Even bigger yuck! I despise the term making love."

"But you don't mind it when I talk filth to you? Seems you've made your choice, then. Fucking you it is. Can I say that in front of people?"

I laugh as she pretends to strangle me. "I don't know why, but '*making love*' forces me to think of making babies or something. It's very off putting," she says, unwrapping her hands from my throat.

"Babies! *Jesus Christ*. That *is* a turnoff. I never wanna have sex again."

She frowns. "Don't be like that. I'm sure there'll come a day when you want a whole tribe of little beasts of your own."

I roll onto the mattress beside her. "Kids? Not me. No way in hell. My childhood was a wreck. I'm not doing that to some poor kid."

I have no idea why I mentioned my shitty upbringing. The only person I ever speak to about it is Nate. And that's only if I'm about to do something real dumb—final and permanent. Jesus. I've gotta get Mia out of here. I don't like the effect she's having on my mouth.

And with that decision made, I pin her wrists above her head and use my lips to torment.

When she tries to wriggle closer, I frame her face with my hands, my eyes searching hers. "Listen, Mia, you know we can't do this again, don't you? Ever. Okay?"

She pats my cheek. "Interesting that you assume I'll want to. Are you going to get off me now?"

Huh? Oh, yeah, right. Time to release her. Set her free.

When I fall back onto the mattress, she gets out of bed and dresses quickly, humming away the whole time. She finds her cell and taps out a message.

Fascinated, I watch her every move, storing the images away for later.

I link my hands behind my head. "So, how you getting home?"

Her phone dings and she checks it, chewing on her bottom lip. I know exactly how great it feels to suck on that thing now.

"Ben's found an Uber. He's coming back to collect me in it."

"*Ben?*" I swing up onto an elbow and push hair out of my eyes. "But he already left. How did you manage to…?"

"We arranged it earlier. It's all good. Go to sleep."

"But…"

"Shhh," she says, strolling back to the bed. She grips my face and bends to plant a quick kiss on my cheek. "It's all fine, South. This is no big deal. It was just a bit of fun. Sleep well."

Frowning, I watch her walk away again. "Yeah, I don't often sleep much."

43

She leans on the door frame, looking chilled and happy. "Oh? Why not?"

"Nightmares." Shit. The things this girl makes me say.

Her expression turns soft. "I'd like to hear about them, but you'll have to tell me another time." She gives me her sunny-smile—the one I like best. And then she leaves.

Thank Christ.

6

MIA

Wedding

Thankfully, South goes on the road with Up Void for a whole fortnight, which gives me time to recover from our bout of mind-blowing sex. Of course, it was everything I imagined it would be and so much more. Devastating. And life changing. Although I won't be letting *him* know that anytime soon.

No way.

I stare blankly at the computer screen I'm stationed in front of, wishing it were already twelve-thirty and I could knock off from my shift at the gallery and get on with my plan. The one that turns South into a friend with flaming-hot sexual benefits.

He's been back in town a week now and suspiciously absent from two social events he'd normally appear at—a bowling night and Friday drinks at the cafe Nico manages. Which means South is officially avoiding me.

Therefore, I need a plan to chill him out, something that will set me apart from all the other girls he's slept with. The desperate ones who hang around believing they can save him from his dark demons.

In all honesty, I'd like to save him, too, but not at the risk of losing our fragile new friendship.

"Mia!"

Huh? Shock jerks my knee into a metal desk leg as Ivy wakes me from my daydream, reminding me that I'm still at Mad Wolf with work to finish, dammit.

She struts over and leans on the desk. Afternoon light streams in through the gallery's massive front windows and sets her red hair aflame, highlighting her smattering of pale freckles.

"So, how's the blog post coming along? Are you finished yet?" she asks, smirking away at me.

"Ummm. Not quite." I slide my gaze away as I speak.

How cute. Ivy is proudly wearing the Burntbad band t-shirt that features her ethereal painting of Nico's face with the song lyrics he wrote about her. I don't think she's too worried about being perceived as a cougar anymore.

She squints at my computer screen and says, "You've only written three sentences! Kendra is going to flatten you and hang you on the wall in an ugly brown frame."

I smile serenely. "Luckily, our boss doesn't despise me the way she does you. I'll sweet talk her into forgiving me."

She folds her arms and hikes an eyebrow. "Unfortunately, I can guess what you've been daydreaming about. Or rather *who*. Let it go, Mia. South will never be yours. Or anyone's for that matter. Nico swears he's too messed up for a relationship. And he's not in the least interested in having one. Not even a casual one."

"I don't care. I'm going to lull him into a false sense of friendship… and then have amazing sex with him again. It was *that* good, Ivy. He's like a drug. I want more. And more. And—"

"When it comes to that guy, there's absolutely no reasoning with you!" She grips my shoulders and shakes hard. "Please, just promise me you'll be careful. That's all I ask."

"I will. I only want to enjoy him while I can and have some fun. No messy heart stuff involved. I promise."

"I think you're lying not only to me but to yourself as well." She sighs, and then grins. "Anyway, go ahead and tell me about the devious plan you're hatching."

"Well, first, I need you to walk away. Then I'm going to call and invite him to the Cossington-Farrar Great Dane wedding down the coast."

"But that's this evening!"

I smile brightly. "That's right, it is."

"No way he'll agree to go—"

"Yes, he will."

"How did you get his number?"

"Your Nico kindly provided it."

She goes cross-eyed and blows a breath through her crimson lips. "Good luck, then. I sure hope you know what you're doing."

"I'm not terrified of getting hurt like you were when you fell for Nico. I'm braver than you, Ivy, and I know how to separate my vagina from my heart."

"Yuck! What does that even mean?"

"Maybe you should ask Nico."

Laughing, she pinches my cheek then dashes toward the office at the back of the gallery.

After I check that there are no customers hovering about who might need assistance, I locate my cell and punch up South's contact.

It rings.

One second.

Two.

Three.

"Yep?"

My stomach flips. "Hey, South."

Two beats of silence that feel like an eternity.

"Mia?"

"Correct. It's your favorite pet wedding photographer reporting in with excellent news."

"Oh, yeah? What's going on?"

"Well, if you happen to be free in around four hours' time, you're officially invited to the beachfront wedding of the very regal Duke and Duchess Cossington-Farrar."

He laughs. "Cats?"

"Unfortunately, no. I realize crazy felines are your thing, South. But these are Great Danes, and they're as big as ponies. I guarantee it'll be one of the best nights you've had in ages."

His voice darkens. "I dunno about that. Not long ago, I had a pretty spectacular night that would be hard to beat."

God, surely he's not referring to our recent explosive sex session.

"But, shit, ever since I found out what you do, Mia, I've been angling for an invitation to one of these things. Couldn't you tell?"

"Not really. Your hints were very subtle. So, are you in?"

"Hell, yeah. But..."

"But what?"

"This is just as friends, right?"

"Of course. Why would you think I'd want anything else?"

There's a long silence, then he laughs and says, "I don't. Is there some kind of dress code for this shindig?"

"Dress up if you want, but your usual t-shirt and jeans will be fine."

Fine. Ha! That's a laugh. He's tall, tatted, and beautiful. Tonight, Jules and Guthrie and their hoity toity friends will choke on their caviar and deviled egg canapes when they get a load of South in all his bad-boy glory. South who prefers to have sex with strangers because he hopes he'll never see them again.

"Are you still there, Mia?"

"Yep, sorry. With the traffic, I think the drive will take

about an hour, and I've got equipment to set up when we arrive. So, I'll need to pick you up at three."

"Can't wait. See ya then," he says, and hangs up.

I can't wait either, but probably for a different reason.

Shoving my cell in my bag, I sigh hard as an unpleasant realization hits me—a wedding is an ideal event for him to meet a girl he'll never see again, perfect for a random hookup. Crap. I really don't want to witness that unfolding.

Oh, well. Too late now. The invitation has been made and accepted.

HOURS LATER, THE bride and groom are looking gorgeous as the sun melts into the sea, painting streaks of hot pink and burnt orange behind them. Duke, his black coat shining, is dashing in a scarlet cape, and Duchess is a vision of… I'm not sure *what* exactly, but she's wearing a charming frothy collar and veil ensemble. I'd wager my generous photographer's fee that the sparkling diamonds in her tiara are real, too. Their owners, Jules and Guthrie, live like royalty.

I dash around barefoot in the sand, snapping photos while the celebrant recites the vows in a serious voice. The well-trained dogs stand calmly next to their owners, and the guests look solemn and suitably moved. All except one.

South's shoulders shake and he frequently covers his extra-wide smile with his hand. It's painfully obvious this is one of the funniest things he's ever seen, and it was most definitely a mistake to bring him. After this, I'll probably never get another job at a society wedding again.

As soon as the dogs are pronounced hound and wife and the groom has licked the bride, I march directly over to the tatted rocker. He looks delectable in perfectly molded pale-denim jeans and a charcoal Burntbad band t-shirt just like the one Ivy wore today at work.

Watching me approach, South bites his full bottom lip.

"How could you?" I ask, folding my arms as my foot goes tap, tap, tap on the sand.

"How could I what?" He does the confused frown that I thoroughly adore.

"You laughed during the whole ceremony, South! You're meant to chuckle on the inside so nobody notices. This is what I do for a living, remember?"

Wide-eyed, he says, "Oh, yeah, of course. Shit. Sorry." Then a devilish grin spreads over his face. "But that red cape on the black dog, and, man, he's about the size of an elephant! Mia, I nearly died from laughing."

"I know. I could see you!"

He cracks up again and, trying not to lose it myself, I lean in and squeeze his arm. "Shh, try and keep it down. I need to get some shots of the dancing in the gazebo. Can you stay out of trouble for a while?"

He sobers. "Yes, ma'am. I'll mingle real politely and tell everyone how great and *serious* the ceremony was."

"Okay, you do that. If I catch you prancing around wearing the groom's cape, you'll be in big trouble."

His smile turns filthy. "Oh, yeah? How you planning on punishing me?"

Shaking my head, I ignore him and walk away before I *punish* him for his hotness by raining kisses all over his wonderful face.

"Nice dress, Mia," he calls to my retreating back. "It's smoking hot."

As I twirl around, I lose balance, nearly falling to my knees in the sand.

Laughing, I say, "What this old thing?" My tight, black dress is thigh high and hugs my curves well, but it certainly isn't old. I bought it the day before yesterday, fantasizing that South would agree to be my pseudo-date tonight. See? Sometimes dreams actually *do* come true.

I get busy documenting the celebrations for my clients—all the disco dancing, canapé eating and business networking. Strangely, for a pet wedding, the guests are mostly human.

Frequently, I catch South's eye and throw him a wink or a cheesy grin. Of course, he's constantly surrounded by females trying to drag him out onto the dance floor. Mostly during the slow numbers.

At nine-thirty, I'm dismissed from duty when the Cossington-Farrars' society photographer takes over, which is a relief, because I really can't tell one senator from the next.

The disco-tune spinning D.J. leaves his post, replaced by the wedding band, a six-piece that plays wonderful old standards by Dean Martin and Frank Sinatra.

After I grab a glass of champagne, I make a beeline for

South who's standing to the side of the buffet table with a bunch of girls hustling for his attention.

I plaster on a pleasant smile, push through the giggling gaggle, and link my arm through his. "Thanks so much for taking good care of my husband while I was busy working. He would have been very bored without the company."

South's jaw drops open, then he snaps it shut when he sees the girls' faces flush red. They say their goodbyes and make fast retreats.

"Don't worry." I laugh. "I swear I'm not getting any strange ideas. You just looked like you needed rescuing."

"Damn straight I did. You wouldn't believe the crazy-assed offers I was getting."

I totally would. "Are you having fun?"

"Yeah. Especially down by the fire on the beach. Mrs. Cossington-Farrar's bridge buddies are nuttier than a pile of squirrel turd. And, therefore, pretty entertaining."

Laughing, I squeeze his arm tightly just because I can.

"It's been great to finally see what you do at these myth-ical pet weddings. You're amazing."

My chest warms and I smile brightly. "Thank you!"

"So, you all done for the night?" he asks.

"Yep. The hired help are packing the car for me, which is so awesome. If I move too much more, my arms might drop off."

The band shifts tempo from a jazzy number to Elvis' version of Blue Moon.

South captures my hand and tugs. "Let's test that theory."

"What?"

"These guys are good. Let's dance."

Shocked, I stumble along behind him.

When we slide in among the well-dressed throng who are shuffling over the temporary wooden dance floor, he swings me into his arms.

Luckily, he holds me close, keeping me upright, because my bones seem to be dissolving.

"I didn't picture you as the type to dance at weddings," I comment as we begin to move.

"Guess you forgot what I do for a living."

The music and dreamy vocals swirl around me, South's spicy scent and body heat drugging me into a lust-induced daze. He stares into my eyes, mouth quirked in the exact expression that made Ivy christen him an *alpha-hole jerk* when we first met him through Nico. And that smirk should look arrogant but right now, his gaze is soft. Sweet, even.

The song finishes and another Elvis tune starts up. Hell's bells! Of course it has to be the soppy love song *Can't Help Falling in Love*. I need to get out of here right now!

Assuming he's as keen as I am to avoid the impending torture, I begin wriggling out of his embrace but, for some reason, he's having none of it and pulls me into a tight cuddle. I have no choice but to press my cheek into his chest as he rocks us gently.

Next he starts humming. Oh, shit, this is horrible and so hot I think my clothes are melting off. Syrupy desire flows through me. I'd like to climb him, bury my hands in his hair and kiss the hell out of him. But I can't do that. No. Because tonight is all about solidifying our friendship. Nothing more.

"South?"

"Hmm?" He maintains the superb bear hug.

"I need to visit the bathroom. Do you think you can release me?"

His head pops back, a crease between his bright blue peepers. "Sure."

I smile as though I'm unaffected by our slow dance. "Listen, when I come back, we should leave. Is that okay?"

Dropping his arms, he steps back, his face serious. "Yeah, sure. You must be tired."

I scamper off the dance floor and spend a while in the restroom splashing water over my face, reapplying lipstick and trying to cool down.

After that, I make my goodbyes to the staff I know from previous pet weddings and circle back to South.

The band is on a break, and he's over by the stage chatting to the suave guitarist about vintage amps from the 1960's.

I make small talk with them for a few minutes, and then draw South toward the cloakroom. "So, have you met the happy couple yet?" I ask after we collect my bag.

"No, not yet. I was chin-wagging to the owners at the bar earlier, but one of their servants had taken them for a piss. The dogs, not the owners."

"Servants!"

"Aren't they? What would you call them?"

Laughing, I drag him toward the beach where Jules and Guthrie are installed on deck chairs, surrounded by the bride and groom and a few elegant friends, all relaxing under a clear moonlit sky. Tonight, not one breath of wind blows a single well-coiffed hair out of place.

"I see Duke managed to get out of his cape," I say as we approach the group.

Jules turns her tasteful silver up-do in our direction. "He thoroughly approved of it in the beginning, dear, but lost patience after a while. Duchess loves her tiara, but it kept falling off, and then she insisted on playing fetch with it. So that had to be put away, too."

Everyone laughs.

"Are you leaving now, Mia?" Guthrie asks as he pats Duchess' giant head. She's draped over his lap like a slumbering dragon. Even though they'd like nothing better, these spoiled animals are really too huge to be lap dogs.

"Yep. I'll email you a taster tomorrow. I got some wonderful shots. What a sunset! Have you guys all met South?"

Everyone smiles and confirms that they have indeed had the pleasure.

I drop to my knees and stroke the dog's head. Her heavy tail thumps against the sand.

"Oh, Duchess, you're so beautiful," I say, my voice pitched to get her tail wagging frantically. "I bet you'll want to wear that tiara when you help the staff bring the shopping in from the Bentley. Right, baby? Right?"

The hefty bride rolls over for a belly scratch, and South squats down beside us. "What? Does she help bring the shopping in?"

"Absolutely loves carrying the bags around, darling, but

only if she's being extensively praised for her efforts and made a huge fuss of." Jules leans over and squeezes South's bulging bicep. "Mind you, not everything she's in charge of makes it inside the house."

South presses his palm against the rough boulders behind us and belly laughs so loud I worry he'll cause the Cossington-Farrars great offense. Thankfully, his deep laugh is so infectious everyone joins in. Even Duke gets excited and rushes over for special rock star pats.

South jostles the dog's head around and rubs his ears roughly. "Hey, there, big guy. Hey."

Duke, in an excited lather, rears up, giant paws bringing down one hundred and sixty pounds of joy onto South's chest, slamming him against the wall of rock behind him. Both Cossington-Farrars squeak in horror and get to their feet.

Somehow they drag Duke off while he attempts to lick South to death. The dog doesn't want to let go of my hot date, and I completely understand.

"Oh, my dear, are you alright? Duke adores you! He only wants to cuddle with you and play," says Jules, clutching her midnight-blue gown against her toned stomach.

Yep. Who doesn't want to play with South?

Jules is in her late fifties with a face that's botoxed into the tranquil smoothness of a calm lake—and it's often hard to tell what's going on underneath the surface.

South rolls forward onto his haunches and rubs the side of his head. "I'm fine. But, that beast is *darn* strong."

He wobbles a little as he huffs out a laugh, and I rush forward so I can press around his skull.

"Ow!" he says when I strike a bump.

"South! You've got a huge lump. Are you really okay?"

"Yeah. I'm fine." He stands and helps me to my feet. "Don't fuss. It's cool."

After Guthrie asks if we'd like their lawyer's contact details and South declines, we bid goodnight to the wedding party and stroll along the beach toward the parking lot.

The waves crash gently into the shore, and the stars shine down upon us. The romantic setting is so perfect for a beach make-out session that I have to constantly remind myself of the reason I asked him along tonight—which is to strengthen our friendship, not have sex with him in the sand dunes.

As he talks, reliving amusing highlights from the night, South bounces along like he's on stage. I wish he'd calm down. I'm a little worried he has some kind of head trauma, because he's not normally this animated.

When he slides into the passenger seat of my car, I flick the overhead light on and lurch forward, squashing his cheeks between my palms. He sucks in a breath of surprise, his glowing, narrowed eyes tracking over my face as I check for signs that we might need to swing by a hospital before we head home.

I release him and start the car. "Well, no blown pupils or eyes going in different directions, so I think you're okay."

"It's a tiny lump. I've had a lot worse. You sure you don't want me to drive?"

"No thanks. I'm good. Listen, I only live one borough over

from you. Do you mind if we roll past my place before I drop you home and you can help me drag a few heavy pieces of equipment inside?"

His eyes widen. "No. I don't mind. Happy to help you, Mia. So, how do you normally get things packed away when you're by yourself?"

"Well, I live alone but my neighbor, Frank, is usually around to help with the heavy stuff. He loaded me up this afternoon and then went away for the weekend. I hate leaving things in the wagon down on the street for too long."

He frowns. "Is Frank like... young?"

"He's only thirty, and he has a rather impressive pot belly."

"Oh. Sounds similar to me," he jokes.

Laughing, I ask, "And how old are you exactly?"

"Almost twenty-three."

"I'm twenty-five," I inform with a smile.

"Hey, you're a cougar like Ivy is."

"Who am I being a cougar too? You and I are just friends remember."

His crooked grin disappears. "Of course. Anyway, to keep your gear safe you need a van that no one can see inside. With a real good alarm system."

"I can't afford one of those at the moment."

"If Up Void gets super rich and famous, I'll buy you one." He clears his throat like he's embarrassed.

He's acting so weird. All evening, instead of being the arrogant alpha-hole I've come to know and lust after, he's been charming and sweet. And much more dangerous to my heart.

During the drive home, South tells stories about Nate in high school. He's funny, and he obviously loves Nate. And he really likes Nico, too.

"So, how did you meet Burntbad's fearless leader?" I ask.

Vinyl squeaks as he chuckles and shifts his body to face me. "Nico was this little emo-kid who used to hang around all our early gigs. He's a funny guy, and cool, you know? We jammed a few times, and I could hear he really had something special. Great vocal range. Catchy song writer. There are heaps of cowboys on the make in the music industry. To avoid them, you need to be able to tell shit from honey, and unlike me, Nico's an optimist. So over the years, I've kinda looked out for him. But then one day I realized I didn't need to anymore—because, suddenly, he was a force to be reckoned with."

Smiling, I turn the radio down. "He's an amazing singer. He and Ivy are so great together, too."

"Yeah," he agrees. "He's real happy these days."

"So the recording of your album is going well?"

"Yup. Most of the tracks are done and we're mainly mixing, but there's one more song that's begging to be written. I can feel it hovering around, can just about touch the darn thing. Fucking frustrating, because I've got plenty of spare songs I could record just to fill the space, but they're not *this* song, you know?"

"Why are all your songs so dark and angry?"

This time, he angles his body away and looks out the

window at the dark paddocks we pass. He shrugs. "Nah, they're not so bad."

"Lined Black? That song's a brain shredder. A heart masher."

"No, it ain't. Listen to the bones of it..." Then he starts singing, and I nearly ram the car in front as it changes lanes without indicating.

He sings slowly, croons the song like it's a sexy lullaby, and my chest tightens, my heart liquefies. And I squeeze the steering wheel tightly and tell myself *no, no, no, please don't fall—whatever you do, don't fall.*

A hot crush on someone is consuming.

Giving in to unrequited love is a fatal mistake.

But, holy frijoles, the boy is like mercury burning through my blood. If I were Snow White right now and South a wicked sorcerer offering me a poisoned apple, I'd take a great, big bite out of it and damn the consequences.

When his voice melts away into the night, I say, "Point taken. Still, the lyrics are dark, and I probably don't want to know what they're about. But, South, please no more singing in that gorgeous voice of yours. It's too beautiful and hypnotic. I'm glad this is my street we've just turned into, because I'm at serious risk of having a car accident."

After we pull up out front, we make a few trips back and forth carrying equipment inside, and then we stand and stare at each other in the hall. This huge hallway is part of the reason why I don't have much spare cash—most of my income goes toward renting my spacious, light-filled apartment.

Having a great place to hang out in when I'm not working is important to me. It doesn't have to be a palace—my studio needs to fit—and me and my cat like a little space to roam as well. I'm used to a much bigger house, though.

I grew up with wealthy parents who mostly ignored me and my sister. Our home was massive but, strangely, I felt claustrophobic and trapped within its well-scrubbed walls. We were never a close family, and now we only see each other for special occasions—Christmases, birthdays and the like.

South clears his throat to snap me out of my trance.

"So," I say, "Thanks for the loan of your muscles."

"Anytime. And thank *you* for inviting me to the wedding. I had a blast." He rubs his messy blond hair. "Except for the head injury."

Silence roars around us while we keep on staring. He looks at my mouth. I look at his, and I know exactly what he's thinking about—the same thing I am. Sex.

Hands in his back pockets, he steps forward. "So, do you want to—"

"Bad idea," I say, even though I'm pretty sure he was about to invite me to lick him all over. Truthfully, I can't think of a better way to spend the next few hours, but the whole point of tonight is to show him that I'm different to his other conquests, that we can be friends. Which means I should offer to drive him home right now.

"Don't worry, Mia. It's just sex," he says, his blue eyes burning bright. "I thought you were into it. Something casual, you know? Just for kicks."

I can't hide my amazed expression. He doesn't sleep with

friends, not once if he can help it and certainly not twice. Has he forgotten his rule? He doesn't seem drunk. Maybe he did receive brain damage when Duke the Great Dane bashed him against the rock.

If I do this, it will make my friendship plan harder to achieve. But, at the moment I don't really care, because it's what I want more than anything else. To be close to South.

Right. Decision made, I step forward, placing a gentle hand on his arm. "I *am* into it. Last time was a lot of fun."

His smile grows.

"But first, I've got to check on Dolphin."

"You have a fish?"

"A cat."

"Huh. How'd it get *that* name?"

"Well, she chirps like one."

"Okay." He chuckles.

We let my cat out of the study and feed her. South picks up the fat, white furball and pets her, laughing at her ridiculously loud purring. He doesn't even seem to mind when, under the guise of being a professional pet photographer, I pull out my cell and snap some pictures of them. Really, I just want the photos to drool over later. I could make a calendar and call it *Hunk with Cat*. I'm sure it'd be a bestseller within a week of publishing.

When I enter my bedroom, I flick on the bedside lamp. A warm glow fills the room, illuminating South standing tall in the threshold. I crook my finger, and he strolls in, shuts my door, and then leans back against it.

Dolphin meows pitifully on the other side of the door as though someone is pulling her claws out one by one.

"Don't worry about her. She's used to sleeping on my bed. She'll give up in a minute."

"Do you want me to let her in? I don't mind."

"As long as you're okay with having your butt ripped to shreds during sex, sure."

He laughs. "Okay, maybe not."

I kick my heels off and sit on the bed. As he watches, the corners of his mouth curve into tiny, kissable arcs. He's yummy enough to eat.

"Woah," he says, checking out the walls. "What an amazing color."

He puts his hands on his hips and looks up. "Man, even on the ceiling! It's incredible."

"Yeah, I obviously really like the color blue. I guess that's why your turquoise eyes turn me on so much."

He does this filthy sounding laugh, low and gravelly. I absolutely love it.

"Take your clothes off, Mia. And do it fast. I need to see you."

Okay, then.

I stand and peel off the tight, black dress. His mouth falls open when he sees the matching lacy stockings and garters attached to my panties. Funny how I wore them when I wasn't planning on seducing anyone tonight. I unhook my bra and let it drop.

He does the *oh-my-freaking-hallelujah* face that nearly every guy makes when he sees a pair of boobs. He shakes his head and points at my panties. "Do they… is it necessary to take them off?"

I smile and spread my stance, revealing the slit that allows easy access to my body.

"Oh, *shit*," he says. "So you can leave all of that on?"

I nod. "Nico's face frowning down at me from your t-shirt is a bit weird. You'd better get your gear off, too."

He looks at his chest and laughs. "Soon, but not yet. Get on the bed."

I climb up and sit against the headboard, cross-legged so he gets a good view of the gape in the material.

He crawls over the bed and mirrors my posture, scooting close so our knees touch. How strange. That's not what I expected. I thought he'd get straight down to business.

Slowly, he tucks a strand of gold hair behind his ear, raising his eyebrows at me. "So, what's it called?"

"What?"

Even in the dim lamplight, his eyes are as blue as the walls. Barely able to breathe, I can't look away.

"The color," he says, "Of your room."

"Oh. Sorry, I don't remember. I'll check and text it to you."

"I reckon it'd be cool to sleep in your underwater room tonight."

I cock my head at him. "What? Doesn't that go against one of your several hundred rules about girls and not getting too close to them?"

"I don't mind breaking some rules with you, Mia. That is, if you don't."

"Okay."

"Like right now I really want to kiss you, and it's definitely against my rules to kiss a girl I like. So, what do you think, should we rebel together?"

"I think your rules are stupid. And one day, I'd like you to tell me why you came up with them."

His big, warm hands grip my thighs. "Maybe I will."

I can't move. I'm too stunned by his calm voice, the look in his eyes. I thought as soon he saw my garters, he'd go crazy, flip me onto my knees, and ram me hard. Fuck me. Hurt me. Punish me for making him want me again.

But, nope, instead I get soft South. Gentle South. A stranger who wants to tease me back. Make me crazy.

His face advances forward, dark eyelashes shadow down on his skin, and he whispers against my lips. "So what's your answer? Is it a yes or a no?"

Before I can speak, his lips brush mine, his breathing unsettled against my skin. Then his mouth presses and opens and I taste him. Warm and spicy. Smell his skin—smoky from the beach fire.

I break the kiss. "I guess it's okay if you want to sleep over. As long as you promise you'll still speak to me when I see you out next in public."

"I promise," he whispers, and then kisses me again. Slowly.

For long minutes I float in bliss while his fingers trail a vibrating current around my ears, my neck, and make every part of me burn. Each move he makes is tender. And shocking.

After some time spent drugging me silly, he glides his lips

away and searches my eyes. "Mia," he groans, warm hands holding my face as he frowns. He glances at my hands clenched in my lap. "Are you ever gonna touch me?"

"Wouldn't that break another rule?" I can't help snark.

"You make me forget them all. I just want you to touch me. Please, Mia?"

Please? I think he definitely has a concussion. Right now, he's behaving so un-South-like that this feels like a dream. Nothing but a fantasy. Something I've made up.

I tangle my hands in his hair and kiss him. He sighs into my mouth, fingers caressing my legs. Through his t-shirt, I stroke his chest, his rippling abs, all the way down to his impressive erection.

Panting, he breaks away. "Fuck. Those stocking things are killing me." Breathing hard, he runs his fingers over the material, dipping between my legs, exploring.

"You're soaked."

Unable to speak, I nod. I stroke his neck. That amazing hair.

South. This is South's skin against mine, his perfect lips, his radiant heat.

The kissing goes on, deep and wet and wonderful, taking me higher and higher until I'm completely evaporated, and there's no Mia left. Only heat and need.

And him.

Only his hands in my hair. Only his fingers moving over my face, skimming down my throat, my arms, and then back up again.

And there's fire.

Fire burning over my skin, making me hotter and hotter. Turning me liquid like bubbling, rolling lava. It's unbearable.

"South, quick, get those clothes off. This is torture."

He inches backward, blasting me with an intense gaze. Then the bed bounces as he leaps to his feet, pulling the t-shirt over his head.

Oh, wow, the body on him. Quickly, I retrieve a condom from the nightstand drawer and throw it at him.

He picks it up and frowns at the packet. "What the hell? This won't fit, Mia. I'm real hurt you think so... *little* of me. I'm gonna have to use one of mine."

I snort at him. Standing there with his hands on his hips, muscles flexing, expression offended, remarkable erection pressing against his jeans, he looks so funny.

And so mouthwatering.

"Luckily, I happen to have a stash on me." He delves into his back pocket, throws three condoms on the bed, and then whips his jeans and boxers off.

And again. The body on him!

He drops down, leans back against the headboard, and slowly rolls a condom on.

Heart thumping hard, silently I give thanks to whichever stars aligned tonight to allow this to happen again.

He gives me a crooked smile. "Come here."

On my knees, I shuffle close.

Greedily, his hands traverse over my breasts, my stomach, and slowly down between my legs. He trails wet kisses over my face, my neck. By the time he gets to sucking and biting my nipples I'm moaning like I'm about to go off big time. Shit, I think I might be.

His teeth graze my lips. "You're driving me crazy here." Then he pushes me backward. "I've been thinking about fucking you again, Mia. Every day. Every minute. I can't wait any more. Are you ready for this?"

The bed creaks as his huge body covers mine. "Yes," I say, almost pulling him off the bed in my haste to get him closer. "Just go for it. Do it now."

With one hand he grips my hair and uses the other to guide himself inside me.

I gasp. The fit is exquisite.

"Christ." He makes a face of agony. It's good pain I guess, because he moans again, breath panting out in harsh bursts. "First time fast and hard, okay?"

"Yes," I say, because it's exactly what I want.

Bringing his smile close, he says, "And the second time can be whatever you want. Anything, Mia. You tell me and I'll do it."

"Okay. Sounds great."

He hikes my knee up and does exactly what he promised, fucks me hard, grinding into me in a take-no-prisoners way. Before long, our movements are shaky, our moans urgent. Sweat slicks between our bodies, the heat intense.

My heart can't take anymore without exploding into tiny pieces that will never go back together the same way. I don't want to be altered, changed, by this, but I am. I can feel it happening with every breath he takes.

I'm his.

My nails dig into his back. "South. Shit. Oh, God. I'm going to come." And then I do, my whole body contracting and releasing in a hot wave of ecstasy.

He goes still as stone, letting my body's contractions work their magic. Then he says, "*Fuuuck*," and comes, too, his muscles shuddering and breath sawing loudly out of his lungs.

Collapsing next to me, he pulls me back against his stomach and kisses my neck. "That about near blew my head off."

I giggle. "Me, too. What a shame it's against your rules to do this on a semi-regular basis. It's good with you, South."

He makes a grunt that could mean anything—agreement or denial—and snuggles closer. "You want to sleep for a bit? Or do you want more right away? I've got some ideas."

Gripping his wrist, I squeeze hard. "Definitely more."

"You always say good things, Mia."

7

SOUTH

Lunch

I drop into a chair, dump my lunch on the table, and then kick back humming in between sips of coffee as I scowl at the walls. I hate the studio control room. It's painted orange, the most annoying color ever.

Ignoring the evil-eyes fixed on me, I send a who-gives-a-shit look around at my bandmates. "Where's Lane disappeared to?"

"He's gone for a beer with Marco. Probably so they can bitch about us," replies Nate, his expression calculating.

I grunt and then keep humming while I wait for the interrogation to begin.

How the hell did Marco convince us to sit in on a

mastering session on our day off? Our A&R guy is a workaholic, totally obsessed. I wouldn't mind meeting the wife and kids who put up with him. They must be crazy too.

"What's that you're crooning there? One of yours?" asks Zave.

"Yep." My boot taps against the table.

"New?"

"Yeah. Something that's started spinning round."

"You should grab a hold of it. It's cool," says Nate, ruffling his sandy quiff into a mess.

"We'll see." I'm not sure I want to, because it's the exact wild chord progression that bruises my brain every time I think of Mia. Of what she sounds like when I'm fucking her.

I stare at my bagel while my bandmates fidget and glare at me. When I can't take any more, I fling my boots off the table and lean toward them.

"What?" I ask.

"Well, thanks for not answering our messages this morning," says Zave, his usual Rottweiler-with-distemper attitude on display. "We had no fucking idea where you were. You walked out of here yesterday afternoon in the middle of a meeting, then didn't show for the agency dinner, and now today you turn up two hours late."

I flick the lid off my takeaway coffee cup and pitch it into the trash. "It's our fucking day off."

Ben grins. "It isn't if you've got something scheduled."

"So where were you?" asks Zave, cracking out an erratic beat on the back of Nate's chair with his sticks.

"Hanging out with a friend."

Nate's eyebrows twist. "Who?"

"What do you care?"

Face flushing as red as his Clash t-shirt, he says, "This is so fucking weird. You never miss anything to do with the album. Ever. You must've been with a girl. Am I right?"

I rock backward in my chair, shocked that Nate's gone with the chick reason. He *knows* I don't hang out with girls.

Palms on the table, he leans close. "Was it Mia?"

A strange heat rises from my gut all the way up to my head, making me a little nauseous.

"*Well? Was it?*" Nate asks.

Biting my lip, my fingers drum on the table. I really don't want to tell him, but I also can't bring myself to deny it. So I don't say anything.

Zave snickers like a fourteen-year-old and Nate's eyes widen. "It was! You did it. You finally fucked her."

"Woah!" Ben explodes up out of his chair and tries to high five me. I duck out of the way. "So, was resolving all that super-hot sexual tension worth the wait, man? Was it awesome?"

"Shut up, idiot." Even though it burns my throat a little, I knock back the rest of my coffee. I badly need the caffeine fix. "It's none of your business."

"Actually, it is," says Zave, pointing an accusing finger at my chest. "You're a loose cannon at the best of times, man. This album's nearly a wrap. We've got shit going crazy over the next few months, and we need you to keep your head on straight."

To fuck with them, I force out a laugh. "What has me getting it on with some chick got to do with anything?"

Nate struts around the table and sits next to me, frowning sincerely like he's my counselor. "We're talking about *Mia*, South. We all see the way you watch her. And then avoid her. If you've done the deed with her, some strange shit is going on inside your head. Or is about to. Take care—that's all we're saying."

"Is this some kinda intervention? Maybe you should call Lane back so he can whine at me too. *Man*. I just had sex with a girl, not started a war. And don't worry, I won't do it with her again."

Nate narrows his amber eyes. I hate the look he's giving me right now. It reminds me of when I was a teenager and he lured me from my shitty home and threw me smack bang into the middle of his happy family. They took me in and raised me up right, undid some of the damage my nutbag mother inflicted. Saved my life basically.

The day I crawled into their home I was like a feral dog, which is why Nate's mom still calls me her wolf pup, and anytime I got out of hand, Nate would give me the exact same look he's brandishing now. Same one you give a puppy when it pisses all over the floor.

"*What?*" I say, raising my arms in surrender. "Want me to sign something promising never to touch her again? Will that shut you up?"

Ben and Zave stay silent and unmoving.

Nate keeps talking. "Look, I just want you to be happy. And to stay sane. Okay? That's it. And I'm thinking with the album about to release and the tour—there's so much at stake —so is now really the best time to start something with the girl you've been afraid of from the moment you set eyes on her?"

What? Afraid of Mia?

Like hell I am!

As I spring up, my chair falls and bounces over the carpet, causing my bandmates' jaws to swing open. "I'm not afraid of anything, Nate. You should know that. And you really need to change the subject. Right now or I'm fucking off home. I could do with some more sleep."

Banging through the door toward the bathroom, the silence resonates behind me like an industrial void. They're nothing but a bunch of controlling assholes—assholes who, most of the time, I happen to love like brothers.

Shit, maybe I overreacted. But, hopefully, I made it clear that Mia isn't up for discussion. They need to stay out of that shit and let me obliterate the Mia-generated weirdness from my life in any way I see fit. Which means I have to start ignoring her again.

Yeah. That's a solid plan right there.

A fucking brilliant one.

8

MIA

Southern Gothic

A week after the wedding, Ivy and I are curled up on the bulky velvet couch in my living room. It's ten-thirty at night and Bram Stoker's Dracula streams on the flat screen. We mostly pay no mind to it, preferring to trade Dracula quotes and giggle into the cushions instead.

Dolphin meows loudly at the door between the kitchen and the lounge as though being apart from us a second longer will be the death of her. She's such a wimp.

"Listen to them, children of the night. What music they make!" cries Ivy in her creepy voice as she slinks off to let my cat in. She returns cuddling the spoiled beast to her chest. "Can I take Dolphin home with me tonight? I wish Nico would hurry up and get back from this tour thing he's on. I so miss cuddling him."

"Is that all you miss? Just the snuggles?"

"And maybe his sexy dimples," she teases. "He's only been away three days, but it feels like forever. Hey, what else have you got to eat? I'm so hungry I could eat chubby little Dolphin here."

"There's another bag of honey popcorn next to the sink."

"Okay, but I'll sample the cat first. She looks tasty." She buries her face in white fluff and then coughs. "Yuck! I think the popcorn will be nicer."

The cat wriggles free, and Ivy turns toward the kitchen, freezing when the doorbell rings five times in quick succession.

"Shit, that might be Count Vlad," I say, wide-eyed.

"We wish. It'll more likely be your neighbor, Frank, wanting help to get his oven going again. Stay there. I'll go this time," she says, and disappears into the hall.

I top up our wine as muffled voices move closer. The door opens and I blink in amazement at South's blazing blue eyes as he stands in front of the couch. The sight doesn't make sense, a tattooed god in my lounge room on a Sunday night and me in my pajamas. I must be hallucinating.

I think of his skin damp with sweat, his lips wet, and the sounds he makes when he comes hard. Adrenaline spikes through my limbs.

"Look, it's South! Not the stove-botherer," says Ivy, standing ram-rod straight behind him. She widens her eyes and mouths the word *fuck* at me.

"The *what*?" he asks.

Ivy waves a *forget-about-it* hand at his twisted eyebrows, and he shifts his attention to me.

With his fists jammed deep into the pockets of his jeans and swaying slightly to a song only he can hear, he looks slightly guilty and a lot adorable. I like his Dead Kennedys t-shirt and the big, red circle on it that looks like a dying sun.

"Hi," he says.

"Hi. What are you doing here?"

Before he can answer, Ivy asks, "Would you like a drink, South? Beer? Some wine? A Flaming Lamborghini perhaps?"

Dropping on the couch opposite us, he laughs. "I'll probably set myself on fire with one of those, so I'll stick with the wine, thanks."

"I'll get a glass," I say, stumbling over the furniture in my haste to flee.

Leaning over the kitchen sink, I gulp down big breaths. What's he doing here?

When he left the morning after the wedding, he reminded me he didn't do friends-with-benefits arrangements and apologized for leading me on the night before. What a confusing guy.

I take a glass back into the living room, fill it up and place it on the coffee table. From his position on the couch opposite, he watches me sit down and then takes a drink.

"So, South, to what do we owe the pleasure?" Ivy stretches her legs out, feet plopping onto the leather ottoman.

Bless her for getting to the point.

"I was just heading to see that band you turned me on to,

Mia. They're playing Silva's tonight and I thought you might be up for it."

"Oh," is all I can think of to say while I wonder why he didn't just text an invite.

"Where are your bandmates?" Ivy asks. "They're not going? I nearly always see you guys at gigs together."

South swirls his glass around, studying the wine. "Uh. No. They're all doing stuff, other things."

"Right." Ivy smirks as she gets to her feet and stretches. "See you later, Mia. I've gotta split to that thing I told you about earlier."

"Liar," I whisper as she bends to kiss me.

She pinches South's cheek on her way out and says, "You be good."

"When am I not?" He chuckles.

She gives him a disapproving look and slams the hall door as she leaves.

Then he traps me in his fluorescent gaze. "Come here, Mia."

Like I'm hypnotized, I traipse over and climb onto his lap, my fingers digging into his inked biceps to be sure he's real.

"You breaking rules again, South?"

"Yeah. Guess I am." His iridescent eyes come closer and then his lips take mine, soft but not gentle, making me float on a sea of sun-warmed bliss.

"Mia," he says, low like a moan. "Why can't I stop thinking about doing this with you?"

"I suppose I'm hard to resist."

Smiling that delicious smile of his, the one that transforms his usual intense expression into sweet-southern hotness, he says, "That's right. You're like pecan pie. I just can't help coming back for more."

The way his gaze burns a fiery trail over my 'puppies of the world' pajamas, I don't think he's put off by flannel—or dogs—and he certainly isn't expecting to be stopped.

"What? No *may I's* and *pleases* tonight, South?"

There's not a trace of sweetness left in his wide smile. It's pure filth. This is wrong. I probably shouldn't make myself so available. So easy. But I want him so badly I don't think I care. We're using each other's bodies. And that's fine by me.

A vivid blue and white tattoo of a great wave curls around his bicep. It looks like a section of an old Japanese woodblock print. An unstoppable rogue wave. And exactly like him, beautiful and catastrophic.

"No, Mia," he says against my lips. "Tonight, I'm just taking."

I frame his face with my hands and kiss him deeply so he'll know it's okay—I want him to take everything.

All that I am.

It's his.

9

SOUTH

Morning After

Light pushes through the weave of the closed curtains, drenching the room in soft blue shadows. I drift to the rhythm of Mia's breathing, my hand molding around her breast. Not to start anything yet. It just feels good.

I can't believe the night has flipped over to another day and, still, here I am—lying in her bed, drunk on her scent. I don't normally do shit like this. Ever. Well, except with Mia, it seems, because this is the second time I've stayed the whole night. I don't know what the fuck is happening to me, but whatever it is—I don't think I like it.

Waking, she fumbles for my wrist and inches her hips

away, putting space between us. Sighing into her neck, I wrap an arm over her stomach and drag her back against me. "Going somewhere?" I mumble.

"The bathroom, if that's alright with you, mister control freak," she says, a sleepy smile in her voice.

"Hey, I ain't stopping you. I've just got a little idea growing." I nudge my dick against her butt.

"That's not little." She laughs. "Toilet first."

In a dramatic show of releasing her, I direct my arm toward the ceiling. "Off you go."

She springs out, giving me an inspiring view as she searches for clothing in the covers, grabs my t-shirt and pulls it on. I settle back and smile at the sight of her drowning in the thing.

She's not that much bigger than my Hummingbird acoustic. I could pack her in my guitar case and transport her around for my convenience, and maybe that would be okay if I were a caveman or hadn't sworn ten thousand times that I'd never touch her again.

When Mia returns, I race to the bathroom, take a leak, and hotfoot it back to her as quickly as I can.

I smile as I enter the room because the curtains are open and the walls shine golden-blue, like a sunlit sea.

Then I frown. "What are you doing?" I ask, trying to hide my disappointment as she pulls on jeans and I crawl back under the covers.

"Isn't it obvious? I'm fine tuning my grapevine for an aerobics competition."

"Oh yeah, nice," I say, sitting up and thumping the pillow

into submission. "I'm good at that move. I can give you a few pointers if you like."

The shit that comes out of my mouth when I'm with her is truly mind-blowing.

I sink back against the headboard. She seems kinda weird this morning, not fluttering her eyelashes and twirling her pigtails at me like she usually does.

On the upside, she looks great in my Dead Kennedys t-shirt. It does something strange to my gut, seeing her wrapped up in my clothes. She probably smells like me, too. The thought of fucking her again becomes all consuming. Sex with her is off the charts—maybe the best I've ever had.

"You should get going. I need to head into the gallery. You do know it's Monday, right?" The mirror reflects her surly expression as she brushes her hair in rough strokes.

"Yeah, I do. I also happen to know you don't start until lunchtime on Mondays." I pat the bed and try out one of Ben's reel-in-the-girls smiles. "Come back in here. You've got time."

She looks indecisive. "I'm not sure it's a great idea. I don't want you to get too attached, South. This is just a hookup, remember?"

My jaw hangs low. Well the suck-up smile was a big fail. I obviously need more practice.

"Of course I remember. I'm not about to propose marriage, I was just planning on having breakfast with you that's all." Well, that's not entirely true. "You want me to make it?" The sheet falls farther down my waist as I lean forward and push off the bed.

Looking back at me, her eyes trail quickly over my chest and stomach before her shoulders slump in defeat.

"No. Stay there," she says, heading for the door. "I'll get something. I don't want Frank to die of shock when he gets an eyeful of Magic Mike through my kitchen window."

Relieved, I start to burrow farther under the covers. Half way down, her comment sinks in and I lurch up. "Hey, it's not... it's just from the surfing and stage stuff. I'm not a gym bunny or anything."

"If you say so." She laughs and closes the door.

At the moment, I feel pretty happy. So what if she compared me to a male stripper? I'm still in her bed and surrounded by soothing blue walls.

After dozing for some time, I jolt awake when the door creaks open and Mia enters looking serious. I sit up, blinking sleepily at her as she passes me a tray crammed with bowls of muesli and mugs of coffee.

"Thanks, Mia. This looks great," I say, pushing hair off my face.

The surprise of watching her remove jeans makes me splutter coffee as she clambers back in beside me.

We dig into our muesli, and I smile as she laughs at how quickly I eat. I'm fucking starving, so I shovel in messy spoonfuls and raise my eyebrows as a rivulet of milk drips down my chest.

"I hope you're not expecting me to clean that off you?" she asks, laughing.

"What a great idea."

She smacks my arm, sobering as she runs her hand over my tattoos of the compass and the curling wave.

"This is nice," she says, her fingertips making bumps over my skin. She'd better stop doing that or I'm not gonna let her finish her breakfast. I nod and scoop more food in.

"Was it hard to decide on? It's from a Japanese woodblock print, isn't it?"

"Yep, good pickup. I haven't come across many people who know about those prints." I use the word *people* but it's the girls I'm thinking of, the ones I want to disappear the second I've blown my load and gotten off. Yeah, sometimes I disgust myself, but what am I supposed to do? No way I want to get close to anyone. And I'm not about to join a monastery any day soon.

"I saw it in art class at high school and knew right away I wanted the wave on my skin. I got it when I was seventeen. Fucking hurt. The compass wasn't a problem at all. Guess I got tougher."

"Why does it say *never lost* under the southern arrow?"

"Huh?"

"I think it's a bullshit statement. You look like a lost boy to me."

Great.

Ignoring her comment, I scrape the last few mouthfuls from my bowl, skull the coffee dregs, and lay down so I can admire her sexy-pixie face. All that platinum hair cascading everywhere is hot as hell. "What's your family like?" I ask, for some reason desperate to know.

She wriggles down next to me, and a dumb smile spreads over my face. This girl makes me do strange things.

We lie on our sides, faces a few inches apart, and I concentrate on naming the rich hues in her eyes. Shades of nutmeg, copper, and pyrite swirl in the light.

"My parents are loaded, both from old-money. They're super-busy and mostly disinterested in kids, so the staff brought up my sister and me. She turned out like them, and I found solace in art and photography and animals. Eventually I put all that together and turned myself into this fine specimen of womanhood you see before you today."

So, she grew up a little like me—no one gave a shit about her. Before I can stop myself, I press the pads of my fingers against her lips. She smiles and nips them.

"Nico says you're an only child. Is that right, South?"

"Yep."

She does the pity face I hate. "Oh. That must've been lonely. I hope you got on well with your folks, that they made up for it somehow."

A dark feeling presses me into the mattress. Looking into her expectant eyes, I draw a breath and try to speak. I actually *want* to speak, but I'm not sure how to put the words together. I never talk about my past.

"South? *Was* it lonely?"

"What? No." I swallow hard against a burning in my throat. "No. It made me self-reliant." I look at the wall to avoid her gaze. "I don't need nothin' from nobody." Shit. Now I sound dumb, like I could throw myself on the ground and miss.

Hand coming up, she smiles and cradles my cheekbone. It feels good to be touched like this. Gently. With care.

Her eyes are soft with understanding, as if she already knows about that pathetic kid I used to be. Did I lower my shields and let her see my thirst for... for what exactly? Fuck, I don't even know what I want from her. But it's something, that's for sure.

"Tell me," she whispers.

And I do.

I start talking. I divulge things I've never wanted anyone to know about—well, other than the people who were on the scene at the time.

I tell her how my mom was sixteen when she was raped by some crazy dude in a forest who beat the shit out of her and left her for dead, how she hated me from the moment she knew I was in her womb, growing like a disease. I fill her in on the way Mom and my step-dad ignored me when I was a kid, let me starve while they drank and smoked crack until I became as feral as an outcast wolf. Always angry and snarling.

I talk, and she cries.

It's fucking horrible and, also, kind of great. And when I'm finished, I feel like a Manhattan-sized boulder has been booted off my shoulders. Shit. I need a drink. Or a good hard fuck.

Stroking my hair, she asks, "So Nate's mom and dad brought you up? That's why you act like brothers?"

"Yeah. He's my brother alright. And if it wasn't for his mom, Abbie, I'm sure my bones would already be dust. Or at best I'd be doing time in some shithole lock-up and getting ass-fucked three times a week."

"Maybe more like daily." She laughs. "Because you're so pretty."

"I'm not sure whether to say thank you or not."

Wiping tears away, she laughs.

"Anyway, Nate's mom is an angel. The best person I know. When I was fifteen, Nate dragged me home from school one day, promising to feed me. I hated everyone, barely spoke, and I didn't want to go anywhere with him, but *man* did I want hot grits and gravy. So I went to his place to eat, did the same the next day, and it was only a matter of time before Abbie refused to let me go back to my dump of an excuse for a home."

"Oh, South. What a terrible story. I wish I could go back in time and hug that poor little boy you were."

"Well, the moral of the tale is that I ain't ever having kids. Fucking ever. No fucking way."

Frowning, she strokes my face. "What's your coping strategy for having a psycho mom who neglected you?"

I cover my eyes and say, "Well, I'm an asshole to everyone and I drink a lot and take drugs and shit. That seems to help." I'm not proud of myself, but it's the truth.

"You're not an asshole. You're a great guy, South. You've only ever been nice to *me*."

She's so wrong. All those months of ignoring her sweet doe eyes as she battered her lashes in my direction, always running away from her, pretending like I didn't notice her.

I noticed her.

"And I've never seen you messed up on serious drugs before," she says, brow creasing like she's thinking back through our past encounters to check.

"Yeah, well I don't really feel the need to get fucked up around you, Mia. I don't know why that is." And I don't know why the hell I said that, either.

She gives me the saddest smile I've ever seen and something tight and hot burns in my chest, corrodes behind my eyes. I don't fucking like it. Nope, not at all. So I sigh and kiss her in a way I've never kissed anyone before. Slow and tender, like it means something.

Bursting through my skin, I drift all the way up to the blue ceiling. Even disconnected from my body, somehow, I'm still aware of each sensation. I didn't know a kiss could make me feel so lit, floating like I'm baked on weed.

Pulling me back, her voice beckons like ripples coming at me over a dark, silver sea. "Are you trying to lure me into having more sex with you?" she asks.

That makes me laugh. *She's* the siren.

"I'm only kissing you, Mia."

Pale freckles sprinkle her nose and cheeks, a sweet contrast to the heat in her eyes. Instead of grabbing, gripping and fucking her hard like I usually do to girls, her face makes me want to be careful and go slow.

Tugging her hair playfully, I say. "I don't need any more." *Seriously?* What the heck is wrong with my mouth?

"Really?" Her hand moves under the covers. "I think you're lying."

Man. I inch my hips away. It's a definite lie. "Ah, ignore

89

that. I just want to kiss you." And ding! Another lie. I'm going to hell for sure.

It's not easy, but I don't push against her or send my hands off on a quest. Instead, I savor the ache. The blue walls must've cast a spell because I've never hung out in a girl's bed before but, right now, I can't think of anywhere else I'd rather be. Which scares the bejesus out of me.

Intent on action, she moves in close, her soft palm stroking my stomach, then gliding slowly up and down my dick. It feels amazing. My hands shake. Forget about just kissing her I'm going back to my earlier plan. I want it all, and I want it now.

I press my forehead against hers, try to think of something witty to say, but all that comes out is, "Jesus. *Fuck.*"

"Well, South, I wonder if you can do more than just say the word?"

"You know I can." I hold her gaze while my heart thumps against my ribs. *Settle down, loser.* Shit, now I'm talking to my organs.

Kneeling, I help her out of my t-shirt. I wouldn't mind making her wear it all the time. *Christ,* look at her body. The sight isn't good for my loser heart. Opposite. I think I'm gonna have a coronary.

I put my hands on her, tease over smooth skin, and kiss her until I've made a mess of her breathing. *And* my own.

When I start huffing like some wild beast closing in for the kill, I stroke into the band of her underwear, slowly pull the scrap of black cotton down her legs, and send it flying across the room. Then I flip her onto her stomach and with one strong heave, raise her to all fours. She yelps in shock.

Oh, yeah.

I make myself stop and consider the angles. Man, this girl is pocket-sized. I grab cushions from the end of the bed and quickly make adjustments. Working a while to control my breathing, I decide to go slow. Yep, I need it to be *real* slow. Want it to last forever.

Knees bracketing hers, I lower my chest over her back and wrap my arms around her middle, squeezing like I'm trying to absorb her. She gasps, and I loosen my hold, the sound of my harsh breathing filling the room. So loud.

Each breath we take together is a beat. A pulse. A song.

The air shimmers, a wild vibration I need to move to. A rhythm to get pounding to.

I want everything. I want nothing. I want to soothe. I want to crush.

But not yet. Not yet.

Still covering her, I use one hand to brace my weight and the other goes to her tits. While I suck and bite her neck my fingers massage and squeeze, then slick through her folds to make her wetter and hotter.

"South," she moans.

And because she says my name like that, rational thought disappears. I'm all animal. Mad. Desperate. But, still, I don't want to rush to the end.

Slow, slow, I remind myself as I reach for a condom on the nightstand, tear it open with my teeth, spit out plastic, and then roll it on. I fist the base of my dick, and then plunge into her wet heat.

Man. It is heaven.

Slow. Slow, I chant in time with her moans.

Spreading a hand over her sternum, I draw my hips back and then plunge deep. Draw back and plunge deep. Her heart crashes against my palm. So fast. It vibrates down my arm to my chest, my gut, and rocks me and rolls me until I'm thrown overboard into a choppy sea. A drowning man saved by a song.

And the song…

It has a verse and a chorus. A riff that grinds me into pieces but keeps on whirling and rolling endlessly.

Go slow. Fight it.

But it feels too good, and my fool idea to torture us both holds for only five more incredible strokes. And then I go at her. Mia's song takes me over and rips me apart.

Gone. Gone. I'm gone.

She says my name again as she comes, and I explode like a meteor shower shooting through space. Falling and falling.

The intensity is death.

The aftermath is life.

Lost and broken into pieces, the song still buzzing through my veins, I try not to suffocate her with my weight.

"Good lord," she mumbles into the pillow.

"You can say that again." Delirious and panting, my arms give way. "I'm a fucking shipwreck."

She looks back at me and laughs. "You are, South. I really can't argue with that."

Well, if I'm debris from a busted-up ship, then what the hell does that make her?

The beginning?

An end?

The song?

I have no idea.

Dark-honey eyes draw me close, and as I lie with my face next to hers on the pillow, an uneasy feeling spreads through my gut. It feels bad. I'd better pretend I never wondered. Just ignore it. Yep, that tactic has always worked well in the past.

Shit.

10

MIA

Pizza

I wait one whole frustrating week before I crack and call South.

After he turned up on my doorstep last Monday and even stayed the night again, I've been hoping he might text to check in or set up another hot session between the sheets. But, nope, nothing.

Yesterday, I caught up with Ivy and Nico. Ivy told me Up Void have been out East, doing a promo run for the album, press and road show-style gigs to drum up industry excitement for its release.

Nico gave me an advance screening of the music clip for the album's first single, *Lined Black*. Seeing South shirtless, singing on top of a moving freight train, I nearly went up in flames on the spot.

Those eyes. That body. And those lips that I now *know* can stretch into a lovely, sweet smile if he feels the urge. I wanted it all, so I called him up to find out when I could get it.

Not really. I just asked him to meet me for a friendly lunch today, and then nearly swallowed my tongue in shock when he immediately said yes, as though it were no big deal.

So now I'm sitting in the sun outside a pizza restaurant near work watching his blond head sail above the street crowds, his eyes scanning the tables for me. He's forty minutes late, but he came.

Bam. Our eyes lock and I get the usual electric shock to the heart. He gives me an adorable crooked smile and weaves his way toward me.

"Hey," he says when he reaches the table and towers over me, looking cheerful.

"You made it."

"When you call me, Mia, it seems I come running." He pulls the chair back and sits, while I grip the table to restrain myself from jumping up and kissing him. I just need to touch him.

"So how was the mini tour thing?"

"Easy. Industry dudes loved it. Me and the guys found all the suck-up stuff pretty entertaining. So all round it was fun."

A waitress appears and bustles a steaming pizza between us. "Here we go, and I'll get some cutlery for your... um, *friend?*" Brown ponytail bouncing, her eyes gleam at South.

There is no way I'll clarify our relationship status so the

girl can flirt with him.

"Thanks." He smiles at her. "And a long black would be great, too, please."

At least he's consistent with his manners.

"What's this?" he asks, pulling a slab of pizza off the tray and hoovering it up.

"A vegetarian. I hope you like anchovies."

"Not really. But for you, Mia, I won't complain." He smirks. "And I don't think it qualifies as a vegetarian once you put those furry things on it. Mmm, but it's not bad."

He licks oil from his lips and the waitress returns to arrange coffee, cutlery, and a plate in front of him.

"Thanks," he says to her, then his eyes move over me. "You look hot."

I laugh, glancing down at my tight-red t-shirt. It's one of my favorites, but I can't imagine it's very lust inspiring. "Really? So, you're turned on by this photo of the cute, little Jack Russell terrier about to blow out candles on a birthday cake?"

Slowly, he inspects my chest. "Yeah. If you're wearing it, sure."

"Excuse us. You're South, right?" Two art student types stand at the table, both very pretty.

He gives them his friendly smile. "Yeah. Hi."

"We're big fans. We love your *Dirt* E.P. God, *so* much! We were at the Old Brewery show the other week. It was amazing. You're amazing! How's the album coming along? Do you like parties? Can we give you our numbers? Because we know of some great parties coming up soon and you could come to them," says the small one at top speed, while her friend nods so vigorously that I fear she's doing permanent damage to her neck.

"Huh." He blazes his smile at them. "That's a lot of questions for someone dozing off in the sun. See, Mia, I told you if I put my face like this no one could tell I was asleep."

Smiling, I say, "I'm so glad you mentioned that, South. Now I know I need to work on my conversation skills a little so I won't bore the next person I have lunch with. Luckily, I don't care if I put you to sleep."

Laughing, he turns his attention back to the girls. "Uh, now what did you wanna know? Oh, yeah, the album—it's awesome. On schedule and sounding great. And parties? Sure, I like them fine." He flicks his head at me. "I've already got this girl's details in my phone, so I reckon I'm okay for numbers right now. But thanks for the offer."

Interesting. If I wasn't sitting in front of him, I'm sure he'd be heading off for a little afternoon menage delight. He must think I'm delusional, that I believe I'm the only girl he's sleeping with right now. I need to set him straight before he imagines I'm like all his other conquests who try to control him.

After looking me up and down, the girls demand a photo with him which I, of course, have to take. Then they prance off squealing into each other's faces.

"Get ready to see that picture on all the socials in about ten seconds," I say, taking a final bite of pizza.

Looking unconcerned, he shrugs. "Doesn't happen much, and I don't give a fuck about Instagram etc."

Soon when Up Void's album is released, and their label's PR machine kicks in, people will be lining up to eat him alive. I think he's in for a nasty shock.

"Get ready to be mobbed putting gas in your car, South. Your life is going to change soon."

Something hard washes over his turquoise gaze—anger mixed with gloom.

I wrap my fingers over his. "I've gotta get back to work," I say softly.

"But I only just got here."

"You were late."

He huffs out a laugh. "Shit. Even though you smile all the time, there's something ruthless about you, Mia. I'll go pay for lunch," he says as he stands, digging into his back pocket for his wallet. "Stay there, and I'll walk you back to Mad Wolf."

I soak up the sight of him, jeans so pale and worn they look like they'd fall away if I touched certain spots, dark, long-sleeve top showcasing his sculpted muscles, that sexy, tousled hair. Yum.

Ten minutes later, I'm struggling to breathe as we travel down a sun-filled laneway around the corner from the gallery. Fruit tree shadows stencil patterns like war-paint over his face as he frowns hard and gyrates his hips slowly.

"South! Stop. I can't get any air in." I laugh.

Hand stuck up in the air, he freezes. "You don't like this one? I thought it was my best."

"I do. It's the funniest, but I'm suffocating. So tell me who that one is."

"It's me. I'm the stupidest dancer out of the whole band."

That's impossible. I've seen him move on stage. He likes making fun of himself, which is a surprising development. He used to seem so frowny, so serious—I had no idea he could be this playful.

"You're ridiculous," I say as I bend and clutch my aching stomach.

When I look up, he's only a foot away and backing me into a low brick fence, a fiery grin on his face. He picks me up and plonks me on the fence top, then steps between my legs and kisses me.

"Mmmm. Pizza," he says, his face close and voice low. "I like anchovies now."

I slap his arm. "That is so not the right thing to say. You taste like pizza, too, you know?"

"Uh-huh. Good." He inhales deep against my cheek, then kisses me slowly, his hands in my hair and body pressed tight.

When my insides turn to hot, simmering liquid and I crave for his fingers to get started on the button of my jeans, I summon the will to disengage.

"South," I say, staring at the luscious lines of his lips. "I've gotta get back."

"Really? Why don't we zip over to your place? Have some fun." Eyes glassy, his pupils swallow all but a bright rim of blue.

"I can't. I really do have to go. And you're probably needed at the studio anyway. I'm sure Nate's about to start hunting you down."

"Well this is gonna be interesting, catching the subway like this." He smirks down at the enticing bulge in his jeans.

"Oh, that's not obvious at all," I lie.

Going by his expression, he doesn't believe me. "Can you punch me in the gut or pull out a few leg hairs? That might take the edge off."

I laugh.

"Don't laugh, Mia, you'd better hope I don't run into your boss, Kendra, out here. It's gonna be difficult to explain why I'm lurking around by myself sporting the most rock solid hard-on I've ever had."

"I think that'd be your problem, not mine. Just keep thinking of Kendra scolding you. That might help."

"Nope. I'm gonna tie this shirt around my waist to distract the public and keep right on thinking about tonight, Mia. I reckon I'll be knocking on your door at about..." He squints up at the blue sky like he's calculating out his schedule. "Probably somewhere around eight o'clock. Yeah, soon as I can get there."

Picturing him on my doorstep, my insides do a happy dance. "Well, in the meantime, I hope you don't get arrested."

Not looking too worried, he chuckles as he ties the top around his hips and saunters off.

Our hookups are becoming absurdly regular. I can't help but wonder how many other bootie-call girls he has set up around town.

Nico always swore South wasn't into repeat sessions. So what the heck is he up to with me?

11

SOUTH

Clouds

This is the coolest position, curled around Mia and holding her tight. Spooning, huh? Stupid name. But, if that's what they call it, I'm fine with being a dumbass spoon. No problem. I can fuck her and not worry about losing my mind and crushing her with my weight. And another bonus, both hands are free to make the most of her lush curves.

Her body is heaven. Hot. Soft. Home.

What? Given my fucked up childhood, *home* is one hell of a weird thought.

Shifting backward a little, I watch my dick glide in and out of her body. Wet and slow. The sight turns me into a trembling mess. To reduce the space between us, I contract my arm muscles and tug her hip. Sucking the heavy air into my lungs, I vibrate all over and moan. This is the best thing ever. Better than drugs. Beer. Anything.

Her fingers dig into my arm. She makes a hot sound that completely ruins me, I feel it, a convulsion to lose my mind to. But I ain't gonna let it happen. Not yet.

I claw at the brink, while that fucking song bombards my brain.

It morphs from the sound of her breathing, becomes the beat that drives us—it gets louder and harder—until it's an all-consuming distortion.

And it booms. It rages.

It urges me on, pushes me higher, burns like lightning through my bones.

No way I'm going over.

Fuck.

I groan, broken and low, balancing on the edge. "No... wait..."

"South," she cries, as she comes hard.

Her voice breaks me. I shatter. Then I soar high—slowly floating down on the breeze of our ragged breaths. Decimated again.

The shipwreck.

Pulling her close, I spread a hand over her chest, covering as much skin as possible. She sighs long and soft, and I nuzzle her neck, amazed at how gentle I am with her. Stunned when I realize she's the only girl I touch these days.

She reaches back and separates us, then turns to face me bright-eyed and smiling.

"So, you should be long gone by now. I have to get to work."

"I don't think so," I tell her, still puffing like I'm some out-of-condition deadbeat. "Last night, you promised me breakfast." I dip my head and kiss her smiling pink lips. "Stay there. I'll get it."

I push out of her cozy warmth, sit on the edge of the bed, and deal with the condom. Then I stumble into my jeans.

"I'll make us some toast. What do you want on yours?" I stand in the doorway, arms raised above my head, fingers gripping the top of the frame.

"Light on the jelly please and heavy on the butter," she says from under the bedclothes.

She's not even looking at me shirtless and suspended there on display. The thought crosses my mind to do a set of chin ups off the lintel. She probably still wouldn't look, and I might crack the door frame. Maybe I should try pulling her hair to get her attention, like a real jerk. What does a guy have to do to get Mia to fall all over him?

"No problem," I say. She's looking now, which makes me grin. I swing my hands down to my sides and pad barefoot along the hallway.

Opening the door into the bright light of a gorgeous, sunny day, I nearly fall over when I see Ivy drinking coffee at the kitchen table.

"Hey! When did you get here?"

"Last night. I often stay the night when Nico's away. I had a work thing, got in late and went straight to bed."

"Fuck, I hope we weren't too loud," I say as I fill a glass with water at the sink.

Pulling her long, red hair over her shoulder, she laughs. "It wasn't too bad. I'm a sound sleeper."

I grunt, take a knife, and slice into a loaf of seedy bread. It's about as heavy as a brick. "So you and Nico are really doing this crazy-parenting thing?"

"We are. Did Mia tell you that I'm pregnant?" she asks, her expression open and happy.

A sick feeling washes through my stomach, but I force a smile. "Hey, cool. Congratulations. Thought Nico seemed extra bouncy lately."

I turn my back to shut down the subject and move quickly around the kitchen, whistling, opening the fridge and cupboard doors, pulling out butter, jelly, and plates and arranging them on the bench. I feel her eyes tracking me the whole way.

"You sure are perky this morning," she says.

I lean back against the sink. "Yeah, I don't normally sleep much, but whenever I stay here, for some reason, I get amazing shut-eye."

"When you're not busy getting off with Mia."

The smile slides from my face. Ivy reclines in her chair, arms folded over her chest and eyes hard.

I give her a cool look back and turn to butter the toast. This is some kind of test and not knowing what's required to pass it, I'm not going to say a word. I finish with the toast and then grab cups.

Ivy glances up from the art magazine she's reading. "There's a fresh pot of coffee here. You're welcome to it." The sharp edge in her voice has gone.

"Thanks," I pour quickly and load everything onto a tray, crashing things together as I go.

"It's okay, you can relax. I'm just trying to get a feel for how big of an asshole you are, South."

"What?"

Shrugging, she slaps the mag closed. "For someone who doesn't do girlfriends, you're spending a lot of time with Mia."

What the fuck?

"That ain't your business, Ivy. You don't like me? Fine. Tell Mia how you feel if it gets you excited. But she's a big girl, and she can fuck whoever she wants."

"You're right. She *can*. Just don't lead her on and spend time with her like this if it doesn't mean anything to you. And you're wrong. I *do* like you. But don't you think it might be best to let her get over you so she can find someone who thinks she's the sun and the moon and the whole universe wrapped up in one gorgeous girl? She deserves that."

I pick up the tray and give her an annoying smirk. "I'll think about it." And as I head back to Mia, I do exactly that. I think about how I feel when I'm with her—light, happy. And how I feel when I'm not—the usual darkness shadowing down, black and bleak, like I'm missing something. *Her.* I'm a dark moon craving the sun's light.

These thoughts are true.

These thoughts freak me the hell out.

I bang through the door to find Mia sitting up in bed, smiling. Coincidentally, on her t-shirt is a black, winter-barren tree with a large silver moon behind it. I stare at it. I'm the moon. She's the sun.

"Yay, here it is! Thank you, South." She stretches her arms out toward the tray, and I place it in the middle of the bed.

I peel my jeans off, climb in beside her, and start on the toast.

She crunches away, too. "You'd better eat it quicker, remember your promise?"

"You know, you don't look like it, but for a small person you're a ruthless hardass. I guess there's no talking allowed, either? Pretty soon, I'm gonna start thinking you just want me for my body."

She shrugs, but keeps her eyes off me. "Well, we both know the deal, right?"

I stare out the window at the apartment rooftops opposite as heat flushes through my blood. *Shit.*

I don't want a girlfriend, but Mia has become a compulsion. During the day, I give myself inconvenient hard-ons, thinking constantly about fucking her, and then without planning to, I end up knocking on her door at night. What an ass I am.

Ivy is right. I should let her go and let her find some other guy who isn't fucked up, who can give her what Ivy and Nico have. Happiness. Commitment.

Ignoring her comment, I finish my breakfast. The shitty

silence and the inside of my stomach feel wrong, so when she finishes eating, I yank her feet until she's lying back down in the bed, giggling.

Curled close to her, I stroke her hair, soothing and appeasing. "What's your favorite thing out of everything in the whole world?" I ask.

After considering a while, she says. "The sky. Stars. And animals."

"Huh. Really? Not, I don't know, rubies? Lasagna? A pair of Vivienne Westwood boots?"

She shakes her head at me, blond hair mussed and sexy as hell.

I laugh quietly. "You're a strange one, Mia. Not at all like the girls I grew up with."

Her fingertips press against my lips. "What about you, what's your favorite thing?"

I have to swallow down the word that's crawling up my throat. *You. You. You.* And then I lie through my teeth. "It's a tie between music and surfing. The ocean bewitches me." Like *she* does.

She smiles like I've just handed her a shiny wrapped present. I wonder what she'd look like if I brought her a cool piece of translucent-green sea glass. Maybe I'll do some beach combing after my next surf and find her some.

"Are you looking forward to the European tour that's coming up?"

"Yeah. It'll be awesome." I tug her ear. "But how will you cope without me for all those months?" Ah, fuck, here I go again. What am I saying?

She looks at me like she's seen a ghost or maybe a complete idiot. I whip my eyes away and focus on the blue wall behind her. I'm not here. I'm under the sea, looking up at the sun as it rays down and breaks up the ultramarine with shafts of gold.

Then, thank fuck, she laughs.

"I'm sure I'll do fine without you, South. I have other options."

A blast of shock explodes inside my chest. *What? Like who?*

To stop myself asking questions I have no right to ask, I kiss her, and then get out of bed and dress fast.

"I'll see you at the gig tonight, yeah?" I say, shoving my wallet in my back pocket.

"Yep, you sure will."

I smile at her pretty face peeking out from the covers and race through the front door as quickly as I can.

Why had I said that crazy stuff to her? I don't want to encourage her to wait for me like this shit is fated. I'm not her guy. I'm not *anyone's* guy.

On the way to the subway station, I duck through the park. The green-tinged light and soft shadows from the trees calm me down, help me think straight.

It's all cool. Mia's not a clingy type. All I need to do is pull back a little, make sure I don't give her any cause to think this is anything more than great sex.

A few laughs with a friend.

And just a tiny break from my usual fucking loneliness.

12

MIA

Mauled

The smoke from the joints that are being passed around the backstage dressing room makes my head spin. My ears still ring from the gig, and South's voice pulses inside my head like a hazard warning. *Danger. Danger. Danger. Don't fall in love with him* my brain warns my heart. Okay, brain, turn it off. You're too late anyway.

I glance over at him slumped against the wall on the dirty floor, looking like a beggar prince. Whatever that is. He pulls on the joint the rock-journo girl holds between his lips. Squinting, his eyes meet mine through a veil of smoke. He stares and exhales a stream of gray through his wonderful lips.

On her haunches, the brunette takes the cigarette from his fingers, pops it between her pink lips, and draws hard. My heart stutters as she leans close like she's going to kiss him, then trickles smoke out. His lips part, and he breathes in. Their mouths are so close. I hold my own breath, waiting for their stoner make-out session to begin.

But it doesn't. She flops onto her butt beside him.

Bright blue beams land on me again. Without breaking eye contact, he drops his head against the wall, gives me a stoned smile and slowly rubs his palm over his thigh—a move I've recently come to realize is a dead giveaway he's thinking about sex.

The word *FUCK* is graffitied on the wall in large letters directly above his tousled blond head. Huh. That's apt. Well, if it's the pretty journo-girl he's thinking of doing it with tonight, I don't plan to stay and witness the show.

After a thorough search through the crowd, I find Ivy and Nico over by the door, standing with Vince from the label, Up Void's manager, Lance, and his purple-haired new assistant, Rita. Perfect, I can say goodnight, and then run home to nurse my broken heart.

It's pathetic to feel like this. I know it's nothing but sex between South and me, but all the same, I can't help the stupid yearning and wanting. And I refuse to hang around and watch another girl touch him.

"Mia!" shouts Ivy. "Having fun?" She slings her arm around Nico's neck.

Vince laughs loudly, sniffing like he's just snorted a whole gram of coke, which might explain why he's giggling like a fool for no reason.

Nico grins at me and flicks sandy hair out of his bright, green eyes. "Cool show, huh? You're not leaving already?"

"Yeah, I'm beat, and I've got a wedding to photograph tomorrow, so I need some sleep," I respond.

An arm comes from behind and wraps around my waist. Then South says to the group, "Sleep, marvelous Mia, is overrated."

Oh, shit.

He swings me until I land against the wall beside our friends, braces an arm over my head, and leans in close. His pupils are huge and the whites of his eyes red.

"How about we get outta here?" he asks, looking extremely pleased with himself. "Go back to yours?"

The conversation beside us becomes loud and stilted. Nico blatantly stares at us, Ivy gives him a worried look, Rita scowls hard, and Vince is so far off in his own world of crazy that he probably wouldn't notice if his hair was on fire.

And me? I've got to get out of here.

I press my palm against South's chest, and he frowns down at it. Then he picks it up, and places it gently against his cheek, holding it in place. Holy crap!

I tug at his wrist. "Don't toy with me, South. It's quite obvious you've already got your dirty dalliance sorted for the night, and I'm not interested in a threesome. So, go on, off you go."

His eyebrows twist and I grit my teeth against how

gorgeous he looks. He tilts closer, assaulting me with booze fumes while his eyes search my face.

"What? No, I'm going with you. Ah'll just get my stuff."

His Southern accent always dials up a notch when he's wasted or upset. It's so hot.

"Wait," I say, stopping him from turning. "I haven't asked you to come with me, have I?"

"What?" He looks thunderstruck. The lazy slur has disappeared, and his fingers dig into my shoulders. "Mia, come on!" he barks.

Nico and Ivy are silent. They've given up pretending to speak to each other.

As I try to wriggle out of South's grasp, a hell-bent glint flashes in his eyes. He traps my face between his big palms, and then kisses me with a let's-get-down-to-business intensity.

Everything falls away, the people, the room. I melt like butter, let him crush against me until he makes a raw groan that brings me back to earth and I realize that, at the moment, I look like every other groupie. Ready for anything. Pathetically willing. Nothing special.

Anger surges through me, and I wrench my head sideways and slap his face so hard his hands drop in shock. His mouth opens and closes like he wants to say something but can't get the words out.

Luckily, the room is packed and the voices and music so loud that not many people notice the commotion. My friends do, unfortunately. I glance at their horrified faces and, without a word, make a dash for the door. The image of South frowning and holding his cheek like the family pet has just mauled him etches itself permanently into my brain.

When I'm halfway up the hall, he calls out, "Mia! Wait."

Do not turn around. Do not turn around. *Damn it!* And somehow, I find myself facing him. My legs have an evil mind of their own. He stands at the backstage door with Nate hanging off his arm.

"Just let her go," Nate says. "I don't know what the fuck you did, but believe me, man, you'll only dig yourself deeper tonight."

"Fuck off, Nate," South mutters, jerking against the restraint. Nate throws his hands in the air and disappears through the door.

Broad shoulders slumped, South walks forward. "Hey. What did I do—"

"Look, I'm so sorry I slapped you," I interrupt. "That was a horrible thing to do. But when I saw you with that girl, I totally lost my cool."

"Mia, what are you talking about?"

"I know this is only a friends-with-benefits deal, but I just can't sit there and watch you do that."

The hall's bright lights make my head hurt as I walk backward, and South follows.

"Do what? What did I do?"

Is he shitting me? As if he doesn't know!

"South, stop. If you keep moving, I swear I will never speak to you again, and that's going to be really uncomfortable at Ivy and Nico's parties over the years. I know you don't want that."

He freezes mid-stride and shakes his head at me. His cheek looks hot, like he's burning up with a fever. *I did that.*

Ashamed, I bolt for the door before I make the mistake of rushing over to soothe away the sting.

13

MIA

What Did I Do?

Love hurts. Nearly all the songs agree. In fact, everyone in the world knows it. I know it, too. So why am I doing this to myself—thinking about South constantly? Picturing his gorgeous face after I slapped it last night, pale with shock and a wounded look in his red-rimmed eyes.

"Mia, have you heard even one word I've said tonight?" Ivy asks, pushing her bowl of noodles away and reaching for Nico's wine.

"Hey!" Laughing, Nico whips it away from her. "You're knocked up remember."

"Oh, whoops. Old habits are hard to break, I guess." She

pours water from a jug then inspects the glass, holding it up to the candle like she's hoping to find a few insects swimming around and won't have to drink it. "I'll stick to this."

Ivy is only a few weeks pregnant and nowhere near showing yet, but she and Nico are giddy with happiness.

"I *was* listening," I insist. "You were telling us about your latest client—the hip-hop artist who wants to pose with his ball python wrapped around his ripped torso, but only if you'll paint snow goggles onto its reptilian head so they match the ones he wants to wear in the portrait, right?"

"Right." She smiles.

Truthfully, I've only heard half the conversation. I can't concentrate.

At ten p.m., we've only just finished dinner and are sitting here at my kitchen table in the warm glow of a candle-lit room. I'm so tired if I shut my eyes, I think I'd instantly fall asleep. Because after making a fool of myself last night in a crowded backstage room and ruining my *keep-it-casual-and-just-enjoy-South's-body* plan, I hardly slept.

So I need to avoid him for a while, let the intensity of my growing feelings settle down, and then I can speak to him, lie to him and say that I don't care who he sleeps with as long as he doesn't flaunt them in front of my face.

Unfortunately, South hasn't got the memo yet about my plan, because he's left three messages today asking me to phone him back. Which, of course, I haven't.

I give myself a mental shake and try to act like a proper host and actually show some interest in my friends. "So when does Burntbad hit the studio, Nico?"

Bang. Bang. Bang goes the front door just as Nico draws a breath to speak.

"Expecting anyone?" he asks.

"No. It's probably my neighbor, Frank, hoping to catch me wearing my sleep shorts again."

Nico rises. "Stay there. I'll get rid of him."

Ivy raises her eyebrows at me as we watch him head up the hallway. After a few moments, the sound of raised voices travels toward us, feet stomp closer, and then the door bursts open. Ivy and I stare at South swaying wild-eyed in the doorway.

"You could at least answer your fuckin' phone."

What? I reach for my cell. Six missed calls from him in the last hour. "Sorry, I had it on silent."

"Bull-*fucking*-shit. You ain't even returned the messages I left ya earlier today, Mia."

Shit, with his drawl as thick as honey and the way he's slurring like a punch-drunk fighter, I'd say he's completely out of it.

Nico slaps his back. "Hey, South. Come on, man, sit down. Take a load off. Great fucking gig last ni—"

"Don't touch me." He swings his arm from Nico's grasp and takes out the water jug, barely flinching when it floods the empty dinner dishes.

Ivy jumps up. "South, shit! What's wrong with you?" She scowls at him and heads for the kitchen.

My cell rings, the name *Gary* flashing brightly over the screen.

South points at it. "And who the fuck is *this* guy calling

you?"

"No one," is all I can say as I turn my phone back on silent.

Ivy returns, glances at the cell I'm ignoring and starts wiping the mess off the table, all the while giving South the stink eye. "It's her friend from art college, not a husband she's been hiding in the closet," she says. "I think you should go home now, South. Nico, call him an Uber."

South steps close to me. "Are you gonna say anything?" he shouts in my face.

Fingernails digging into my palms, I bite my lip hard.

Nico's thumbs tap fast over his phone screen.

South narrows his eyes at him. "Make that call and you can forget about doing the Hollywood Forever show with us."

"Fuck you. I don't care about that. Just go home, dude, and get some sleep. Talk to her when you're straight and can remember what crap comes outta your stupid mouth. Believe me, I feel your pain. I fully understand what you're going through here. But, I'm telling you, you are going about this the wrong way."

The soft love song streaming through the speakers makes a ludicrous background track to the scene—South pacing in front of the table, his hands digging through his already wrecked hair, us stunned and watching silently.

Suddenly, he freezes, drilling his eyes through mine like blue lasers. "Why don't you say something, Mia?"

I want to, I really do, but I'm too shocked by the state he's in. My chest tightens. A dull throbbing starts up behind my eyes. I take a deep breath. "Will you go if I speak to you for a minute? In the hallway?"

Ivy's spine straightens. "I don't think that's a good idea!"

Nodding, South drags a hand down his face. "Yes. I just want you to talk to me."

"We'll be right here if you need us," Ivy calls after us as we venture into the hallway and close the door behind us.

South races past, bounces off the wall, and then keeps going in the direction of my bedroom.

The old floorboards creak as I jog to catch up, and then grab his arm. "No, not in there. Sit. Right here." I point at the floor.

Skin turning gray, he slides down the wall and closes his eyes.

"You need water. Don't move." I grab my bedside glass and fill it from the bathroom faucet.

When I return, I pass him the drink, and he skulls it down without a word.

"Mia, please..." he whispers.

I lean back on the opposite wall, the plaster cool against my skin. "What? I don't know what you want, South. Or even what you're doing here."

"Fuck. I don't know either. It's just... ever since we fucked, I can't seem to think about anything else."

"Okay. Truthfully, I kinda like the sound of that. But you're a mess right now, drunk, stoned, whatever you are... so why come here like this? It doesn't make any sense."

"Because you won't fucking talk to me. Like an idiot, I call and call, and you act as if I don't exist."

"I *am* talking to you," I say, dropping to my knees in front of him. "I just… I needed a little space after seeing you with that girl last night. I was jealous. I felt things I have no right to feel, and that scared me half to death. Understand? So, I needed to protect myself. That's all I'm doing."

"Why? I ain't fucking no other girls right now. It's just you, Mia. Why do I feel like I went and did something wrong when I haven't? Tell me what to say so you'll look at me how you always do—all soft and sweet. Not like this…" He waves his hand around my face. "…not like you're fixin' to run away from me."

The lost boy, the intense frown, he is breaking my heart into jagged pieces.

Large palms cover my thighs, heat searing through denim to my skin, and it's nearly enough to make me lean closer and give in. Eyes on his lips, I lick my own dry ones.

"Look, I'm sure you can parrot words back at me, but we both know you wouldn't mean any of them. You're watching me pull away to save myself from heartbreak and normally I throw myself at you, South. Always. From the moment I met you. And, right now, you're just aching for what you can't have. That's all that's happening here. It's simple."

"No, that's bullshit. Hey. Hey, Mia. Let me sleep in your bed tonight, okay?" Blue eyes wide, his fingers dig into my flesh. "I just wanna sleep is all—with you close. It's all I want."

I draw in a slow breath, hoping I'm making the right decision. "Another time, just not tonight."

His eyebrows twist into an anguished shape. "But when

I'm with you, I don't dream bad. I forget stuff. All the shit. My fucking mom calling and acting all crazy-like—crying one minute and telling me she hates my guts, then asking why I don't go see her anymore. She forgets that she's the one who dumped me! That stuff freaks me out, gives me nightmares. But *you*—you give me good dreams, Mia." He clasps my face and pulls until our lips meet, and for a few moments, I kiss him.

I kiss him and the world stops spinning.

He tastes of alcohol and something chemical, sharp and bitter.

Heart pounding, I draw back. "I'll call you a cab. The best place for you right now is in your own bed."

With his hands buried deep in my hair, he kisses me again. Hard and punishing as though he wants to swallow me whole.

Then he shoves me away and says, "Fine. Fuck you, Mia," and stumbles to his feet. Without another word he walks through the door, slamming it behind him.

I stand in the bright glare of the hallway and stare at the door. It hurts to see him leave like that—an angry mess— because I want nothing more than to drag him into my bed, rub his temples with cool fingers and sleep with an arm wrapped tight around his chest. And tomorrow fix him perfect hangover-cure food.

Now he'll probably never speak to me again. Some people can't handle rejection, and it seems like South is the king of them.

14

MIA

I need a Lover

"Fucking South!" says Nico, trying to stab his last few mouthfuls of rice onto chopsticks. "I'm so over his shit."

"I think if you coax the rice just a little there, approach them with care, they might be willing to get on your sticks, my love. They know you're angry and they're scared." Reaching over the table, Ivy digs chopsticks into her bowl of eggplant hotpot and wearing a smarmy face, shows him how to do it right.

It's just past ten on Thursday night, and me, Ivy, Nico, and Burntbad's lead guitarist, Linc, have to yell to hear each other over the noise of the other diners.

The food at the Green Tea Inn is awesome, so we don't allow ourselves to be put off by the dated eighties decor. It's brown and gray, and ugly air-conditioners hang on fake-wood paneled walls. To maintain blood supply to your butt, you need to move around constantly on the hard office-style chairs. But a smidgen of discomfort is a small price to pay for the salt and pepper calamari.

"What's he done now?" I ask, not really wanting to hear the answer.

Since he left my place in a huff last week, I haven't heard a thing from him. I've been dying to call, but at the same time hoping I never see him again so I can wean myself off him. So far my pathetic love vibes are getting worse, not better.

Linc flicks black hair away from his dark eyes. "He's outta control. Just wasted all the time. He sometimes has spells like this when his past comes knocking, but I've never seen him this bad before."

I have trouble swallowing my noodles. "So you were hanging out at the studio today, right?" I say. "Did they get the new song, Singing Eyes, finished yet?"

Linc gulps wine. "Shit no. What is it with that track? Even with him a mess over the last week, he's nailed everything else no problem. But this fucking genius of a song... it defeats him every time. He can't get through it. The Up Void guys are ready to kill him."

Pouring the last of the wine in our glasses, Nico says, "And the worst thing is, the album's done. Fully mastered. Ready to go except for this last song that he insisted on adding, which it turns out he can't fucking sing."

Diners at the next table over break out in a drunken chorus of the *happy birthday* song. I yell louder to be heard above them. "I feel sorry for him. Something is very wrong."

Nico leans closer. "Yep. Some bad scene is playing out on him and I feel like I should be doing something to help him, but at the same time I just wanna strangle the prick."

Ivy stops applying lipstick. "So explain why we're about to head off and see the asshole? It sounds like it'll be a train wreck. I don't think I'm in the mood for that tonight. And it'll only upset Mia."

Feigning outrage, I smack her arm. She's always seen through my South facade. Always known that what I feel for him is so much more than lust.

I check the time on my phone. "Well, if we're going, we'd better go now; they're on at ten-thirty."

We pay the bill and file down the internal stairwell, emerging into busy Chinatown and a steamy, hot night.

While we amble toward the graffitied alleyway that the grungy Tyr Bar is tucked into, my mind races. What will I see on that stage tonight? It's worrying because even as a mess, South is a scorching hot one.

His current anguish only fires up my nurturing instincts. All I can think about is feeding him a bowl of soup, tucking him up in bed with a goodnight kiss and a whole lot of forehead stroking.

When we arrive, the erratic swagger of their song *Lined Black* gallops roughshod over my heart before I even pass through the door into the band room. Up Void are already on stage.

The special invite-only gig, judging by the lack of space between bodies, is the popular ticket of the night. We can barely manage to push politely through to where Marco stands in front of the bar, sipping the vodka straight up he rarely deviates from.

Nico and Linc give us wicked smiles and disappear into the thick of the crowd, heading for the front.

The band thumps and smashes at their instruments. South circles over the stage like a tornado, his fingers grating over the guitar strings in a blur. Boy, he looks angry.

I think of those calloused fingertips and what they feel like drawing patterns on my body and bumps break out over my skin.

The spine-tingling sound, South's wildness, and the stifling heat, all contribute to an atmosphere of menace. Tonight feels wrong. Maybe I should leave. Well, maybe in a bit. Where are the emergency exits anyway?

The music and vocals suddenly disappear on one synchronized beat. Hair dripping with sweat, South tips himself against an amp and jerks his guitar around in front of it. The crowd roars their approval at the screeching feedback. He lets the howl die out, and then throws himself at the mic.

"This one's for Mia," he says in a clear, deep voice, sneering out at the sea of people. "She knows why."

What? My heart stops beating while I wait for South to drop his bomb. I'm not expecting to hear a love song.

The drummer, Zave, makes a *what-the-fuck* face at him and Nate bends backward into a soaring guitar riff. I want to run, but my feet feel bolted to the floor.

Heads bounce in the crowd and people smile as South begins snarling out the words to Ugly Kid Joe's early nineties hit *Everything About You,* a not very subtle little ditty about hating someone. Pain explodes in my chest. They've punked the song up, and South spits it out like he means every single word. Wonderful. What a shit he is.

"Oh my God!" Ivy yells into my ear. "What the hell is he doing?"

"Being a prick, obviously. He wants to broadcast that we've slept together and have everyone witness him telling me to piss off. This has done it. If he thinks I'm ever going to be his hot bootie call again, he's crazier than he looks right now."

South growls out the end of the song. Nate's guitar screeches to a fade, but Zave keeps riding the beat into a fever pitch of aggression.

My mouth drops open as South, in a frenzy on the ground, smashes a cymbal stand into the floor speakers. He seems to be on a mission to destroy them. As angry as I am, I can't stand to see him get hurt.

"I'm outta here. This is nuts, and he's a bastard," I tell Ivy.

"That cymbal is lethal. I'm coming home with you. I'll text Nico when we're out of here. He can get a ride home with Linc if they make it out alive."

We push through spreading hysteria and out into the fresh night air. To clear my head, I tip my face toward the sky. No stars. The clouds will force the heat earthward all night. It'll be difficult to sleep.

"What a maniac. That was insane," says Ivy. "That's not a

normal part of their show. He has freaking lost it. What's wrong with him?"

"Everything, it seems. He's mad with me for being the first girl to say no to him, I guess. But why did he dedicate that heap of crazy to me? In front of everyone! If only I'd listened to you in the first place and kept away from him, then I wouldn't be feeling like this."

"He's either determined to hurt you badly or he's just so out of it that he doesn't know what he's doing."

We head for the shopping strip where we'll have no trouble finding a cab. "I hate him. But even after that horror show, I still want to take him home with me. I'm pathetic."

"You're not, Mia, you just need to go out with someone, anyone, to exorcise him. He's bad news."

Scuffing my feet against the pavement, I shake my head.

"Listen, it will work I promise. Sleep with some other guy. Even if your heart's not in it. At the very least it'll distract you from thinking about him."

"You're probably right. I know you are. I should. Right now, though, I want to go to bed and never get out again. I'm the biggest fool who ever lived, thinking I could control my feelings for that beast."

15

MIA

Organic

"He's here!" whispers Ivy, pulling me to a stop in front of the broccoli at our local grocery store.

"Oh, please, no," I say, clutching my canvas shopping bag. "Please don't make me do this."

"You're not backing out now, my friend. You need to exorcise that beast South from your heart before he does irreparable damage. This is simple, eye contact and smile. You do remember how to smile I presume?"

I nod.

"Good. Whatever happens, don't stop doing it."

Ivy takes my arm in a tight grip and leads me down the aisle past the carrots, the potatoes, and all the other colorful vegetables that only have to sit on the shelves completely at their leisure. *They* don't have to front up to someone they're not particularly attracted to and charm them into asking them out. I don't know why I agreed to this idiotic scheme.

We keep marching until we reach the refrigerated shelves and Liam the clean-cut architect. He's here too, staring at the milks and cheeses and tapping his foot in an annoying fashion.

"Hi, Liam," Ivy calls to his red-shirted back.

Of course he's wearing a collared top on a Saturday. Always so smooth. He does have on some nicely faded jeans that fit him well, but they hardly make him look like a bad-boy. His dark hair is short around the neck and ears, but a little tousled on top. It's okay, I suppose. Personally, I prefer a guy's hair to be longer and messier like... South's. No! Don't think about him.

Liam turns to place a jar of goat's cheese in his cart, brown eyes fixing immediately on me and widening. As they always do every single Saturday morning.

"Ladies! Lovely to see you on this fine day. It's exactly how you like it, Mia, isn't it?" He smiles, and I stretch every face muscle I have, grinning like an idiot.

"Hi, Liam. Yep, it's the best. Not too hot and sweaty."

"Oh, crap, I've gotta grab that what's-a-thingy..." Ivy waves her hand around vaguely and races for the other end of the store.

"How have you been?" I ask, making sure to look him in the eye and keep the voltage high on my grin.

He leans against his cart. "Great. Signed a new client this

week for a design on a huge, spaceship kind of home. And I went to the Veggie Bar for dinner during the week and had their brilliant mee goreng, the peanut sauce was spot on. It was all dimly lit, and I could barely read the menu. Very atmospheric."

"Yum. I love that place. I haven't been for ages. I should go soon. You've made me really feel like it." Eye contact. Big smile. More eye contact.

Liam's eyes grow wider. "Yeah. Me too. I could go again. Tonight. Should we... maybe go together?"

"I'd love that, but I've got some wedding photos to edit. How about tomorrow night?"

In obvious shock, he seals the deal before I can change my mind. "Okay. Great! Text me your address and I'll come by around seven-thirty."

"Perfect. I can't wait to hear about your new project."

I whip around and walk straight into the corner of a food aisle, upsetting some oranges from their neat pyramid.

As I scramble toward Ivy, who's paying for a small bag of groceries at the register, I'm planets away, thinking only of golden hair and sky-blue eyes.

I've had no contact with South since the horrible song-dedication gig on Thursday night. He hasn't called to say he's sorry for being an ass and begged for forgiveness. He hasn't told Nico or Linc or anyone that he's sorry. And now I've got a date with Liam.

Tomorrow.

16

SOUTH

A Good Guy

It's Sunday, four-thirty in the afternoon and stinking hot. I'm at a cafe down by the marina, alone and battling the indecision that makes my gut hurt like someone's stabbed it. Should I go to Mia's and make a damn fool of myself as soon as I've finished this coffee or wait a few more days?

I can't decide. After the way I've been acting, she'll probably take one look at my sorry ass and boot me all the way down the stairs.

To sort my shit out, I need a surf. When things settle down a little with the band, I'll head straight for the ocean to calm the crazy thoughts that are spinning through my brain. Most of them are about Mia.

I pull my t-shirt away from my chest, wishing I could take it off. Despite the fact that I'm wearing loose skate shorts and have my hair piled into a kind of man-bun thing, messy enough to make Ben proud, I'm still sweating. It was a mistake to sit in the sunny window. Been making a lot of those lately.

I push the music magazine I've been pretending to read away in disgust.

"Can I get you another coffee?"

I look up with a start into the sloe-green eyes of the waitress. She's definitely hot, all piercings and tropical hair color, tight body—a stranger, too—and yet my dick doesn't even stir. Lately, it only pays attention to a certain sweet-smiling girl with platinum pigtails, the one I've recently been a complete asshole to.

I can't stop thinking about her.

I'm fucked.

I smile at the waitress. "No thanks. I've gotta get going."

She puts a hand on her hip. "Now that's a shame. Where you from?"

"Tennessee originally."

"Ah, that explains the hot accent, then." She raises an eyebrow and licks her red lips.

I'm not even tempted.

The distorted guitar of Nate's ring tone throbs out from my back pocket. I dig out my cell and answer. "Hey." The green-eyed chick sighs and rolls her bony hips away.

"So, are you going to Mia's or what?"

"I don't know. Yeah. I think so. What if she tells me to fuck off?"

"Then you fuck off and keep trying. Like Nico did with Ivy. You haven't gone through days of feeling like shit to straighten out just so you can mess it up again by being a jackass."

"True. That'd be real dumb." I watch people parade by, couples holding hands and smiling at each other. Some stop to look through the second-hand book bins out the front of the cafe. Watching them makes my chest ache, but in a good kind of way. Because maybe with a little groveling I can have that too.

Even with the heat, I decide that it's a fine spot here at the wooden bar, right in the window with the gold light slowly cooking me like a hog on a spit.

"You know, South, you might have fucked up royally the other night, but just remember that you *are* one of the good guys. No matter what your bitch of a mom says. Okay?"

"But am I? I don't feel like much of a stand-up guy right now."

"Fuck, of course you are. You want me to ring Abbie, get her to sort your dumbass head out for ya?"

"Jesus! *No.* Don't call your mom, man. She'll jump in her truck and drive five hours just to tan my hide."

"No way. She never could punish you for acting up, bro. You'll always be the precious wolf pup she rescued from hell who can do no wrong. Now shut up and listen, I gotta tell you something you ain't gonna like much. So keep cool. Got some news from Nico. He didn't wanna tell you in case you went apeshit, so instead he told me and left me to decide if you should know or not."

My gut twinges and I take a deep breath. "Then spit it out."

"Well… it seems as though Mia's got a date with some fancy architect man tonight. He's picking her up at 7:30. And Ivy's been telling her that if she sleeps with him, it'll be a sure fire way to exorcise you from her system."

Words get trapped in my throat. The thought of some guy taking her somewhere, touching her, makes my brain sizzle. Because, if that dude's smart, he'll find out pretty darn quick that she's special.

And she's mine. I want him to know that. And I *need* Mia to know that. Now. Before she does something stupid.

Shit, I feel sick. Hot then cold. Then both at the same time.

"South? You still there, man?"

"No, I've gone to feed the fucking seagulls. What do you think?"

"Okay, quit snarling."

"Well, I reckon the architect's decided it." I quickly check the time again. Five p.m. It's not too late. "I'm heading to Mia's right now."

Nate wishes me luck. I kill the call and throw a twenty on the bar before rushing through the door.

My old Chevy truck is parked down the block, and I run the whole way so I can leap in and spark the engine to life, almost breaking the key in the ignition with my frenzied jabbing.

For once the river of traffic flows obligingly, and it takes just under fifteen minutes to get to Mia's apartment block. I turn the radio up loud, but I can't name one song I hear. The only thing my brain can hold onto is the blazing hope that, even though I don't deserve it, she'll allow me the chance to speak.

By the time I get to her front door, my heart is pounding like a bass drum, and it's not from climbing the stairs. I take three deep breaths and bang on white-wood panels.

On my fifth knock, the door opens and there she is—Mia, looking amazing in black yoga pants and a matching tank top.

"South?" she says, her amber eyes wide.

Greedily, I soak in the sight of her. Her hair is twisted into a sexy shield maiden kind of plait, and she looks hot enough to start a wildfire.

I smile and point at her outfit. "Well, you don't look like you're getting ready to go out anywhere special."

"That's true. And you look all casual and relaxed like you're dropping in on a friend, which you've recently told me and a whole roomful of Up Void fans that I'm not."

"I'm real sorry about that, Mia. Real fucking sorry. Can I come in and apologize properly?"

"No. You don't deserve to come within ten feet of me after that song dedication the other night. You said you hate everything about me, remember?"

"But here's the thing, Mia, that song was a load of hogwash. I don't hate even one thing about you. I like it all. It's just when you kicked me out of your house, I went kind of nuts, you know? It hurt bad. On top of that my crazy mom's been calling again, completely off her tree, one minute going on about how much she hates my guts and the next screaming and crying. It makes me insane. And I don't want a girlfriend. I've *never* wanted one. But I sure as heck want something from you. And I know I'm gonna want it every single day. All the time."

Her eyes get wider by the second, but she's not smiling like I want her to. Or jumping into my arms. Am I fucking doing this wrong? Isn't she into me anymore?

"Sex is what you want."

"Shit, yeah, at least twice a day and ten times on Sundays. But not only that. I'm here to beg you not to go out with that architect. Come here and let me kiss you instead."

"Who told you about Liam? Was it Nico? Well, I've already changed my mind. I canceled the date because it wouldn't be fair to go out with someone I'm not even attracted to."

"Awesome! Best news I've ever heard. So come on, Mia, let me in. Let me show you how much I'm into *you*."

"No, South. You're a mess."

"How am I?"

She crosses her arms. "Well, one—you have no idea what you want from me. And two—when things don't go your way, your solution is to get wasted and turn mean. Now, how is that appealing?"

"Okay. It's not. I get that."

"You don't deny you take drugs and fuck up?"

Oh, man. The only way forward here is full disclosure. It's

a risk going with the truth, but I owe it to her. "No. It's true. Any drug you can think of, you can bet your ass I've snorted, swallowed, or shot it into my veins."

"South!" She stiffens, looking horrified. I don't blame her one bit.

"But I don't do that all the time," I say quickly. "Whenever my past catches up with me, I push people away. I wipe myself out so I don't remember who I am. Or who I was. I kinda never gave a shit if it killed me, you know? But you make me care. Let me show you that I can be one hundred percent sane with you."

I stop breathing while she chews her lip.

Finally, she speaks. "I deserve better."

Closing the distance between us, I frame her face with my hands and speak softly. "You *do* deserve better. I know you do. And I can give it to you. Just give me a chance. You're the only drug I need from now on. Just you, Mia. Help me. Save me. With you, I can be who I want to be—all the time."

Surprising me, she moves first and presses her lips against mine. Fireworks go off in my chest; my whole body burns hot as the sun. I kiss her deeply, needing to demonstrate what I feel for her with each slow glide of my lips and tongue. "Be mine, Mia. No one else's. Just mine. Say yes."

Her dark eyes are glazed, her expression soft. "You only want this now because you heard about the date. You're jealous, that's all. When you calm down and think it over, you'll be glad I didn't let you in."

"Damn straight I'm jealous." I step back, weave my fingers through my hair and tug hard. *Shit.* No way she's in the listening mood right now. And that's fair enough. I should be punished for what I've put her through.

"Okay, fine." I say, walking backward on the landing. "I'm leaving. But don't forget the gig tomorrow. If you don't show up, I'm gonna come find you."

Hip resting against the door frame, she gives me her usual smile, the sweet one that makes my dick as hard as a mic stand. "I'll think about it."

"You better be there. I've got stuff to tell you that you'll be wanting to hear. Real important things."

She leans forward. "Well, tell me now!"

"Nope. You ain't in a listening frame of mind. Have a good night, Mia."

Then, without another word, I turn and amble down the stairs, whistling like all is perfect in the world.

It fucking well better be.

17

MIA

Show Me

"South," I think as my head hits the bathroom's tiled wall. I try to say it out loud but, before I can, his mouth is on mine, sweet and brutal. He grips my face, angling it to suit him, and presses into me. It feels amazing.

Pulling back an inch, he glares scorching blue fire at me. "You, Mia..." he starts, then leans in again and kisses me hard. "...are mine."

"What? Is that all you wanted to tell me? That you don't want me to sleep with any architects or car salesmen from now on?"

He shakes his head, smirking, then presses forward and

does something wicked with his tongue. "Yeah, but that's not all I want. I need you to be my girl."

My heart gallops around my chest like it wants to break free. These are words I never *ever* expected to hear come out of his mouth. These words make me weak, give me hope and restore my faith in the idea that dreams can come true.

Hoping I look composed, I raise an eyebrow. "And you're mine too? As in the boyfriend-girlfriend scenario you've avoided your whole life like it's a death sentence."

"Uh-huh." Wearing a crooked grin, he says, "That's exactly what I want. Exclusivity. Only you. Only me. And no one else. When I'm with you, Mia, I feel like I'm home and when I'm not, everything is just wrong. Bleak. Colorless. Fucking boring. You can't deny we belong together."

The words to agree wholeheartedly won't come out of my mouth. All I can do is nod, wide-eyed, and hope I don't faint from shock.

"Promise, Mia? Just us?" His hand spreads against his chest, right over his heart. "And I promise I'll never hurt you again, like I did with that dumb song dedication."

"You'd better not. I may be crazy about you, South, but I'll walk away from you without a second thought the next time you treat me badly."

"Okay. But do you promise? Just us, yeah?"

Smiling, I grip his arms tightly. "Yes. I promise."

"Me too." He tugs my t-shirt. "Now take this off."

"*What?*"

"You heard. Take it off."

"But we're in a bathroom. A *shared* bathroom. Anyone could—"

"I really don't care." He walks to the door and cocks his head at it. "Huh. You're real lucky, Mia, it's got one of those stupid snib things on it. If I turn it, no one will be able to bust in here and watch me fuck you."

I stare at his lips as he says the word. A long F-sound, hot, to match the flame in his eyes. He should come back and kiss me. No, first I should tick him off, say I don't like it when he speaks like that. It's so coarse. Not attractive at all.

What a liar I am. I love it.

He prowls forth, eyes gleaming and smile dangerous, his jeans hang low on slender hips. A black Poison City Records t-shirt is stretched tight over broad shoulders. A precious heart beats hard in his chest. And it's all mine.

Apparently.

He's a gorgeous creature, and also right, the beast, we *do* belong together. It just took him a little longer than me to work it out.

"Actually, you'd better take *your* top off," I advise. "Vince from your record label nearly faints when he sees you wearing the competition."

"Well, you know me. I'm all about the underdog. Speaking of which, I'm drooling here." He wraps a long chunk of my hair around his fist. "This faithful hound needs a treat. Badly."

"Faithful hound, huh? We'll have to wait and see how that pans out."

Up Void's album has only been out two days and it's

bulleting up the charts, purchases, streams, you name it. As I stand here, pressed against him, his life is changing—a new world of temptations growing by the second.

"You'll see. I never cheat at anything and I sure as hell ain't gonna start with you, the best thing I've ever had. Now, take the top off."

"You're due on stage any minute. And don't you think this is a bit sordid?"

He tugs my hair. "No, I don't think."

"But we can be back at my place in a few hours and—"

He moves closer and pulls my top up while I pull down and we have a mini tug-of-war. "South, I—"

"You don't wanna take it off? Fine. I can work around that." Fighting laughter, he yanks the neckline below my bra, bends and kisses me hard, his breathing all over the place. Just like his hands. In two seconds he has the bra below my breasts.

Wrenching my mouth away, I glance at the door. Nate has enough muscle power to push through it. Vince could walk in at any moment.

South smiles and sinks his teeth softly into my lip, fingertips creating tingling bumps all over the skin he's revealed. Silver fragments explode behind my eyelids.

Oh, who cares about crazy Vince?

Stars rain down, igniting flames, and I pull South closer and pant into his mouth. "Oh, *fine*, go ahead. Go for it."

"You sure?" he asks, glazed eyes sparking mischief. "You really don't seem too keen on the idea." Gently, he wrestles my bra back into place, putting my boobs away for later, I guess. Now that won't do at all.

My hands tangle with his, pulling the material in the opposite direction, trying to bring the goods out on display again. He laughs low.

"No, South! It's okay," I say, panicking that he's changed his pig-headed mind. "You're right... let's... Why should we wait? After all, this is a celebration of you coming to your senses."

"That's right. We're sealing the deal." He gives me a victor's smile, hand moving slowly down my body to rub over my panties in a torturous, whisper-soft rhythm.

In a husky voice he says, "Hmm. Feels to me like you *can't* wait. You know, I'd be real happy to help you out with that. So, what do you think? Do you want me to, Mia? Don't feel pressured or anything."

I long to kill him. Or at least wipe that smug grin off his face. As thrilling as it is. "Okay, you can stop dicking around, you pest, and start... utilizing your actual dick. *Now*, please."

Laughing into my neck, he drawls, "Yes, ma'am."

Heat flares right through me. God, the *hick-boy*. I have a massive crush on him. The Southern talk is a sure sign that he's reeling internally. Losing control.

He hikes my skirt up my thighs, then my body up the wall, and with a hand supporting my butt, probably strains tendons to pull my panties aside. He grapples with his jeans and the difficult angles for a few frantic seconds, and then pushes into me.

"God," I say, faint with relief and yet mortified at what

we're doing. It feels so good. But we should stop. Wait until we're alone. It's tacky to do this in a backstage bathroom. Isn't it?

But this is South's sweat-sheened skin sliding against mine. His breath panting all over me, creating shivers. The one guy who makes me weak inside. The *only* guy who is impossible to resist.

Pulling back slowly, he groans into my hair. *"Oh, man,* that's so—*hey* hang on! What the fuck are we doing?" He stares down between us. "No condom."

I stop his hand from digging in his back pocket. "Wait. I take birth control. And I've had my health checked recently. It's only been you since then, South."

"I'm clean too. Do you trust me?"

"Of course. Now get moving."

"Thank Christ. I'm gonna go slow here because I've been waiting and I wanna savor it and… *shiiit—"*

"No you're not. Get cracking." I wriggle to urge him on.

"Okay. Your command… my wish." His laugh turns into ragged gasps as he grips my long plait, adjusting my head so he can move those perfect lips between my neck and my mouth with ease. "Shit, Mia, I've never felt anything so good… I am not gonna last here."

The friction of skin on skin, no latex between us, is incredible. So perfect. "Don't worry, I'm right there with you."

Thunder booms inside my head, perfectly timed to his thrusts. *Geez.* Wait. No. It sounds like someone is—

"Hellooo. Anyone in there? Can you open the door please?"

"Go away, Rita." With one hand, South grasps my face, giving me a desperate look—a wry smile mixed with a grimace, and then ignoring his manager's new assistant, he keeps moving.

"South? Is that you? What are you doing in there?"

"*Hell...*Oh... nothing much, just knitting sweaters for poor oil-spill penguins." He keeps pumping, and shaking, and breathing like a horse galloping down the homestretch. "Go away, would ya?"

"Lane's looking for you. Your ass is due on stage."

"Be right out."

Shit, Rita might come in. But that doesn't matter. Right now, frankly, I don't care. Just as long as he keeps moving. Making me melt. And shake. Turn liquid, like hot oil about to burst into flames. Burning. So hot. So...

He grunts and slaps a palm on the wall above us. "Oh, fuck, Mia, I'm gonna blow... I can't..."

On a long, loud groan he comes inside me, and I muffle my own shaky moan into his chest, shattering right along with him. He tugs my head up and stares deep into my eyes while white-hot waves wash over me.

A surprised "*Oh!*" sounds on the other side of the door. "*Right*. Sorry! I didn't realize you had company. But you have to hurry up. Nate's spitting chips."

"Okay. Okay. Just go." South laughs. Still breathing hard, he says, "Man, that girl could wilt the dick off a bonobo monkey."

"Don't be so mean." I push his chest away and fan the air between us. "Whew, it's hot and sticky."

"Yeah." He grins happily as he withdraws slowly from my body. "That's just how you like it."

I pinch his cheek hard. "Anyway, she's gorgeous!"

"If you like crazy-eyed girls who constantly wield gig and sales stats at you, then, yeah, she's great. Hey, can I move some stuff into your place tomorrow?"

"Really? Shouldn't we see how the dating thing goes first?"

"Nope. The album's going nuts. I'm gonna be away a lot, and when I'm home, I want to be with you as much as I can. You're it, Mia. I'm not messing around here."

"This is crazy."

Gripping my face with both hands, his eyes gleam a translucent blue-green, like chunks of raw beryl.

"It's the sanest thing I've ever done. How can I say it? You're the water. The wave. The whole ride. You're everything. I mean, I think this has to be..." As he trails off, his fingers dig into my waist, gaze dropping to his feet.

"What? What is it?"

"Love." He says the word like he can hardly believe it's true.

An explosion of joy detonates inside me.

"Put me out of my misery and tell me you feel this madness, too."

I nod, and he laughs. Then he kisses me, soft and slow. "Yeah? You do?"

"Yes. I love you, South."

"Don't fuck with me now. Are you sure?"

"Yes! I was a goner from the second I saw a photo of you. *Wham*—just like that—love at first sight."

"I am one lucky guy, then." He sighs into my mouth and kisses me sweetly. "Guess I'd better go and do the show, huh?"

"Yes! Go get 'em, Tiger. But first, maybe you should pull your zip up."

Grinning, he looks down at his softening hard-on. "What? You don't think this is a good look?"

I laugh, then smack him and race for the toilet cubicle.

18

THE WATCHER

Shadows

Eyes fixed on the movement of his shoulder blades, I'm draped in shadows so no one will notice me. Not the band, not the crew, and certainly not South's new girlfriend.

Hypnotized, I watch every ripple of muscle, angle and glide of bone. The perfect curve of his butt in those faded jeans. The golden hair falling in messy waves around that face. The sinful lips.

All of it mine.

All of *him*, mine. Well he's not mine *quite yet*, but he will be very soon.

Not Mia's, the cow who he's been lusting over for weeks

and weeks.

Mia. What an annoying name.

He prowls to the front of the stage, eyes scanning the swarming crowd, and the drone rises, rushing into my ears so loudly it hurts.

To distract myself from the wildness, the zapping inside my head, I concentrate on his fingers turning guitar pegs, adjusting and feeling into the sound, like he always does.

Watch him.

Watch *him* and don't think of anything else. *Especially* not Mia who's standing next to Lance side-of-stage, blond plaits bouncing as she enjoys the show. Enjoy it while it lasts, bitch, because you won't have him for long.

My eyes tear back to South as he shouts into the mic, long and deep. "Hey! Y'all hot enough out there?"

The crowd reaches fever pitch, and he turns and grins back at Nate. His laugh stabs at my chest. An attack I have no desire to protect myself from. I'll happily drown in an ocean of blood as long as he's the guy who creates it. Sick, I know. But that's just how things are with me and South. Overwhelming. All consuming.

And he has no idea.

Yet.

The endless sea of fools wanting a piece of him scream. And scream. They lurch and push forward, fingers reaching and mouths gaping like black holes. All of them wanting to swallow him up.

I know the feeling well.

Except for my head nodding in time with the drum beat, I stand motionless, bobbing my fake grin up and down.

Down and up. Up and down. Always in a steady pattern, so I won't look out of place.

Who am I?

No names yet.

Think of me as the watcher.

Because that's what I do best.

I watch.

19

SOUTH

Soundcheck

"**S**hit!" I say, my fingers blurring over guitar strings and the sound bouncing around the arena's hollow space.

Soundchecks are weird these days. The sight of around sixteen thousand empty seats, a little depressing. Those seats won't be empty tonight and though I feel grateful, I can't help wishing we were playing some dive bar instead of this soulless joint.

With no clear destination in mind, I stomp across the stage. At the very least, I'll get away from the mic. I can't concentrate on this new song at all, and I can't stop thinking about Mia.

A month ago, I pretty much moved into her apartment.

We had three freaking amazing weeks, crazy shit going on with the record label, the album going nuts—and me always hanging out for the day to end so I could return home to Mia. Now we're on a mini East Coast tour and I haven't seen her for a week. It's fucking with my sanity.

Raff, our tour manager, stops jawing at the sound engineer and glances up from the desk. "It's cool, South. So you fucked it up again. Don't worry about it. Take a break."

Yeah it's cool for Raff. He's not the one getting painful nodules on his vocal cords. Plucking strings, I lean against a speaker and watch a team of venue staff move chairs around on the floor. From up here they look like tiny fucking ants.

"Why did I write this dumb song?" I say to no one in particular. "It's almost outta my range. Every time I sing it, I end up screaming."

"You wrote it because it's awesome, that's why." Zave whips his t-shirt off, uses it to soak up the sweat dripping down his chest, and then throws it at me. "What's it about, anyway?"

It's hotter than forty hells this afternoon, and whatever air conditioning the cavernous venue has isn't working.

"Sex," I say, catching the shirt and throwing it off the stage to be walked on by the roadies.

"Hey!" Zave yells.

"Are any of your new ones *not* about fucking?" Ben grins happily now that the conversation has turned to his favorite subject.

"Nope."

"Don't knock it," says Nate. "Clearly, fooling around with

someone he actually likes is still a trip for him. We're all reaping the benefits of that cozy situation, because the new batch of songs are as intense as—"

"Fuck?" I suggest.

"You are a one syllable guy this afternoon." Zave laughs. "Don't sweat it. We won't put that one in tonight's set. Problem solved."

"But I want to try it on a crowd. See if it flies. It's just hard to sing though. Hurts even."

Nate kicks his pedal board. "Shit, the overdrive's moving. Raff! I need a cable tie. Let's hope no one likes it and then you'll never ever have to do it live again."

Sighing, I drop to the floor. I play a haunting riff that echoes out over the arena and makes everyone stand still.

Nate laughs. "Purple Rain?"

I smirk and sing the opening to Prince's opus. The lines about not wanting to cause trouble or pain. When I get to the part about wanting to see them laughing, Nate uses his boot to push me over.

"Listen, you lot might not have lives, but I've got places to go," whines Ben. "Get up off the floor and finish this shit. And stop looking like such a sad little baby foal."

"There's no such thing as a baby foal." Tuning my guitar to open G, I glance up and laugh. "It's just foal."

Ben looks around for backup. "Bullshit. Baby foals are a thing, aren't they, Lane?"

"No," booms our manager from the front row seats. "They're just foals."

"Whatever." Ben lifts his guitar over his head. "You're so basic."

I snort. "You are." Then raising my eyebrows at Ben, I play the opening riff to our song *Dirt*, knowing it'll piss him off.

"Jesus, speaking of babies. I'm not wasting any more time on your stop-start diva crap." Sneering, Ben shoves his bass on a stand. "I'm outta here. Bouncing big time."

"Okay, sure. Could you do me a favor and go directly to a streetball court? Someone there might bounce you on your fucking head for us. And don't forget about the live Instagram thing at the hotel later. I'm not doing it by myself," I growl at Ben's back.

Without turning, he gives me the finger and keeps walking.

"Chill, man," says Nate. "I can do that interview with you if he doesn't show."

"I hate it when he says bounce. He sounds about as dumb as a watermelon. Shit, he's worse than Zave these days."

Zave thumps his kick drum. "Hey, man, I can hear you."

"Well, you hate a lot of things this last week," says Nate.

A roadie, layers of muscles testing the seams of his dirty, white tank, passes Nate a cable tie. "Thanks, man. And now we're down a bass player. So you can hate that too."

"I also hate this diva tag he's throwing at me all the time. I'm really not that bad."

"He only does it because all the girls he sleeps with at the moment ask to be introduced to you. It's a jealously thing."

"*Sh-it*. Let's try this damn song one more time. Mia loves

it," I say, ignoring the comment about girls. "Raff! Can you *bounce* on up here for us and be Ben for a bit?"

"Bounce means leave, you idiot." Nate heads for his mic.

"Yeah? Well, it also means to strike the ground and rebound. That's more Ben's style. Wait. Actually, it's all three. Strike, rebound and *then* leave."

"As long as he doesn't bounce himself right out of the band, I'm okay with that." Nate waits for Zave to count him in. "Now get yourself in front of that microphone and whack this song out of the park before I start calling you a diva, too. Or a baby foal."

"Yes, sir." On my knees, eyes screwed shut, I let out one long, low roar.

Who cares if it hurts? Might as well go for a bit of self-sabotage, give myself a vocal cord hemorrhage right now. That way they might let me go home to Mia.

20

THE WATCHER

Spark

My drink glows orange in the strange lights of the funky bar. Little sparks like luminescent red sperm dart through the liquid. One moment they're alive, racing, and the next gone. Light extinguished.

Dead.

I spark on the inside, too. I flash and flare in hot waves that corrode and burn. Sitting here, watching like I always do, I'm unhappy. And also excited. Overflowing with a billion volts of electricity, I'm a lightning bolt needing to earth. I search the crowd for South, yearning to strike him hard. Over and over.

The bar is packed. Music thumps, but I can't make out the

song. The song doesn't matter. Only he does. *He* matters. And tonight, post gig at the West Hollywood hotel bar, unbelievably, South is here. And Mia, hallelujah, is back home photographing one of her stupid pet weddings.

All the Up Void members stand separately, each surrounded by little packs of industry sycophants. A journalist here. A music exec there. And he, of course, is surrounded by girls that giggle while their hands claw softly at him.

Eyes gentle, he smiles and laughs as if he has no clue what they want. Everyone else knows. And Mia. Mia knows, too. Luckily she's not here to witness their fawning.

I keep on watching and wait for him to break. Because I'm certain that it's just a matter of time. One fuck. A quick one. And why not? Without a doubt he must be horny, all that fiery energy he pulsates with on stage. And off. And Mia would never know.

Ah, now—what is this?

A girl in the pack surrounding him, blond and shining and almost as sexy as he is, has given up the subtle game. Fed up with getting nowhere she pulls him by the neck, pushes back golden waves to whisper in his ear. His face doesn't change. Polite interest. A half smile. Done whispering, the girl turns her face and takes his mouth.

Oh, my. Lucky her.

For two seconds, he's frozen. Even his lips don't move. I watch very, very closely to be sure of that. And then he's shaking the goddess off, saying 'no' and trying hard to smile. He seems shaken, which doesn't make sense. The guy looks like a sex machine who'd screw anything with a pulse, but he acts like his dick would disintegrate if it touched anyone other than Mia.

When *she's* around he's like a mutt near a bitch in heat, oozing come-fuck-me vibes. Why?

What dark spell has Mia cast? What's in the potion she's fed him? Whatever the ingredients, they make a powerful magic. Because he sees no one else.

Watching the blond girl push through the crowd, her face a stony mask of disappointment, I sigh and then smile. Because it will be different for me when Mia's out of the picture. When that sweet day comes, there won't be any failure.

Only South.

21

SOUTH

Want

"Rita. Hey, Rita!" Vince leans around me and slaps Lane's assistant's arm.

Swiping purple bangs out of her eyes, she clunks her wine glass on the bar. Chardonnay no doubt. It's all she ever drinks.

Not one to be intimidated by loud-mouthed big-shots, Rita raises an unfriendly eyebrow at Vince. Personally, the guy gives me nightmares.

"See the dude that Marco's talking to over there?" Vince points through the crowd at a guy with a handle-bar mustache and long red hair cascading around his shoulders.

Rita nods.

"That's Axl Rose's son. Go talk to him. I know you're burning a torch for his father."

"What rot! Axl hasn't got a son, has he, South?"

Noticing she didn't deny the crush, I smile. "I think the closest he got was a few dogs and a step-son."

Opening a packet of chips and sneering, Ben gives me a once over. Here we fucking go. He's been riding my ass ever since I got together with Mia.

"So, what… are you like the go-to guy for celebrity gossip these days?"

"I think you'll find that South *is* the gossip," says Vince. "He's just so super-hot right now. Everyone wants to know who he's fucking and how often. Who cuts his glorious hair. What kind of underwear he stores his junk in—"

"Do you realize you're obsessed with undergarments?" My head pounds. "It's a sickness, Vince. Every time you open your mouth you start banging on about them."

Vince grins. "Don't try and distract me. Now where was I? Other than your stripy Calvin Kleins, what else does the regular girl on the street wanna know?"

Hooking my thumb into the waistband of my jeans, I peer down. Yep, I'm wearing the stripy ones. "How the hell did you know—"

"And the million-dollar question all the fans want the answer to…" Vince narrows his eyes at me. "Is that kooky blond-haired bitch *really* his girlfriend?"

What? Fists clenched, I step forward. Vince may be the high and mighty managing director of String Power records, but in about thirty seconds he'll be history. And flat on his ass on the ground.

"Whoa there, Tiger." Ben shoves a palm on my chest and laughs at Vince. "Better choose your words more wisely, Vince. I don't think he likes hearing his girlfriend called that. See the blue lasers shooting out of his eyes? They're telling you to start running."

Vince sips his straight scotch. "Ah, relax. I love the girl. He knows that. I'm just repeating what everyone else is saying."

I shake my head at him. Every single muscle in my body aches and then some. "I'm going to bed."

Rita shoves her phone in my face. "But it's only quarter to two. Stay and hang with us."

I do a quick survey of the hotel bar. Too bright and swanky. Too many assholes wanting to give me their cell numbers. Talk contacts and projects. Mention how great they are at sucking cocks. And would I like to sample their skills? No thanks.

Leering at Rita, Ben, the man-whore, says, "Or we could hit the sack, too, Rita. What do you think about an extreme fireworks show back in my room? Sound good?"

"One day I'm going to say yes and your balls will explode in shock. You're exactly my type. Problem is, I've got a very strict policy on not sleeping with co-workers." Hand on Ben's shoulder, Rita pouts at him. He goggles back at her.

For once, Ben is speechless and, by the look on his face, he's just swallowed one of his chips sideways. I laugh, and it only makes my brain squeeze tighter.

The background music changes from some soft rock

rubbish to The Strokes' debut album. Weird. It doesn't fit the sterile atmosphere of the bar, and even though the first track always gets my blood moving, it's not enough to keep me here. There's something I can't wait to do back in my room.

Sliding my beer along the bar, I say, "You're all pretty funny, but unfortunately not entertaining enough to stop me from heading for the elevator. I need some sleep."

"Night-night, South." Ben nudges Rita. "Him and his right hand are off for a long, hot night of chaffing the skin on his dick. Tell us who you think about when you do it. Is it always Mia or do you spice it up now and then with a bit of variety?" Ben wraps an arm around Rita. "Maybe sometimes you even think about raunchy Rita here."

My eyebrows shoot high. That's a low blow, even for Ben.

As I clap Vince on the shoulder, I meet Rita's gleaming dark gaze. She holds eye contact and licks her lips. I look away. *Jesus.* I've never once thought about fucking her. Sure she's cute and maybe a little creepy, but Mia keeps me amped around the clock. Why would I need to think about anyone else to shoot a load off?

"See you comedians tomorrow." I tip my chin at Vince. "And, *you*, don't forget to call your wife. I really don't want her ringing me at four in the morning again while you're out on another bender."

The look on Vince's face says '*fat chance of that happening, buddy*', the calling, that is. The bender is a certainty.

I turn and head for the lobby.

Accosted by grabby hands all the way, I'm lucky to make it through the crowd and into the stark foyer with my clothes and dignity intact. I glance around. Stone and glass and not a splash of warmth to be seen.

Staring at the elevator, I try to recall what the heck floor I'm on. Was it twenty-four? Nope. Thirty-four?

"Shit!" I flinch as my left butt cheek is squeezed and a barely-dressed girl, all dark curls and bovine-sweet eyes, molds herself to my side like a wet rain jacket. I hadn't heard her approach. The groupies get stealthier every day.

Reaching a black-painted nail toward the buttons on the wall, she says, "What floor are we going to, South from Up Void?" The smile on her face is anything but sweet.

I laugh. "I'm working on that information right now. Just need my brain to co-operate."

Her hand drags down my chest, my stomach, and then she palms my balls. Instantly, I'm hard.

"Well, I'm ready to co-operate. And even if your brain's lagging, another part of you feels very willing."

Twenty-five! That's my floor. And room 302. One finger stabbing at the button, I move her aside. "Oh, right. Yeah. Listen, do me a favor and wait there for a minute."

I step into the elevator, pressing another button quickly. Her jaw drops as I wave goodbye. The doors whoosh shut and I'm shot upward so fast my tired brain spins in my skull.

Surrounded by mirrors, I sag against the back wall and make the mistake of turning my head. The elevator jolts to a halt. In the mirror, I see my hard-on trying to bust out of my jeans at the exact moment an elderly couple stumble in laughing like loons.

Holy shitballs.

They look about ninety-five and, as Mia would say, well pissed. Hands clasped in front of my jeans, I nod at them and try to look casual.

If they speak to me, it might deflate the persistent boner. So far, sharing the confined space with them is having zero effect.

The lady pats her bouffant ginger hair, scanning me from head to toe. "Have you been to Club Rodeo yet?" she asks in a down home accent.

So that explains the guy's cowboy hat. Kind of. I smile and shake my head. Squirming under their scrutiny, I check out my dick. Still hard. *Damn.* Where's Mia when I need her?

"Well, we just about danced our pants off tonight. Didn't we, Clive? And I nearly busted my gut I laughed so hard!" Pressing the button for floor seventeen, she says, "Do you dance, young man?"

Clive shakes his head at me. "Katie, would you leave the boy alone? Whatever you're thinking, stranger, I suggest you do *not* say yes to her."

She reminds me a lot of Nate's Aunt Patty. Sweet thing.

What I do on stage, does that qualify as dancing? I sure like slow dancing with Mia in my arms. Pressed tight. Practically carrying her around. I can't lie to Katie just because Clive says I should. "Yeah, I guess I do dance—"

"Well, we're heading back to the club real soon. You should come check it out."

The doors open and they step into the silver hallway. "I'd love to see a strapping fella like you take on that bucking bull thing. Oh, my, what a treat."

Folding my arms across my chest, I laugh.

Her gaze sweeps down my body, eyes widening. "Although, in your condition, it might not be the best idea. You don't want to do yourself an injury. And, darlin', I sure hope you've got a woman waiting back in your room. Or a man, if that's what inflates your dinghy. No. It looks like you've got more of a canoe there."

The doors close. My mouth gapes open.

By the time I arrive at my room, I feel weak with exhaustion. At least my dick has finally wilted. That's a relief.

As I enter, my cells rings, and I throw it at the fake-fur blanket covering the bed. I get tangled in my t-shirt, wrestling it over my head. When I'm free, I lounge back on the purple and gold armchair that looks like a throne and answer my phone.

"Hey," I yell over the racket coming down the line. "What do you want, Zave? It sounds like you're at the circus."

"Yeah, I am. A naked one."

"So, this is a pocket dial?"

"No, man. Just thought I'd check in. Heard Ben's been a constant prick to you. Are you alright?"

I stroll into what the hotel staff call the 'zen room' and take a piss. Huh. It's a very jazzy looking toilet. If that's what it is. The perforated holes covering the floating stone bowl look like they might jet out steam. Maybe it gives facials. Well, if that's what it does, the next person who has one is in for an unpleasant experience.

"Shit, thanks, Zave, but don't worry. I reckon I can handle it."

"Well, if you want me to sucker-punch him for ya, I'd be happy to do it. Please tell me you're not *pissing* right now?"

"Fine. I'm not pissing right now. And instead of worrying about me, you should go get laid."

I hang up, drag myself back to the bed and flop over it. I arrange the pillow against the headboard and lean back against it. Thumbing over my cell, my stomach muscles clench. She'd better answer.

"South!"

I grin as half of Mia's face fills the screen and then disappears. She's shit at FaceTime.

"Hey, Mia. You still at the pet wedding? Sounds pretty wild. Can you go somewhere quieter? And hurry."

I hear a squawk, get a flash of red lips, and then everything blurs as she moves quickly through the crowd.

Two minutes later, there she is, her laugh echoing around a shiny, gray bathroom. "Hi! Oh, South. *Hi, sweetheart!*"

She's definitely tanked. It's the only time she uses soppy endearments.

Other voices chirp in the background. Hand dryers roar.

"Are you already back at your room? It's only two—"

"Go in a cubicle, Mia."

"But I don't need to go to the toilet and—"

"Quick, just go in. I want to talk to you."

Ivy's face peers over Mia's shoulder. "Is that South? Oh, hi, South. Wow! Good God, you are looking fine as always. Shirtless and everything!" She rolls her eyes dramatically.

"Hey, Ivy. How's it going? Put Mia back on, will ya? It's kinda urgent."

"Oh, yes. I can see that."

What? Yeah, okay, so my hard-on is back, but she can't see that. Can she?

Everything goes fuzzy. I hear creaks and bangs, and then there's Mia's smiling face framed by a gleaming, white toilet cistern.

"Mia. You look beautiful."

The little softy's eyes tear up. She's wearing the red velvet dress I love. It hugs her curves just right and when she moves, the wrap-around top reveals glimpses of pale, succulent flesh. I plan to make the most of the sight. Breath ratcheting up, I undo the button on my jeans.

"Thank you!" she says. "You're sweet."

No, I'm really not. "Hey, tell me who's there tonight?"

"I was allowed to invite friends to this wedding, so everyone!"

"Yeah, like who?"

"Well, Ivy and Nico, of course. The rest of the Burntbad boys are hanging out, making us laugh. They're quite mad."

"They're certifiable. And the architect? Nico mentioned he might be tagging along. Is he there?"

"Yep, *Liam's* here."

"Uh-huh." *Dammit.* "I wouldn't mind smacking him."

"Why, for crap's sake?"

"Because I'm jealous."

She clicks her tongue. "You're so silly."

"Sounds more like a party than a work night, which is great." Except for the architect being there. I sure was bummed when I heard about him inserting himself into Ivy and Nico's social lives. I'm keeping my eye on him.

"Yeah, these guys know how to have fun. They've even got a Cuban band playing, South. They're amazing. And was your gig good? What else has been happening?"

I really don't want to tell her what's been happening. She'll only worry. To distract her I say, "Man, I should have grabbed Lane's computer. Then I could get a better look at your bra."

She looks down. "What? You can't see that!"

"Not yet."

"Anyway, you can't even work Lane's computer. You do strange things and make it freeze up almost every single time."

"Yeah, well, talk to the Mac people about that. They've gotta fix their dumbass programs. It's not *my* problem."

Mia laughs, and I feel it in my groin. *Man,* I just want to touch her. Her laugh must have mucked with my head, darn it, because, before I can stop myself, the wrong words tumble out. "Mia, she rang again yesterday."

"Your mother? No! Why? Are you okay? Did she say what she... Look, South, whatever you do just wait right there, honey. Okay? Please don't go anywhere... I'm going to hop on a plane. Right now, I'm heading for the airport."

Heart bashing against my chest, I shake my head. "No, you don't need to do that. I mean, I want you to. Fuck, so much. But not for that reason. I'm fine. She was drunk. She spoke shit. I listened for two minutes. Then I hung up and turned my phone off. I don't want to talk about her. I just want to think about you. How gorgeous you look."

"*You* look beautiful, South," she says, giving me a sad smile. "I wish you were here."

"Man, me too. You know, I'd pay just about anything if I could fuck you right now."

"Geez, what a romantic!" She crosses her eyes at me. "Way to make a girl feel like a prostitute. And do you think you can put a top on, please? Your bare chest is very distracting."

"I'm hot. I'm not putting a top on."

Her gaze moves slowly over my body.

"You know it's only as the words are coming out of my mouth that I realize I could probably use better ones. But by then it's too late. Hey, Mia?"

"Yep?"

"I love you. You know that, right? I'm trying to learn how to speak pretty to you, but I'm not much good at it yet. I just need more practice."

"You do fine."

Really? *I* don't agree. All those feelings that build warm and sweet behind my ribs, they're hard to put into words without sounding like some corny quote. Give me a guitar and then it's easy. Turning feelings into music—now that's cool.

But I lied to Ben at soundcheck today. Sure, a lot of the new songs are about what it feels like to fuck someone I love. Better than drugs. But mostly the songs are maps of feelings, wild emotional rides sparked by laughing golden eyes. Sweet sensations. Hot surges. Lost meanderings. Oozy, sticky, scary fucking feelings.

"So, do you love me?" I smirk. "I notice you didn't reciprocate when I told you before."

"Shut up. Of course I love you. And I'd give away everything I own if I could sleep cuddled up next to you tonight."

I huff out a laugh. "Sleep, huh? Is that all you want to do?"

Her smile turning hot, she says, "No, first I'd lick you all over, then make you come so many times you begged me to stop."

My pulse hammers. "Wow. That sure sounds fun. Give me a taster."

Motionless, she blushes. Then trails fingers down her chest.

I grin while she loosens the material and pushes it away, revealing her bra. Releasing a long breath, I cup my hand over my jeans, applying pressure to my dick. "Fuck. You're wearing the red one."

She runs her nails across the lace and just the sight of her nipples, dark and hard, brings me to the point of no return.

"Jesus. Keep doing that."

"This?" she asks as she puts her hands on the sides of her tits and squeezes them together. Oh, Man, I could weep with frustration. I *need* them in my mouth.

Groaning, I try to get my zip down fast without doing any permanent damage, then I set my hand to work. It really won't take much effort. I battle against my eyelids. They kept trying to close, but I don't want to miss a second of the visuals. When she speaks, I can barely hear her over the sound of my breathing.

"Do you ever get tired of having a short girlfriend?"

"What?" With my brain on a fast train to Orgasm-Central and about to pull into the station, it takes a moment for her words to sink in. "No. Of course not. Why would I?"

"Well, always having to contort yourself. Bending over. Cricks in your neck—"

"Shh. You're the perfect size. I can pick you up any ol' time you're being objectionable and hardly feel the strain. It's great. Can you lean forward some more? Oh, yeah, exactly like that." I put my hand back on the job. In a rough voice I say, "And if you were any bigger, I wouldn't see so much of you in this tiny, little screen… and…what I'm looking at now has me ready to blow in record time."

She laughs. "Always with the sweet words!"

"Mia!" a voice shouts. "You still in there?"

I freeze. Ivy again. That girl has the most inconvenient timing. "Mia! Don't answer her—"

"Hey, Ivy." Mia clears her throat. "Yep. It's me. I'm just, you know, going to the toilet."

"Well hurry up about it. The host needs you. He's about to do the goodnight speeches and he wants you to shoot some photos. You still talking to South?"

"Yeah. I'm saying goodbye to him now. I'll be out in a sec."

"Mia, no. *Please.* Wait until she goes."

"I can't," she whispers. "I'd better go help."

"Help *me* first!"

She laughs, swinging blond hair over her shoulder, and then rearranging her dress. "I'm fairly sure you can help yourself. What are you going to do when I hang up? Other than the obvious. Sleep I hope. You look really tired."

"Ah, so you lied before?"

"No, you idiot. You always look amazing. Even back when you were a messed-up pain-in-the-butt marauding through my house."

Frowning, I say, "Shit. Why did you have to remind me of that? You're killing my buzz here."

"Seriously, what are you gonna do after I say goodbye? Your mom called. I can't help worrying about you."

Running my eyes over her, I say, "You guessed right. First, I'm gonna finish thinking about that red bra, the soft velvet dress, and the smoking hot girl wrapped in them. Then I've got a song to work on."

That perks her up. "Another new one? I can't wait to hear it! What's it about?"

"Jerking off." I laugh at her pursed lips. "Nah." Smile gone and frowning hard, I say, "It's about how, right now, my chest feels like it might bust open from missing you so bad."

"Mia!" yells Ivy.

"Go on get out of here. Go and do your job and let me get on with mine. It's a very important one." I grin down at my dick so she'll know precisely what I have to work on, and then I bring the phone close. She does the same. Perfect. Now I can see the gold sparking in her eyes. "Love you, babe."

Expression sweet, she tells me what I want to hear, and then we spend about ten seconds smiling at each other before we press end call on the count of five.

22

MIA

The Garrison

Up Void's dressing room looks like a battle zone. Earlier in the day, it had been the venue for a food fight between record label staff, assorted drunks from at least three other bands, and a guy in an Ant Man costume. The outdoor festival clean up team will be cursing them at bump out time.

Right now, the guys are tearing up the stage, but Ivy and I have zipped back to the trailer to use the bathroom.

Frowning at the filth surrounding me, I push away a pile of clothing and settle on the couch. "Ivy, hurry up! They're playing *Dirt* and they're absolutely shredding it. Listen to the crowd!"

Ivy stumbles out of the tiny bathroom, zipping up her sequined shorts. "How did you cope in there, Mia? It's disgusting."

"Grab that setlist for me." I point at the opposite wall. She swings her head around. "There. See it?" I say. "It's gaffered above the table."

Ivy plucks it off, and then yelps, shaking her hand. "Ew, I do not want to know what that gunk is on it. Holy batshit!" She wipes her hand on South's battered denim jacket and flops next to me.

"Quick, let me see," I command, bouncing in my seat. "What song's next?"

Ivy scans the list while I peer over her shoulder. In the right-hand corner of the sheet, South has drawn a cute black dog.

"Aw, look, Ivy. South's drawn Roxy." The faithful mutt has been Nate's mom's constant companion since her husband, Mason, died from a sudden heart attack last year. Both close to him, Nate and South are still reeling from their loss.

"That's cute. But the other picture, hmm… not so much."

I squint hard at the paper. What is that scrawled in the other corner? Ah, yes, of course. It's Zave's signature sketch —a floral-patterned dick and balls. He's such a jerk.

"So after *Dirt* they're doing *Lined Black.* Um, then it's *Mess Me Up* and bingo… this has to be what you're looking for, right? *The Garrison.*"

"Yes! Quick, let's go. If we leave right now, we'll have plenty of time to push our way down near the front."

"Absolutely not! If anyone recognizes you, you'll be cruci-fied. Stomped on and torn to pieces by thousands of little South-ettes."

"Come on! It's *The Garrison*, Ivy. That hypnotic start that builds and builds until South chucks his guitar. Then he's half naked on his knees, screaming like a whole tribe of berserk-ers. It'll go off. Tell me you don't wanna be in the crowd for that?"

"Look, if you wait until tonight, I'm pretty sure he'll give you your own private mosh session back at the hotel, and that way his fans won't get a chance to tear all your hair out."

"Come on. No one will notice me."

"Rubbish." Eyes wide, Ivy pats her ear. "Darn. I've lost an earring." She eyes the toilet. "Unfortunately, I'll have to take a look in that disgusting hell-hole. Send a search party if I'm not out in thirty minutes."

After shuffling to the bathroom door, she spins around and says, "South has given you your orders about this kind of thing. It's different now that he's public property. People can easily find photos of you online and then try and stab your eyes out." With a dramatic flick of red hair, she stomps into the toilet, slamming the door behind her.

It's unfair. All I want is to be down in the crowd, my heart soaring as the music takes me high. It's utter bliss. Why should I miss out?

"Mia, over here," comes a voice from the trailer steps.

My head whips up.

Lane's assistant, Rita, grins at me. "Come on, hurry up," she says, and disappears.

Sending a guilty glance at the still-closed bathroom door, I bury my bag under South's jacket and sprint after Rita.

When I catch up, she gives me a wicked smile and tugs me past artists' chill out zones, tropical-jungle bars, and food tents wafting mouthwatering smells. "We can easily make it down the front before *The Garrison* starts. I've got very sharp elbows."

23

SOUTH

Missing

"You seen Mia?" I yell, leaning into the guitar tech who's standing side of stage.

"Yeah, I watched her and the red-haired chick disappear about twenty minutes ago laughing like a couple of hyenas."

Weird. Mia hates to miss a set.

Zave thumps his kit hard in a series of slow pounding beats, shoulders tensed to crack into *The Garrison*, one of Mia's favorite tunes.

I look over my shoulder and, dammit, there's Nate urging me back on stage, flicking his head and wriggling his eyebrows like a jackass. I *should* get out there, but Mia not being side-of-stage feels wrong. Every single time I push myself to the edge of goddamn insanity with that song, I do it just for her. Knowing how hot it makes her.

"Pete!" Out of nowhere, Ivy hurtles past Nico and Linc, who are standing in the wings, and shakes our techie by the arm. She looks freaked.

Nate starts the song extra slow and paces in ever-widening circles toward me. Shit. I'd *really* better get out there, but I can't tear my eyes off Ivy jabbering at Pete.

She points at the crowd, and I do my best to lip read while moving closer, straining to hear over the racket of my band.

"No. She's not with me!" Ivy shrieks. "She wanted to get down the front."

"Who?" I yell.

Two heads swing my way. "No one," Ivy says at the same time Pete growls, "Mia."

"What?" I can't have heard that right.

"Mia," says Pete. "That's where she is. Down there."

Brain spinning, I gaze out at the swaying sea of people Pete is pointing at. Nope. Mia isn't a massive risk taker. She wouldn't do that.

I look back at Nate who's getting his message across loud and clear in angry shrieks of feedback. *Get out here. Get out here. Get out here.*

Loping across the stage, Ben bounces mad licks off his bass. Zave looks bored as he thumps his kick drum.

"Has she lost her fucking mind?" I yell. "Have you seen how small she is? *Fuck.* She'll be *minced* out there!"

Ivy jams her hands on her hips. "Would you chill out? I'm

not sure she actually *is* down there. She's probably just bumped into someone backstage and can't escape. Anyway, she's not silly, South. She wouldn't go off by herself."

I remove my death glare from Ivy and shrug my guitar into place. With steam coming out of my ears I start roaring, barreling toward the microphone, fingers attacking guitar strings.

Well, that's a different start to the song. The fans seem to dig it, though, so that's cool. Far from cool myself, I feel like a blazing fireball of fury.

Man, if Ivy can't even manage to look convinced by the tale she's spinning, then why the heck should I swallow it?

As I hit the mic, my howl comes crashing back at me from the monitors. And, somehow, while choking on Ivy's words, I manage to pull back, throttle down, and coast into the first verse, eyes scanning the crowd as I sing.

If Mia is down there, I'm gonna kill her.

24

MIA

Found

Five rows deep in the mosh, I turn and check out the crowd. What an amazing sight. Ten thousand people with their arms in the air watch South, who's clutching the mic in a fury, his body jackknifing in a violent rhythm. Up Void are on fire and South looks insane. Crazed. A Viking god made flesh and bone.

Without warning, he drops to the ground.

Holding Rita's shoulder, I yell in her ear, "What do you think he's doing?"

Still on the floor and dripping with sweat, South's chest presses into his knees like he's doing the child pose in a grungy hot yoga class. The microphone lies discarded at his side.

Zave launches into the familiar thumps that signal the beginning of *Singing Eyes*. My song. The song he wrote when we first began sleeping together. Every time I hear it, I want to cry. It's about him falling in love and drowning in emotions. It's about me. It's about *us*.

Seeming in no hurry to start the number, South stays low and crawls toward the front, scowl fixed on the first few rows.

"He's looking for someone!" Rita shouts.

What? Hopefully not me. For the first time in my life, I'm grateful for my lack of height.

"*Fuck*," South snarls, lurching onto his feet. With his chin raised and chest pumping, he stares at the audience, and like a seething mass of seaweed, people sway and scream and reach their arms toward him.

Pete passes South his Hellcat acoustic. Prowling to the mic, he slings it over his neck, fingers plucking at the strings. He exhales long, loud puffs of air that I can hear even over the crowd's roar.

The Up Void boys face their singer, watching his every move. A hum of excited chatter and the lilting notes South picks float through a mild dusk breeze.

He takes a massive breath, and a hush descends. Everything goes silent, even the insects.

Then South sings. "Wait." And the crowd erupts. "Wait and make…wait…wait and make me…wrecked."

One hand rubbing the middle of my chest, I wipe my

burning eyes. *This song. This song.* It takes me right back to the searing heartache, the pain of wanting South, finally having him in my bed. And thinking he'd never be mine.

"No. No," I hear Rita say to three girls standing on her left. Grimacing, she turns to me. "Your name is Steph if anyone asks. Especially this lot next to me. I think they're on to you."

Well *that's* a brilliant development.

Nate punches out distorted power chords, and then backs off. Picking up the mic stand, South shoves it near the edge of the stage, then keeps playing, eyes scanning the crowd again. He looks disturbed. And incredibly sexy.

Zave pounds slowly on his kick drum, then settles into a hard, steady beat, a perfect foil to South's pretty guitar riff. Hips rocking, his knees bent, a frown of agony in place, South and ten thousand Up Void fans sing together.

"Take."

"Take."

"Will you make me yours?"

"A ship."

"A ship that's wrecked I'm..." In the middle of a line, his voice disappears.

Suddenly, I'm trapped by the flaming heat of South's furious gaze. Singing abandoned, fists clenched at his sides, he sways toward the rim of the stage. Front-rowers squeal and laugh, reaching across the safety barrier. The rest of Up Void keep playing.

I look left. Right. Down at my feet, and then back at South. And he looks... absolutely terrifying.

Time slows, sweat oozes from my pores as I watch him struggle with his impotence, rail against the knowledge that if he speaks to me, he'll be throwing me to the lions.

Slowly, he shakes his head, takes a chance and mouths, "Get. Out."

"No," I say as I raise my eyes to the stars. Then back to South.

Glaring at a guy four people to my left, he yells, "I said get out of there. Now! I ain't fucking joking." He's two meters away from the mic, and yet his every word is crisp and clear.

Excitement builds as news ripples back through the outdoor amphitheater that things are getting weird.

Voice shrill over the din, Rita says, "Mia! I think you should split. He's about to go ballistic."

I stare at her. Is she mad? She just said my name out loud. Yelled it while pointing at South. And now several people are pointing at me.

The mob pushes and I stumble to stay upright. The girls Rita spoke to earlier shriek, *Mia. Mia. Mia.* And it sounds wrong, like mice squeaking. And then I'm pushed forward and back.

Hands over my ears and completely helpless, I watch South erupt. Bellowing my name, he leaps from the stage into the security pit and swings over the crowd barricade into chaos. Oh, shit. He's going to be ripped apart.

Then sounds become muffled, and I feel like I've been dumped by a brutal wave. Dragged under, I'm drowning in a sea of limbs, gasping for breath.

Nate calls for calm. *"Let South through. Let him get out and we can keep playing."*

And suddenly I'm crowd surfing, being passed along. Jolted and jostled, I hit the barrier. A guy in a yellow vest pulls me over, and I look back into the fray and see South behind me surrounded by five security guys tearing girls off him. Swearing, he jumps into the pit and yanks me into his arms.

"Mia. Mia," he says, hands gripping my face. "Oh, man, are you okay? Are you trying to give me a fucking heart attack?"

My eyes flutter and I can't keep his face in focus. "You look lovely, South."

"What?" He glowers at me. "You're making about as much sense as tits on a bull... *Shit.* For fuck's sake can someone help me over here!"

I'm pushed right. Then pulled left. From a distant planet, I hear South say, "No fucking way! Take her over the stage. *Right now.*"

"She'll get to the tent quicker through the pit," says a deep voice I don't recognize.

"I don't fucking care. Over the stage. Get a doctor on the side. *Now!*"

And then I'm passed along, riding the wave again, up, up, in a smooth swell to be beached on the floor side-of-stage.

Lane and the Up Void crew shout around me, but I can't understand a word. And South. South's hands twist into my clothes as he snaps at the others.

"No way," he says. "I'll go back on if she stays where I can see her. If she needs the medical tent, then that's it, I'm pulling the plug."

Oh, God. If I don't die in the next few minutes, Lane will definitely kill me for ruining the gig.

A doctor arrives and prods away at me. When he finally ceases his torture, he confers with Lane while South, whose lap provides a rather comfortable cushion, looks on anxiously.

"What?" he yells in their direction.

"Shhh!" Lane swipes a hand at him.

Not easily put off, South interrupts again, "What's he saying? Is she okay?"

"Well if you'd shut your mouth for a damn second, I might be able to find out." Heads together, Lane and the doctor mutter on.

"I'm fine, South, really."

He puts a hand over my mouth. *Shhh* I can't hear—"

"Okay!" Lane struts back, his Hawaiian shirt flapping in the breeze. "It's just a bit of shock and a few bruises. She's fine."

"She's fine. She's fine." The band members and road crew echo like a Greek chorus.

Fingers loosening on my top, South blows out a long breath.

"Get her a chair," hollers Lane, and everything around me dissolves in a blur of motion.

Next, I'm plucked up and deposited in a wheelchair, wrapped in a blanket and handed a bright orange drink. Grimacing at the chemical sweetness, I slurp through the straw and smile at South. The way my heart clamors and head spins, I'm probably about to go into respiratory shock from an aspartame overdose.

Hands on hips, South frowns at me and then turns away to consult with Lane and the Up Void boys. "How many numbers have we got left?" he asks them, looking dazed.

"Only two," replies Nate.

Ben pops his gum. "Plus an encore."

South looks my way. Dopey grin fixed in place, I wave. Scowling hard, he shakes his head at me.

"I dunno what to do." South folds his arms over his chest, tats and muscles rippling. "Hey, Lane, what did the guy say about noise? Will that be okay for her?"

"Don't be such an old lady. It's got nothing to do with her ears. She'll be fine."

Ivy and Nico step close. "We'll take care of her." Ivy's arm wraps around my shoulders. "She'll be fine."

Fine seems to be the buzzword of the day.

"Why'd you do it, Mia?" South asks. "Go down there on your own? It was fucking stupid. You could've been ripped apart."

"But I wasn't alone! Rita came with me."

Turquoise eyes narrow, the skin over his cheeks turning darker. Big whoops. I shouldn't have mentioned Lane's assistant.

"But *Rita* should know better," says Nico.

South glares at me. "I'm gonna strangle that little—"

"Hey, South. Let's do this." Zave clicks his sticks together. "Fucking listen to them out there. They're begging for more."

The chant of Eyes-Eyes-Eyes grows louder by the second.

With his hands braced on my chair, South contemplates the stage for several moments, then bends and kisses me like he's about to head into battle. From two inches away, blue eyes scorch into mine.

One second. Two. Three. I start to squirm.

Without warning, he nips my bottom lip, smirks, then unfurls muscle and bone until he stands at his full, impressive height.

When he takes two steps away, I sigh in relief. Then he spins back around and stabs a finger at me. "You're in big trouble, Mia. And don't think I'll let you off the hook easy. You could've died out there."

I swallow hard. He's being melodramatic.

"Move her closer," South instructs some poor underling in a voice like thunder. "I want to see her."

Then he stalks onto the stage.

25

SOUTH

Reckoning

With my ears ringing and the crowd's roar at my back, I leave the stage and make a beeline for Mia. "Feeling better?" I ask. Palms on the wheelchair, I drop my face close and rock her back and forth.

Looking kinda worried, she says, "Um… yep?"

Someone from behind whacks my back. "Unreal show, man." I wave my hand in their general direction.

Thank fuck, Mia looks okay. Laughing in relief, I spin her around and push the wheelchair forward. We cruise through corridors, down ramps, scattering the usual post-show well-wishers and back-slappers with ease.

The chair is an effective tool for pushing through hogwash. Maybe I should make her sit in it at every gig. That'd sure teach her. Nah. I've got a much better punishment in mind. One that I'm going to relish delivering. Actually, I can hardly wait to get started.

As the night air hits my sweaty skin, I look up and check out the sky. Like a billion glitzy sequins afloat on a black sea, the Milky Way glows bright overhead while down on earth the wheelchair bumps and rolls over grass.

"I feel ridiculous in this thing," says Mia.

"Yeah, well you *look* ridiculous too." That's a lie. As usual, she looks adorable and infuriatingly fuckable.

"Can you stop, please? I feel fine and I'm happy to walk."

I chuckle. "Nope. *I'm* happy with you stuck right there."

"Hey, the dressing room is that way!" She leans left, pointing to where the party is already in full swing.

"Yep."

"But—"

"You don't get to go to a party. Not after your behavior which was… I'm gonna speak plainly here, Mia." I lean close and whisper in her ear, "completely unacceptable."

"*Geez.* That's a bit unfair. With the stuff you've gotten up to in your past, you shouldn't be chastising me for cutting loose for once in my life."

"This is different. It could've had a fatal outcome."

She twists around to blast me with her outraged expression. "Says the hypocrite who used to get messed up on whatever drug was nearest when things weren't going his way and—"

"Hey! Enough. Don't remind me." I shake my head, trying to eradicate memories of my past fuck ups. Being created by a rapist and a completely psycho mother, I've always felt like I had plenty of reasons to live dangerously. And, yeah, before Mia, I mostly didn't care if I never woke up to see the next day. But things are different now. Now I want to see them all—every sunrise I can—with *her*.

When we reach the tour bus, I hoist Mia into my arms and race up the stairs. While I fumble with the door, she scrunches her nose at me and asks, "What are you planning to do? Put me down for a nap or something?"

"Or something." I grin. "You're not getting off that easy. You could've been killed for Christ's sake. Then what would I do?"

As I walk through the bus, she buries her face in my neck and kisses my skin. That's brave. I must stink like a polecat.

"Why are you going into the bathroom?" she asks, trying to wriggle free while I maneuver us into the black and gray-tiled room, flicking on the fluorescent light.

Unable to contain my laugh, I turn the lock on the door and prop her up next to the basin.

"Are you planning to what... maybe wash away my sins?"

"Not exactly. You okay balanced there?"

"I guess. But... this isn't what I was expecting. I think I'd like my lecture instead, please. What are you..."

Gently, I push her back against the mirror, perching myself on the edge of the low shower wall. Yep, just as I'd hoped. A perfect alignment.

"South!" She tries to shuffle forward, but I press my palm on her chest.

"Hell, woman, sit still!" I say. Or maybe I yell. The temper I've banked since leaving the stage currently flames hot.

Making an effort to be cool, I say, "Please don't move. If you do, I promise the lecture you'll get instead of this will go on for several days. And you'll also get one before every single show, long and loud, and I won't care who the fuck's standing next to you. Do you want that?"

"No! Okay. See? I'm still as stone. What are you going to do to me?"

She'll find out soon enough.

"Good. Make sure you stay that way. And if you utter even one word before I'm finished with you, you'll be getting the lectures as well."

She sighs and slumps back against the mirror.

There's a whole lot of creamy skin on display between her knee-high black boots and the hem of the dark red dress, and I slowly inspect it all. The boots can stay. In fact, I can probably manage fine without removing a stitch of clothing.

I scoot forward, put my hands on her hips and pull her to the edge of the counter. Mouth and eyes wide, she gasps.

"Uh, uh. Remember, no words," I warn.

As though I've got all night, my eyes trail over her entire body at a leisurely pace. I push her knees wide. She gasps again, and when I move my fingers to her panties, she clutches my arms hard.

Gently, I pull the purple material aside. I want to look at

her face, see it change, but it's like my eyes are stuck watching my thumb stroke over her glistening flesh. *Jesus.* The throbbing in my pants right now is unbearable.

This probably isn't the best way to make her pay for scaring the life out of me. Who am I kidding? It's most definitely my dumbest idea ever, because I want to fuck her senseless, not torture myself.

I put my mouth on her, inhaling her incredible scent, and suck and lick. She shakes hard, her every breath resounding in the small space, a filthy soundtrack that makes me huff raggedly over her skin. I hook my arms under her knees, wrap my palms over soft thighs and use my teeth and tongue to get her shaking harder. To make us both squirm.

When she rocks forward, panting *god-god* with each exhalation, I pretend I can't hear it, stop fighting my own moans and look up at her.

Eyes closed, head thrown back and lips parted, blond hair curling down her writhing body, the sight pushes me to the brink. Man, it won't take much more to make me shoot in my jeans. Best if I keep that exciting news update to myself.

"You're so close you probably wanna make some noise, huh? Maybe even say my name. But, Mia, you'd better not."

Looking miserable, she nods, threads her fingers through my hair, and tries to get me back on task.

I resist. "Well, because I'm a good guy, I'll do you a favor. If I keep going here, I can tell you're gonna start hollering. So I'll stop. That way you won't get the lectures as well. I know you don't want them."

Laughing at her face, I take one last look at what I'm missing out on and get to my feet. I throw her over my shoulder and make for our room at the rear of the bus. I stride in with purpose and bounce her on the bed, then turn away.

"South, wait! I think I do want the lectures. I'll take every single one of them without complaint if you'll just come back here now. I promise I won't mind."

Man, that's exactly what I want to do. To stop myself from leaping on her, I grip the door frame hard and force out a laugh. Then duck to avoid the pillow she lobs at me. "Hey, bad shot," I comment with a straight face.

"Oh, shut up! So is this the punishment then, you beast? To leave me hanging like this?"

"Nope. I'm just putting you down for that nap like you suggested. I figure you must be real worn out after your little adventure in the mosh."

"For your information, you're *not* a good guy! You're a horrible one. Stop smiling! Where are you going, anyway?"

"To take a shower. Then I'm gonna find Nico. He owes me a few beers."

"Well, don't be surprised if I'm not here when you get back. I won't be hanging around just because *you* told me I should."

"I know, but I reckon you'll stay right there because you can't wait for me to come back and finish what I started."

I slam the door on her furious face and fall backward against fake wood. Breathing hard, I try to calculate how long I'll need to wait before I can justify racing back to her. An hour? Maybe two?

Shit. I'm no brilliant strategist that's for sure. I really hadn't thought the so-called *punishment* through at all, because however long I stay away, each minute will drag like hell.

And be complete and utter torture.

26

MIA

The Wave

"I think that coffee I just had tasted better without sugar in it!" I declare with a self-satisfied smile.

"Yeah?" South moves away from the woodblock print he's been standing hypnotized in front of for the last five minutes. "That's because it's got a big, fat dollop of smug in it." He drops next to me on the gallery's cube-shaped couch, laughing as he bumps my shoulder.

"You be quiet," I chide. "You're just jealous."

"Look, if you're fool enough to cut the good bits out of your food, that's fine, but don't start on me. I wouldn't last a day without the sweet stuff." He leans in and nuzzles my neck, licking and biting and rasping my skin with his stubble. "Mm, you're so tasty."

Giggling like a happy fool, I push him away. Maybe he's right, giving up sugar probably *is* a bad idea.

Since I ditched it from my diet a month ago, around the time of the music festival incident, I've barely been able to keep my eyes open after ten p.m. Not that I blame my adventure in the mosh on my permanently sleepy state, but South still holds a grudge about the event, reminding me of my reckless behavior whenever he's home.

With Up Void's album exploding into the stratosphere, he's only been around for a few days here and there before shooting off with the band again, leaving me aching and trying to keep busy to distract myself from the pain. It's not easy being in love with a guy you have to say goodbye to all the time.

As of today, he's been back for six-days of bliss and, currently, we're checking out the Hokusai exhibition at a city gallery. South is a sucker for the Japanese artists' wave prints, hence his tattoo.

I'm a fan as well, but even surrounded by incredible art, I'm so tired I could curl up in his lap and easily nod off. I gaze down at muscular, denim-covered thighs with longing. Yes, South's lap, and everything in it, is so very tempting.

Grinning, he says, "What are you looking at? Wanna find a column to hide behind and make out for a bit?"

"No! Is there any place in the world you think unsuitable for getting it on?"

"You already know the answer to that question." He

waves the catalog at me. "Hey, says here that Hokusai used around thirty different names over his lifetime. Mostly ones he made up himself."

"Maybe you can use one of his spares now that the limelight's getting a little intense."

"Huh. Maybe. How about Gakyojin? I reckon it suits me."

I pull the brochure from his hand. "Um, let's see... apparently that means *'man crazy about drawing'*."

Trailing heat up my thigh, he runs his finger over the paper in my lap and asks, "Is there one for *'man crazy about sexing up his girlfriend'*?"

I laugh while he gazes at the art gleaming bright against the dark-blue wall.

"What is it about that wave, Mia? I fucking dream about it. It's weird."

It's because it's you, South, I think. Seductive and dangerous, even now that he's become so familiar. So dear and necessary to my happiness.

While he studies the print, I soak him in. The inky wave tendrils curling around his bicep, the tattoo's bright blues and stark whites. Then his strong jaw, the high cheekbones, and those eyes like blinding gemstones. I love the warmth of his denim and t-shirt clad body beside me. His smell. Citrus and delicious boy.

Wrapping my arm around his shoulders, I squeeze hard. He smiles at me and tucks strands of hair behind his ears.

Over in the corner, whispering and giggling, a group of high school girls check out all his good parts too. *Crap.* Looks like another photo session looms with me acting as the shoot producer, props manager, and lifestyle photographer all rolled into one. Maybe this time I'll duck out and leave them to it.

"Hey, I'm just going to find the restroom." For some reason, weeing is my number one occupation lately. Probably should see a doctor, because visiting the bathroom seven thousand times a day surely isn't normal.

I press my lips to his cheek, and he turns and kisses me slowly, warm hands framing my face, making my limbs molten and heavy. This is sure to outrage his fan club hovering in the corner. Yep, going by the several petulant scowls that follow me as I stride quickly across the room, I think they're pretty cranky.

In the bathroom, I grimace at my reflection in the mirror, the shadows under my eyes enhanced by the harsh lighting. More spaceship than ladies' room, it's decorated in the hues of a storm. Black granite sinks, gray fittings and tiles. And then there are the purple bags under my eyes. *Yuck.*

A mother wrangles a toddler in the cubicle opposite. I can hear her cajoling and wheedling, telling little *Finny* to leave the door alone. To wait. She's not finished yet.

A scream rents the air, high-pitched and about as long as an emergency siren. *Oh, my God.* Will the child ever take a breath? Hands over my ears, I head for the toilet at the same time the cubicle door opens and the red-faced brat comes shrieking out, legs pedaling fast. He looks about three and is very cute.

The heavily pregnant mother follows, struggling to fasten her pants and keep hold of several bags. She probably started the day well put together, her inner-city bright red hair, expensive maternity tunic in glowing swirly patterns, all getting limper by the hour.

The child pushes on the outer door. "Finn! Oh you little—"

"I'll get him." I grasp the would-be escapee by the armpits and swing him back to his mom.

"Thank you! When you birth a child, an extra pair of arms should automatically begin to sprout. They'd be so useful. How will I cope when this one rears its lovely head?" She gestures to her very uncomfortable looking stomach. "I guess I'll find out in a matter of weeks. Would you mind hanging on to him while I wash my hands? Then I can put this rubbish in the stroller."

She laughs at my face. "No! Not him. I meant the bags. Got any kids yourself? Silly question. You look too fresh. You're like a pretty wildflower."

I bounce the squirming child on my hip and wipe a stringy patch of drool from my shoulder. "Oh! Thanks. I feel positively wilted at the moment. Ancient. I've been completely stupid and given up sugar. I must be detoxing because it's only made me feel sick. Can't stay awake past ten o'clock and everything aches including my boobs!"

The woman pulls paper towel from the dispenser and raises an eyebrow in the mirror. "Got a man? Sounds like you're pregnant."

What?

Laughter peels out of my mouth, an unhinged noise

someone in extreme shock makes. "No, not me. No way! That's impossible."

The lady holds her arms out for the child. "Not as impossible as you might think. Thank you for helping me with this little monster. Are you peeing a lot?"

Numb, I nod.

"Get a test, find out for sure." And she shoves the stroller through the door, leaving me shattered. Brain exploded into gloopy blobs—I can't think. My body is a quivering mess— can't move. One hand is on the sink. But where's the other one gone? Finn must've taken it with him.

Without knowing how I got here, I'm sitting on the toilet seat, jeans around my ankles, staring at my panties. No period again today. *Shit.* That makes it… two weeks late, and my last period, more spotting than anything, had barely qualified. I'd just thought… *Oh, fuck!*

My palms press into my breasts. So tender. But it's not possible. I'm on the pill, and I've never missed a day of taking the silly things. Not one.

I push my stomach. It feels tight with a strange pressure that I'd thought might be the beginnings of a bladder infection. But over the weeks it hasn't progressed, hasn't turned into anything. A dreadful heat burns through every cell in my body as reality hits like a sledgehammer. I feel faint.

I am knocked up. In the family way. *Preggers.* It's true—I just know it.

Now everything makes perfect and extremely frightening sense.

I am carrying South's baby, and it will be the end of life as

I know it. The end of South. As if he'll stay. Since we've been together, he's made it more than clear that a child is the one thing he cannot handle. Doesn't want. *Ever.* So, if I plan to keep him, then that leaves... termination? What a word. What a thing to do. Nope. No way I'm doing that. I won't.

I need to speak to Ivy as soon as I can. I have to hide this from South until I've had time to think. Then I can work out a way to present the news that might make him see reason.

After I relieve myself for the twentieth time today, I stumble out of the cubicle. Thankfully the washroom is empty. Hands shaking, I splash water over my tears, scrub paper towel over my face, and try to calm my heartbeat.

It will be okay. South loves me. I know he does. He'll be shocked, but he'll listen.

Eventually.

No.

No, he won't listen to reason. South's greatest nightmare is now my very own living hell, and I'll have to suffer in it alone.

Sniffing back more tears, I blunder through the gallery past paintings of blurry waterfalls, liquid blossoms, vibrating mountains, a ghostly octopus.

And there, over by the Great Wave off Kanagawa, is South, surrounded by giggling girls who squeal and fire off questions in high-pitched voices. Some even dare to reach out and touch his t-shirt. His arm. A brave one reaches around from behind him and fluffs her hands through his hair.

"Hey," he yelps, turning and laughing at the delighted girl. He's always so kind to them no matter how peskily they behave. And, believe me, with Up Void's new-found success, the fans are becoming more painful every day.

I place a gentle hand on my belly and watch him make them laugh. He's all smiles, maximum charm. And I'm a walking secret, a miracle on trembling legs, because deep inside, right under my palm, his child grows. And he has no idea.

Smiling, he looks up, notices me and waves. I shiver under the icy gazes of around fifteen hostile-looking girls. This may go badly.

As I near the group, one of the two tucked against his sides, says, "Is that lady your wife? Is she? Is she your wife?"

A wall of cell phones comes up in my face, and all but the girls wrapped around South break ranks to surround me.

Are you his wife? Are you married? I bet she's part of management. She's not pretty enough to be his wife. No! That's his girlfriend, we've seen photos, Sonia. Don't pretend you haven't stalked him online.

South pushes carefully through the hysteria and pulls me close. I relax a little. He won't let anything bad happen.

"This is my girlfriend, Mia," he says, wearing a broad smile.

I plaster on a cheesy grin and wave both hands at them like a clown.

"She takes great photos. So if you're really nice to her, I bet she'll shoot a bunch for us."

The atmosphere changes instantly from hostile back to over-excitement, phones coming at me from all directions.

The tall queen bee, who has reattached herself to South, pops her gum and asks, "So is he any good in bed?"

Screeches of laughter make me cover my ears, and South's expression turns cocky as he fixes a grin on me, waiting for my answer. Like the girls are.

So, do I tell the truth? Try and deflect? Maybe I can say that he's really great at making babies and has amazing contraception-defying sperm.

"Well?" asks bubble-gum girl, flicking blue hair off her face. "You'd better tell us, and we'll know if you're lying."

Not sure how she'll tell, but I'll go with the truth anyway. "Well, I'd have to say he's about as good as he looks."

South, who is surprisingly clueless about how gorgeous he is, bites his lip in confusion. The girls, who understand completely, all go *wooooooo* and fall over each other like a bunch of hysterical howler monkeys.

I point at a spot on the shiny floor halfway between the hot rock star and me. "Okay, so if you line up here, you can take turns standing with South, and I'll get a few shots. Then you'll each have a photo with just you and him. How's that sound?"

Quite good going by the answering yelps.

The static crackle of a two-way radio mingles with the squawks and honks. A guy in uniform, who looks like he's never learned how to smile, sidles up to me. "I have to ask you to move along. You're too close to the art. And too noisy. You're blocking others from seeing the wave."

The girls bleat loudly at him.

Smiling patiently, I take the security guard aside. "Can I

just shoot a few photos, please? We'll move a little farther away."

"Sorry you'll need to leave the exhibition unless you disperse—"

"No, it's okay, we'll move on. Sorry, they're just really excited."

"Who is he? Celebrity or something?" By the look on the guy's craggy face, being a celebrity would have to be one of life's more repulsive fates.

"He just sings in a rock band. Plays guitar. Is there somewhere else we can do this perhaps? It will make the girls' week. They're pretty thrilled."

He eyes the preening gaggle with distaste. "I have a teenage daughter. He got any songs I might know?"

"Um, I'm not sure. *Singing Eyes* is playing around a lot, I guess."

"He's in *Up Void?*"

I laugh. "Yep."

The guy stares at South, his eyes wide. "Well, shave my legs and call me Grandma! They're my daughter's favorite. I thought all that golden hair looked familiar. The Great Hall happens to be free right now. Come with me. I'm getting in that photo line."

Freaking wonderful. Resigned to my fate of snapping photos of girls groping South while I smile like an idiot and think about the fact that very soon I'll be a heartbroken single mother, I sigh and follow craggy-face, gesturing at everyone to fall in line behind me.

After the cozy photo session, South and I will go home

where we'll grill salmon and bake crispy potatoes for dinner, and I'll try and pretend that everything is okay with the world and all peachy between us.

Hiding this will be the biggest challenge of my life. If I can pull it off, if he suspects nothing, then I should change career and head straight for La La Land, because I will truly deserve an Oscar.

For best actress in a melodrama.

27

MIA

The Award Goes To

I take my eyes from the harbor view sparkling through the floor-to-ceiling windows and scan the party. Bingo. South's height makes him easy to locate in a crowd.

Standing in a tight circle, Vince babbles at top speed to the bass player from the latest Green Day wannabes, a willowy diva currently making a big splash on the dance charts, and South.

Ivy follows my gaze. "What's he doing? Why is he bouncing like that?"

Yep, every few seconds South's head rises even higher above the group. "Haven't you noticed he does that whenever he wants to run? Folds his arms over his chest, stands wide and goes up on his toes periodically. It's a sure sign you're either pissing him off or boring the shit out of him. But look, he's still trying to smile at them. Sweet, isn't he?"

"Mmm, don't know if that's the exact word I'd use." Smoothing down her emerald frock, Ivy raises an eyebrow and grins. "I guess he's antsy because Up Void only qualified for one award tonight. He probably wanted to win more."

I laugh. South doesn't give a hoot about awards.

"You should stop laughing, take him back to the hotel, and tell him the good news. This is getting ridiculous."

A week ago, I informed Ivy of my predicament. To get through the tear-filled confession, I broke my sugar fast and ate two bowls of hazelnut ice cream at breakfast time. After-ward, I felt ill, but it was a relief to unburden myself. Hiding it is sending me mental.

In essence, South is still a lost boy, learning to love, to be vulnerable and rely on someone for the first time in his life. It's horribly wrong to lie to him.

Stomach souring, I say, "*Good* news? Yeah, right. You're just happy I'm joining the mother-to-be ranks with you."

"Of course I am. It's so exciting! Our kids can grow up together."

"Nice idea, but you've got Nico who couldn't be more devoted to you. I'll most likely be a single mom. Big differ-ence in our situations. So yeah, I can't do it tonight. But I will soon, I promise. I'm not ready to let him go just yet."

I'm not sure I ever will be. South is the only man I'll ever love.

"You won't have to, Mia! There's no denying how he feels

about you. He wouldn't want to get rid of a baby of yours. It doesn't fit with the kind of guy he is."

Thankfully the horrible jazz band in the corner and the loud coked-up crowd mask the content of our conversation.

"But he's completely scarred. Think of his childhood. It probably—"

"Won't matter when he's faced with the reality of his own bun cooking in *your* oven."

"It's not a good time. Look at him. He's exhausted. Always working, constantly hassled by everyone around him, everyone he meets. And he hates all this suck-up stuff. If I tell him tonight, it won't go well."

"Oh, you're such a chickenshit. Tell him! He might be thrilled he's going to be a dad and—"

"Who's gonna be a dad?" Nico's bright-green eyes and killer smile pop over Ivy's shoulder.

I spurt drink out of my mouth, soaking the front of my red silk dress. Shame. I quite like it. Putting my glass on the table beside me, I proceed to cough through Ivy's stuttering.

"Oh! My Aunt's husband. No, that's not right. I meant to say... her daughter, my cousin. Well, he's having a baby. *No*, I mean *she's* having the—"

"Woah, babe, stop!" Nico waves his hands in Ivy's face. "I don't know what the hell you're talking about. Sounds like you've been doing lines in the bathroom. Except you're pregnant, so I *know* you haven't."

Out of nowhere, a hand thumps three times on my back. "You alright there?"

Fuck! It's *South*. I cough harder.

"Whose cousin is doing lines in the bathroom?" he asks.

"Um?" says Ivy.

With a thumb, South wipes away a tear that's streaming down my face. "Here, Mia, have some of my water."

"Water?" Nico frowns at South. "What are you drinking that for? You pregnant or something?"

Oh, sweet Jesus, kill me now. I dig my nails into my hand while a final round of coughing wracks through me. Then I take South's drink and sip, trying to settle my crazy heartbeat. Surely, he hasn't heard anything significant.

Now, how to make my face look normal? A smile will do it. I stretch my lips wide. No, too bright and fake. I feel like a constipated weather lady. I turn the lip-wattage down and pop my head on the side, going for a look of pleasant interest. No. That's too fatal attraction.

Ivy pinches my arm, and I squeak like a dog toy.

South raises an eyebrow at Ivy. "From what you just said, for a freaky second there, it sounded like Mia had a nasty little surprise for me."

"That's a shocking thing to say! What's the matter with you? What if she did?" Ivy flicks her red locks over her shoulder, looking like she wants to belt South.

I wouldn't mind knocking *her* out cold—to stop her speaking. What the crap does she think she's doing opening up this dangerous topic?

South snarls and gives her a mean laugh, the kind that makes my skin crawl and panic roll through my gut. Then fixing his vibrant blue gaze on me, he says, "Mia would know better than to spring that kind of horror show on me."

Oh, holy hell. This is disastrous. My head spins, and it's impossible to get any air in. I can't faint, though. That'd be even more suspicious.

"And I reckon she'd be smart enough to sort out a problem like that pretty fucking quickly. Or prepare her goodbye speech."

Looking stunned, Nico stares at him. Hoping to disperse the tension, I force out a deranged laugh, and Ivy places a soft hand on my back. Probably to stop me from collapsing on the floor in a wailing puddle of misery.

Frowning, South brings his face close. "What's wrong? You look strange, like you've had an electric shock or..." His eyes flick down, and he smiles at my boobs. "Hey, nice touch with the wet-top thing you've got going on there. It's very stimulating, but you really don't need to ruin your dress to get my attention."

"Look out, Mia, he's doing the thigh rub thing," says Nico as he hooks an arm around Ivy's neck and snuggles her into his side.

South gives him daggers and turns to me. "Did you have to tip him off about that? Fuck, *I* didn't even know I did it." He steps closer. "But, honestly, it's a little hard to be mad right now. With that dress all wet you're looking more tempting than anything on that dessert table over there. And, Mia, you know I'd do just about anything for chocolate. So what'd you spill on it, anyway?"

"Wine. White wine," I insist loudly.

Bending down, South inhales. "You sure? Smells like nothing, like water."

That's because it *is* water. Tonic water to be precise.

"Hey, guess what? I begged Vince to release me for the night and asked him to get the car brought around. Fed him a heap of shit about being on the brink of a meltdown, and he ate it up. We can leave!"

That's a relief. I'm nearly asleep on my feet.

Ivy frowns. "But there are two more after-parties to go to after this after-party! It's all about the afters tonight, and they're not over yet."

I yawn. "Please don't say *after* again."

"I'm sick of the afters as well, so I'll be taking Mia back to the hotel for our own private party. Under the covers. She looks half dead."

"Oh, thanks!"

"Fine," he says. "Let's go to two more parties and I'll cart you around on my back. You can snore in my ear while I get chatted up. Sound fun?"

"No thank you. Let's make tracks."

Up Void's lead guitarist appears out of nowhere. "Wait," Nate says, amber eyes gleaming. "I'm coming with you guys. I'm gonna FaceTime Suze at the hotel."

Nate is impressively faithful to his girlfriend. He and South are so similar. Both loyal and solid amid all the craziness. I make a note to personally praise Nate's mom, Abbie, for the way she raised them. They're great guys. Well, except for South's one humongous flaw—his intention to unceremoniously shuffle me off should I ever be unfortunate enough to be pregnant, *as I am*.

We bid goodbye to Nico and Ivy, and wearing a foul

expression, South nudges his way through the crowd, shaking hands and slapping people's backs but never once stopping to chat. I follow, and Nate trails in our wake.

When we get out to the valet parking area, Nate says to South, "Hey, what's with the lemon-suck face?"

"Do you have to come with us? I was gonna try for limo-sex on the way back to the hotel. But you've fucked that up for me."

What?

"Aren't you into threesomes?" Nate elbows him.

"Shut up, man. I should say, *sure let's go for it* just to jerk a knot in your tail."

"I wouldn't believe you anyway," says Nate, laughing. "As if you'd share her."

Over his shoulder, South gives me a crooked grin. I force a smile back, wondering how I'm going to live without him looking at me that way after I break the news.

A hot shiver runs down my spine. With me being exhausted, he'll be completely happy to do all the work tonight, and I can lay back luxuriating in the bliss. What a guy. He's so wonderfully agreeable like that. About most things, actually. As long as I don't count that one flaw. The one that will soon ruin my life. And my baby's.

Hopefully, he can stop me thinking about how close to disaster we came tonight. Imagine if he had heard the whole conversation. Found out, right there at an industry party in some beige and gray colored mansion, that what Ivy taunted him about is true.

It can't go on like this. He'll work it out for himself before too long. Perhaps I had better get back on the sugar quick smart. Get a dozen-donuts-a-day habit. Then I might have a plausible excuse for my soon-to-be expanding waistline. Because I won't be informing him tonight that he's going to be a dad.

And probably not tomorrow, either.

28

MIA

007

A week later, I lie back watching my baby, a grainy swirl of white, roll in the dark sea of amniotic fluid. Already, it's just like South, bopping constantly to some inner beat. Its arms flail, legs kick, mouth opening and closing as if it's working on a song.

Dear God, South should be here to see this. I can picture him—blue eyes glowing, face filled with awe, skin abuzz, and maybe even holding my hand tightly.

"Bub looks perfect," says the obstetrician, studying the ultrasound screen. "About eleven weeks. Maybe a bit over. Or perhaps he's just an enormous kid. Is the father a big guy?"

"Yes," I croak, turning my head away to hide the tears. Wow. Ivy is around nine weeks pregnant, shit, I'm due *before* her.

When I force myself to meet his gaze again, the doctor frowns. He's tall and lanky, has a Scottish accent, and even looks a bit Sean Connery-ish around the eyes. The whole procedure is like being pushed and prodded, examined thoroughly by an alien James Bond. Quite surreal.

"How are you feeling?"

"So much better over the last week. Nausea's pretty much gone, but my clothes are already getting tighter."

"All normal. You'll feel a lot more flutterings from now on. You've got a little mover there. Wait until you get a proper kick in the ribs. I imagine this one's probably gonna give you hell."

South's child. No surprises there.

"And it all happens so quickly. Before you know it, you'll be awake all night changing diapers. So, make sure you enjoy this part. There's nothing quite like a first pregnancy."

Oh yes. It will be so enjoyable, living with the fear and uncertainty.

No.

No more uncertainty. That's something I can put an end to. All I have to do is spring it on South. My tiny protruding gut tells me it's time. Maybe even tonight. I can show him the video, and when he sees his baby suck its sweet little thumb, how can his heart not soften to the idea?

007 wipes sticky gel from my stomach, throws his gloves in a bin, and washes his hands. "I'll leave you to get dressed.

Wait in reception to get your next appointment date. We'll email you the video and photos. And take care, won't you? You should bring your husband next time. I'd love to meet him."

"Boyfriend."

He nods. "How does he make a living?"

Silent for two beats, I stare at his ear. "He makes um... donuts?"

His eyebrows shoot skyward.

Boy, that came out so uncertain. "Um, yeah. So, you know, he's got a bakery and they're his specialty. Donuts. And... um, also buns."

He gives me a wide smile. "Oh, great. I love donuts. Get him to bring some in next visit."

"Sure. Fine! He loves to take them places... See you then. With the donuts."

"And your boyfriend."

"Right."

Swiping at tears, I weave unsteadily down the hall, eyes stinging and barely able to see a foot in front of me. At least I know I'm heading in the right direction because I can see all the other mothers-to-be lolling around the waiting room reading magazines. And... Rita. Rita is out there, too, lounging back reading Maternity Style.

Rita?

What? No! No way. It can't be. But just then, can't-be-Rita looks up and makes it quite clear that it is definitely, one hundred percent the *actual* Rita sitting there with her eyes round as saucers, waving happily.

Shit.

My head swinging around wildly, I search for an escape route. As I turn the first handle I blindly grasp, Rita calls out, "Mia? Is that you?"

Crap.

Ignoring her, I step through the door and close it behind me. Shaking in my sandals, I survey my cramped refuge. The light is on. That's good. The sharp stench of cleaning products burns the inside of my nose. A utility room. Not so good. Well, I can't stay *here* all day. Best to get it over with then.

The fake smile I plaster on as I walk into the hall feels like it will crumble off my face any second. I frantically shuffle through reasons I might have for visiting an obstetrician's rooms, other than the obvious one, but before I can decide on an excuse, I arrive in front of Lane's goggle-eyed assistant.

"What are *you* doing here, Mia? I thought I was seeing things. You gave me quite a shock!" Rita says, moving her bag and patting the seat beside her.

As I drop into the chair, my lunch rises up my throat. Funny, Rita doesn't look shocked. She seems strangely thrilled, almost vibrating with pleasure. Or anger. It's hard to say which.

My eyes fix on a bright patch of purple in Rita's hair. "Um... I... So I've been having period issues and—"

"Mia Heughan?" the receptionist calls as she holds out an envelope over the counter, her smile blindingly white. "Here's some pregnancy literature and we printed out a few shots of the bub for you."

I wobble toward her.

She clears her throat and speaks even louder. "And because this is only your first appointment, the doctor wants to see you again in two weeks instead of the usual four. There's an appointment card in there, too. Take care."

Take care? By throwing her words around so recklessly, the lady has made that impossible. Now the cat is out of the bag and I'm the mouse about to be hunted, toyed with mercilessly, and probably savaged to death.

When I turn around, I'm met with a set of gleaming, hostile eyes. "Mia! *Oh, my fucking God!* Congratulations. I can't believe it. What does South think? Is he excited?"

Words won't even form.

Rita is the one who looks overly excited about my condition. "Oh, I *see*. He doesn't *know*, does he? Oh dear. Pretty soon, when your belly starts to pop, it'll be extremely obvious. But, then again, men are so *stupid*, aren't they? They only see what they want to see. Tits and asses and wide open... mouths."

What?

"Don't worry. Your tiny secret is safe with me. But it won't be tiny for long, though."

"Sorry, Rita." As I turn around, I trip over the glass coffee table. "Whoops! Sorry. I've gotta race. I'm due back at Mad Wolf... see you soon."

Without turning back, I fly away as fast as my trembling limbs will allow.

It's not until I'm behind the wheel of my car, melting in the afternoon heat and stabbing the key clumsily at the ignition, that I think to wonder what on earth Rita was doing at the clinic herself.

It felt like she was expecting me—as if she knew I'd be there.

But that's impossible.

Isn't it?

29

SOUTH

Karate Kid

"Shit, Nate, stop. *Stop*. I don't know what the heck you're doing there. Can you play it through for me again?"

"What? All I did was run the chorus three times with chords and then the last time with just notes. I told you that's what I was gonna do." Nate squints at my guitar. "Why haven't you got your capo on, man? That's your problem right there. Christ, you're out of it today. Are you high or something?"

"No!" Fuck Nate. I don't do that shit anymore. Not now that I know my life's important and worth something to Mia.

"Wanna go again?" asks Tony the engineer, his hand thrust deep in a bag of Doritos.

Nate cranks through the opening again, and I sing half a verse before pulling the headphones away. "Shit! Tony, can ya turn the guide vocals off? I fucking hate them."

From the control room Ben laughs, delighted by my inability to get through a take.

"Don't worry. You sound great," says Nate, always the good guy. "Hey, I think I need to change this riff, listen…"

Arms folded, I watch Nate's fingers. "Oh, shit, yeah. Where it changes up. It's *A-Punk*. That's funny, you've just ripped off Vampire Weekend. No wonder, because it's a damn catchy song, and it's probably smarter than pilfering something by The White Stripes. I reckon they have sharks for lawyers."

"Well, *I reckon* you two should quit your fussing and just lie down for a bit. Go take some nanna naps."

"Good idea, Ben." Aiming for his open mouth, Tony tips the junk packet upside down and spreads crumbs all over his shirt. "Let's take a break."

"Hey, did you know Sad Hank and the Planks are next door cutting tracks?" Zave asks me as we push open the door to the control room.

"Nope. I didn't know." I whack out a *jab-jab-cross* boxing combo right in his face.

"Quit that! You're gonna take my head off. You're just like Henry fucking Rollins was in his prime. Too fit and ripped."

Offended by the insinuation that I spend all my time

working out like some kinda show pony, I drop my fighter's stance and say, "It's just from the surfing."

"Are you doing sit ups on your board or something, Bruce Lee?" asks Zave. "And do me a favor, will ya, and put a shirt on? My inferiority complex escalates every time I get a glimpse of your stomach."

"What? I'm sweating in there."

"Then stand still for three minutes." Ben sniffs at me. "No one's watching. You don't need to go all Iggy Pop."

Tony laughs. "We've got the Karate Kid jumping around in here and next door they're doing goddamn speedballs."

"Hey, South, you should go and pay them a little visit. Start doing push-ups on the ground next to them while they're peaking hard and talking shit to you. Show them the benefits of clean living."

I snicker and collapse on the couch. Yeah, that could be pretty funny. Or not. Speedballs are hardcore. I'd probably have to call an ambulance before I got the chance to take the piss out of them.

Hanging my head between my knees, I moan loudly. I'm running on hardly any sleep and feel like shit.

Nate settles next to me and bumps my shoulder. I let myself slide sideways until my cheek hits vinyl.

"So what's up with you, then?" asks Nate. "Don't stress about the track. There's no pressure, remember. This is just for kicks. We're back on the road soon, and the label doesn't need us to put down anything serious until the U.S. leg of the tour's done."

"It's not that." I pick at the frayed waistband of my jeans. "It's Mia."

The room goes quiet. Even Ben looks up from his phone wearing a dubious face. "Trouble in paradise?" he asks. "Is she feeling insecure? Want you to lay a ring on her or something?"

"No. She's just... I don't know... acting weird. Not been herself the last couple of weeks."

"Ah ha. That explains your punk moves, then. You've got a bit of steam to blow off." Nate raises his eyebrows. "Weird how?"

"Well, like today, she's gone somewhere with our neighbor Frank. But she didn't mention it to me, only said she had a work meeting on. But I overheard the fucking phone call, heard her organize this... *thing* with him yesterday. And the strangest part is that she spent ages convincing him to take a bag of donuts with him. She even insisted he buy them from a specific shop and transfer them into a plain paper bag. And for the life of me I can't work out what the fuck they might be doing with them and why she couldn't tell *me* about it."

"Donuts!" Zave laughs with more enthusiasm than I'd like to hear, even going as far as to slap a thigh.

I glare at him and he sobers, clearing his throat.

"Sounds to me like one of those pastry-fetish affairs," suggests Tony. "They must be getting it on and require well placed donuts as props."

"Yeah, not helping, thanks." I throw an arm over my eyes.

"You know the logical thing to do, don't ya?" Zave says.

"It's simple. You just need to ask her about it. Honest and clear communication is always the answer with any relationship issues."

Clearly, our drummer has lost his mind. And maybe I don't want to hear her answer. "Been doing a counseling course in your spare time, have ya?"

"I'm serious. Just ask her. I mean, it's Mia, right? As if that little sweetheart would be fucking over her own boyfriend. That's you, by the way. Don't look so confused. *You're* the boyfriend. You know, the guy she loves?"

"Shut up. I know what you mean." I knead my aching neck muscles and roll onto my back, something dark humming through my blood. *Jesus*, the ceiling needs a paint. It's disgusting.

It pains me that Zave is right. I should speak to Mia like a normal boyfriend would do. Hopefully, there's a good reason for the secret meeting with Frank. But the doubt is killing me.

There is *one* thing I'm certain of, though—I sure as hell won't be eating any goddamn donuts for a while.

30

THE WATCHER

Ease

I lie in bed sliding my legs against crisp hotel sheets. Dusk hangs as heavy as a shroud outside the window. Night falls and rain looms. Cars honk, trams rattle.

I roll onto my back and press hard on my stomach. It's soft and yielding, not tight. No baby grows there yet. But one day soon it might. When it does, it will be South's child. I'll make sure of it. And I won't hide it from him like that foolish girl is doing. When I tell him, he'll be pleased, so happy. He'll kiss me, then hug me. Hold me way up high.

And then they'll both be mine. The man and his child. And he'll make me feel like this all the time. Horny. Alive. Smiling, I trail a hand down my restless body and stroke softly, softly over tingling, hairless folds. Each breath I take burns my throat.

He won't even remember the other one. The child that almost was. But wasn't. Never will be. Can't be.

Won't, won't, won't, won't. Won't ever breathe a breath of air.

It'll be easy. With Mia so gullible, so trusting, the little simpleton will believe anything. And then she'll leave and fall apart. Her child will die. Or maybe in her anger, she'll kill it, do the unthinkable and get an abortion. And when she's gone, South will suffer. And suffer. And suffer. I know it won't be easy for him. But I'll be there to help.

And because Mia is going to soundcheck tomorrow afternoon. Because she's always on time. And because the first thing she'll do when she arrives is use the backstage bathroom to relieve her stressed bladder, I only need to wait. To listen. And then speak.

And then I'll be the one. The one who's there day and night, night and day.

At home. On tour.

There. There. There.

Always there to ease his pain.

Me.

The only one.

Rita.

31

MIA

The Bargain

I t's five p.m. and the air is still hot and humid. I'm strolling down the city street, feeling uncomfortable in my new dress because it's a little too tight. I smile down at the printed cowboys who ride horses all over the burgundy material. I'd bought the retro-style dress because of them, and because South likes it, too.

Shaking his wet hair all over me this morning, he leapt out of the shower and interrupted my lipstick application, talking like a cowpoke between delicious, sloppy kisses.

His hands had roved over my curved belly, and I nearly fainted from lack of air trying to suck it into flatness. His hotly whispered threats to lasso me with his towel and drag me back under the water might have made me a bit weak, too.

Currently, the dress is stuck to my stomach, making me paranoid that every single person on the street can tell I have a secret tucked beneath the soft cotton. A secret that Doctor Oh No, as my neighbor, Frank, christened him yesterday, advised was about the size of a lemon.

Yesterday! Now that was one of the more stressful days I've lived through. Thirteen weeks pregnant and a fortnight after my first disastrous visit to the obstetrician's office, I fronted up for the second appointment with Frank and an oily bag of donuts in tow. Both as hard evidence that I hadn't fabricated my thrilled-to-bits baker boyfriend. Unfortunately, all I proved was that my mental state was incompatible with motherhood.

During the consultation, the doctor eyeballed height-challenged Frank with suspicion, then me with great concern. Having failed to produce the *big guy* who had clearly been expected, he diagnosed me as completely delusional. I could tell.

And then there were the donuts. Frank hadn't quite pulled off the *oh-yes-I-am-definitely-a-baker* attitude, either. Impossible to achieve, really, sitting there in his expensive work suit looking like a trendy business owner. An unfortunately *short* one.

As I pass by an old art deco movie theater, I check out the Wonder Woman poster hanging in the window, the word *courage* emblazoned in gold letters over it. Yes, that's exactly what I need to help me break the baby news to South tonight. A massive injection of bravery.

I can't keep him in the dark any longer, no matter the outcome. He trusts me. Loves me. I know he does. Even though I feel sick merely picturing his face when he learns the truth, if I have to break both our hearts, the sooner I get it over with the better.

Tonight, Up Void are playing the Harbor Arena, which is fortunate for two reasons—it's in our home town, and because they've played there twice before, I know exactly how to find their dressing room fast. I've just jumped off the subway from work, and I can't wait to make use of the band's bathroom.

Arriving outside the huge glass building, I trot up the stairs and then duck around back where trucks are still bumping in equipment, and enter the stadium via a heavy metal door.

Showing my access-all-areas pass to security staff along the way, I take the elevator up to the second floor and wind through passageways until I reach Up Void's VIP area.

The guys are already on stage for their soundcheck. Through the floor I hear South laugh and rap into the mic, guitar riffs stop and start, and then *Dirt* explodes in an avalanche of noise. The song has me grinning and bopping my head as I move through their empty changing room toward the white door at the far end.

I stride into the massive bathroom, stopping at the unexpected sight of Lane's assistant with a phone pressed to her ear. Instead of being front of house with the crew, she's preening and patting at something in her hair. "Yeah, South gave it to me," she says into the cell, her voice bouncing off the white tiles.

"Hey, Rita."

Her head jolts up. "Oh, shit, Mia! You're early." Face glowing bright red, she drops her phone on the counter top.

Something sharp stabs and twists in my chest, and I don't know what makes me ask about the dragonfly clip in her hair that she's patting so fondly. "What did South give you? Surely not the hair clip?" I'm the one who loves dragonflies, not Rita.

"Yes...I mean..." Rita stutters, her eyes flitting between the tiles and my face.

Again, not knowing what possesses me, I stomp over and peer down at the phone. She covers it with her hand but not before I see South's address appearing on repeat in her in box.

I laugh. "What are you hiding? Show me."

Rita shoves the phone in her pocket. "You don't want to see that, Mia. Believe me."

"Why the hell not?" That came out a little too shrill. I think I'm losing my grip. Perhaps on my whole reality.

Silent, Rita shakes her head at the floor.

Hand on my hip and heart pounding, I say, "So, what, he's giving you jewelry and sending you emails you don't want me to read? Why would he do that?"

Rita's expression hardens. "Oh, come on. Don't be naive. Why do you think?"

And then I can't speak, can only stare, only feel the

ground drop away. Swallow bile as my world collapses around me.

"But he wouldn't—"

"He would. He did. And he *has* been screwing me. Frequently. At every opportunity."

Tears burst out of my eyes. Ugly, messy ones.

With a hand on my shoulder, she steps close. "Oh, I'm sorry. It must come as a great shock, especially in your condition. I feel terrible—"

"Get your hands off me!" I spin away from her.

"But you can hardly blame me. He's too good for you, Mia, and I'm sure deep down you know that."

On unsteady legs I head for the door. I'm going to kill South. He promised—only me—he put his hand over his heart and swore it. It was meant to be just us, for always. And I was stupid enough to believe him.

"Mia, you can't tell anyone about this. I need this job. And *you* need *me* to keep your little baby news safe from South, too, don't you? So I think we'd be wise to make a bargain and keep each other's secrets for a little while longer. If you don't tell, then I won't. And when you finally come clean about your pregnancy, he can decide who he wants."

"I'm not agreeing to anything," I spit.

"Fine. But if I get the slightest inkling that South knows you know about us, then I won't hesitate to tell him about the baby you're hiding from him. I doubt he'll ever speak to you again, let alone provide child support."

"Maybe I won't care if he doesn't." Blindly, I stagger

through the door, wind along corridors, and topple into the alleyway, wiping at tears as I go.

South, the treacherous bastard, won't be home for hours. *How awesome.* I'll have the apartment to myself and can fall pathetically and noisily apart while I pack an overnight bag.

So, I don't have to face him later, I'll send a text and say that Ivy is sick and needs nursing while Nico's away with Burntbad.

On the subway I shove my ear buds in hard and turn an all-girl punk band up loud. I can't breathe. I can't breathe. Ignoring fellow passengers' stares, I try to think straight and devise a plan.

What the crap am I supposed to do now? I'm pregnant to a cheater. That asshole has trampled my heart. Pulverized it.

Well, one thing is certain—the choice I've agonized over for weeks, the baby or South... with his shocking betrayal, he's made the decision an easy one. And to think I'd planned to tell him tonight.

From now on, I'll put every bit of love I have into the tiny life that's growing inside me and harden myself against that wretch, that slayer of love who dares to call himself my boyfriend.

He's no partner, no devoted lover. No way. He's nothing but a man-whore betraying seducer. A rock star ruined by the trappings of success. News flash—it's now confirmed—South is ruled by his dick. Certainly not by his heart.

As if we're living in a fairy tale, I thought all he needed was love and that I could be the one to save him with a happy ending. What a joke.

It's clear to me now just what South *needs*—a million hard kicks to the butt and several thousand slaps in the face.

And *I* need to wake up and find that the last hour was nothing but a sickening nightmare. But that won't be happening—only a heart breaking for real could feel this bad.

Hugging my belly, I pray hard that Ivy won't say *I told you so* too often tonight. From the beginning she warned that South would break my heart, and blinded by his turquoise eyes and high-voltage sex appeal, I refused to listen.

Well, I'm a fool.

And Ivy was right all along.

32

MIA

Jam Donut

"You can't just run away and never see him again. That's his baby you've got tucked up in there," says Ivy, pointing a threatening finger at my belly. "You know, an actual future child and all, not a freaking jam donut."

I've had enough of donuts—jam, cinnamon or iced, and frankly, I'm done with them forever.

"I'm well aware I've got a baby on board! And I know I have to tell him." I look at the bright-blue sky above us— same color as his eyes. "At some point in the future."

This morning, I'm having trouble steering clear of the pedestrians bustling over the busy strip mall. I step sideways to avoid a girl who's wielding over-stuffed designer bags around like weapons and wince as the sharp edges jab my thigh.

"When I think about how South came into this world. Unwanted. Unloved. And the whole not knowing his psycho-rapist father thing. His mother barely bothering to care for him. Cripes! No wonder he doesn't want children. But he does still need a chance to be involved. An opportunity to love this kid. Doesn't he?"

"Well, otherwise it's a bit too close to history repeating itself. Ooof!" says Ivy as her shoulder connects with a rabid bargain hunter elbowing her way through the crowd.

Ivy is right. The current situation has a spooky parallel with South's past, and I'm having nightmares over the fact.

"Yes! And I keep thinking, what if it's the answer, the very thing to heal him? He deserves that chance, doesn't he? Even if he is a faithless, cheating prick."

"Mia, I don't actually think it's possible that he is one. When I first met him, I doubted his ability to ever be a one-woman guy but since you've been together, I don't. He barely looks at Rita. And if you're in the room, he can't see anything else. It just can't be true."

"Rita admitted it yesterday. Tried to act all sorry and everything, but I could tell she wasn't."

"What a heartless bitch. Do you know how lucky you are? Look at *me*. I'm two weeks behind you and my belly has already begun to pop out a little. It must be my cougar punishment for forcing a gorgeous hunk of a guy like Nico into parenthood at such a young age," she jokes. "You're not showing at all."

"I know, but South *has* been touching my stomach a lot lately, which is weird."

"It probably feels nice to fondle." Ivy leans over and has a go herself, rubbing over my belly. "Yeah, it's a bit rounder and firmer. It's lovely."

I pull her toward a bench seat that's positioned right out front of an edgy hairdresser's. Inside the shop all I can see are dreadlocks, rainbow colors, and tattoos. "Slow down, Ivy. Geez, sit a minute. I need a rest." And a lobotomy.

"What you *need* to do is confront South. You can't keep avoiding him." Ivy hugs her grocery bag tight. "Oh, shit, look at that schnauzer in a tutu! That's hilarious."

The dog *does* look silly, but its owner looks pretty damn pleased with himself. Probably just the type to go for a pet wedding, too. If I wasn't feeling like jumping off a bridge, I'd be foisting my business card on him.

"I have to get out of here. Go away for a bit and get some perspective. Cry out an ocean before I can face telling him."

"Didn't staying at my place and lying about me being sick last night tip him off that something was up?"

"No, when he got my text, he rang back immediately all sweet and sympathetic, even asked if he could come over to help out after their show!"

"That's a laugh. As if I'd want all that sexiness holding up the puke bucket. He's so clueless sometimes. You know the obvious answer, don't you?" Ivy asks.

"No, of course I don't!"

"Abbie."

I stare dumbly.

"Go to Abbie's."

"What? There is absolutely no way Nate's mom will protect *me* over South. No way in hell. I mean, we get on great, but she practically raised him, and he's her golden child who can do no wrong. I'm amazed Nate hasn't knocked him on the head with a shovel and buried him somewhere on the farm out of jealousy."

"Lucky for South that Nate's under his spell, too."

"Aren't we all?"

"Yeah, I guess we are. But *think,* Mia! The wolf pup's child. Abbie will be beside herself with joy. She'll do anything to make sure it's born. Anything. And with Mason not around, Nate said she's lonely. I bet she'd love having you there to fuss over all the time while plotting how to get you and South back together."

"I don't know. If it wasn't for this baby, I'd be okay with curling up in bed and letting myself starve to death. I've never in my life felt so gutted. I trusted him and he's totally broken my heart. What an idiot I've been." And, dammit, the tears start flowing again.

Ivy wraps an arm around me, squeezing my shoulder. "Look, once the European tour starts, Up Void won't be back in the States for two and a half months. You'll be nearly six months pregnant by then. Then the first leg of the American tour goes on for a month. South and Nate will be so busy they won't make it out to Abbie's before it's over. Gives you time to work up the courage to tell him, and then all you need to do is make sure you're back home in time to have the baby so Nico and I are around to help and everything will be swell."

Oh, sure. Swell.

Swearing, I hunt through my bag.

"What are you doing?"

"Finding my phone so I can call Abbie. Shit, and Kendra too. I'm gonna have to fess up to her about the baby so I can get some leave from work. Will you look after Dolphin for me while I'm away?"

"Of course. You know how much that cat loves Nico."

"How am I going to get through this dinner tonight at Vince's place?"

"You'll figure something out."

"I think I'll meet South there. That way I won't need to see him beforehand," I say, wiping away another pesky tear. But I *will* have to sit through a meal with Vince's family and the Up Void crew, laughing and pretending that my soul isn't bleeding out of my ears. And somehow try to smile at South when all I want to do is put my hands around his throat and squeeze hard.

Then later tonight I'll need to speak to him, look him in the eye and tell him that it's over.

Stuff what Rita wants. I'm going to tell South that I know about his despicable, cheating ways, and then take my baby to Abbie's where I can lick my wounds and work up the courage to spring the fatherhood news on him.

So, that sounds like a plan, a terrible one, yes, but better than the jumping-off-a-bridge one.

33

SOUTH

It's Not Working

"**S**hit!" My heart pounds as Mia's arms come out of nowhere and wrap around my waist, her head nestling into the curve of my back. She can move about as loudly as a shadow when she wants to.

"Hey." I drop the knife on the counter, twist to get my arm around her and pull her against my chest. I bury my nose in her hair. All warm and sleepy, she smells like home. "Did I wake you?"

"No. I couldn't sleep." She makes this long sigh into my skin. It's a resigned sound. A sad one. The air around my body drops a degree or two, and my heart thuds slow and hard.

Stepping away, she peeks at my plate lying on the counter next to the sink. "That looks revolting. What's on it?"

I grin, tear off a piece of bagel and wave it under her nose. A blob of gunk drips on the floor. "Jealous? You want some?"

"No!" She swipes it from my fingers and prises it open. "Yuck! What is that? Nutella? Marshmallows?"

"Yep. All grilled to gooey perfection. This'll be my second."

"That's type two diabetes on a plate. How can you still be hungry after the massive dinner Sal put on tonight? She spoiled you big time."

Yeah, Vince's wife outdid herself alright, cooked all my favorites. And the least I could do in return was full justice to the mountains of spicy fried chicken, cheese grits, corn pudding, sweet potato pie, and homemade ice cream. I piled my plate high. Fuck, okay, so it was plates. And even Ben had shaken his head at me, and he eats like a whole team of pigs at a trough, so I guess I must've overdone it.

"I'm not sure why I'm still eating." I smirk as I look her over real slow. "But if I have to give a reason, I think it might be all that sex you insisted on earlier. You were ruthless, and it created a calorie deficit."

"I find that hard to believe. Your fuel consumption at dinner was enough to get you through a whole week of non-stop surfing."

Laughing, I glance at the clock on the wall. "Shit, it's after three. Go back to bed. I'll be finished this in about thirty seconds, and then I might come looking for something even sweeter to finish up on. Keep you awake a bit longer."

I pull her close, let her feel what the sight of her hot curves, barely covered in a tank top and black panties, do to me. "Sound okay?"

She gives me small smile and I frown because, like the sun, Mia's smiles are *always* full blast, never dimmed down or half-hearted. Except for tonight.

At dinner, I watched her go through the motions, like she was pretending to have a good time. I'd wondered. Then I dismissed the dark feeling as paranoia. Convinced myself she was only exhausted from looking after Ivy. But it's clearly more than that. Something is wrong.

Whatever it is, I'm sure I can fix it. Wrapping my fingers in her bed-messed hair, I tip her head back and indulge in a slow, deep kiss. Two seconds into it and I'm totally gone. Food forgotten. Worry evaporated. My only thought is the need to get her back to bed so we can fuck again. So her sighs, her warmth, can dissolve the darkness inside me.

One second she's right here with me, limbs loose as she makes noises that get my blood simmering, and then she's squirming. And not in a good way.

"South…"

"Huh?" I pull back so I can see her face, keeping my arms locked tight around her and breathing roughly.

"We need to talk—"

"What?" Shock twangs through me like the mid-song snap of a guitar string. The pitch of her voice is off. It's too high and shaky, and it makes me feel real bad. Sick, even. "Talk about what? What's going on?"

"Sit down."

Sit down? In the history of the world, nothing good ever came after that introduction. She nods at the chair, and with my eyes stuck on hers, I shuffle into it, lean my elbows on the table and swallow hard.

Then I wait, racking my brain for what could be coming, wondering what might make her pace like that and frown at the honey-colored floorboards. With her palm, she rubs circles over her stomach.

Maybe she's unwell. Yeah that makes sense with how quiet she was at Vince and Sal's tonight. She's probably just coming down with the same bug Ivy has.

"I…" She trails off as she stands there staring at me. My pulse races faster. A few seconds pass before she speaks again. "Okay, I think I'm just going to come out and say it. So… I want you to tell me how long it's been going on for."

"What? Eating toasties in the middle of the night?"

"How long, South?"

Shit. Well that joke crashed and burned. "How long *what*, Mia? I don't know what the heck you're asking me."

"Rita."

"Rita?" Sludge moves up my throat, a sound like a plane taking off roaring in my ears. "What the fuck about her?"

Mia slides her palms across the table until her fingers almost touch mine. Her golden eyes are close as she says each syllable slowly. Like I'm a moron. "How long have you been sleeping with her?"

"What. The. Fuck?"

"How. Long?"

"Is this a joke? You think I've… what, fucked *Rita?* You

really think I could…Jesus." It hurts to draw air into my lungs and, even though I want to, I can't get any more words out. This isn't happening.

Needing to be next to her and not knowing what else to do, I get up and take hold of her arms, backing her against the fridge.

"Well, she's just the one I'm aware of. Who knows how many others you've got off with while you've been out on the road with the band?"

Behind her head, standing out bright against the white fridge, is a selfie we'd taken at the beach on our first weekend as an official couple. Almost hallucinating from sleep deprivation because we'd stayed up all night fucking, I'd never felt more alive than at that moment with Mia leaning back against my chest, her body nestled between my legs.

Safe. I'd felt safe.

"South?" Her fingers dig into my arms.

I can't take my eyes from the photo, off our laughing faces framed by the pinks and purples of a violent sunset. Or off my dumb fucking grin. It looks like it might split my face apart it's so wide.

"And this thing with Rita… I hope you used protection, because it's not fair to risk anyone's health."

"Protection? What do you mean, like a rubber?"

Nodding, she lets out a shaky breath.

"No, Mia, I didn't—"

"*What?* But how could you not—"

"I haven't used a condom since we decided I didn't need to. *Because, Mia,* it was just going to be us, wasn't it? No one else. That's what we agreed to. Do you even fucking remember that conversation?"

"But if you changed your mind and slept with someone *else* then you have to use one!"

A growl rumbles in my chest. I weave my fingers through chunks of my hair and tug hard. "I didn't need to use one because I've only been sleeping with *you!* Fuck! Why are you saying this shit?"

I grip her arms again, forcing my fingers to relax when she winces. "Who's telling you this bullshit? All these… dirty fucking lies."

"So, you're absolutely denying it?"

"Yes! *Yes.* Of course I'm fucking denying it! You're the only one, Mia. Only you. Like we said when we started this thing. No one else. Just us, remember? *Fuck…*"

I turn away, pressing my hands hard into the table's wooden surface to stay upright. I want to let go, collapse on the floor, and howl like a dying wolf. But I won't. Not yet, anyway.

She stands close behind me, each soft sniffle as she cries breaking my fucked-up heart.

"Mia," I say turning and dragging her against my chest, holding on for my life. "Don't do this. I'm begging you not to do this." I say it over and over while she sobs, warm and perfect against my skin. Small and soft and mine. The one who loves me right. Or so I'd thought.

I frame her face with shaking palms. "Please…" I draw in a shuddering breath. "Please, Mia. Listen to me. I'll do anything. Anything to prove it's not true. You *know* it's not true. You know *me*. Fuck, better than anyone. And you know I wouldn't do that. You have to believe me. You're the moon, and I'm the sky you burn across. I can't do this shit without you. I love you more than anything."

"I know you do." She pushes away, and my skin chills further as she walks toward the living room. "But I don't think it's enough."

"It *is* enough. *You're* enough. You—"

"No." Leaning in the door frame, she says, "I can't do it, live the same way my mother has—with an adoring, gorgeous husband who, even though he loves her, gives in to temptation over and over again because it's so easy for him to do so. Always wondering. Always knowing that at any time it's a possibility. A monk would have a hard time resisting all those girls who want you, South... I can't cope with the stress. They can have you."

Anger flames through my gut. My head spins. She's throwing me away like some piece of garbage. Just like my mom did. Why? Because it's easier? Because I'm not important?

I get up close. "I fucking knew it! I knew this was too good to be true," I yell.

She flinches and I try to cool down, try to lower my voice and get a handle on my fury. But I can't. "You don't want this anymore? You don't want *me*? Of course you fucking don't."

I fling around and stare at the dirty dishes in the sink, muttering low, "Why would she want you, idiot? You're just a worthless piece of—"

"South? Who are you talking to? If it's me, then I can't hear you properly."

Fuck. Did I say that out loud?

This is my darkest fear brought to light, taking form in the shape of the only girl I've ever felt anything for.

She doesn't love me. Not really.

She knows I'm tainted. Rotten inside. How can a person like me—formed from madness and cultivated in hate—be anything else? I'm nothing. A filthy piece of shit. Rejected. Humiliated. Afraid and ashamed just like when I was fifteen. If my own mother didn't want me, why would anyone else?

"Listen, if you don't want me, all you need to do is say it. You don't need to make shit up. Make up stories... just... just fucking tell me, Mia."

Our ragged breathing fills the air. She trembles, and I take a step forward out of habit. If Mia suffers, I'm the one who can fix things and make her smile. But not tonight. My fists drop, thudding against my thighs.

Nothing I do tonight will help.

"Okay, fine, I'm telling you, South. I've had enough. So, I'm going to go and sleep on the couch. In the morning, you should call Nate about getting your old room back. It's still empty." Her face crumples. "I'm sorry. I really am. But I can't be with someone who cheats. No matter how much I love you. I just can't. And right now, I can barely even look at you."

A *cheater?* She actually believes that... And she's making me leave. She's killing me.

"Fuck this shit," I say. Nausea rising, I make to stride past her, but of its own accord my hand shoots out and my fingers wrap around her throat. So gently, barely touching her skin.

While I lose my mind to the staccato beat of her pulse, chords and notes winding through my head, I pin her against the wall. I do it slowly, the way a lover would.

Face close, my eyes search hers, looking for a sign, a flicker of warmth, anything that might give me hope. Man, I should be kissing her, running my hands all over her. Not leaving. Never that.

"Why wait for tomorrow?" I whisper. "Ah'll go now." *Listen to me! The cowboy has taken over.* "Then you won' have to look at me again. That should make you real happy. And all I've wanted, Mia, is for you to be happy. Maybe from now on I just won't give a damn."

My thumb trails down her throat, and then I try to lift my fingers from her skin, from the hypnotic pulse of her jugular vein. I bite my lip hard.

Go, you dumbass. Go now.

But instead of pushing away, I press my mouth to hers, taste her tears mixed with my blood. A madness whirls in my head while I wait for her lips to part.

One cymbal crash.

Two.

Three.

Four.

Then, finally, her lips move, and in a warped version of mouth-to-mouth, I exhale a laugh into her lungs, and then use the hate I feel for myself, the full shitty force of it, to wrench away. To let go of her and walk through the door.

In the bedroom, I stumble into jeans, stuff a t-shirt into my back pocket, grab my phone from the bed, and then stagger down the stairs and into the abyss on the street outside our home.

The stars hang low in a clear sky. It fucking hurts to look at, because I know I'll never again feel any joy in a beautiful night.

Shuddering like a wet dog, I stare along the empty street through a fuzzy haze. Something is wrong with my eyes. The air is cool. My chest bare. Heart broken. Now what? Now fucking what? Still shaking, I try to make sense of the situation. Work out my options. But my damn head is nothing but a jumble of misfiring signals bouncing inside my skull. Nothing makes any sense.

Think.

Think.

There's that all-night bar a few blocks away. At this time of the morning it will be full of lost causes, so I should fit in well. Or I can walk to Jackson Street. No doubt there'll be a junkie or two awake looking to share the misery with someone.

Fuck. I drop to the curb, hang my head between my legs. My eyes burn, then fill, and a fat fucking tear splatters on the filthy concrete. My gut heaves, and I hack up a mess of Nutella and marshmallows. Well, I reckon they'll be off the midnight-snack menu for a while.

So, this is love, huh? This is where giving your life over to someone, trusting another person, gets you... homeless and aching and throwing up in the gutter like a loser.

I tug my t-shirt out of my pocket and use it to scrub my mouth hard, then pull out my phone and stare at the massive list of contacts that blur in front of my eyes. My thumb flicks over all the options. Which one should I choose?

The phone numbers are all symbolic crossroads leading to vastly different destinations. A thumb press down on any one of them could change my fate in unique and mostly unwholesome ways.

Choices. Choices.

I can call up some druggie friends and get loaded.

Phone a girl.

Or ring Nate.

Hey, I'm the king of my destiny! Yeah, bullshit. I'm more like the jester of Fuckwit-land because if I could choose any path at all right now, it would be the one that takes me straight up those stairs and back to her.

Right. Fuck it. Guess that decides it then.

I press the number and wait. Nothing happens. I kill the call and try again, same number. This time it doesn't take long for him to answer.

"This better be fucking good. It's nearly four—"

"Nate. It's me. I need… I'm in big trouble."

"South? Where the fuck are you?"

"Home." Even to me, my voice sounds thick and warped. "I'm out front… in the gutter."

"Where's Mia? What's happened? Is she alright?"

"She's the one who put me here!"

"*What?* Hell… don't move, okay?"

Silence.

"*South?* Promise me you won't move."

Nodding, my mouth pulls into a grimace. A terrible sound, song-perfect, rumbles from the pit of my stomach and through my lips.

"*Fuck, South.* Just say it. You won't move, right?"

"I won't move."

"Okay. I'm on my way. And if you're gone when I get there, I swear I'll sic Abbie on you."

He will too, the fucking snitch.

"South? You hear me? You don't want that now, do ya?"

He's right. I'd rather have my balls removed with a blunt shovel.

"Hurry," I grunt, and then hang up before he can bitch any more.

34

SOUTH

26th of April

Two full days and nights is exactly how long I manage to stay wiped out for, practically comatose as I drown my pathetic sorrows. I only raise my head from the mattress every half hour or so to pack the weed bowl, slug some bourbon and collapse backward. But no matter how deeply I suck the smoke into my lungs or the quantity of booze I swill down, my head continues to spin with images I don't want. Mia's smile. Her dreamy eyes when I'm inside her. Memories thrash. The way her laugh flows through me. The taste of her tears.

Will this shitful pain ever end?

Back in the house I share with Nate and Zave I'm
disgusted by the sight of my white bedroom door, so I flip
onto my side. My body aches from passing out in strange
positions that would give a chiropractor nightmares—neck
twisted and lying half-on, half-off the bed. I wriggle onto my
back and stare at the ceiling. It's a very annoying gray color.

Why does today have to be the 26th of April, the most
depressing day of the year?

As a kid, nothing special ever happened. There'd been no
cakes with candles. My mom, somewhat drunker than usual,
only ranted and raved a little more. And presents? Until I
moved in with Nate's family, I never got any of those. Well,
that isn't entirely true. The year I turned thirteen I received a
second-hand snow shovel. And maybe it had been ungrateful
of me to chop it into firewood but full of fury, I longed to
smack my smirking step-dad over the back of the head with
the damn thing.

Instead of giving in to savagery, shame corroding my gut,
I burned it to ash, finally understanding that there was something wrong with me. Something that made me unworthy of
the birthday gifts the kids at school boasted about, skate-
boards and bikes and days out at theme parks.

Then two years later my mom told the story, the story that
confirmed just how horrifically wrong I *am*.

A mistake. Unwanted. Conceived in violence and fear. A
product of man's worst nature, base and evil. I'm utter filth.

Sickening heat rising, I push the quilt off to cool down.
Cradling my head, I press my arms against my ears, trying to

block out the sound, because I'm right back there in Chattanooga in that mess of a tiny kitchen, shaking on the floor while she screams. And screams. My hate for myself spreading through my body like a cancer.

Pity I ain't got any firearms here in the city. Wrapping my lips around some cold metal is about the only type of kiss I deserve right now. And what sweet relief it would be.

Maybe not. Because, after all, there *are* my friends to consider. They'd have to deal with the mess, and not just the kind made by blood and brain and bone fragments. These days I've got people who care, who might suffer for years if I ended in such a brutal way. My band. Abbie. Maybe even Mia still.

And like Mia always says—the past is dead and every day I get to choose a new future. Why not try for a good one?

Like the happy-family scene I witnessed a month ago at Marco's place. At the birthday party for our A&R guy's twin daughters, there'd been an excess of good things. Food, laughter, friends, and an insane number of candles sparkling on a gigantic silver princess cake. And so much love infusing the air that I was practically marinating in it. And I have to admit it felt damn good.

With my phone turned off, Mia pulled close, and nothing else to do but eat and talk crap, I'd actually had fun—at a kids' birthday party. Un-fucking-believable!

A shaft of light flickers against my bedroom wall and memories from later that day project themselves over it. At home after the party at Marco's, I'd kissed Mia back into bed for a long afternoon of my favorite pastime. I remember the sweet ache, the hot shivers of anticipation and… *Ah, man. No.*

With the amount of depressants in my bloodstream, my dick should be dead, even with my brain transmitting a porn movie onto the wall. But no, the stupid thing is raring to go.

Three good punches into my pillow, and then I throw it over my shoulder. My phone goes off again. I hate my phone. It woke me at ten this morning and hasn't stopped bleating since. My voicemail must be full of messages from people making asses of themselves singing that damn birthday song. Without listening to any of them, I'll just delete the lot.

Unless… what if one of those messages is from *her*. In fact, I need to get a look at the screen straight away and see who the latest caller is. Just in case. Because if she's going to ring on any day, this will be the one.

In a panic I dig around the bed trying to find my pillow, because the last time I saw my phone it was lying underneath it.

Christ, where has my pillow gone? How the heck could I lose something so big? Muttering, I crawl through the covers, my palms making frenzied slaps over them.

The phone goes silent. *No, goddamn it.*

Scowling so hard it hurts, I freeze and remember hefting my pillow off the bed not even a minute ago. I sweep my eyes over the floor and spy the cell on top of a pile of clothes. Lurching forward, I make a grab for it and slide head first onto the gray boards.

Righting myself, I rub my skull, flip the phone over, and

nearly black out when I see her name on the screen. Shit! She's left a voicemail.

Maybe she's calling to say she's on her way over or, better yet, waiting out at the front door. My sweaty fingers slip over the screen until, finally, I hear her voice. It's only been a few days since she booted me out, but word from Nico is that she's skipped town and isn't even in the same state anymore.

"Um, hi, it's me...," she says, and then goes silent for a few beats. I wait. "So when I woke up this morning, I remembered what day it is and, South, I..."

Blood roars in my ears while I wait for more. Speak, woman! Knees pulled tightly into my chest, I sit shaking and hoping. *More. More. More.*

And then... "I just wanted to say Happy Birthday, and I hope... I wish you well. I want so much for you to be happy and... shit this is hard. I got you a present ages ago. You might not want it now that we're not together. But I guess I'll give it to Nico to pass on. You can throw it away if you want. Oh, South... I'm so sorry." Her voice breaks, and then it's just silence.

The traffic rumbles outside. All my blood rushes into the thudding lump of muscle in my chest, and I long for her to say she's made a terrible mistake. To say she loves me and believes me, realizes that psycho bitch—whose neck I'd pay good money to wrap my fingers around and squeeze until her eyes bulge—is a liar.

For ages I wait like a brainless idiot, my ears straining for something to cling to. Words that might spark a hope. When I realize how dumb that makes me, I pitch my phone at the wall, and stumble down the hall to the bathroom.

After guzzling water from the faucet, I brush my teeth, inspecting the wreck I've made of myself in the mirror. Despite the blue eyes faded to gray, pale skin and aching chest, I feel a little better. So the rumors must be true then, alcohol isn't as hydrating as good old water. Funny about that.

Back in the bedroom, I slide to the floor, lug my Hummingbird onto my lap and smash my fingers over it, growling out words in a gruesome drawl. "Happy Birthday to me... Happy Birthday to me..." Shit, I sound like a lunatic. A twelve-year-old one.

Palms covering my face, I dig numb fingers into my forehead and try to straighten out my thoughts. While my brain scrambles, my chest contracts, eyes filling with a watery heat. I am *so* fucked.

Enough.

No more of this pity-party shit. She called, didn't she? Said she'd woken up thinking of me. That's good. Must mean she still cares a little about what happens to me.

Think.

What do I know about Mia, about what kind of person she is? That's easy. She's caring and kind, and hates making others unhappy. The best type of person, really.

Has she ever loved me? That has to be a yes. You can't fake the warmth, the electric sizzle, the uncontrollable blaze we make together. All that smiling and laughing, all those feelings. They're real.

And have I done anything wrong? Anything to change what we are together? Nope. I haven't.

So maybe, if I can get my head out of my ass, there's a chance I can fix this. Maybe all I have to do is stop falling apart and go and find her.

An idea begins to form, a bright light firing in the murky depths of my brain. Muscles tense, I sift through the bourbon-and-pot-fueled sludge and chase after it.

Fuck, of course! Before Mia, I hadn't known love was something I could earn. Prove myself worthy of. *Deserve.* Now I do. So, instead of getting wasted, falling back on bad patterns, I should have been convincing her that I'm faithful. Doing anything, *everything* to show her. And eventually she would believe me because it's true. I've got the facts on my side. *Shit.*

Forgotten, my guitar clatters against the boards as I get to my feet. For starters, I need to speak to Marco. *He'll* know where Mia is because he's tight with her and Ivy. And because he's loyal to *me*, there's a good chance guilt will make him spill the beans.

Once I have a location, I'll tell Marco to get that fucking girl, that lying piece of garbage called Rita, to tell the truth.

A tingling starts in my chest and spreads to my toes, my fingertips, until I'm nothing but a vibrating ball of energy. Okay, a wasted, only just functioning, dumbass, buzzing ball of energy. But a dumbass who's had an epiphany and is now on a mission.

All I have to do is get my shit together and simply *be* the guy that Mia deserves. The guy who makes her smile and laugh. If a girl like Mia ever loved me, I can't be a bad person like Mom always said I was.

And no one is ever gonna love Mia more than I do. Or make her happier.

Well, even if I'm not entirely certain about the second part, I'd better make damn sure that *she* believes it's true before some jerk like Liam, *America's most radical architect*, as his website proclaims him, makes her think that he's a better guy for the task.

I stumble to the window, flinching against the light, and squint out at pale leaf-covered trees. The sun is out. It's a beautiful day, but I'm too wrecked to drive. No way I'm taking the subway. The idea of people staring at me while the carriage clangs along to Marco's place isn't very appealing. And there's always the possibility that an Up Void fan could be on board, too, and it really ain't a good time to pose for happy snaps and shoot the breeze. Crying on some young dude's shoulder might be a traumatic experience for both of us, and I don't need that on my conscience. I've got enough to worry about.

Right. I'm calling a cab.

An hour later, I lean against the massive crimson door to Marco's converted warehouse, one hand pounding on it and the other thumping over my pants for my phone. Hoping I haven't left it in the cab, I scowl at the ground. Damn, I forgot to put shoes on. How have I only just noticed that?

The door creaks open and there's Marco looking frazzled, dark hair a wild mop partially obscuring his raised brow.

"Hey! You're the last person I expected to see on my

doorstep. Happy Birthday, buddy. Hell, you look a bit worse for wear."

"I feel even worse than I look, man." I shake off Marco's restraining hand and push past him into the spectacular atrium entranceway. The angled sheet glass above us creates a weird magnification of the sunlight, making it brighter than outdoors. I've never wished for my sunglasses more. "And anyway you can't talk. You ain't looking so hot yourself."

"I've been hassled by the two terrors all morning. They took a day off school, and to be honest I don't think it's a good idea for them to see you like this. You're not exactly looking like a model of good behavior right now."

"Neither are you letting them ditch school. In fact, that's very irresponsible parenting."

A piercing, whirring sound starts up. I wince, then smirk as I peer around Marco's shoulder. "Too late. Here they come."

Shouting like a whole posse of Avengers, Marco's girls, Aster and Bloss, fly down the stairs, dressing gowns billowing behind them like capes.

"Ooof," I say as they smash into my legs and wrap their chubby arms around my knees. I bend and lift them into an unstable embrace, balancing one on each hip.

Marco frowns. "Hey! You're gonna drop them. Put them down."

I laugh.

"Girls, South isn't feeling very well. I'm sure you don't want to catch whatever bug he's got and end up having to stay home again tomorrow, do you?"

Wearing a sassy smile, Bloss says, "Yep, *I* do."

After Aster slops kisses over my cheek, she asks, "Is it *really* your birthday?"

"Uh-huh."

Bloss wrinkles her nose. "You smell funny." She buries her face in my hair and sniffs. "That's not how you smelled at *my* birthday party."

"True. I might have spilled some grown ups' drink on my clothes this morning."

"Yuck!" Aster tugs my ear. "How old are you?"

"How old are *you?*" I counter.

"Guess!" they both yell.

I deposit the dark-haired twins on the gold and slate colored tiles and examine them, doing my best not to smile. "Ah let me think. Well, you..." I say, pointing at Aster's serious, freckled face. "I reckon you're about, maybe twelve?"

Aster giggles.

I turn and grin into Bloss' sparkling green eyes. "And you bouncing up and down there... I'd say you're probably... um about thirteen and a half."

They squeal.

"You're silly," Bloss says, jamming tiny fists on her hips. "We're both six! Don't you remember the candles on our cake?"

"Six? No way. That ain't true. I just saw your noses grow right then."

Little hands reach up to pat at adorable faces.

Marco spins them to face the stairs. "Back you go, please.

You've got one hour to get that painting finished or there'll be trouble."

"Can he sing for us while we do it, Dad? Aster wants to hear *Dirt* acoustic, South," says Bloss. "She thinks it'll sound good that way."

Luckily they have no idea what the song's about—my pre-Mia dalliance with hard drugs. It ain't a pretty scene.

"Not this time ladies. I've gotta pour some coffee down his gullet and then have a special man-to-man talk with him."

"What does gullet mean?"

"It means South needs a drink, Bloss," says Marco. "Preferably of the non-alcoholic kind."

"What's a nanocolic?"

"I really don't know, Aster. Now get outta here!"

Waving and blowing kisses, the girls pad backward up the stairs.

"It's disgusting the effect you have on females, even when you look like something the cat's dragged in. I'm warning you now that you won't be allowed over here when they're fourteen."

Back stiff, Marco struts off, grouching over his shoulder, "Aster's already got you pegged as her future husband, and believe me, I lose sleep when I think about that."

"I wouldn't worry. I plan to be off the market again by then," I say as I amble toward the industrial, open-plan kitchen, wondering what the big deal is.

Going on what I see in the mirror, I'm just a guy with two eyes, a straight nose, and a normal mouth. Sure, I'm pretty fit, but so are a lot of people. Must be the singing thing.

"Sit." Marco points at a metal stool that's positioned smack bang in the middle of a shaft of light that beams down through a roof window like a fucking spotlight. Awesome.

I sink onto the seat, slumping over a huge, antique wooden table that probably cost more than the entire budget for our upcoming tour, and watch Marco crash around the kitchen.

"So, confession time! I'm sorry about this but we haven't planned anything for today. String Power, I mean. We've got nothing organized to celebrate your birthday. We thought you'd still be in bed."

"Thank Christ," I mumble into the cup of coffee Marco places on the table.

When I glance up from the creamy froth, I find him sitting opposite and eyeballing me hard. It's kind of his specialty, unwavering silent glares.

I grab my cell, flick my eyes down, and listen to the seconds click away on a nearby clock.

After Marco spends far too long watching me scroll through texts, he asks, "Well?"

Okay. Here goes nothing. I take a big breath. "So where is she?"

Silence.

I heave a loud sigh.

"How would I know? I'm just your record label guy."

I laugh at the bullshit he's trying to feed me. "Cut the crap. I know that you know, Marco. Everyone close to the band probably does."

He raises his hands in surrender. "Fine. Of course we

fucking know where she is. And believe me, not one of your Up Void buddies will tell you."

I open my mouth.

"Shh, just listen. If you keep your shit together until the end of August, get through Europe, then the U.S. dates, *I'll* fucking tell you."

"Really?"

"Yes, really. Word of honor. But no fucking up. You have to kick ass at every show. And I mean every single one. So if Lane tells me you don't, you can forget about me helping you."

"But August..."

"It's the best offer you're gonna get. If I have to betray Mia's confidence, I need to get something out of the whole mess. Got it?"

"Unfortunately, yeah, I do."

I sit forward, fingers wrapping tight around my fairy princess mug that has Olivia written on it in large, glittery letters. Huh? That's strange. No one by that name lives here.

Four fucking months. It's way too long. Somehow, I'll find her before then. Nate will break before August, because, bless his savior's heart, the sucker will do almost anything to keep my head above water. His worst nightmare is to watch me drown, feeling like he somehow failed me. And if Nate refuses, maybe Nico will reveal all if I hassle him enough.

I nod slowly. "Okay, I can do that. But one thing... can you please just tell me... Do you know if... Shit. Does Mia..."

"What?"

"Hate me?"

"No, man, she still loves you."

A mega-cocktail of endorphins floods my system, making me lightheaded. "Are you sure? I'm begging you not to lie to me about this, Marco, just to get me to do the tour."

"Of course I'm sure."

"Did she really say it?"

"Yes. Yes, she told Ivy who told Nico who told me. It's gospel. But full disclosure here, she still believes Rita's bull-shit story even though we've all told her, all sworn that out on tour you're as chaste as the freaking Dalai Lama."

Moaning, I let my head fall into my hands.

"She won't always think that. Trust me. It's tied up with her asshole parents, self-esteem stuff. You know all this. But she *will* see the light."

"Why won't you let Lane kick Rita's butt all the way back to the Boston hole she crawled out of like we've been begging you to? Or at least make her speak to Mia and tell the fucking truth. That one's not right in the head. Why are you making me put up with her on this tour? Maybe you're deranged, too."

"South, it's complicated. There's stuff I can't disclose right now, but I promise you there's a logical reason, a very *big* reason, in fact, why we can't get rid of her yet. And why you therefore have to play along and pretend that you don't know she told Mia that you and her were supposedly engaged in a non-stop fuckfest on the road. Just keep out of Rita's way, and it'll all make sense when you see Mia again."

Watching my knuckles turn white, I squeeze the mug harder. "What is this, the freaking X-Files? Is *Rita* some kind of alien? How about Mia, am I hung up on a chick from Kepler-186?"

"Jesus, man, knock it off!" Scratching his chest, Marco shuffles in his seat. He doesn't seem able to get comfortable. "You're not doing... you know..."

"What? Doing what?"

Raising an eyebrow, Marco drops his gaze. "The hard stuff."

"What? No!" I turn my palms up, sliding my arms across the table. "Look. Clean, see? I rarely did that shit, anyway. And I haven't done anything but get a little buzzed on booze these last months I've been with Mia."

"You're a very creative guy, South. There are plenty of other places to inject. I've told all the crew if they get you any of that rubbish, they're out on their asses—"

"Fuck, come on. As if I would." Sighing, I press my thumbs into my throbbing temples. "I promised her, Marco. Never again. Sticking needles in my skin would be the easiest way out of how I feel right now. But maybe I don't want easy anymore. I reckon I'm ready to fight for what I want."

"Well, good for you, man. It's about fucking time. Now go on, piss off and get some rest, and I'll cancel that acoustic TV session we had lined up for this afternoon at your place."

Rubbing at my frown, I push onto my feet. "No, man, I'm fine. Lane's already sorted this anyway. Nate's gonna come and hop into bed with me. We'll do a love-in John-and-Yoko style. I won't let you guys down."

Marco looks worried. "What song are you doing?"

"Eyes."

"What? Mia's song? Are you fucking insane? Jesus, you certainly like to whip yourself when you're lying on the ground, South."

"Well, someone's gotta do it. It might as well be me."

35

MIA

Abbie

"You have to tell South, Mia. You're four and a half months along now, and you haven't spoken to him since you left home. This is crazy." Abbie fans out her playing cards, squinting at me over the top of the them.

It's been a mild day, but we've lit the pot belly stove to counter the cool night air circulating through the drafty farmhouse kitchen.

"I know. Soon, Abbie."

In her baggie denim jacket over a multicolored boho dress, Abbie looks more earth mother than a determined force-to-be-reckoned-with. But when you get up close to those warm whiskey eyes, you see the truth and the strength burning in them. That's when you back away slowly.

"You tell him tomorrow. Or I will… Rummy!"

I frown at the cards as she lays them on the table. "You must be cheating. That's the second time you've won that way. Why do I bother playing with you?"

"Don't ignore me. He needs to be told. It's only fair."

Yep, she's right. It's more than fair.

Since leaving home a month and a half ago, I've been staying with Abbie at the Sequatchie Valley property Nate, and South from his teenage years, grew up on. Dear Abbie, who won't accept any rent money and only dishes out a mere handful of lectures when her desire to throttle me must be overwhelming.

"I know. I know. Just a little longer. I promise I'll tell him soon. Why haven't you told him yet, Ab? I still can't believe you've taken my side over his."

Abbie's eyes harden. "Make no mistake, I will take that boy's side at every turn. I'm only doing what's best for both of you in the long run is all. And looking out for his child."

Patsy Cline croons in the background about falling to pieces, and I yawn loudly. Patsy is a nice change from Tammy Wynette. If I have to hear *Stand By Your Man* a third time tonight, it might push me over the edge.

Abbie doesn't believe in subliminal messages. Next she'll be placing placards around the house that itemize all South's good points. Probably with attractive photos plastered over them.

I've already been subjected to numerous family album

viewings, dying a thousand deaths as my eyes blur over photographs of a golden-haired future heartthrob smiling as he cuddles kittens, rubs down horses and chucks out the barn. Talk about emotional blackmail.

"I told my family about the baby today."

Abbie raises an eyebrow. "And?"

"My sister, Greta, is thrilled, but my folks? Nope. I spent ten minutes begging my dad not to launch a seek-South-and-destroy mission. Which is bizarre considering how disinterested he is in my life."

"It's not South's fault! You can't kill a guy for having sex with his girl."

"I don't think they want a rock star's genes polluting the family's blue blood. At the moment, my dad believes he'll be doing a community service if he strangles South."

"You're the bad guy in this situation, hiding a pregnancy, not South."

My face heats as I nod my agreement. Even though he's been unfaithful, in the greater scheme of things, hiding an impending baby is worse.

"Mark my words, that wolf pup's gonna be growlin' and foaming at the mouth when he hears the news. And you'd better be the one he hears it from, too. He'll take it much harder if someone else dishes this up."

Burying my face in my forearms, I say, "I know. I worry day and night that Nate or Zave will slip and tell him. I need to do it. But I'm so scared, Abbie. So scared. Shit. Shit. Shit. What a mess." Slowly, I lift my head from the table. "Why do you call him that still? He's the furthest thing I know from a cute, little furry pup."

"If you could've seen that child the day Nate lured him home from school with the promise of a hot meal. Lord, he was snappin' and snarlin' at us and about as beautiful a mess as ever there has been. It damn near tore my heart up to see him like that. Almost broken. And try as I might, I just can't rid myself of the picture of that skinny feral boy all hungry and unloved."

"If he was so wild and wary, how did he end up staying with you?"

"That woman, his mother, and that's a loosely applied term in her case, she was too messed up and drunk to care a hoot about him. I reckon she barely remembered he existed, let alone thought to cook a supper for him."

"Where is she now?"

"Rotting away in some meth town east of Nashville. Probably got more tattoos than teeth by now, I reckon."

"Does she ever contact you?"

"She must have some sense left in her fool head, because she hasn't done so in a long, long time."

Shivering, Abbie buttons up her jacket. "Now what was I saying? So first off, South came for the meals because he was near to starving. Made himself sick on three gigantic plates of my biscuits and gravy that first night. So it was the food he wanted. And then, Mia, then he stayed because of Nate's guitar. Nate had been learning it about a year, and he brought it out on South's third visit. Nate sat across the table from him right there where you're plonked down now, watching South stuff himself. After a bit Nate started playing, something by a Pixie I think it was…"

"The Pixies."

"That's right." Abbie tucks long, silver hair behind her ears. "And the second it began South went still as stone, staring at Nate. Even stopped eating. After that he was here every day begging to be taught. It made him realize that he had to act civilized to people if he wanted their help. That was a game changer for him, because I got the feeling he'd rather roll around in a tub of pig shit than owe anybody for anything."

Abbie sighs, and then smiles. "He was a real fast learner, too, and he did jobs around here so he could save up and buy a guitar of his own. He worked like a demon he wanted it that badly, and within a matter of weeks, he'd done it."

The chair scrapes against the floor as Abbie stands, rubbing her neck. "I'm as dry as a chip. You want some water?"

"No thanks. I'll be up all night peeing as it is." Or asleep and dreaming of South's hands on me.

Wearing a sad expression, Abbie drifts over to the sink. Almost a year has passed since she lost Nate's dad, Mason, and although she's only kept the horses on, the old farm-house is a lot of work. Luckily the small-town community is close knit and she's got a horde of supportive friends and neighbors ready to lend a hand.

Abbie sits back down, sipping her drink. "And then… oh, Mia, he started with the singing. I will never forget hearing that voice for the first time. He sat out there on those porch steps, all alone, feet bare in the dirt. And it wasn't someone else's song he was crooning. Oh, no, it was one of his own, full of pain and anger and as dark and beautiful as a night sky. It was the way back for him. An outlet and a kind of healing. Music saved that boy's life."

"No, you did, Abbie. The music helped, sure, but it was you who saved him."

"Well, you need to take some credit, too, girl, because falling in love granted him peace. Letting love in will be the key to fully healing from the damage his mother did."

"But I'm about to cleave his chest apart with this latest bit of abhorrent-to-him news. God, I wonder how he's doing? I can't stop Googling him, and I can't tell much at all from the gig photos that appear online every five seconds, other than the fact that he looks like sex on legs. Sorry, Abbie. That's too much information."

"No, it's just an unhealthy obsession, especially when all you have to do is call the boy to find out how he's doing first hand."

I want to do that so badly, hear his voice, tell him I miss him and love him. My heart bleeds for him with every beat, but if I *do* hear his voice, I'll tell him about the baby and then it will be over. For real and forever.

Abbie sighs. "Well, Nate tells me that South is doing okay. Apparently, he's still under the impression Marco's gonna crack at some point and spill the beans as to your whereabouts."

"Marco's stringing him along. There's no way he'll tell him."

"Well, South's got it in his head that if he can see you, he can convince you that he didn't sleep with that girl. And, of course, deep down you already know that he didn't. Don't you, Mia?"

"No. I don't know it! Of course you're all going to say he's a sweet innocent lamb. That's his power, isn't it? People do what he wants all the time. He kids himself that's not what's happening, but it is. The people closest to him worship him the most. It's sickening."

Abbie reaches for the cards, shuffles, then deals them out. "Maybe we treat him like that because we know him well. Know who he is beneath the skin, in his heart. And because the sweet soul that he is deserves that level of trust and faith. Lord knows he had no one extolling his virtues for the first fifteen years of his life."

The cards swish across the table as I push them away too hard. "I don't want to play again. My brain can't handle the intricate scoring thing you do. Have you considered the fact that he and Rita only needed to be a little discreet and the band and crew probably wouldn't have noticed a thing? A late night slip into a hotel room and who'd know? And why would she lie about something that serious?"

"Well you're very naive if you can't work that one out."

"Look, even if he didn't do anything with her in particular, it's only a matter of time until he gives in to the temptations of the road. How could he not? Girls throw themselves at him constantly. It's a smorgasbord of shiny boobs and butts. I can't compete with that."

"You know little of him if you believe you're in competition with those girls. It makes me sad to hear you talk like that. You ever seen one of them flea-bitten dogs lucky as all hell to find their way out of a vicious home, used to nothin' but beatings and neglect?"

I nod.

"And then seen 'em after they've found a true friend? Someone who loves them, values them, and treats them right?"

"Yep."

"You won't ever find a more thankful hound. I reckon they'd rather chew off their own leg than be disloyal to their new owner."

"That's true! One time I was at this country bar and there was a gorgeous greyhound—"

"Mia, *wake up*. South's that dog. And you're the new owner. Get what I'm saying?"

"But that dog you're talking about there didn't have thousands of people vying to take it home, all offering pulled pork sandwiches covered in gravy, and pumpkin pie, and—"

"Shh. Right now, I feel like slapping you to sleep and then slapping you again for sleeping!"

"Abbie, I need an uncomplicated relationship. I don't want to suffer the way my mom always has, living with my slick playboy father. And a few years ago, I had a psychopathic narcissist boyfriend who lived solely to torture girls. He ruined me. And I know South's not cruel. He's not like that guy. But I'm stupidly terrified of having my heart broken."

"You can say that again. But the fact is, you're miserable without him."

She's not wrong. All I do day and night is fantasize about South's touch. His kisses.

"And your baby will be wanting a father so—"

"It's way more complicated than me either just believing or just forgiving him. Look what I've done! I've hidden a pregnancy. That's not sane, Abbie. He'll kill me when he finds out. The tables will turn, you wait and see."

"Well, then, so be it. It's time, Mia. Time you face reality and help South get through this baby thing. Being a father sure won't be easy for him. But—"

"But it just might save him," I say, squeezing my temples hard.

Abbie smiles. "That's right. You got it."

36

NATE

On Fire

I feel sick. I could hurl right now, christen my new black Vans with a mess of spicy taco vomit. I may as well ditch my guitar and walk off stage because the Detroit not-so-hidden secret club show that should have been a breeze is turning into a shit-storm.

At soundcheck earlier, when South chose *The Wasted* as our pseudonym for the night, he probably had his breakdown all planned out. He's totally smashed, and the gig's a fucking disaster.

At least the crowd is getting off on the mayhem, that's something, I guess.

I stomp on my overdrive pedal, kicking up the distortion, and scan the onstage chaos.

Ever the optimist, Ben continues to bang out the opening to *Dirt* on his bass. Good luck getting our singer's attention.

Lane, the bastard, is standing side-of-stage, keeping his useless manager's eyes averted. I wave urgently at him and get no response.

Looking bored, Zave crush rolls over his snare drum on repeat.

South hasn't moved in at least five minutes. Maybe he can't. His gleaming, sweat-covered torso hangs into a pit of awestruck girls who grip his hair, trying to raise his head so they can suck on his face.

The audience cheers, screams, and laughs like they're at a fucking carnival. I 'spose they are.

What was Lane thinking to let South go on tonight? We should have canceled. I knew this was gonna happen sooner or later. I'm just surprised he kept his shit together this long.

It's mid-August, three and a half months since Mia kicked him out. During May and June, he somehow stayed sane through back-to-back shows in Europe. After a three-day break in London, we jumped on a plane for L.A. and are now ripping through five weeks of Stateside dates. Everyone's exhausted and pining for home. Or at least a decent rest. And, tonight, South has finally cracked.

"Nate," Zave yells into his mic, eyebrows wriggling like a jackass.

Squinting at our drummer, I amble over, kicking leads out of the way.

"What the fuck is up with him?" Zave tips his chin at South.

"Didn't you see him nursing that bottle of bourbon backstage and dragging on joints? He's shitfaced."

"But just before he went on, he started joking instead of growling. I thought things were looking up after the grunty-caveman he was at soundcheck."

"Check out the bottle on the speaker. Not much left."

Zave looks. "Shit."

"Yeah. I begged Lane to pull the plug, man, but he thinks South's fine. Or at least thinks the carnage will make great press."

Still thumping his bass, Ben joins the huddle. "Why'd he have to crack tonight? He's so close to Marco's deadline for good behavior. It's fucking sad."

It's true. Over the last few months, South has kicked ass at every single gig. Outwardly, he seemed to be doing okay. But not so much now. Why did he have to lose it so publicly? This will definitely get back to Marco. And then South will be fucked.

Okay. Time for damage control. "We need to get him off stage," I yell over the racket.

Zave and Ben look as if I've asked them to do something impossible, like lick their own elbows. And they're right. The only way to get South to do what you want is to make him think that he came up with the idea himself.

Right now, a pretty blond has him in a headlock, trying to mash lips with him. He wrenches his head sideways and shoves the mic between them, mumbling about soaking wet sheets and a freight train.

I laugh. Shit, he's singing Springsteen's *I'm on Fire*.

"I've got an idea," I say, and quickly bring Ben and Zave up to speed. Then I head to the front of the stage.

"South," I yell at our wasted leader. No response, only mutterings about '*bad desires*'. I crouch next to him, push the girl away gently, grab South under the arms and haul until he sits slumped, legs hanging off the stage. "Hey, great idea, man. I love that song."

Carefully, I remove his guitar and place it on the stage. "Why don't we play it from the top? We'll make it dark and edgy. Just how you like things. It'll be epic. You can stay right there and sing. Here, take the mic."

Obediently, South wraps his hands around it, smiling up at me like a glazed-eyed pig in shit.

"This will be our last number, okay? But make it a good one. I hate it when singers butcher classics."

With those words, South's *who-gives-a-fuck* expression transforms into steely-eyed determination. He surveys the crowd with a bloodthirsty gaze, swaying like a drunken Thor about to go into battle.

An electric energy builds, buzzing in the air with a charge as lethal as a category five hurricane. Well, it looks like he's about to blow every single mind in the club.

Skin prickling, I face Zave and Ben, and yell, "Make it real slow… and fucking depraved."

Ben pops gum. Zave wipes sweat off his brow, tips his chin, and then clicks his sticks together.

One.

Two.

Three.

South draws a long breath then his growl vibrates through the floor to the soles of my feet. Like always, his voice brings the darkness. Down, down, down it descends on every living soul in the room. Charged and heavy, it's a hot blanket of pain. Black and sticky, it tars us in his loss, feathers us in his twisted love as he drowns in self-hatred and we sway along to the beat.

Effortlessly, he glides into the high notes at the end of the song, and I'm ripped in half by his agony.

I feel weak.

I feel like I could take on the world.

Shit, how does he do this?

A chant hammers through my head. It becomes a prayer that I repeat until South throws the mic across the stage and feedback shrieks through the room.

This is it:

Come back, Mia.

Mia, come back.

Come back, Mia.

Mia, come back.

Before it's too late.

37

SOUTH

Freight Train

Why the hell are Nate and Mack the roadie hauling me around like pains in the ass? Or is it asses? "Hey, can you losers put me down?"

I fly through the air, and then I land hard on the dressing room couch.

"*Fuck*," I complain as my brain bashes my skull.

"Just stay there and don't move," says one of the scowling Nates. All three of them hover above me, their arms folded and expressions pissed.

I wave them away. "Ah'm fine."

"Sure you are, bonehead."

Huh. Awesome. Seems like Nate number one has bought my sober act, but the jury is still out on the other two.

He stabs a finger at my chest, shoving me against the cushions. "You're so fine right now I bet you could walk a tight rope all the way between here and New Jersey and not fall off once."

"Are you mocking me?"

"Oh, I wouldn't dream of it," he says with his lips all twisted funny. "You look great right now."

Just as I open my mouth to bitch at him, my body slides sideways, cheek connecting with cool vinyl. Shit, maybe I'll stay horizontal for a while. It feels real good.

"Jesus, South. The room's full of people and look at you. You can't even sit up. Way to appear like a bad rock cliché, dude. I'm gonna find Raff. He can get someone to take you back to the hotel."

"What? I ain't going in no boat."

"Huh? *Shit.* You are *fucked up,* man. Look, just do me a favor and don't talk to anyone, okay? When those people hovering over there swarm at you, ignore them. Pretend you're asleep. If you have to speak, just say the word *tired,* nothing else. Keep repeating it."

The three Nates step away, and I laugh until one turns back. It's the angriest Nate, unfortunately. *Oh hell… go away.* I push my palms at mad-Nate.

"Do you need a sick bucket? You're a very strange color. What exactly are you doin' with your hands?"

Laughing, I pat over my pockets. "Phone," I say.

Nate, who obviously has no clue what's going on, screws

his nose up. The dickhead. What is wrong with his ears? "Phone. Phone. *Phone,*" I shout to clarify the situation.

"Oh, right! Lane's got your cell. You're not planning to drunk-dial Mia are you?"

Mia.

Pain like a jagged knife twisting through flesh and viscera pierces my heart and shreds it to a pulp.

Mia. Mia. Mia.

Nate watches while I writhe in agony.

"Stop staring," I growl. "*Phone.*"

"Alright, E.T., just hang in there. I'll get it for you." He spins on his heels and trots off through the crowd.

Fucking finally.

I close my eyes and sink slowly back into the abyss, float-ing, consumed by golden eyes and hot sighs, platinum hair cascading over my chest. *Mia... Mia... Mia...*

"Shit, South!"

Damn. I crack an eye open. Why the heck is Nate back so soon? "What?"

"Will you get off her?"

"Who?" I glance down, surprised to find myself wrapped around a girl and almost choking on a mouthful of teased blond hair. She's not a bad cushion and has a real sweet smile, all pink lips and large white teeth. How the hell did my head get on her shoulder?

My nose smashes into the sofa as the girl gets up without warning.

"Yeah absolutely," Nate says to the smiling chick, his own smile not reaching his eyes. "Yep, sure, I'll tell him. You should probably get going. The only thing he's capable of tonight is sleep."

"Oh. Alright," she says. "He's *lovely*. Like a sexy angel, isn't he?"

"Oh, yeah, an angel. You have no idea." Nate turns her to face the drinks table, prods her back, and she limps away in skyscraper-heels.

He frowns at me. "That girl you were sleeping on just told me that was the best version of Springsteen's *On Fire* she'll ever live to hear. I really don't know how you pulled that stellar vocal out in your condition. It nearly killed me."

"Phone. Phone." Man, I sound like I've been double tracked to within an inch of my pathetic life.

"Yeah, yeah. Drink this first and then you can have it."

Yes. Just what I need, a vodka straight up. I grab the glass and guzzle down the liquid. Huh? That just tastes like…

"It's water, South, not a martini. Here, take your interstellar communication device and phone home. Or wherever." Nate flops beside me, and I snatch my cell, stabbing it with my finger. "This fucking won' work."

"Give it here. Your phone's fine. It's you who isn't working right now. Who you trying to call?"

"Marco."

"Marco? I'm not sure that's a good idea."

"Marco," I insist.

Unsteadily, I grope my way onto my feet. Stuff Nate. I'll find Zave. He'll definitely help me. Holding the phone out like a blind person's cane, I get ready to crash through the crowd.

Nate pulls me back and pushes me at the sofa. Muttering, he fiddles with the phone and then passes it over. "Good luck. And don't hate me tomorrow for helping you put a noose around your neck."

The second our A&R guy's voice growls down the line, my head clears a little. Praise be to angry-Nate and his sobering water.

"Whadda you want?" Marco asks.

"Did I wake you?"

"Nope. I'm still in the studio. And you sound hammered. Impressive, hey? It only took four words and I could tell."

"Shit, man. Have I fucked it up? I tried real hard, Marco. And I'm callin' to tell ya about it myself. So's y'all don't have to hear it from fucking Lane. Our manger's a real whistle... whistle-blower."

"Relax, South. Anyway, what's with the *y'all* shit? It's just me you're talking to."

"What? I thought you might have had Emma on the watchya call it..."

"Line? Speakerphone? Em's my wife, not my personal assistant. She's got better things to do than follow me to work in the middle of the night."

Yeah. That sounds fair enough. I must be more loaded than I thought because my brain ain't computing things right, such as the bizarre sight before my eyes.

A meter away, Ben mimes a bass riff down on his knees in front of some famous guy. Actor in that... uh... that...

"South?"

Oh, shit. *Marco.* Right.

"Listen, man, I can't do it anymore. It's too hard. I need to see her… and now I've gone and killed any chance I had of you helping me, I might as well just go and—"

"Hey! No! You listen to *me*. Did you get back on the hard stuff? Fuck some groupie?"

"No! I wouldn't. I don't want any of that shit. I just want Mia back."

"Then you're fine. Look, South, you've been dealt a shitful hand with this whole Rita fiasco. I can cut you some slack. So settle down."

"You're a really, *really* fucking good person. Have I ever told you that?"

"*Hot damn.* Shut the fuck up and go get some sleep." Marco hangs up.

I look around at the hipster crowd. So many man-buns and beards. And shit, look at that! One beard has purple streaks in it. Huh. That's cool.

All of these people look interesting. And nice. I wouldn't mind giving every single one of them a hug, which is a weird feeling. But first, I'd better find Nate real quick, before he makes any further progress on his strange boat plan. That's the dumbest idea I've ever heard. Why would I want to go freaking fishing after a gig?

Tonight, the only thing my hook might catch is one, or possibly both, of my eyebrows.

38

SOUTH

Why?

Damn. Last night I must've left the blinds up and the hotel door unlocked, because when I crack my eyes open, I'm greeted by three unpleasant things. A searing beam of sunlight, a grinning smartass bassist, and a sulfuric-sweet smell that makes me wish my nose had an off button.

Ben throws a greasy parcel at the covers, most likely a hamburger, going by the stench, and crawls over the bed.

"Ow! That's my—"

"Shit. Sorry, didn't mean to knee you in the blue balls," he says, settling back against the wall. His legs stretch across the bed and rest over my curled up body.

"What am I, a convenient ottoman?"

Snickering, Ben shoves his long, black hair off his face and bites into his lunch. "Eat something," he mumbles.

An arm shielding my eyes, I shuffle onto my back. "I feel sick. And it stinks bad."

"Well, you did it to yourself, dumbass. You know what you're risking, don't you?"

"It was a one-off and you're not exactly an altar boy, so you should probably shut up."

"What were you pumping on last night, anyway?"

"Jack and pot... and those pills that front-of-house mixer dude was passing round. I don't know what they were. Downers, I guess."

"You were pretty messy. I thought you were back on the junk."

Groaning, I thrash and wriggle until I'm propped against the headboard. "I'm not ever doing that rubbish again. No matter what. I promised her, Ben. I'd rather shoot my brains out than go back on my word."

"Don't talk like that, man! D'ya wanna be put on suicide watch or something? What an idiot." Ben plies his burger bun apart and peers between the cheesy layers. "Way too much pineapple. You're gonna love yours."

"What am I, the Pineapple King?" I croak. "Why would *you* care what happens to me anyway? You've been such an asshole lately, I feel like you hate me. And why the hell *is* that exactly? Just because a bunch of girls wanna jump my bones instead of yours? Who cares, man?"

"I've had more than three lifetimes worth of girl-action

over the last few months, so believe me, that's not the problem. Look…" Ben takes a big bite, chews and swallows recklessly, eyes tearing up in pain.

"Maybe chew it a bit longer."

"Yeah, good idea." He dumps the burger on his lap, shreds of lettuce slopping over the covers. "I can see I'm gonna have to fess up. Not that I want to." Stalling, Ben picks the dreaded pineapple out of his bun. "Honestly, at first I didn't even *know* why I was so pissed at you. But I think… What you mentioned before? I've been worried about that."

"What do you mean?"

"Well, just before you got with Mia you were out of control. I woke up every morning wondering if that would be the day I got the call from Lane saying you'd been found dead in a bathroom somewhere. And then—"

"That was never gonna happen."

Ben stops chewing. "Get real. You were putting all sorts of shit into your body, and when you got a girlfriend you cleaned your act up fast… and maybe I was jealous that you wanted to be steady for her, but not for your friends. Or for the band. And I didn't think the thing with her would last. Like it hasn't. And so I've been getting some distance, so if something bad happens to you, I won't care. But you've lost your shit again and I've realized I don't want you to go back into that sinkhole. I don't want you to die, man. So if having another friend is gonna help prevent that, well I guess I want you to know that I'm here for you."

I stare open-mouthed at Ben while he inspects his knees.

Jesus. This has turned into some kind of men's group thing, with an actual risk of emotions and awkward guy-hugs. Still, if Ben's made the leap, 'spose I should jump off the cliff too. This is the most he's spoken to me in months. Like Abbie says, when it rains it sure pours.

"Ben?"

Not looking at me, he shoves more burger in. "Yeah?"

"I'm okay, and I promise I won't do any of that stuff again. See? That's an oath. One I've sworn to Mia *and* you. Two people I care about."

"Yeah, well look where that's got you. You're alone and acting crazy again. Thank fuck I've never been into a girl like that."

"Yeah. It makes you feel like you've been chewed up and spat out. But if she feels the same way about you, then nothing beats it. No drug. None of this fame shit. Nothing. So what I had with Mia? I just want it back. I *need* it back." Rubbing my silver pendant between my fingers as if it's a talisman that will take me back to her, I say, "Last night, missing her just got too heavy, you know? I needed to blow off some steam is all, get a little wasted."

Ben laughs. "A little, huh?"

I stick the chain between my lips and suck on it like it's a pacifier. "As I told you, I'm done with the hard stuff. I'm gonna see Mia again soon, and everything will be fine."

"And meanwhile, you should grab a few of the girls lined up waiting to jump in your bed, put them in it, and fuck away your misery."

"Now why would I do that? I'm real happy cleaning my own rifle, thanks," I say, hoping I don't sound as bitter as I feel. "I love it."

"Trust you to use a gun euphemism at a time like this. Good job, dickhead." Ben squints at my throat area. "Is that the birthday present she gave you after dumping your ass?"

I pull the chain out of my mouth and look down at the silver necklace. "Yep, it's a cicada wing. Means transformation. And also, get this, the males, they sing their mates back to them."

"Huh. So it was a very prophetic gift, then." Ben leans close. "And what's that engraved on the other side?"

I huff a low laugh. "That *fucking* wave, of course."

"Hm. Like a good little cicada-boy, I hope you're working on a killer song for her this time. One that'll bind her to you forever and ever, man."

"Don't worry, it's coming."

"Got a name for it yet?"

"Yeah. It's called *I Don't Wanna Play Cleveland Tonight*."

Grunting, Ben pushes off the bed and then heads for the door. "Well, Lane's gonna love that one. Eat your burger, numbskull." He slams the door and disappears.

Nope, I do not want to get on stage tonight. If I had a choice, I'd caffeinate the hell out of myself and get behind the wheel. If I drive nine hours straight, I can be at Abbie's just past supper time. And if anyone can help get my head straight, motivate me to hang on and stay sane, Abbie is the person for the job. She practically has a degree in smacking some sense into me.

Rubbing my palm over the wave tat on my bicep, I stretch back on the bed. Yep, that's a real fine plan. I'll go see Abbie.

But first, I've got to get through tonight's show. Shit. I'd better get a little more sleep.

39

RITA

Tour Bus

I pull open the door and enter the tour bus. It's cool and dark, the curtains drawn over nearly all of the windows. And it's also empty.

An unusual silence permeates the space that is normally filled with noise. South says silence has a sound, different each time, depending on the mood, the setting.

This particular silence is slick, tightly strung, and wetly pulsing. If it were a song, it would be about sex. This means *he's* in here somewhere. Alone. Everyone else is off stuffing themselves full of rubbish, calling home, pissing and shitting.

But not South. He's here. I know the feel of him so well,

how he changes the vibration, even the taste of the air like a storm waiting to break open the clouds.

I glance over at the couches in the lounge area. No. He's not there. Maybe he's in the bunks. Fingers trailing over cloth-covered head rests, I walk down the aisle, the pad of my feet soft as a whisper.

The buzz in my stomach gets stronger. I stop. There he is, down near the back, asleep in a row of chairs. Curled toward the window, his golden head rests against the black curtain.

Oh. My whole body melts.

I move closer and then gently lower into the seat next to him, my blood spiking as I take in the mouthwatering picture. The long legs enclosed in pale denim, green Sorority Noise t-shirt riding up displaying skin and muscle, his lost-boy-asleep expression, the dark honey-colored lashes casting shadows on high cheekbones, so sweet. No. He's not sweet. He's sizzling hot.

What a fool Mia was to walk away.

He must be exhausted. So tired after last night's show in Cleveland, performing with a brutal hangover and only two hair-of-the-dog beers to ease his pain. Even still, like an earthquake, he rocked the venue into the ground. He needs some relief, and I'm just the girl to give it to him.

Through all the identical cities, the highways and back roads, the gigs and hotels, he's kept his distance from me. It's because he feels it too, the pull between us, and doesn't want to jeopardize getting back to Mia. But *that's* never going to happen.

Once I give him a taste of the real thing, Mia will be forgotten.

Smiling at his strong hands curled against the window, my eyes track slowly over muscled arms, all those hot tats, and then down, down to his hard-on, a tantalizing shape covered in worn denim. Maybe he's even dreaming about *me* right now.

I swallow, and then inch my hand toward him. I rest it softly over all that hard heat and wait, studying his face.

His hips shift slightly. Then nothing. I curl my fingers, press down a little. He shifts again, but this time he flings onto his back, head still turned away, legs spread wide, giving me better access. I squeeze, and his lips part, chest rising and falling quickly.

With skill, I stroke, watching his face change, his closed eyelids tighten. He grows harder, bigger even, and triumph zings through every cell when his hips rock into my hand. The ragged breaths panting past his lips make me wet and feverish. This is it, what I've always wanted. It's finally happening.

Wrapping my other hand around the base of his skull, I pull his head until his mouth meets mine. And then he's moving forward, his face, his pelvis, pressing into me. He changes the angle of the kiss, huffing warm breath into my lungs, and I'm flying so high I might pass out.

He moans and his eyes flash open. For three beats I'm swallowed, drowning in the turquoise heat of his stare. Then he yelps, "Fuck!" and flings backward against the window like he's been shot in the chest.

He stares at my hand that's still somehow resting in his lap and uses both palms to push me away.

"What the fuck do you think you're doing, you psycho nut job?"

What? This is wrong. No way he means that. He was loving it. He was so hot for me.

Heart hammering, I say, "Come on, South, you were totally into it. What's the harm in having a little fun?"

"My dick would be into a bit of action from a sock puppet, right now, it's that much of an idiot." He grabs the back of my head. *Yes, finally.* He brings his lips close, ocean eyes all I can see, and he whispers, "But *I* wouldn't. Not from you, *Rita*. Never with you. You got that? Touch me again, even if I'm passed out in a ditch, and I will fuck you up." He stands and struts into the aisle.

"South," I call. "I know you. You'd never hurt a girl."

"No, but I'd rat one out to Lane."

As his broad shoulders disappear through the door, I feel a quick stab of panic. Shit, maybe he *will* tell Lane and I'll be out of a job within the hour.

No. He won't do that. He'll change his mind now he's had a taste of me, now he knows I'm the one.

Why wouldn't he?

40

ABBIE

Hound Dog

I sit at the kitchen table, my hand wrapped around a mug of hot coffee, kidding myself that I'm looking through the local paper for some cheap wire mesh to mend the chicken coop with. In all truth, I'm on the hunt for a nice juicy article to help me forget about all the post-lunch chores that need doing. Unfortunately, the horses aren't about to water or groom themselves any time soon, but surely they'll have the decency to wait a little longer.

The phone on the wall rings, the shrill sound making me clutch my chest like some lily-livered ninny.

"Want me to grab that?" Mia shouts from the adjacent living room.

"No hon, I'm waiting on Carl next door to call me 'bout that hay delivery," I say as I creak out of my chair and make for the pine bench that runs along the green wall. I pluck the phone out of its cradle. "Mornin', Carl. How's that—"

"Abbie, it's me."

Oh, boy, if it ain't my wildest rebel rouser. With the golden tones of South's voice warm at my ear, I glance up to see Mia standing in the door frame, smiling and rubbing that ever-burgeoning belly of hers.

I take a slow breath to settle my nerves, school my features to relax, and hope I look normal. "Well, hi there, darlin'," I tell him all casual like. "Can you hang awn there for a sec?"

I press my hand over the mouthpiece and say to Mia, "You mind getting a start on watering them horses? I'll be out there in a flash to give you a hand."

"Sure," she replies, beginning to turn away. Then she stops. "Since when do you call Carl 'darlin', Abbie?" She gives me a saucy grin and then, thank the Lord, waddles out.

Heart thumping, I wait until the screen door bangs twice. "South! How's my wolf pup?"

"I'm alright. Who's that you're bossing round just now?"

"Oh, no one. Only Carl come to give me a hand with the horses."

"Well don't go riding him too hard or he may not stay keen on being your ever-loving good neighbor. Do you realize he's kinda pleased that Mase is finally out of the picture?"

"South! Really, only you would say something that

299

wicked. When I'm still grieving an' all." I can't keep the smile out of my voice. I've always adored his teasing. No matter how inappropriate. "Now tell me where you are. And more importantly *how* you are."

"You first," he says.

"I'm fine. Looking forward to seeing y'all next month. Nate tells me you've got a few days off now."

"Yeah. And I'm practically around the corner."

Dear Lord! My heart near jumps out of my mouth and bounces across the floor in shock. "Oh? And where, pray tell, might that be?"

"Don't know for sure. Some gas station. Everyone else is loading up on hot dogs, Mac-N-Cheese Bites, and pop, and I'm in a paddock out back with three very angry sheep. I wouldn't mind knowing what I've done to offend them. I've been sleeping on the bus for a while, but I'm still so freaking tired."

"Hon, what you need is a great big rest."

"You sure are right about that. Anyway, wherever we are I reckon it's only a few hours outta Cleveland. Tonight Nate's heading upstate to Suze's folks, and all I want is to come home to you, Ab."

"I'm not sure that's possible because—"

"Just for a couple of days. I—"

"South, remember what Lane asked of you? That you don't go and drop your bundle until the tour's over? He wanted you to stay with him and the crew until this first leg's done. It's only a couple more weeks now."

"Why? I don't get that at all. Shit… I'm telling you, Abbie,

I really need to see you. Heck, I'll probably just lob in a bed and stay there for the whole time anyways."

"Oh, darlin', I think you should wait." At least until I can work out what in the high heavens to do about Mia. Should I warn her so she can prepare herself or just let South come down on her like one almighty angry surprise?

A hard sigh sounds down the line, and then nothing for a bit.

"I'm… I nearly screwed everything up. Two nights ago… I lost it. It's just getting too hard to hold on because she hasn't even tried to make contact. There's been nothing, sweet fuck all. And that has to mean she doesn't care anymore, doesn't it? That it's over."

"No, honey. It's not over."

"Marco says he'll tell me where she is when we finish these shows, but what's the point? I'm barely holding my shit together here, you know? I can't do it much longer. I'm so tired of it. Of everything."

"There *is* a point, South. Believe me, sweetheart."

"How do you know that? And I just got molested on the bus by that freakazoid. It was very traumatic." He laughs, but the cold sound of it makes my chest ache.

"Man, I can't stop thinking about wiping myself out. I don't want to feel like this anymore."

He's conning me. Still, even hearing his hustler's voice, the situation isn't good. I'll never forgive myself if I let him down when he's vulnerable, that poor kid who's learned to survive with no one having his back. The mess he'd been when he came to me at fifteen, thinking he wasn't worth a damn, broke my heart.

Against all odds, his own heart is made of gold, and I'll never be able to turn him away. Well, then, it looks like trouble with a capital S is heading our way and Mia will have to do her best to wrangle him.

"Okay, git yourself here to me, then. Come home. As soon as you can."

"Really?"

"Yeah. Just don't go doing any ol' fool thing in the meanwhile. Get your butt here so I can kick it up and down the hill a few times first. And please don't tell any of those old worry warts where you're going. Make something up. We don't want them followin' you here and making a fuss."

"Sure, I can do that easy. I'm just gonna steal me that car over by the bus. It looks like one hell of a sweet ride, and then I'll be burning rubber."

"South!" He's joking. Hopefully. Trouble is, I'll be waiting a while to know for sure, because the devil-child has gone and skedaddled off the phone.

Shaking my head and praying that I won't get a call from some law man anytime soon, I swipe my hat from a hook beside the door and make for the barn.

And Mia.

41

MIA

Home

I hate vacuuming with a passion, pulling the stupid, cumbersome machine around the house, getting caught on corners and twisted in cords. The industrial noise of it. Yuck.

Right now I'm wondering if seven months is too early in the pregnancy to be nesting. Because it might explain why I'm spending a gloriously mild Saturday evening cleaning the house.

Still, the whole process makes me grumpy. That's why when a roaring sound comes over the drone of the machine, I smile as I turn, glad for any interruption. Even if it is from a grizzly bear out on a rampage.

The beast in front of me is golden-haired, dressed in a muscle shirt and ripped jeans, and vibrates with fury.

Blasted by the extravagant blue of his eyes, I stumble as I push the vacuum cleaner off with my foot, then straighten and stare. Shit. Both the South-beast and the machine stop bellowing.

In the silence, my brain catches up. Oh, no. It's *South*. Unsuspecting father-of-my-child South, not a bear. Dropping the vacuum-cleaner hose on the floor, I take a step backward and he steps forward.

"What the hell is *she* doing here?" he asks Abbie, who has suddenly appeared at my side.

Oh, if only he *were* a bear, not a bear-shifter-book-guy but a real wild-animal type of bear. One that couldn't speak. Or make sense of what's jutting out toward his eyes from the middle of my body.

"South, honey!" Abbie darts forward and hugs him. "Well, ain't you a sight for sore eyes."

He stands rigid as a corpse, one who has died from a fit of rage, going by the snarl and the white-knuckle clench of his fists.

Abbie presses her fingers to his lips. "You'd better shut that mouth of yours or flies will lay eggs in there."

He lets his backpack drop to the floor. "You've been... Abbie... Have you been *hiding* her here? Why would you—"

"Oh, relax. This is exactly what you wanted, isn't it? To see Mia. Well, here she is!"

He swallows. Does the lost-boy frown I love so much. My

heart squeezes, and I long to rush at him, leap on him, tangle my hands in all that glorious hair.

The frown turns into a full-on scowl, then it disappears. The corners of his mouth lift and what could almost be called a smile flickers. And then... and then his eyes move from my face down, down until...

His jaw drops even further. He points at my bulging stomach. "What is *that?*"

Well, obviously, it's not a bowling ball stuffed up my top.

Abbie clutches my arm. My heart smashes against my ribs. Speechless, South keeps staring.

For five long seconds I shrivel under his glare. Then his eyes roll back and, holding his stomach, he sprints to the tiny bathroom off the kitchen.

"Stay calm. Stay calm," Abbie chants while we listen to him heave.

"This is bad. This is terrible! Should I go and help him?"

"Goodness, Mia, no! Stay there."

The toilet flushes and water gushes from a faucet before South appears in the doorway wiping his face. He opens his mouth to speak, and then flings around and marches out the door.

I look at Abbie.

"He'll be back. Be patient."

Several seconds later, he reappears in the doorway and hurtles toward us. When he's a meter away, he yells, "Who fucking did this to you? You better tell me, Mia."

I scurry behind a wooden dining chair. He strides over, grabs the chair, and then throws it aside. "Tell me!"

Shaking my head, I shuffle backward until my butt hits the table and I can't go any farther.

"South, that's enough now." Abbie's voice seems to come from a great distance, the moon maybe. "You have to calm down. Pitching a fit ain't helping none."

His eyes flick briefly to Abbie, and he flinches like he's surprised to see her. "You'd better tell me now, Mia, because whoever did this is a dead man."

"Now, South, that's ridiculous, you know how I feel about suicide. Surely you're not gonna go that far." Amazingly, Abbie sounds amused.

"What?" he asks.

"You're not planning on murdering *yourself*, are you?"

If I wasn't panicking, I'd laugh at his dumbstruck expression.

"Since *you* did this to her and all. And you've just now vowed to put an end to the person responsible."

"What?" he says again.

"Tell him, Mia. The boy's slower than molasses running up a hill."

Oh, do I have to? Can't I run and hide under the bed instead? Or jump in the car and drive twelve hours straight? It really doesn't matter in which direction.

I look at the floor. I look at Abbie. Then glance at the door.

"*Mia*," he growls, nostrils flaring like a bull about to start pawing at the ground.

I take a long shuddering breath and a shaky step forward, just a little closer to him. "You did this, South. No one else."

Eyes widening, he shakes his head. "No."

"Yes. You and I together, *we* did it. There is no guy to maim. Just us."

"That's not possible. You were taking those pills."

"It's still possible. Here's your proof."

"You… but… how long have you known?"

I swallow.

This is it, the moment I've been dreading for months. But there will be no more lies. I can't do it to him anymore. "Um, so… kind of since the Hokusai exhibition."

"*What?* All that time and you didn't think you should tell me? *Jesus Christ*, Mia! What's wrong with you?" He falls into a dining chair.

After wringing her hands for a few moments, Abbie makes for the sink and starts filling it with water. I've already washed those pots. There's only the impossible lasagna tray left to tackle.

"Ah, *fuck*, Mia, are you trying to kill me?" Shoulders hunched, he rocks and shivers, goes to stand up, collapses back down on the chair. "You said you loved me. I don't understand… this doesn't make sense. Why didn't you tell me?"

"Because you said over and over again that a child was the last thing you wanted. You made it more than clear that it would be the end for us. And because I love you, so I couldn't risk losing you. But you have to believe that I had it all planned out to tell you but it turned out to be the same day I found out about you and Rita."

"*Rita*," he yells, pushing both palms toward my stomach, warding it off like it's about to attack him. "I don't wanna hear that name. And I don't want *this!*"

Dish cloth thrown over her shoulder and still scrubbing at an already clean pot, Abbie says, "It's only because you're scared. Give yourself some time to adjust to the idea and—"

"Damn right I'm scared—"

"Well, people say facing your greatest fear is a surefire path to happiness."

He glares at Abbie. "Who exactly are *these people* that you're always going on about who seem to know everything? You only talk about *them* when you can't think of anything better to say."

"South, can't you just try and see it from my perspective? Just a little? I couldn't tell you after I found out that you'd been getting it on with *Rita* of all people. What was I meant to say to you? Oh, so you accidentally slipped it to one of Up Void's admin team one night? Easy mistake. No problem. And that must've been a trial for you, too, because you were always talking about how you didn't even like the girl! Oh, and by the way, good news—we're going to have a baby—after you'd always said you never wanted one and went on and on about it in front of Nico and Ivy at the awards party. So, yeah, that's exactly when I should have told you I was pregnant!"

He springs out of the chair, paces across the length of the kitchen twice, then stops in front of me. "I did *not* sleep with that fucking psycho. And since the night ah first touched *you*, I ain't touched no one else!"

Uh, oh. Whenever his accent goes way down south, it usually means he's about to go nuclear.

Breathing hard, he turns to face the curtains, and Abbie clangs the pots in the sink louder.

I stare at his shoulders, broad and beautiful and...hang on, what? I can't possibly have heard him right. "Oh, sure, as if you haven't slept with anyone while you've been out on the road."

"I haven't," he says, finally looking at me. "Other than having unsatisfying times with, you know, just myself."

As if that's true. He can't possibly mean he's had no sex over the last four months. That would be a miracle. Are his parts malfunctioning?

From only a meter away, his eyes bore into mine—powerful and intense—his gaze shines pure and *honest*, filled with the light of the *truth*. A truth that burns so brightly, it blinds me momentarily, and when my vision clears, I *know*, I just know he's not lying.

I need to stop kidding myself. South is loyal. Trustworthy. Abbie, Nate, Marco—everyone—they were right all along. South wouldn't sleep with anyone else while he's with me. Or even while he's *hoping* to get back with me, it seems.

If anyone is a liar, it's Rita. And now me, of course. I'm a liar, too.

He looks at Abbie who is hunched over the sink, busily throwing suds around. "You should go and do some felting. Hang out in your craft room for a while. You don't need to hear this shit."

"I probably do need to hear it. If you think I'm gonna

leave Mia all alone to be terrorized by you having a dying duck fit, then you're surely dumber than a—"

"Bucket of hair?"

"I was gonna say box of hammers, South, but that'll do fine."

"I've heard enough of this crap. I'm going to bed so I can lie there in shock for the next ten hours. Can I sleep in Nate's old room? I can't stand looking at that fucking *betrayer* over there for one second longer."

"Well, ain't you just a peach." Abbie smiles sadly, shaking her head at him. "You always did like to run off when things weren't goin' your way."

"Wait," I say, inching closer and speaking quickly in case he self-combusts in a dark cloud of rage. "Can't you sit down again? Just for a few minutes? Let me tell you everything. You'll understand when—"

Before I can blink, he's up against me, fingers biting into my arms and voice loud. "Don't worry, Mia, I already understand!"

And then Abbie is between us, her hands gentle on our backs, her words soft. "Quit that yelling. I don't mind you touching her if you go gentle about it, because she's yours as much as anything ever has been. I can see what it's like between you two as plain as day, but, South, you keep on acting like a bully right now and I'll get Carl to come around here and sort you the hell out."

That's an interesting picture, burly farmer Carl, who is at least seventy if he's a day, up against a wild-eyed South. Hopefully he'll have a couple of his sturdy sons in tow.

"At this moment," Abbie continues, "I'm ashamed of my part in raising you up. And you should think of that poor baby in there listening to your hollering, making its momma quake."

"Well, I don't want to think about that thing. I didn't ask it to get in there! It ain't got nothing to do with me."

Abbie steps back, her mouth a thin line. "You addle-pated dummy. You are gonna live to regret every fool word that comes out of that mouth of yours tonight. My advice is to shut your trap and listen."

Body convulsing with each hard breath he takes, he stands scowling, angrier than I've ever seen him. "You... you..." he says, and then trails off.

I wait for more words.

The new fridge hums, the old clock ticks as South struggles to get breath in. Has he developed some kind of asthma in the last few months? It really doesn't sound good.

"You..." he says again.

This is torturous. I want to help him. It's like busting to say the words for a stutterer, but knowing it would be the worst thing to do.

Again, I glance at Abbie. Not my best idea, because Abbie seems to be shrinking, all the love and pain she feels for the boy she claims as son shining clear in her red-rimmed eyes.

"You accused me of being a liar and a traitor. And what are *you*, Mia? Tell me what the fuck are you?"

Without thinking, I cover my belly with my hands, soothing over it. South stares in horror. And then with a roar that makes me feel like I'm watching him from the center of a heaving mosh pit, he turns to the table, picks up a vase of daffodils, throws it hard at the floor by the wall, and walks away.

I move to follow and Abbie says, "Wait. He's as mad as a seething pit of snakes. Just let him go and sulk. It's always best when he gets in a snit. Although, maybe snit's not the right word on this occasion."

Glass shards, red and purple, cover the wooden floor, not jagged, but all blurry seen through my tears.

"Oh, darlin' it will be okay." Abbie pulls me into her arms.

It won't be okay. Without South, nothing will ever be okay again.

"You go get some rest. You have to think of that sweet baby in there." She strokes my belly and tries to smile.

"No, you go, Abbie. I need to clean up this mess up. I caused it. And I won't sleep anyway. It'll help calm me, truly."

After Abbie leaves, I turn the light off and sit in the dark, staring at sharp pieces of glass on the floor illuminated by a moonbeam shining through the roof window.

Well, that wasn't an ideal first encounter for a child to have with its father's voice. The baby should have heard the honeyed tones of a lullaby. South's warm laugh. Or one of his slow-teasing tales told in that meandering deep drawl. Not the roar of a wild animal emanating shock and hate. No, that was far from optimal.

As I cry, I wish over and over that I'd had the courage to tell him about our child a long time ago. Like any sane person would have done.

How will he ever forgive me?

42

MIA

Sulking

Two hours later, there is nothing but darkness underneath South's bedroom door. Lucky him if he's managed to get to sleep already. I shuffle past, moving slowly down the hallway toward the bathroom. My head throbs and my throat burns from crying. I've put the kitchen to rights again, so that's one good thing that's happened since he arrived.

While I brush my teeth with a shaking hand the harsh light above the mirror washes over my skin, making me look sick. Well, that makes sense. I *do* feel ill.

I spit water into the sink and stare at the shadows beneath

my eyes. I look like a strung-out junkie. Well, if I'm coming down from anything, it's from *him*.

Seeing South again was a terrible thrill, and I'd known he would react badly, finding me at Abbie's, and then the shock of the baby. Shit. Who wouldn't freak out?

If I'd been prepared for him to burst into our Saturday night, I might have taken a sedative in advance. Probably not wise while pregnant, but perhaps better for the baby than the extreme levels of stress hormones currently walloping through my system.

South seems fine with the idea of never seeing me again or never laying eyes on his child. How will I break through such a rock-solid wall of hate? A wall that he has every right to build high. To keep me out.

But what about our baby? She doesn't deserve South's anger. Unlike me, she's innocent and blameless.

It's unbelievable that he's asleep in the room next to mine, our beds close, lined up against the same wall. And I want so badly to touch him. To hold him. And kiss him.

Wait a second, what a great idea—that boy—he adores getting it on. He's happiest when we spend whole days and nights in bed, eating, talking, having sex... so, maybe that's the answer. There's no way he'll turn down an opportunity to get off. I should throw myself at him shamelessly.

Abbie will be asleep by now, too, and she's all the way over the other side of the house. She won't hear a thing.

Stalling, I stretch the hem of my baggy top over my panties and laugh when I look down. Shit, I'm wearing the rainbow-magic unicorn t-shirt that always makes South laugh. Is that a good sign? I'm not sure.

Stumbling on weak legs, I creep down the hall and push his door open before I change my mind. The bed creaks as he rolls over.

"South?" I wade through the dark, arms out feeling for obstacles, and head for where I think the bed might be.

"Mia? What the hell are you—"

"*Shit!*" I say as I fall onto the mattress.

"Are you alright? *Fuck.* Get off the bed, will ya?" He sits up, a hulking shadow in the gray light, and steadies me.

Linking my hands tightly behind his neck, I lean in, ready to whisper against his mouth, but he pushes me away before I can get any words out. Ungracefully, I launch myself at him. He makes a lucky grab in the dark, grasping my wrists hard.

"Ow!"

"Shit," he says as he releases me. "I'm sorry. I didn't mean to hurt you, but you've gotta leave. Right now, okay?"

This isn't going well.

I stare at the outline of his body, my eyes slowly adjusting to the dark. Oh, crap. His sculpted chest is bare, and the need to touch his skin is so great that I feel like an addict yearning and burning. But I don't. I just sit there as an eternity passes, our overloud breathing the only sound in the room.

I'm not very fond of rejection, but I need to make him feel something other than anger or pain, help him remember how it is between us. The magic. The blissful intensity of our joining.

It's now or never.

Shuffling closer, I press my hand against the base of his throat, and he flinches as if I've struck him. Probably in shock, he sits as still as a mountain, and I run my fingers along warm, smooth skin, muscles as hard as granite, down to his lap and grope around in the covers.

This will wig him right out. An hour ago he was yelling at me, and here I am going for his dick. But I'm desperate to get him fired up, and it's usually such a simple task, never taking more than a look or a certain smile. Dammit, I can't see a thing as I fumble about.

"What the hell are you trying to do?" His voice is rough as he backs away.

He's going to force me to say it, make me tell him what I want. "South, I just... I just really need to feel your arms around me again. So much." I clear my throat. "And I want us to have sex."

He makes a choked sound. "You have got to be fucking kidding me. Have you forgotten you've been hiding a *baby* from me? Get the hell out of here."

"No, South, please just listen," I say in a shaky voice. "You don't even have to do anything. Lay down, close your eyes. Pretend it's someone else if you want. I don't care, but just let me touch you and use my mouth. Remember how much you love that. And you know how bad you feel right now? I can make it all go away. You'll feel good. I promise."

"No I won't," he whispers.

"*Yes.* You will! Or we can do anything you want. Right now. Just tell me—"

"Shit, Mia, that's pathetic. And hell, I don't wanna *fuck*

you!" The lamp clicks on, the orange light revealing the dark-sapphire glitter of his eyes. "I'm mad as snakes, remember?"

"I know that," I say, taking in his messy, golden hair, tense muscles, that frown I love. "And you've got every right to be. I know you do. But I've missed you so much. And this feels freaking terrible. I can't bear it another second. Help me, South. Help us both. We'll feel so much better."

"*I* sure as hell won't feel any better. I'm never gonna feel good again, thanks to you." He points at my belly. "And anyway, look at you! *Shit*, can you even do it in that state?"

"Of course. I just can't lie on my back for too long. The weight of the baby—"

He grimaces and waves his hand around to shut me down.

"It's either a me-on-top situation or we can spoon. I know you like both of those options a lot."

"How the heck could you know those positions work in your condition? Been testing them out with some other poor sucker, trying to cuckold me?"

I almost laugh. "As if I'd—"

"I don't fucking *care*. You can go nuts cuckolding as long as you get out of my bed. I probably couldn't get it up even if I tried. Knocked up isn't much of a turn on."

He's lying.

"Well, what's that pushing up the covers, then? A zucchini?

"Yes." His lips quirk like he's trying to hold back a smile as he rearranges the quilt.

"South, please—"

"No. Fucking. Way. I can't believe you've hidden this from me, Mia. Have you got any idea what it's like for me to go in one instant from every breath I took being just for you, the only purpose of each heartbeat to get me back to you, to this... finding out you're nothing but a goddamn liar? It makes me sick to even look at you."

I glance down at the covers again. Evidently, not *too* sick.

He stares at a framed photo on the dresser of him and Nate on the same tall horse, tousled-haired teenagers, grinning madly. By the dreamy look on his face, I'd say he's gone back in time, consumed by memories. Okay then. If things are going to proceed it will be entirely up to me.

As I peel off my t-shirt, he closes his eyes.

"So, look at me now and check if you still feel sick."

"No." He flips onto his back, faces the wall, and closes his eyes.

The covers down to his hips, every muscle is unyielding, like cold, hard marble. Goosebumps prickle my skin, and it's not from the cool night air. It's the sight of South, the electric current that always thrums in the air around him.

Feeling like a swollen battery about to explode, I take a long breath and reach for his wrist. I pull hard to bring it close, and he resists until I say, "Ow," straining my neck.

In an instant his body loosens and I vault forward. When I straighten up, I tug his arm with all my strength, aiming his hand at my belly, and he lets it happen.

Head still turned toward the wall and jaw tight, his palm hovers only an inch above my stomach. I press it onto my skin and watch his eyes open wide. Breathing fast, he whips his head around and looks into my eyes. The agonized frown he wears makes a tear spill down my cheek. Hopefully, in the dim light, he won't notice.

In the silence he keeps his eyes locked on mine while his chest pumps. I can tell he's fighting the urge to look down. I wait and count.

One.

Two.

Three.

Four.

Five, and then it happens. His eyes flick to where our hands meet over my tight, round stomach. He makes a rough sound and turns away.

Well that's some progress at least. He looked.

While he pretends I'm not here, I move his hand over the bumps and dips of my belly, the baby's shoulder or maybe a knee poking out, and his eyes stay squeezed shut.

A great wave shudders over my skin. "Fuck!" he says as he pulls away and curls up facing the wall, arms bracketing his head.

"What the hell was that?" he asks the pillow. "It's like a horror movie. That Alien one."

I laugh. "It's okay, the baby is just moving around. Getting comfy."

"Well *that's* disgusting. And don't say that word either."

"Which one? Comfy?"

He flings onto his back and laughs. *Yes.* Here's my chance. But I'll need to try a different tactic.

As I lean forward, he says. "Mia—"

"Shhhh." I take his face in my hands, the stubble on his jaw rasping my fingers. "I love you," I whisper against his lips. He tries to turn his head, but it's a feeble attempt.

Yes, *this* is the way. Why hadn't I thought of it earlier? Having spent most of his life starved of tenderness, he's a total sucker for it. This is the secret I could sell to all those groupies. A tender touch and sweet words would get them so much further than over-perfumed flesh and a writhing pole dance.

"I love you so much, South." I stroke his beautiful face, his tousled hair, letting my feelings show in each move I make. "Nothing else matters. Only you."

And the baby.

One hand warm against the wild beat of his heart, I press soft kisses over his eyelids, his entire face. Telling him with every breath I take that it's him, only him, who makes me happy, only him I love, and that I'll do anything to fix things.

With each vow I make, the current from his skin vibrates harder, hotter, and I sink deeper into a trance. And the spell works on him, too, because after a while, between each whispered *I love you*, his lips move over mine oh so gently, making my skin burn. His fists are still clenched, and he doesn't say a word—but he's kissing me back.

Quickly, I shove the covers down and straddle his hips, shaking at the feel of his hard length, heat and wetness rushing to my core. He clutches my hips too tightly, slaying me with his deep blue gaze. His hard frown only makes me more determined to have him inside me, claiming me, punishing me. Even if it's the last time ever.

I want this. And no matter how angry he is, I want *him*.

Always.

Forever.

South.

And, right now, he wants me too.

While I've got him shaking beneath me, I raise up, reach into his boxers and grasp the base of his dick tightly. It surges in my grip. Then he's panting like some great beast who is, finally, on board with the program, and he yanks my panties aside. I lower down in one long, shuddering breath.

Overcome by shock, the intense feeling of being skin to skin with him again, I stare, lost in his blue-fire gaze.

He's dazed, drugged, and staring at me like he wants this badly, too. Right now is the perfect chance to create a conditioned response. Pregnant Mia equals fantastic feel-goods. It might be unscrupulous, but I'm not going to waste the opportunity. I may never get another.

I unwrap his fingers from my hips, placing his palms on my stomach. I startle when he lets out three harsh breaths, sounding like he's been thrown into an icy surf. I hold his fingers down so he won't take them away and rotate my hips.

Moaning, his eyes close for a second, and then open as he locks a fierce gaze on me.

"Fuck, Mia." He tangles his fingers in my long hair, wrapping it around his wrists. "Jesus," he says, clenching and tugging, hurting me.

As slowly as I can manage with quaking thighs and my big stomach unbalancing me, I glide up and down, drawing out the pleasure. Unguided by me, he releases my hair, his hands traveling over my round belly. His eyes roam between the baby, my face, and my breasts.

"I… oh, hell, you feel so good," he says in a rough voice, straining into me and picking up speed.

"You, too, South. God, you too."

I can't take my eyes off his face. I'm stunned that he looks so into it, biting down on his lip and moaning. It's turning him on—my body so ripe—I'm sure of it.

I lean forward to change the angle, and it must be just right, because he breaks rhythm, arching up off the bed, stroking deeper. A moment later he freezes and asks, "Will… so can this hurt the…?"

"No," I say, giggling. "It can't. Go as hard as you like."

He flashes a grin that makes my heart falter, grits his teeth, and lifts me by the waist to a kneeling position. What is he doing? Oh, of course, more room to get pounding.

I bring my hands beside his waist for balance and, slowly, his palms make gentle patterns over my stomach. And he keeps looking at my baby-belly, making desperate, lost boy sounds. And he goes on making them until I come undone.

A series of shocking waves swamp over me, battering my body, weakening me and making me cry out.

"No. Fuck, no," he says roughly. "Mia, please…"

I don't find out what he was about to beg for because his big body tightens, stills, and he shakes, fighting his climax. Then, with a loud groan, he explodes, shuddering and quaking as his cock pulses inside me.

Breathing roughly, I go to lower myself on his chest and am surprised to find my gigantic stomach in the way, amazed that it even exists. South makes me forget everything but him. Always has. Always will.

Never mind lying on top of him, I'll kiss him instead.

He kisses me back, tenderly and sweetly as he comes down from the high.

Mesmerized by his gem-bright eyes, I say, "I love you."

Expression blank, he holds my gaze. I want him to smile back at me, but he doesn't.

When my breathing finally settles, I shift awkwardly off his lap, and then curl against his warm skin, inhaling his scent deep. As I wrap my arm over his chest, he turns his back on me.

That's unusual. He loves to snuggle. Or at least he used to.

"South?"

"Go away, Mia," he murmurs.

"But—"

"Don't think this changes anything," he tells the wall. "I'm still mad at you."

"But, I didn't do this on purpose! I didn't plan to fall pregnant."

His narrowed gaze burns through to my soul, crushing it. "That's not the point, Mia. It's what you *didn't* do when you found out."

"But running away and hiding this... baby from you... Everything bad I've done is because I love you. I did it out of hurt and fear, yes, but also out of love. Because I didn't want to lose you."

"Yeah? Well, you know what I've been lying here thinking about?"

"No," I say, heart thudding faster. "Tell me."

"Before you decided I'd been shoving my dick in strange people, you had like, what? I reckon around a month where you knew about that... thing. For a whole fucking month you knew that you were *pregnant*... and you lied to me every day. You lied when you looked in my eyes, you lied every single time you spoke to me, you lied on the phone, you lied in my arms, you lied when you—"

"Okay, stop!" I say, a sob escaping my throat. "I did it because I love you. I love you so much."

"Yeah, and I loved you," he spits. "You make me fucking sick. Now get the hell out of here before I lose it."

And I do. Without another word, I leave, my head hanging low, heart shattering.

I return to my room and cry acid tears until first light, the whole time obsessing over his words.

He loved me.

He *loved* me.

Loved.

Past tense, not present.

It's over.

South hates me.

The only man I'll ever love can't stand the sight of me, and I can't blame him one bit.

43

MIA

Step One

"Get out of it, Rox. You'll make yourself sick eating that, it's too greasy. Not to mention stinky!" Pushing the dog's head out of the lasagna tray and her stocky little body off the chair, I turn to Abbie and say, "How much garlic did you put in that, anyway? It smells like something died."

Back on the kitchen floor where she belongs, the dog looks up at me, tail wagging wildly, silly grin in place and oil dripping from her mouth. I reach down and pat her shiny black head.

Hunched over the table, eyes fixed on a magazine, Abbie

says, "Well, it's South I feel sorry for, having to kiss you probably half of all last night after you'd eaten that."

"*What?* He did not kiss me..." I lie. "What makes you
think *that* happened?"

Abbie stops flicking pages and studies a photo of a
woman frolicking dreamily through purple fields. "I like *this*
one a lot. It's very fine. Not too fussy," she says, pointing at
the white, bouffant dress that if I ever made the mistake to
put on, would give me the look of an albino wench out gath-
ering herbs, smiling witlessly at a tree for reasons unknown.

Wanting a closer look, I walk over and squint at the
picture. The girl really shouldn't look so pleased with herself,
the dress is definitely way too 'fussy'.

"And what on earth are you doing reading Southern
Weddings magazine for anyway?"

"Oh, I always read it. Ask Nate if I don't. One day we are
gonna have a real fine wedding here, Mia, just you wait and
see. Maybe even two." Abbie lowers her voice and mumbles,
"It's just a question of who'll be the first."

I hope she's referring to Nate and Suze or maybe even Nico
and Ivy. "Speaking of questions, you didn't answer mine."

"About how I knew that you crept into his bed last
night?"

Not really wanting to hear the answer, I nod.

"Well, I'm thinking our wolf pup's fur is a little smoother
today. It ain't sticking out every which way like yesterday. He
ate up all his breakfast and even smiled at Roxy this
mornin'," Abbie says, looking smug.

To escape, I bolt for the sink and start scrubbing the tray.

Abbie murmurs, "And there's something that says *well satisfied* in his look, too, if you ask me."

"No one did."

She laughs. "You know, he's sitting outside on those shed steps right next to the horses. Looks like he's just waiting on someone to come and stroke his fur some more."

The darn lasagna is cemented on the spatula, and my scouring isn't achieving much. "Oh, come on, Abbie! I'm sure he doesn't want *me* to go out there. He totally ignored me when I said good morning to him."

Craning her neck to look through the window, Abbie says, "Uh-huh. But he's looking mighty peaceful right about now with the sun softening him up nicely. Very approachable."

"Geez! You're relentless." I throw the spatula into the sink. "Come with me, Rox, at least he'll be happy to see you."

The dog bounces on the spot three times, yapping constantly as we head for the back door.

Roxy has the wrong idea. This won't be any fun at all.

44

SOUTH

Step Two

Today's Sunday and my favorite kinda sky, blue and cloudless, ranges overhead. Pity I ain't in the mood to enjoy the sunshine warming up my skin as I sprawl over the barn steps, keeping the horses company. This morning, I've got more of an appetite for murder and mayhem than for sunbathing.

All five of those grass-chomping horses in the paddock right alongside me don't give a hoot that I've got to leave on Wednesday to meet the band in Chicago. And I'm not sure how to feel about it either.

I'm conflicted.

I want to go. I want to stay. I want to sink deep inside Mia again, fuck her, hug her. But, mostly, I want to shake her until we both wake up and find out the last few months were nothing but a shitty nightmare. Not real. Not real.

Anger burns through my blood. I wouldn't mind throwing some hay at those horses, fucking bales and bales of it. Or chopping up something that isn't meant to end up as firewood. Like Mia's bed for example.

One minute I want nothing more than to get in the rental car and drive like a lunatic and the next I'm rooted to the spot, brainless, mouth hanging open and seeing nothing but *her* as she was last night. Above me. Round and soft and panting hard. For months I've been dreaming of that moment. Minus the extra round bits, of course.

Man! She's fucking knocked up. My life is a clusterfuck of insanity. Musically I've got the world at my feet. Personally— I'm screwed.

For some reason, I picture lying underneath her while her hands close around my throat, slowly squeezing the life out of me while I fuck her. How sick am I, needing her to end the misery for me? Damned if that little fantasy isn't proof of just how completely that girl weakens me.

Before Mia, I was numb and heartless, and happy enough to live that way. Kind of.

Now, I can say I'm a guy who's experienced both sweet-soaring feelings and gut-wrenching loss. And, despite what she's done, I love her still. But I regret every moment, every single breath I wasted wanting her, needing her. Because thanks to Mia, these days I live like my skin has been peeled away, my insides raw and exposed.

Right now, I don't know what the hell I want. Although, I *am* sure of one thing, dreaming up crazy shit about sex and strangulation means I'm losing my damn mind.

A strange snorting noise pulls me out of my black thoughts, and I look up to see the dog hurtling at me from the direction of the back door. Roxy is going so fast she's nothing but a dark smudge, almost invisible until she lands on my chest. "Get off me, Rox! Man, you hit about as hard as a bullet."

She leaps all over me, each time I push her away, launching a fresh assault. My dog-wrestling efforts diminish as I catch sight of Mia marching toward me. *Shit.*

Mia. Mia.

Hellfire and damnation. My mouth waters at the sight of her blond pigtails bouncing, piping-hot body rocking and rolling its way across the yard. *Hot body?* What the fuck am I thinking? The woman is *with child* for crying out loud, *my* child, apparently.

Ever an opportunist, the dog takes advantage of my distraction and slathers her tongue over my face, making me gag. "Fuck's sake!"

"Roxy! Off," yells Mia.

Unfortunately, I ate enough of the hash Abbie cooked for breakfast to fill three stomachs, and now I'm about to chuck it all up in front of the girl who taught me how to love, then ripped my heart from my chest. Awesome.

"What the heck has that dog been eating? That was… Christ!" Wiping dog slobber off my cheek, I glance up into Mia's laughing eyes. I'm amazed she can even look at me, what with all the guilt she must be feeling right now.

Sneaker scraping at the dirt, she says, "I know. It's foul, isn't it? Abbie put stupid amounts of garlic in the lasagna last night. It's kinda fermented or something, and Roxy just licked the pan clean."

Fantastic.

"Can I sit?"

I stare ahead. Maybe if I stay silent, she'll go away.

She flops down next to me, way too close for my pulse to keep its usual steady tempo. I inch over, aiming to get some space between us.

"Come on, South. You can't keep ignoring me."

"Who says I can't?"

"Well, *I* just did. But if we ask around, I'm sure we'll find others who'll agree with me."

"Go away, Mia."

She puts her hand on my arm and it gets harder to breathe. "We need to talk."

"Nope," I say, shaking her off.

"You can't just avoid me and hope the pregnancy will disappear. It's too serious a thing to pretend it's not happening. Can you at least try and think about the future? I mean do you *want* anything to do with this child. Actually, I should say *your* child—"

I interrupt her with a hard laugh. "*My* child? Yeah, right." I glare at her, thinking my moronic outburst might put her off, but, no, she keeps right on talking.

"Well, do you think you'll want to see her when she's

born?"

Anger fries my brain and I explode like a steam-pipe. *"She?"* I yell. "How the fuck could you possibly know that? You mean *it*, don't ya? When *it's* born." Feeling like the world's biggest jerk, I dig my fingers into the dirt beside me and try to get a handle on my breathing.

Blinking sweet, golden eyes at me, she plucks strands of grass. "Or when she gets older, you might want to see her at times or even be around a lot. And there's this thing called an ultrasound, you goose, that shows you the sex of your baby. People have been having them for decades. Anyway, to me she *feels* like a girl."

"I know what an ultrasound is, Mia. I'm not a total hick."

"I was joking." She gives me a dreamy smile and hugs her ridiculous looking belly. "But I don't need to be told the baby's sex in advance. I want a surprise."

"Well, personally, I wouldn't recommend one of those. Last night, I had a really big one, and it wasn't very good. Fuck, Mia, why do I even have to think about this? And you were right before. I do want it to disappear, okay? I don't want a kid. I don't want to decide if I plan to see it or not. I don't want any of this shit." I pick up a rough stone and throw it at the water bin. I'd love to take a rifle and shoot holes through the fucker. "All I want is you."

"What?" She stops pulling at the grass and looks at me. I look back, seeing her properly for the first time since I arrived. Her gold eyes are dark, the skin puffy underneath like she's been crying.

Shit. I have to tell her the truth. It's only fair. "I need you,

Mia. Exactly like it was when we were living together. Nothing feels right anymore, and I don't know how to fucking fix it."

Her breathing changes, now shallow and fast.

"*I* know, South. I know how to fix it. All you have to do is put your arms around me and stop being angry. That's it. It's actually very simple."

"No, it's definitely not simple." She has no idea of the gravity, the foolishness of what she's asking of me. I'm too messed up by the hellhole I was born into, ruined by the monster who rejected me no matter how hard I begged her to love me. Thanks, Mom.

I can't take care of a shitting kid. No way.

Hands shaking, I look up at the blue sky for warmth and inspiration, but my brain shorts out, and blackness descends, cloaking me in past horrors. Fuck. I'm back in the dark wardrobe with my knees pressed tight against the door. The smell of musty clothes suffocates me. Outside the closet, my Mom screams, my step-dad laughs, and dirtbag visitors yell things like *you-dumb-fucking-broad* and *pass-me-the-pipe-already*. I'm hungry and scared, so I start praying for food, for someone with a kind smile to find me, to disappear forever, to be swallowed by the universe, but then—

"South? Hey! Where have you gone to?"

Flinching, I whoosh back into my body and feel Mia's soft hand on my shoulder. "Nowhere. I'm just thinking about how unfair everything is."

"But that's life. It throws stuff at you that you don't wanna catch all the time. At everyone, not just *you*."

I stare into her tired eyes. *"Why?"*

"To test your mettle, maybe? Teach you things? I don't know."

"That don't mean I have to deal with it if I don't want to."

She does the pity expression I fucking hate. "Think of how your mother dealt with almost this exact same situation. That's what you want to do, is it? Repeat her mistakes and let another child grow up unloved by its parent? She had more reason to spurn parenthood than you do. If memory serves, I believe the sex we had was consensual. And wonderful. In fact, one could even argue that this child was conceived in love."

Love.

Conceived in love.

She's right.

It was.

It fucking was.

Every time I'd touched her, fuck, even looked at her, it was with love. This thing… this pregnancy is nothing like how *I* was made—in terror. A screaming, fucked-up mess.

This is different. This baby was made out of love—part of her—part of me. An expression, made flesh and bone, of what we are together. Or *were.*

Head spinning, I drop my face into my hands to hide from the horror, the horror of what I'm rejecting. I try to stop my shoulders from shaking, but I fucking can't. I can swallow down the ache, but I can't stop the shaking. She'll know for sure that I'm not laughing.

An age passes while I fight to keep all sound inside. The

air is hot on my skin, so hot it burns like hell. Lyrics warp through my mind. *Black blood makes dirty rain. I ain't. Ain't insane. Water chokes. Water chokes.*

"South," she whispers, rubbing my back gently. "All you have to do is take my hand. Here, look at it. Right there on your knee. So close. Take it and we can at least be friends. It's a start, and you can be with us whenever you want. All the time or some of the time. It doesn't matter. You can even pretend it's someone else's child if that helps. Just stop hating me and we can see what happ—"

"*What?* Are you crazy? I am never gonna pretend that's some other guy's child. Shit, Mia! You break my fucking heart."

I shove her arm off and stumble up, wiping the wetness from my face. "Why are you the only person who can make me feel like this? So completely… wrecked." I meet her gaze and let my shields drop, so I stand raw and bleeding, and so she can see what she's done to me and fully understand the damage.

"South, please," she says, lifting her palm out. "I believe you about Rita—that you didn't sleep with her."

"Oh, that's great. But it doesn't change the fact that for *months*, you fucking didn't!" I whip around and bolt for the shady trees in the next paddock over. I need to get away from her. Away from Abbie, too.

Leaning back against an ancient oak, heart slowing down a little, I pull out my cell. I know what I'll do. I'll call Caleb. His family's biodynamic dairy farm is only an hour's drive away, and they're always happy to see an old friend. Especially one whose muscles can handle hours of hard labor. It's exactly what I need.

Sweaty farm work and no talk, talk, talk bullshit.

45

SOUTH

Manure

Caleb will not shut up. He's even worse than Abbie. Watching him pull one side of the long paddock gate closed, I hope he stops flapping his jaw soon.

A hokey straw hat covers his dark hair, casting a shadow over his smiling, freckly face. His pale green eyes are the same as they'd been back in high school, clear and direct. He looks good. Healthy and happy.

"Grab the other one, will ya?" Caleb asks. "You know what you need to do, South? Just go back to your girlfriend and give her a smile and a hug. That'll solve all your problems."

If only it were that simple. Rolling my eyes, I shut the left side of the gate and fumble with the chain, trying to lock it.

Caleb makes a complicated pattern in the air with his hands. "Just loop it through like that."

I do as instructed and lean over the top of the fence, staring at the peaceful, sunlit fields. Framed by distant gray mountains, sixty or so Jersey cows chomp happily away at the lush grass, their udders not long emptied and tails swishing idly at flies. Unlike me, they're not bothered by any heart-crushing, life-changing decisions they have to make. All things considered, the cows have the better life.

"Come on." Caleb claps my back. "Let's go shovel some shit onto Gran's compost heap."

We collect wheelbarrows over by a row of massive solar panels, and then make for the stables.

Whenever Nate and I stay with Abbie we make sure to spend time at the farm with Caleb's family. The natural rhythms they live by are a far cry from the shambles of a rock band's life on the road, but the toil and the sweat sure are similar.

As we go around to the back of the barn and park our barrows next to a great pile of shit, Caleb says, "So, have you been attending my lectures properly? Do you understand what you need to do now? Just forgive Mia for hiding being pregnant, be happy, and enjoy your life."

Smirking like a pain-in-the-butt, I lunge toward the shovel he reaches for. "Oh, sorry did you want this one?" I ask with a straight face.

As Caleb nods and tries to snatch it back, I yank it away,

laughing. "You can't have it. It's mine. In case you forgot, I did manage to get through college. So you don't need to talk to me like you're philosophizing to the livestock."

"Well the stories I'd been hearing about you before you went and got yourself a girlfriend, drugs and the like, did make me wonder if you knew shit from Shinola, buddy. Speaking of crap, let's see how quickly you can load up."

Grinning at each other, we strip off our t-shirts and start shoveling. Like a typical ex-footballer, Caleb's still as competitive as a gladiator.

Minutes pass with our grunts filling the air while we work. It's an improvement because, finally, farm-boy has quit with the counseling. Then, like a moron, I reopen the cozy heart-to-heart session myself. "But pregnancy aside, how could she ever have believed that I slept with that freak. That I cheated on her!"

"But, she believes that you didn't *now*, doesn't she?"

"Well, she says she does. But how could I have felt that close to her…" I fix my eyes on the manure before I speak the next words. "And, you know, *safe* with her, yet all that time she didn't actually trust me? I don't get it."

"It's not that hard to work out. Like you told me, her first serious boyfriend and her parents made a mess of her. Her dad had affairs. Because of Up Void, you're apart a lot and you've got all those easy opportunities to hook up on the road. Or probably even when you buy milk at the store these days, now that your face is every-fucking-where. And when the shit hit the fan, you hadn't been a solid couple for all that long. See the problem?"

"Sure. But this baby news makes me want to regress and just get fucked up again."

"But you're not going to do that."

"No. Probably not."

"So, just forgive her for making a terrible decision already. That's what you do for people you love. See? It's easy. Your love life is fixed. And what's the other thing you were whining about? Right, you're gonna be a father. Big deal. What's so bad about that?"

"What's so good about it? I was thinking on this yesterday driving over here. The only thing I could come up with was that having a kid surrounds you with this aura that you've kinda had sex successfully—at least once in your life—so I suppose that's one good thing."

Leaning on his shovel, Caleb laughs. "I don't think anyone's doubting you on that front, man. And I reckon fatherhood's got a little more going for it than that."

"Really? Like what? And what's the point of bringing kids into this abysmal world anyhow?"

"Woah!" His back gleaming with sweat, Caleb gouges at what's left of the pile of crap on the ground. "Talk about negative. Look around you. Look at this place. Smell the air. This shit, even. All the happy animals. They smell great."

I freeze mid-shovel, shaking my head at my friend the evangelist. "So you guys have worked your butts off to create your own four-hundred-acre piece of paradise. Good on you. And I'm not saying that other pockets of beauty don't exist in the world. But as a whole, seriously? I mean, as a species we're making a mess of everything. We're nothing but a bunch of assholes."

"Man, you need some Prozac or something."

"Yeah, well, at the moment I *am* depressed. There's no doubt about that."

Wiping sweat out of my eyes, I pause to catch my breath. It's a pretty warm day.

Both wheelbarrows are now full to the brim. Laughing, we try to scrape shit from each other's blades, fighting over a final couple of shovel loads.

"You're loving the sweating, at least. I can tell it's doing you good. You're in a much better mood than yesterday. Your energy feels lighter, not so dark."

"Jesus. Listen to you. This is exactly the kind of emotional rubbish I was running from over at Abbie's. What's happened to you?"

"I told you, I got married. Love will—"

Throwing my shovel down, I say, "Stop right there. I need a drink before we take this over to the garden."

And a break from talking about girls. And love. And painful goddamn feelings.

"I'll bring back a jug of something cold." I retrieve my t-shirt from my back pocket and wipe my face.

"Hey, honestly I'm surprised to hear you sounding like a love cynic." Caleb calls to my back. "I've been listening to your music, South, and sure there's a paddock-full of anger in it, but I knew your mom, so I reckon that's fair enough. But there's also a mountain-range of beauty in those songs. So, you know, you should go with that. Focus on the good stuff. Creativity and love."

I snort and keep walking. So that's what being brought up by earth-loving hippies does for a guy, turns him into a metaphor-spouting optimist.

Man. I should have stayed at home and listened to Abbie's lectures. They're filled with the exact same crap that I'm getting here, a full hour's drive away at an infernal dairy farm. And from the former high school linebacker, for Christ's sake!

Well that's settled it then. Looks like I'll be leaving today. I stride through lime green grass and up a gentle hill into the yard. I had planned to stay two nights so there'd be less time hanging around Mia, feeling mad. But nope, I'll get out of here asap, go home, and… try and avoid Mia some more.

Well, maybe after I've eaten Caleb's mom's awesome roast dinner.

The farmhouse gleams white in the sun, and the mouth-watering smell of a cake baking lengthens my strides toward it. Grandma Josephine had been missing in action from the dinner table yesterday. According to Caleb, she'll be here tonight and, no doubt, salivating in excitement as she prepares to deliver me a tongue lashing. But the food at the farm is so heavenly it's worth getting my chops busted some more. If I can make my face look unaffected, Grannie-Jo will quit her nagging fairly quickly. Hopefully.

I can practice my innocent smile as I beg for a jug of lemonade. Yeah. That's a good plan.

Plastering on a grin, I bang through the screen door into

the kitchen and see Caleb's mom washing dishes. Perfect. Hollering out a growly version of the chorus to *Rosie*, I make my way toward her. She's a massive Jackson Browne fan, so she'll be well buttered up by the song.

Just as Rosie turns from the sink, laughing and raising an eyebrow at me, I recall what the song is about. Masturbation. *Damn.* My cocky smile disappears.

Hopefully, she'll still let me have a piece of that cake. It smells like buttery pecans.

For some fool reason, that makes me think of Mia.

Double damn.

46

SOUTH

Punish

Enveloped in blackness, I stand in the doorway, staring blindly in the direction of Mia's bed. But not for long.

Light fills the room, soaking up the shadows as she flicks on the lamp. She draws a shocked breath and sits up, staring dumbly at me as I lean, arms folded casually, against the door frame. Looking like an asshole, I hope.

Man, this is the exact picture that plagued me all day long at the farm. Mia in bed, looking sleepy and mussed-up. I spent a lot of time today trying not to see this image, and then wanting to see it in the flesh something fierce.

"South! What are you… what do you want? It's nearly midnight."

Wearing a hard smirk, I say, "Sex."

"What? Where?" She looks around the room.

"Your bed will be okay, I guess."

"No! I meant to say *why*. Why are you telling *me* this?"

"Well, I thought you might like some warning before I went and got in there with you."

"What? I don't understand…*Why?*"

"You sure are asking some dumb questions, Mia. Truth is I'm kinda horny, and you've made it pretty clear that you're more than up for it. Also, it's a long drive into town to find a proper hookup, so this might be better than scratching the itch myself. Although, there is the rather *large* issue of your condition to consider. Bit of an obstruction really, but I guess I can work around it."

Eyes sparking, she looks smoking mad and like she wants to throw something breakable at me. Perfect.

A hot wave of satisfaction flushes over me as I watch her work hard to give me a wobbly smile instead of launching a book at my head.

With that fake smile in place, she throws the covers open. "Come on, hop in then."

Not waiting to be asked twice, I peel my t-shirt over my head, taking long strides forward. This is too easy. Speaking to her like this, I deserve a smack in the mouth. And *she*… she deserves a throttling for her filthy, deceitful lying.

At the very least I should ride her rough. Punish her in a way that will, in truth, be no real hardship for either of us. In fact, it'll feel freaking fantastic. But will I feel better afterward, when I come down from the rush? Probably not.

"How was your stay at your friend's dairy farm? Did you have fun?"

Avoiding looking at her, I quickly shuck my jeans and boxers. "Nope."

"So, what did you get up to over there?"

"Shut up, Mia. I don't wanna talk about that shit." Eyeing her frown, I make plans to turn her to face the wall, picture sinking into her heat. I'll do the whole thing fast. And hard. A couple of times might be okay as long as it's just fucking.

When I snuggle in close against her skin, I get the usual warm blast of endorphins, and I make the mistake of looking into her glistening eyes.

While my heart thuds like a bass drum, in a cold voice, I say, "You ain't gonna cry now, are ya?"

She shakes her head. "No. Of course not."

I cup her cheek and before I can stop myself my mouth meets hers way too gently. My pulse is an erratic contrast to the slow, molten movements of my lips and tongue.

It's frustrating not to have the whole length of her tight against me, and I have to curl in a weird way around her stomach, but, man, the kissing feels good. And the touching. I've missed it so bad.

With her hands in my hair, I'm fully charged and buzzing like an amp on ground loop. She sifts through the thick layers, then grabs a fistful and pulls like she wants me closer, deeper.

I tug her blond locks. "I like your hair this way. It's cool."

"Sorry, what?"

"The two-tone thing. The top half is this pale honey color, and the rest is white."

"I can't dye it anymore because of the chemicals. Because I'm pregnant."

"Oh. Right." Sorry I mentioned it.

Back to the kissing thing. I reckon I could lie here all night with my mouth over hers, just kissing her. Nothing else. I'm so into the hot, wet feel, the stroking, the *sound*.

No, forget that. I need to be inside her asap, to conquer and control her and… wait… this isn't going how I planned at all. She's the one who needs to be desperate for this, not me.

I pull away and kneel over her, puffing so hard I'm practically wheezing. *Great.*

"Take this off." Now that sounds better. Nice and gruff. I try not to drool on her while she struggles out of her t-shirt. I get to work on her panties, throw the red scrap over my shoulder, then press her knees apart.

"South… wait. I can't stay on my back, remember? Want me to go on top?"

"No way. I'll—"

"Or I can go like this," she says, rolling onto her side.

Fuck. That's one helluva nice view. I don't want her to know how much it affects me, so I lick my lips, and say, "Man, your stomach is *huge*."

She says nothing. Huh. Shame, I wanted a reaction. Might have to try a bit harder to get one. I send my palm skimming over her hip, the curve of her butt, and down further to tease through soft folds and make her even wetter.

"Is that the worst thing you can think of to say to me?" she mumbles into the pillow.

Um, yeah. It kind of is. And I'm pretty sure she's hoping to sound unmoved by my asshole comments, but I'm not fooled. I know her too well. Guilt twangs in my gut. It's not my thing to get off on hurting people, especially girls. And Mia—I've never wanted to make her feel bad.

But now I'm conflicted because I want to shake her and fuck her and squeeze her and kiss her, all at the same time. And none of those options are good.

Maybe I should split while I still can, go back to my room and jerk off to this incredible vision—Mia, hot and ready, waiting for me to touch her. Yeah, right. I'm not going anywhere. I'm gonna stick to my plan and show her how I used to fuck girls before I met her, hard and without mercy.

She waits for my next move, shuddering every now and again like she's cold. I touch her hip. She's warm and soft. Unable to stop myself, I run my fingers over smooth skin, follow luscious curves, stroke over her stomach.

When my gut and my balls feel so heavy they hurt, I drag her knee higher and get up close in the space between her legs.

The amazing view of her ass makes my dick pulse. With a firm grip, I work it inside her. No. That's wrong, there's no effort involved. I slide one hand between the mattress and her hip, support her stomach with the other, raising her pelvis a little.

As I push in to the hilt, her breath hitches. "And... I'll be even bigger in two months, just before the end."

I try to scoff, but it comes out like a groan. "I cain't even believe that's possible," I murmur, starting to pull back and then push in slowly. Pull back and... wait. *Cain't?* Christ, listen to me. What a redneck.

"You get any bigger there, Mia, and you might explode like an over-ripe melon and... uh, shit." This feels like heaven. I bite my lip and swallow down words, words of praise, of love.

Have to stay angry.

Maintain the rage.

Suspended in my grip, she's in the perfect position for me to use her as if she's only a vessel for my lust, for my burning wrath. Yeah, that's the right way to think of it. Now I'm back on track.

Hate the betrayer.

Fuck the liar.

Make her cry.

Wanting to get off before she does, so I can be a real prick and leave her hanging, I pick up the pace. Despite the giant belly, she's so small, and I feel like a shaking, shuddering mountain. Or a rutting dog. But, man, it feels so good that I can't stop myself from slowing down to savor it.

Sweat breaks out over my skin as my brain battles my body. Go slow. Go fast. Hate her. Love her. Shit!

Hand clutching the sheet, she tries to look back at me, and I start pounding into her to avoid her gaze.

"God, South," she moans.

"Are you… does this hurt?"

"Only in the best of ways. For pity's sake, please, don't stop. Go faster."

Fuck, my stomach, my balls, thighs, shit, even my toes go hot and tense. I ramp up the speed, pulling her against me, and then pushing her body up the bed with each thrust. Down. Up. Down. All in sync with her moans.

And the whole time, no matter how often I tear my eyes away, I'm drawn back to her stomach, to the baby as if by some insidious force. And instead of putting me off, like some dumb caveman, I lose my mind at the thought of that kid in there. The notion that we've done that together. That *I've* done that. And that it makes her mine. No one else's.

Mine.

Breathing ruined, she shakes and cries out, and all through the convulsions of her body tightening and releasing around me, the same chant spins through my skull until, dammit, it's on my lips.

As the tension explodes and I break apart, I exhale the word *mine* like prayer or a vow.

No. *No.* Shit. What am I doing? So much for showing no mercy.

While lightning crashes through my gut, I hope like hell her ears stopped working when she came. I'm sure I've read about that happening. Or maybe I dreamed it.

It better fucking be real, because the last thing I want is for Mia to know the truth about me.

That I'm in love.
Heartbroken.
Hers.
Always.

47

MIA

Rain

Beautiful music draws me from my afternoon snooze and, in a trance, I follow it down the hallway to the living room. The sound mixes with the rain on the tin roof, filling the air with a crackling energy.

I stand in the doorway and watch South as he kicks back against the sofa folded around his guitar, disheveled hair curtaining his face, and sings.

The song is made of opposing forces. Pain, then love. Then more pain. On it goes, making my heart bleed and thud, and then bleed and thud again. Like a thundercloud, positive and negative charges separate within the beautiful boy I can't look away from, and at any moment he might change into pure lightning.

My skin heats as I recall what we did together last night. What *he* did to me. Like cruel razors his words cut deep, and then he used his body to heal my wounds.

Afterward, when he left my room, he said nothing to give me hope, but the pain instead of anger burning in his eyes made me think that maybe—just maybe—it might all be okay.

One day.

But, of course, he's leaving tomorrow. Who knows when I'll see him again?

A low growl, a sound wrenched from the depths of a nightmare, chases the final note that vibrates from his strings and rings through the air. Eyes still screwed shut, hair curving in sexy waves around his chin, he sits on the green sofa in the shadowy afternoon light looking like he's cast out of bronze.

Thunder cracks and a horse whinnies in the distance.

"South," I say gently.

He flinches, then freezes, eyes still on his fretboard.

"That was amazing! Just… so sublime."

Swallowing tears, I walk toward him, and he slumps back against the cushions wearing a cold half-smirk. I falter, then take another step, stopping when I'm a foot away from his spread knees.

"Wait until Lane and Marco hear that one. They'll be so excited they'll probably pee on each other in joy just like little puppies!"

"Oh, yeah, and you can photograph it. It'll go great with your latest pet wedding shots. Make a collage."

I hate his tone, the way he speaks to me, each word a barbed arrow meant to pierce deep and cause pain.

I attempt a bright smile. "And Nate will love it, too. He'll go nuts—"

"Yeah, well, I won't be playing this one to any of them. It's just mine. In fact, that's what it's called. *Mine.* But you can read the lyrics if you want, Mia." His smirk turning into a sneer, he slaps his palm against the Hellcat's ruby-red veneer. "But I have to warn you I don't think you'll like them much."

"Is it about how mean and horrible I am?"

"Something like that."

I glance down. A yellow envelope and its contents are spread over the coffee table next to him, the ultrasound photos I had printed and the CD video of the baby floating about in blackness like a large-skulled alien.

"South. Come on, this is crazy. Stop being like this. Let me in. Let me speak to you properly."

He pushes the guitar off his lap and I try to take its place, but he grips my waist firmly and plonks me beside him. Feeling brave, I stroke his hair and then his cheek while he stares ahead like I don't exist. His chest pumps, he swallows repeatedly, but he doesn't push me away.

Fingers hooked into his sharp cheekbone, I turn his face and stare into icy-blue eyes. I count to ten before I see a glimmer of something warm in his gaze, then I look deeper to be sure. Yes. It's not my imagination.

Next, I try smiling at him and, miracle of miracles, his lips stretch slowly until his eyes glow, and then he laughs. Sweet relief fills my chest.

"Come outside with me," I whisper. "Where Abbie won't hear us. Please, South."

He watches sheets of water stream down the window overlooking the yard. "I'm not going out there. It's pouring."

"It's just a little bit of hard drizzle. Nothing to worry about."

Huffing his silent laugh, he shocks me by standing abruptly and zigzagging through the collection of well-worn chairs and couches and out through the door. Holding my stomach, I scurry to catch up.

He takes long strides to the middle of the yard and then swings around and stares at me, his hair dripping and plastered to his head.

The sky is a dramatic silver and black, and a gusty wind whips my tunic around. I move close enough to see the beads of water darkening his eyelashes.

"Is this wet enough for you?" He points at my belly like it was *its* idea to come out here.

I study his scowl and then the sad-looking skull on his sopping wet t-shirt. The words 'angry, young and poor' are printed in white letters over a black background. At least the slogan's only wrong about one thing.

"Yes. This'll do fine."

"Well? What do you want?"

I stroke my belly and his lips twist. "The baby... I'm seven months along now and—"

"Really, you don't say? I'd forgotten you were knocked up."

"I can't talk to you if it's going to be like this, you interrupting every few seconds just to be awful."

"I'm always awful. I like being this way."

I sigh. "Right. Fine. I'll cut to the chase, then. I've booked a plane ticket. I'm going home the day after tomorrow."

"What?" His fingers shoot up to cover his eyes, then his arm drops, palm smacking his thigh. "Ah, you're a real fucking piece of work—"

"You should be happy! I thought you couldn't wait to see the back of me."

He takes a long step forward, blinking against the rain, and bends to yell in my face. "I'm fucking ecstatic!"

No, he isn't.

"But you're going back on tour tomorrow anyway. It's not like you'll *be* here."

Shaking his head, he spins on his heels, ready to stomp off. I wipe tears and rain from my face and say, "Wait!"

He stills, shoulders rising and falling and his hands clenched.

When I touch his arm, he flinches, eyes burning into mine. Is it pain or anger I see? Probably both.

I suck down a big breath. "Listen, please believe me when I say that I *know* you didn't do anything with Rita. I *swear* with all my heart that I believe you."

His eyebrows dart high.

"And if you say you haven't slept with anyone else since

you and I have been an item... then I believe that, too. It must be true, South, because you're not a liar. You're not."

Silent and unmoving, he stares, the look in his eyes hard and intense. It's difficult to get more words out, but I need to say them.

"And... I'm so sorry. I'm sorry I doubted you. And most of all I'm sorry that I lied to you about the... you know..." I point at the baby. "You're an amazing boyfriend and lover, the best friend a girl could ever want. Genuine, caring, funny. And so many other things, South." Like heart-achingly beautiful inside and out. Better not bring that up right now, though.

The anger in his eyes dissolves, but the intensity remains.

"When I found out I was pregnant, it was such a shock. And I was so scared of losing you. So I handled everything badly. I *know* I did. And then I stuffed it up even worse by not trusting you. Not having faith in you. You're the best guy, South, and I was wrong. So wrong."

In answer to my awkward apology, something sparks in his eyes—relief, then heat—and he seizes my arm and jerks me forward until I'm pressed against him and then he kisses the living daylights out of me.

Thunder rattles the sky again. I'm drenched and cold and feverish, drowning in the heat of his lips, his mouth.

He breaks off to rasp, "The stables," and yanks me toward the nearby hulking barn.

The horses shuffle and snort when they see us and no wonder, because what two-legs in their right minds would be out in this dreadful weather?

South crushes me against a stall door, and I feel Annabelle the big chestnut mare's hot horsey breath on my shoulder. "South... the horses."

"Goddamn it," he says, directing a dark scowl at the poor beasts as though they're the ones trying to mount each other in his living room while he eats a TV dinner. "Over here." Linking our fingers, he tows me to the feed area.

Dust motes swirl around the bales of hay stacked chest high in front of me. "I can't lie on top of that. I'll fall off."

"You can lean on them. See? It's the perfect height." He drags a low stool over and guides me onto it so I'm facing away from him. He places my hands on the straw, gently urges my shoulders lower, and starts grappling with clothing. The sound of his zipper coming down grates, then he pauses. "Shit, you look incredible. Why haven't we done this before?"

"Um, let me think. Probably because you haven't had time for it in your super-busy schedule of hating me and..." I trail off, groaning as he slides inside my body, filling me perfectly. My knees weaken as he drags slowly back, then plunges forward, the warmth of his skin against my butt making my head spin.

"You okay?"

"This hay's a bit scratchy but, please, don't stop." Dropping my face into the bale, I let out a long sigh.

"Don't worry, you won't be there long." His palm sweeps over my bulging stomach. "Ah!" he yelps, flinging his hand away as if the baby bit through layers of flesh and took his finger off. "It just moved. I felt... It was like it turned over or something. Should I stop?"

"No!" I put his hand on my skin again and guide it back down the path it had been traveling. Not needing much coaxing, he sets calloused fingers to work in sync with his thrusts.

Within seconds I pant his name, going still as every part of me tightens and then breaks apart. My muscles clench around him and he convulses, breath shuddering loudly in my ear.

"Oh, *God*. Fuck," he says. One last hard push into me and, seated deep, he shakes and groans long and loud.

I savor the feel of his big body wrapped around me and wait for our ragged breathing to settle. Then I laugh.

"What?" he asks, breath hot against my ear.

"It's just I rarely ever hear you say *God* during sex. It's always *fuck* and *shit* and *so fucking good*."

"Well, I'm pretty sure I said fuck, too." He pulls out, and then turns me carefully. Grim faced, he folds me into a deliciously warm bear hug and huffs hot breaths into my hair, making deep, raw sounds like sobs. Wait. *What?* No, that can't be right.

Going up on my toes, I squeeze him tighter. "Oh, South, honey, don't do that. Everything's okay, my love." I stroke his hair, dig my fingers into his skull, but he keeps trembling.

Holding his cheeks, I push his head up. "Tell me what's wrong."

"I don't want you to go so far away." Looking ashamed, he glances over at the tools, the muck rakes and forks, shovels and odd bits of horse tack arranged on the wall. "I mean... isn't flying dangerous? What if you have the baby on the plane?"

This is the first time he's called his child something other than *it*. So that's some progress.

"I've got two months left. It'll be fine. I need to be at home for the birth where Ivy and Nico are."

"But what about me? I've got this fucking tour to finish."

"So, you've decided you want to be a father now?"

Shaking his head, he whispers, "No."

"Well, you've got what? Another month of gigs left before you get a break?"

He nods.

"I won't chase after you like I did in the beginning, South, so if you want me, come home when you can. And preferably when you've realized that we're happiest together and that being a father isn't the worst thing that can happen to you."

"And meanwhile you're not gonna go and marry that idiot Liam or anything dumb like that, are you? Because let's face it, good ol' Architect Man will be blowing his load at the thought of swooping down in his shiny pants to save you from your predicament."

"No! Of course not. Geez."

"Good." He tugs my arm. "Come on, let's get you and that lump dried off."

At least the rain has stopped. The grass squelches and squeaks underfoot as we make our way across the yard. My toes are cold, but I don't care, because his hand is warm and strong around mine and I can smell him on my clothes. But mostly because he'd cried at the idea of me leaving.

When we reach the back door, he freezes, drops my hand

and turns to me. Looking at the ground, he bites his lip while I wait.

Finally, his gaze travels slowly up my body, lingering on my stomach. When his eyes meet mine, he says, "You tell Liam for me that if he touches you or my kid, I'm gonna come and flatten him. And I mean that most sincerely."

He gives me an *I've-got-my-mojo-back* smirk and ducks inside the house.

The sun comes out and turns the water drops on the trees into glistening gems. I watch them sparkle, wondering how I'll cope over the next month or so without him, and how long I'll need to wait before he'll come home to me. Hopefully it will before the 26th of October, or he'll miss seeing his daughter born.

At the moment, he probably doesn't much care about that, but some day he'll regret not being there. I'm certain of it.

48

MIA

Purr

It's a warm day, and I'm at the local pool, busy gawking at all the swimmers enjoying the afternoon sun. I've only completed three out of ten planned laps and have settled in behind my sunglasses for a session of people watching. It's *much* more fun than exercise.

South says that beaches and pools are great equalizers of humanity, the way everyone comes together to hang out the second the temperature rises. Being a surfer, he's always singing the praises of water.

Darn it. I need to think of something else quickly before I ruin my relaxed Friday afternoon vibes. Now let's see. What's the biggest positive in my life right now? Cutting back my shifts at Mad Wolf has been good, although I'm desperate to do another pet wedding shoot, I miss it so much. But I've got loads of free time at the moment, which is brilliant, and I couldn't be happier.

Bullshit! I'm not happy. I'm terrified of becoming a mom. And possibly a single one.

At least in five weeks' time, when I'm not hefting around an over-sized fetus everywhere I go, my bladder will be a lot more comfortable.

Wriggling, I try to hoist my boobs back into my fifties-style swimsuit, afraid to glance down at the mountainous cleavage that I'm certain is on display. Sadly, I look less retro-pin-up-girl striking a pose and more Free-Willy-the-whale with my chest straining toward the open ocean. South, a die hard breast-man, would love to get an eyeful. If only he were here to enjoy the spectacle.

If only.

Missing-South-horribly has been my number one pastime since arriving home three weeks ago. With his baby constantly beating up my insides, he's difficult to forget. And this place brings back too many memories of the times we came here together, when I idled away hours watching him write songs in his head as he stared down at the water's dappled patterns on the bottom of the pool. His fingers constantly tapped and shaped chords against his thighs as he wrote songs in his head, whispering the words.

Deep water. Water deep. Deep down. Found. Find me. Dark deep. Still water. Trouble found.

Gazing at the water now, all I can think of is amniotic fluid, big babies, and, of course, South.

I pull my phone out of my bag and check emails, heart leaping at the sight of one that's only four minutes old. From him! I stab at it with my finger, preparing to read a funny tale from the road about Zave falling off his kit again or a retelling of a recent Lane-lecture on toilet seat etiquette.

Oh, hells bells. It's only two sentences long but, hopefully, he's still awake. Laughing, I read the email.

From: wolfpup666@gmail.com

　　To: Miagracelovessouthb@gmail.com

　　Re: Cats

　　Today at 3.37 pm

Hey Mia, do you know why cats purr? You're the animal expert, right?

Sent from my iPhone

I start a text message.

Me: Probably. But more importantly, two tiny sentences don't really make an email, you goose. Text me.

When my cell pings a few moments later, I fist pump the air.

South: Sorry, what? You want me to SEXT you?

Me: Good heavens, no. I still haven't recovered from the last time.

South: So... I repeat, why do cats purr?

Me: Coz they're happy. Obviously.

South: Nope. Well, yep. But also coz the vibrations relieve pain and even heal wounds.

Me: Wow. Thank goodness you got in touch with that information.

South: I love to help. But I'm telling you this for a reason.

Me: ?????

South: I'm teaching myself how to do it.

Laughing, I snort loudly.

Me: Teaching yourself to sext? Good idea. I think you could do a lot better.

South: LOL LOL LOL!!!!

Me: You only need to write it once, dummy. Or preferably not at all.

South: Not in this case.

Me: Okay, I'll bite... why are you teaching yourself to purr?

South: I'm trying to heal my broken heart.

Me: Seriously?

South: Yep.

Me: Aw poor you... what has Ben done now to hurt your feelings?

South: LOL!

Me: You may look like a big bad wolf on the outside but inside you're soft and sweet.

South: Thank you???

Me: Where are you right now?

South: Tour bus… driving… on a road. I mean THE road. Fuck knows where. Brain not functioning so T.I.R.E.D.

Me: It must be late. What's with the acronym?

South: Yeah, it's nearly 2. I miss you. Totally. Irked. Really. Exhausted. Dead.

I picture him lounging across some seats as the bus hurtles through a dark landscape, his face reflected ghostly white in the window. And probably rubbing his eyes like a kid as he always does when he's bone weary.

Me: Only another week until Up Void's done and then you can jump on a plane.

A minute passes with no response. Maybe he's fallen asleep.

Me: South?

South: So what about you? Where are you now?

Me: At the pool showing off my colossal-sized boobs. I'm talking burlesque plus plus plus.

Again nothing. I wait a few moments.

Me: Earth to South. You still out there?

South: Sorry… you're setting quite the scene for me. It's, ah, let's just say a welcome distraction from staring at the back of Zave's head. Yeah.

Me: I know what you're thinking and I doubt you'd be thinking it if you could actually see me.

South: Trust me. I'd be thinking it. And doing it.

Me: Physically, I don't think you'd manage to somehow. Bovine is a very unsexy look.

South: Quick. Send me a photo. Don't think. Just do it. PLEASE.

A blurry photo appears on my screen, only the top half of South's face, bright-blue eyes pleading.

Ok. Don't think. Don't think. Just do it!

I grab my phone. Without changing to selfie mode, I point it in the general direction of my boobs, take a photo, and then examine the result. Hm, it could be worse. I press send and wait.

One second. Two seconds. Three. Four.

Shit. What is he doing? Then at last, the typing dots.

South: I'm managing it.

I laugh.

Me: You are not!

South: Yeah, I am. Hard as titanium. Now send me one of your face. And smile.

Oh, crap. I do as requested and then wait, and wait some more.

South: Uh... speechless. Shit. That's made my heart problem a lot worse.

Mine feels pretty bad at the moment, too.

Me: I love you. Can you please come back to me soon? I need you here.

I squeeze water out of my hair while I wait again.

South: Gotta go. Can't keep my eyes open. I'll dream about you and call you tomorrow. Love you. Xxxxxx.

He adds emojis of guitars, waves, hearts, and kissy lips, and because he quite enjoys a slap in the mouth, a whale. Pity he's not close by to receive his whack of outrage.

Wiping away a tear, I scroll back through the texts just to make sure. Yep, it's exactly as I thought. He completely avoided the issue of what he'll do when the tour finishes, the question of when or even *if* he'll be heading back to me.

Standing and stuffing things into my bag, I contemplate what to make for dinner tonight. Something healthy like salmon and a salad? Maybe comfort food will be better—yeah—macaroni and cheese.

In five weeks the baby is due, and there's a slight chance she might arrive early, too. From what I've read, a mother's stress can cause premature birth, making me an ideal candidate. Either way, it seems like South may be too busy hiding on the other side of the country to make it home in time to see his child born.

The coward.

That makes two of us. All those months ago when I discovered the pregnancy, I should have been brave and told him immediately. But I hadn't. And now I'm paying the price.

It's hypocritical to be mad with him when my own behavior has been appalling. If my conscience was clear, I could hate him, forget about him. But the way things stand I can't help wondering how much my mishandling of the situation—what a freaking understatement—contributes to his refusal to commit to a future with his child.

My gut feeling tells me the answer is—a lot.

Right, guess I'd better go home and wallow in my guilt, which means make myself sick with a tub of salted caramel ice cream.

49

MIA

Mystifies Me

"So can you give me some warning when you think you're about to burst? I don't want any of that *amybiotic* fluid on my shoes." Vince grins at me, and then winces when Ivy digs her elbow into his ribs.

"It's amniotic fluid, you dope," she says, tapping her foot along to the folk song that three stunning sisters are currently crooning from the candle-lit stage.

"Well, I'm not a frigging baby doctor, am I?"

"And for *that* all women in this city are thankful." Ivy sips water, then crunches ice. "Mia's got two weeks to go and I've got four before we pop, so there's no need to look so scared, Vince. You guys are such wusses around birth and babies."

"That's a little sexist," I say.

"You'll find out soon enough when Mr. Hotstuff is falling about the floor while you're hard at work pushing out his jumbo-sized kid."

The baby jabs a limb into my bladder. *"Ow.* South will hardly be feeling faint if he's still in a different state when this one comes out."

"My point exactly." Ivy sniffs.

I survey the crowd. It's a Thursday night, and the hip downtown bar is chock-full of music industry types enjoying showcase performances by a bunch of String Power Records' bands.

The acts are stripped back, semi-acoustic, so the sound isn't likely to vibrate my baby out of the womb early like a normal rock gig would. That's kind of a shame because I'm feeling over ripe.

A guy in a black t-shirt stands near the toilets nodding along to the beat, his impressive psychobilly quiff almost as high as Nate's. I gaze longingly at his back. He makes me miss Up Void. And South.

I dig in my bag and check the time on my phone. Ten thirty. Is that all? I thought it was at least two hours later than that. Bored since being unemployed for a whole week, it's a treat to be out of the house, but I wish it didn't feel like the middle of the night already.

Nico pushes through the crowd, blaring his dimples at us. "How you coping there, girls?" he asks, throwing his tattooed arm around Ivy and biting his lip ring.

"I loved Burntbad's set, Niccy, but—"

"Hey, don't call me that. It's boring." His bright green eyes flash at me. "Apparently, Prince Harry's mom called him *Your Royal Naughtiness*. Now that's a better nickname."

Nico and his weird fact-spouting habit—you never know what he'll come out with next.

"I had no idea you were a royal watcher." Ivy snickers and raises an eyebrow at him. "But if you like, we can call you that from now on."

I laugh and swat her arm, wishing I had my own well-muscled rocker here.

"As fun as it is to be out with the grownups," I say. "I think I'd better head home and get some sleep."

"No!" Ivy yells, taking hold of my arms and steering me toward the bar near the stage. "You can't go yet. You're going to love this next act."

Act? Is a juggling clown about to go on? Or a fire-eating stick twirler? That might be entertaining.

"Here, sit on this stool, and I'll get you some refreshing water. Good view, hey? You can see the stage perfectly from here. I've got an idea for a new painting. Can I take a few shots of you while you kick back and relax?"

I sigh and nod, watching the trio leave the stage. I didn't love their performance. The songs were a little too depressing for my liking, but the girls are talented and beautiful and going places fast.

While I rummage through my bag, the crowd erupts in sudden hoots and whistles, clapping like they're super excited. The fire-eating juggler must be setting up.

Why is my silly satchel so huge? All I want is a stick of lip balm to soothe my dry lips, I shouldn't have to delve about in muck for fifteen minutes to find it.

Foisting a glass under my nose, Ivy says, "Okay, now take a big breath."

Wondering what on earth she put in the drink, I grimace at the liquid.

"Not of that you fool." Ivy points at the stage.

"What?" I look up and stare at the lone guy getting comfy with his guitar on the chair.

No. It can't be.

The glass slips out of my hand and bounces along the wooden floor.

I must be seeing things, or maybe I've lost my marbles. Not knowing what else to do, I gaze into the interior of my bag. If I don't look, the painful apparition will go away.

Then the voice comes through the mic, and I begin to shake.

"Hey, how y'all doing?" that voice says, and then laughs as the audience screams and yells back at him. "Hi, Mia."

Shit! Heart pounding, heat rippling through my blood, I force myself to look up.

Holy hot baby-makers! It really is South sitting there smiling at me, looking all chilled out with his fingers hanging over his guitar in a relaxed fashion, like he's lounging on a veranda in the tropics. He laughs into the mic. "Well... *surprise.*"

My hands cover my gaping mouth.

He turns back to the crowd. "I can't tell if she's glad to see me or not. You look a bit shocked there, Mia. Do you guys think she looks happy?"

Yes, three hundred people tell him.

"I sure hope you're right, because I'm pretty happy to see her." Still smiling, he raises his eyebrows in my direction.

I nod. His smile grows.

"A while ago, some of you here tonight had the misfortune to attend a gig where I dedicated a song to Mia. At the time I was pretty messed up. I won't bore you with the details, but you know how it goes when guys are half-wits about girls."

The crowd goes wild. They know what he's talking about.

"So, because I was an idiot and had lost my fucking mind, it wasn't a very nice song."

Boos and laughter fill the room.

"Fair enough. I know I deserve that." He huffs another laugh into the mic while he fiddles with his guitar pegs. "Ah, man," he says, shaking his head, probably remembering if not that mad night, then his hangover the next day. "Tonight I've got a better one for her."

Smile gone, his eyes lock on mine. "Mia, once in your blue room you told me that this is the most romantic song you'd ever heard… so I'm gonna play it for you, and I hope you like it. I'm real sorry about that other one."

Looking back at the crowd, in a clear, deep voice he utters the exact words he'd said at the Tyr Bar all that time ago. "This one's for Mia. She knows why."

Chaos erupts in the audience, but they quickly bring themselves to order when the beautiful intro to Son Volt's version of *Mystifies Me* comes ringing out of South's guitar. The warm energy of the alt-country ballad mesmerizes, casting a spell over the room.

Then he sings in that golden voice about needing me to give out signs, tells me he'll learn anything I want him to, and that I mystify him like no other does.

And though I try hard not to, I cry hot tears of confusion and happiness, sadness and joy because he's here. *He is here.* And I'm really not sure why.

50

MIA

Bathroom

"**I**n here, quick." South drags me into a bathroom off the backstage hallway, and then throws himself at me.

"Careful," I say as I'm pressed against the tiled wall. Then I can't speak because it's all kissing and hugging, and kissing and laughing, and big, calloused hands wiping at my tears.

After he spends some time getting reacquainted with my mouth, he gives my bottom lip a final slow suck and takes two steps away like he's planning on going somewhere. Abruptly changing his mind, he swings back around to smash his mouth against mine, making my head rush and my heart pound.

He pulls away again. "I'm gonna... wait there..." he says, and walks to the door.

Studying it, he says, "Damn, no lock." He stalks back, a thumb hooked into his jeans pocket, hand pointing to his...

"So I guess you're pleased to see me, then?" I nod at the prominence growing in his jeans.

Closing in on me, he thumps his chest with a fist. "Every part of me is pleased to see you—mind, body, and soul. I'm having an integrated experience here. It's kind of like a spiritual awakening."

"You geek," I say as he lifts me up next to the sink.

Eyes wide, he rubs my stomach. "Jesus, look at you. Fuck!"

"I know, it's crazy, isn't it? And, South, it's *so* uncomfortable. I can barely walk. I can't sleep, and my back aches and—"

"*Shit*, the whining has started already. Marco warned me about this."

I smack his arm. "You're really lucky that I'm far too happy right now to wallop you properly."

"Wanna know how to make *me* 'too happy' right now?"

"I can already guess. But there's no way I'm doing that in my current state."

"Wait. What? You can't fuck?" His blast of shock practically gives my hair a nice blowout.

"You should probably start practicing not to swear so much. For the baby's sake. And I can have *sex*, it's just—"

"Hallelujah for that," he says, looking mischievous. "Because I haven't had *intercourse* in nearly two months! To say I'm looking forward to getting real close to you, Mia, would be the understatement of the century."

Miracles *do* happen then.

"I'm getting turned on staring at shiny table tops and eating delicious oranges and—"

"I feel for you. I really do. I'm just not going to have sex with you in my state…"

Eyes widening, his eyebrows twist hard.

"…in a public bathroom."

He pushes up tight against me, plants juicy kisses on my mouth, and I can't stop myself from dragging my hand slowly down to stroke over his hard-on. His rough sighs thrill me, as does the magnetic pull in the air particles between our bodies, our lips.

Eyes flicking from my face to my explosive bosom, he pulls back and licks his lips. "Right, I can't take any more of this. Let's go home. And as soon as we get there, I am gonna give you one hell of a back massage and then an even better internal one."

"That sounds disgustingly medical! I'm thinking of my obstetrician at the moment."

"Well, you won't be soon." He smiles and pushes long strands of blond hair behind my ears. Hand going still at my temple, he frowns. "Hang on… what does that guy do to you, anyway? Should I be worried?"

I laugh at his crossed eyebrows. "I can't believe you're here. I nearly had a heart attack out there. So you must definitely be okay about the baby, then? About being a dad? You still sounded wishy washy on the phone the other day."

"Nothing's changed. I'm definitely *not* okay about it. Shit, I don't want to be responsible for a child. Look at me."

I look, and I see no impediments to fatherhood. He's perfect in every way. Smiling, I stroke his cheek. "What on earth are you doing back here, then?"

"It's been nearly two months since I've seen you, Mia. Phone calls aren't enough. I can't stand it anymore. I've been done with Up Void for two weeks and I tried to stay away, because I don't want any part of this kid situation that you never gave me a freaking say in. You just decided to have it yourself." He covers his face, rubs it hard, and then drops his hands so he can glare at me. "But I can't stay away. I just can't do it."

"Oh, so if you'd known earlier about the baby, if you'd had your chance, you would have advised murder—"

"No! I don't know. The only thing I *do* know is that I can't be away from you anymore."

"So, what happens when she's born and is upsetting your perfect rock star life? What will you do then? Run away? Pretend she doesn't exist?"

Rubbing his own stomach for a change, he winces. "I don't know!"

"What's wrong?" I delve under his t-shirt, blood simmering at the feel of the ridged muscles covered in warm skin.

"Stomach ache. It's nothing. Nate said it's because I ate too much on the plane. I think he's right."

"I thought I saw Nate out there. That's fantastic that he's home, too."

"It's really not. Abbie's got him following me around acting like some super-cautious old dude with a fire extinguisher. As if I'm gonna spontaneously combust at any moment. Why doesn't anyone trust me?"

"Well, I guess we're worried about you." I pat my tummy. "Your biggest trauma-trigger is about to pop out any day now, so…"

"I don't want to talk about that. Not yet, anyway. Can we please go home? I'll catch up with everyone soon. Right now I just want to see the blue room. With you in it. Hopefully not wearing much."

"Who's not wearing much? Me or you?"

He snickers. "What sort of a question is that? Both of us, of course."

51

MIA

Emergency

"That'll be five hundred and seventy-nine dollars, thanks. I gave you ten percent discount because you got so much stuff," says the girl at the register, inspecting my belly haughtily. Perhaps *Mackenzie*, as her name tag states, shouldn't work at a maternity store if she's so disdainful of the condition.

"Thanks so much. That's kind of you."

With only ten days to go until the baby is due, I've decided to stop ignoring the fact that life is about to change forever. It's time to get organized and that means stocking up on baby supplies. Ivy and I have overdone it, of course, traipsing around stores all day, and now I ache from my scalp all the way down to my toenails.

My cell rings for the third time since we've been in the store, and because I want to escape this hell hole ASAP, I plan to ignore it again. What urgent matter has turned Linc into such a persistent pest?

"Until Nico and I started shopping a couple of months ago, I had no idea diapers and baby clothes cost so much," Ivy says, adjusting the sunglasses on top of her wavy, red hair. "We got a lot of bargains online. But you've kind of left it too late for that." She nudges me out of my daze. "Are you sure you've got enough money to cover it?"

"Oh, yeah. That's not a problem. Luckily mister-you-know-who has been regularly topping up my bank account."

"Really? Sorta like giving you an allowance or pin money?"

Passing my card to the girl, I nod. "Yeah, I guess."

"That's very Regency-husband of him."

"Or very sugar daddy."

Ivy snorts. "Did someone tell him to do that?"

"No. He came up with that one all on his own. His way to absolve himself from the guilt of still not being sold on the idea of being a dad, I suppose."

Mackenzie's eyes widen.

"He wasn't interested in coming today?" Ivy asks, stuffing the receipt in a bag. "Casting his creative eye over the color selection for all the teeny-tiny t-shirts?"

"That's hilarious. As if! I didn't even mention it to him."

"I'm amazed you're allowing yourself to spend his money."

"Well I haven't got any. And believe me it took around two hours of Nate's nagging to convince me to let my sugar daddy pay for—" My phone pings loudly.

Linc again.

The text says, *emergency—pick up NOW*, and just as I finish reading it the cell rings.

"Geez, Linc, what's going on? Don't tell me Nico's cut you off from the vodka martinis again—"

"It's South. Now don't freak out, Mia, he's not dead or anything—"

"What? South!" I yell, moving away from the counter.

At the mention of his name, Mackenzie's ears prick. Darn it.

Linc rattles away at full speed while I pace in a circle, hoping to find somewhere to flop down. The low display stand with a frighteningly high-tech stroller perched on it looks good. I need to buy one of those things soon. I collapse next to the stroller wheels and try to make sense of Linc's story.

Apparently, when the Up Void boys went surfing this morning, South got sick. Or *sicker*.

"—and because of that they're worried his appendix will burst." Linc takes a big breath. "So, he's in the hospital."

"For the love of Pete, he's had that darn stomach ache since he got home so that's... four days. I told him to go to the doctors this morning. How can he ignore pain like that?"

"Well, Nate reckons South was probably feverish on the

drive to the beach, all red faced and squirming in the car. When they arrived, Nate begged him not to get in the water, but you know what South's like when he's told he shouldn't do something. He almost drowned, Mia. You'd better waddle on over to the hospital, girl, because they're gonna operate any minute."

"Wait, Linc. Why did Nate call *you*, not me?"

"Well, he didn't want to worry you. He wanted someone else to do it instead, and he couldn't get a hold of Nico, so here I am. Those Up Void guys are fucking pussies."

That's not true. Linc's jealous of all their muscles.

Hanging up, I meet Ivy's narrowed gaze. "South's about to have emergency surgery to get his appendix out."

"Oh, shit!" With her arm wrapped tightly around my shoulders, she guides me toward the exit. It's hard to under-stand what she's saying, something about appendix opera-tions not being serious. South will be fine. Blah blah blah.

Stepping out into the sunlight, I glance back inside the store—just in time to see Mackenzie lift her phone and snap photos of my backside lumbering away. Well, that will look nice on Instagram.

Just perfect.

52

MIA

Hospital

Seven doctors—five male and two female—sit at a hospital cafe table opposite mine, hooting like drunken barflies. When they arrived ten minutes ago, quiet and serious in their white coats, I prepared to eavesdrop on a difficult case meeting full of juicy medical details. Instead, their conversation is like an episode of Grey's Anatomy.

Doctor Deep-Voice made out with a girl at a post-punk gig on Saturday night. Everyone is impressed. Doctor Bushy-Brows is in love with the new Star Wars movie and outraged when Doctor Pretty-Dimples announces that Disney owns the franchise. Then it's a free for all with the Mickey-Mouse-in-space jokes.

Keen to get back to South, I quickly drain my tea. Yuck. Somehow, I accidentally ordered it with sugar.

I drag my feet all the way to the elevators. I'd love to pick up speed, but with an advanced case of pregnancy, it's out of the question. It's also six o'clock, practically bedtime for me, and my brain has already called it a day.

When I landed in South's room an hour ago, he was still out cold. But, hopefully, he's conscious now. To be sure he's okay, I need to hear him utter a few words, and then I can go home and collapse. After a day spent shopping for baby supplies, my back now aching and stomach heavy, bed is all I can think about.

As I near his room, girlie giggles drift up the hallway, confirming he's awake. Leaning in the doorway, I watch two nurses fawn over him while he entertains them with whatever silliness comes out of his sexy mouth. I clear my throat loudly.

"Hey, Mia!" In full-on party mode, he points at me and then blares at the nurses, "This is my girlfriend."

The nurses stare at my belly as it sails toward them. Sometimes, I wish I could store it behind me, like a handy backpack.

Smiling, I wave, and they make space next to South for me.

"You're sounding pretty happy for someone who's just had an organ ripped out," I say.

His hand taking mine, he gives me a lopsided grin.

"Congratulations," says the more matronly of the nurses as I move tousled hair off his forehead and press my lips against his warm skin.

"When are you due?" asks the younger one. She looks like a finer featured P.J. Harvey, wild black hair escaping her bun and green eyes intense.

"In about ten days. But I wish it was sooner. I'm so uncomfortable."

"No you don't," the older lady says as they waltz toward the door. "Make the most of any sleep you can get. And enjoy as much time alone with your man as possible."

"Good advice," I agree, watching South's palm rub over his thigh in his signature *I'm-thinking-about-sex-right-now* move. Unbelievable. He probably wouldn't say no if I tried to mount him right here on the hospital bed. Even with the nurses watching.

He frowns at my expression, follows my gaze, and laughs down at his hand.

"I'm doing that thing again, huh? I better not tell you what I was picturing. This is freaking awesome, you being here and all. I've never been stoned and happy at the same time before. Everything is perfect." He glances at my stomach. "Except for that..." His finger stabs near the offensive body part as I dare to press it up against the bed.

Mother of pearl, he is totally off his face. "This better not be giving you any ideas on how to spend your down time," I say, shaking my head at him. "How does your stomach feel?"

Wearing a stupidly wide grin, he tries to pull me close.

"Great! Never better. Come here… why are ya so far away? Hey, that nurse looked kinda like Ben, didn't she?"

I sigh. He's so out of it he's practically cross-eyed. "No. No, she didn't. She wasn't even the tiniest bit like him."

"Oh." He pouts at the tree swaying outside the window, then turns back, smiling again. "Know what, Mia? I'm *real* hungry."

"You probably can't eat anything yet."

"Hell, yeah, I can. I could easily throw down a pizza and a large coke."

The muscles in my back spasm, and I wince. "That's not the point. I don't think you're *meant* to eat anything right now. Maybe tomorr—*ow!*"

"Hey, what's wrong?" he asks, putting a hand on my hip and rubbing soft circles with the other over my belly. That's nice. So far, he's only braved touching it during sex, when he's completely gone.

"Is it those Braxton Hiccup things again?"

"Braxton Hicks, silly."

"I know. But I reckon hiccups sounds better. Are you okay?"

"No, they really hurt. They've been happening all day, but they're getting worse instead of better."

His eyes sharpen. "Fuck. That sounds like you're in labor. Do you think that it might be the… is it the—"

"So you *have* been reading those birth books, then."

Smirking, he says, "Yeah, in between reading Metamorphoses in the original Latin. I'm not a total lamebrain." He reaches for the call button. "Shit, Mia, I'll get the nurse back and she can take a look at you—"

"No! Really, there's no need. I'm fine." I rub his chest to distract him and watch his eyes roll back in his head. "But I should go home and get some sleep. I'm just tired. And you need to get some rest, too." I lean close, and with a teasing smile say, "Ivy and I got lots of cute baby things today."

His face scrunches up. "Shit, don't *tell* me about it. Kiss me properly before you go instead."

I do.

And then not wanting to worry him, I get out of there as quickly I can, before the next torturous wave shatters all the vertebrae in my lower back and makes it impossible to hobble down to the car.

An old lady scowls at me as I shuffle past the nurses' station rubbing my spine. I wonder what she's thinking?

It seems South was right, because the waves of pain racking through my body are just how I imagined labor would be, fierce and unstoppable.

Well, Ivy and I are in for one hell of a big night, then, because my baby is definitely on its way, and South is getting exactly what he wished for—to be excused from attending the birth of his child.

I hope he'll be happy.

53

SOUTH

Oh, Baby

The next morning, hungry as a wolf, I try not to drool as a nurse lifts the lid off the breakfast tray. I'm hoping to see mashed potato and gravy, fried chicken, and a big ol' slice of pecan pie.

She pushes the plate toward me, revealing a pile of gross white and orange colored gunk. "What the hell is *that?*" I flop back against the pillow, wincing in pain. "It looks like... yogurt and pureed something-or-other!"

"It sure is, darling." She smiles and tucks escaping strands of frizzy, red hair back into a tight bun. With her soft, round body and plump cheeks, she looks like a kindly grandma, but she sure as heck ain't one.

Despite how pissed I am, I give her my best pleading frown. "But I'd really like some toast, thanks. With lots of butter and jelly."

She laughs at me. "Would you now? If you behave yourself, maybe tomorrow."

I check her name tag. "Please, Martha? I can't eat this rubbish. It's sour and disgusting."

Her expression softens a little. "I suppose I can get you a little honey to sweeten it some."

"No, don't bother. What I need is guys' food. You know, something with gravy on it."

Shaking her head, she says, "Flashing those bright blues at me like that won't work. While I'm in charge, you'll eat what's best for you."

The puppy dog expression slides off my face. Man, this lady loves her rules. She's all *now, young man, it's time for this and now, dear boy, it's time for that*. Tick. Tick. Ticking away at her charts. *Isn't that better?* No, it really fucking isn't. My stomach hurts, and the meds they've given me today are rubbish.

"Smile," she says, floating over to the door. "You'll be okay with the yogurt. You look strong enough to cope."

My scowl disappears as she collides with Nate who barrels into the room as though he's running from a pack of wild groupies. I laugh hard, holding my stomach because it hurts like crazy.

Quiff bouncing and amber eyes dancing, he looks hyper. Maybe he's on something. Whatever. I'm so hungry my belly thinks my throat's been cut, so I spoon white gunk into my mouth.

"Congratulations," he yells when he lands at my bedside.

"Huh?" Grimacing at the taste of my disappointing breakfast, I force myself to swallow. "For what? Still being alive after surgery?"

"No, man. You've got a daughter!"

"I've got a *what?*" For some fool reason, I shove a second spoonful of white stuff in my trap.

"Mia had the baby last night. Or this morning. Quarter past two to be exact."

Brain on fire, I can only stare, then I spit yogurt back into the tray before I choke on it.

"*Shiiit,*" says Nate. "I'm not sure I did the right thing by telling you. You've gone white like you're in—"

"*Shock?*" I yell, trying to push off the bed. "Ow! *Fuck.* Help me get this damn trolley out of the way. Is Mia okay?"

"Yep, she did good. It took a while, but everything went fine." Crossing his arms, Nate watches me struggle.

"And the baby?"

"Big and healthy."

And a girl just like Mia had thought it would be.

I freeze.

A baby. A healthy baby.

Desperate to get up, I resume wrestling with the bed linen and the trolley, but they won't do what I want. "Cut me a break here, will ya, and help me. Don't just stand there like you're watching something amusing on Netflix!"

"Well, what am I supposed to do? You're not going anywhere like that—"

"I fucking well am."

"No you're not. You're definitely not going anywhere today."

Sagging backward and pressing my palms over my gut, I jostle the trolley weakly. "I've gotta get out of here."

Like he's got all the time in the world, Nate lowers himself into the bedside chair, smirking up at me. "Just chill. You have to wait. There's absolutely no point literally busting your gut about it. When are they letting you out of here anyway?"

"Fuck. Friday." I scowl. "Or maybe Thursday if all goes well."

"That sucks. But, look, today's Tuesday so Thursday's not really that far away. Guess you'd better be a good boy for the nurses."

"Nate, it's not funny. She'll need me there."

"Now *that's* hilarious. She didn't even want us to tell you. Didn't want you to freak out and hurt yourself. Like you're kinda doing now."

Strangling the sheet, I stare at the veins on my hands, turn them over, and inspect the callouses on my fingers.

I've got a child.

A daughter.

Man, I feel nauseous and Nate studying me like I'm a science project really isn't helping.

"She'll be fine. Nico and Ivy are there with her and,

anyway, you've spent weeks telling me you didn't want this. That you weren't planning on being at the birth and—"

"But see? This is my punishment for saying all that shit. Abbie was right. There definitely is a god and I've pissed him or her off big time. Would you please tell me what I'm meant to do now?"

"Lie back. Eat your food and keep your cell close. Ben and I are heading over to the *other* hospital now. I'll give you a full report after I've seen Mia. *And* your baby. I'm pretty excited."

"Yeah, me too. I'm fucking thrilled for you," I grouch. "It's so nice that you get to see my kid before I do."

"Tough. Want me to send you a photo?"

"No, thanks." I heave a sigh. "I'll wait to see the real thing. Marco said fresh outta the belly ones look pretty gross, kinda like wrinkled pecan nuts."

"It's probably not gross if it's yours, though." Nate gets to his feet. Rubbing at the back of his neck, he says, "Are you alright?"

"*No.* No, I'm not alright."

Instead of offering sympathy, he laughs all the way to the door. Before he disappears through it, he turns back so I can see his smartass face. "Just relax. Watch some talking cat videos. I'll get Ben to send you through some new ones. He's always collecting them for you."

"Yeah. Awesome. Thanks so much," I say loudly. "Dickhead."

He stuffs his hands in his pockets and strides off chuckling.

After staring at my breakfast for ten minutes, I decide I'll eat it slowly and scrape the spoon over the bowl until it looks like I've licked the damn thing clean. I'll even drink my fake-tasting juice. I plan to do everything nurse Martha and her cronies say, no matter how stupid their orders are. I'll eat anything, even a cat, if it'll get me out of here by Thursday at the latest. But first, I need to call Mia.

If I don't hear her voice soon, I'll go crazy.

54

SOUTH

Gold

Thursday afternoon, I'm in the birth center, pressing my hands over my guts to stop them spilling out while I glare at Mia as she lies in bed, propped against pillows.

"You called her *what*?" I try not to yell but fail miserably.

"You heard. Sanne."

The nurse gives me daggers and tucks the blanket tighter around the lump that I guess must be the kid. "How do you pronounce that?" she asks, her lips no longer pursed but stretched into a kind smile as she looks at Mia.

"Sah-na."

The nurse's smile grows even sweeter. "Oh, it's lovely—"

"But people won't know how to say it! I'm not calling her that. No way. You have to change it."

"It's not *your* choice, South. I'm not changing it. And coming straight from your hospital bed doesn't give you the right to be mean. In fact, you can go away if you're going to be horrible."

Nope, I'm not going anywhere. Fuck that.

I rush toward the bed, then stare down at Mia, taking her in. Her hair is a mess, eyes a flat dark brown, no gold sparking in them like usual, skin pale. She looks as exhausted as I feel. Probably best not to mention that right now. She might throw the baby at me.

The baby.

"Do you want to see her or are you just going to stand there gawking at me?"

Shit. I clear my throat and shuffle my feet. "I guess I—"

"Well, come around here, then." She pats the space next to her on the double bed. It's just a plain white piece of waffle blanket. Seems okay. Pretty comfortable. I look at the floor, back at her again. Swallow.

"Hurry up. We're not going to hurt you if that's what you're worried about."

Christ, she's right. I am scared of babies. Kids. Anything in a stroller, really. They drag me down into nightmares—the insides of dark closets, beatings. Parents who never gave a shit and caused pain and fear.

I take a big breath.

Chest tight, I crawl onto the bed, lean against the head-board and keep my eyes fixed on my boots.

The nurse shakes her head. "I'll leave you to it, honey. Just holler if you need anything."

"Thanks Claudette. I will." Mia smiles at the wide back, stiff with disapproval, as it leaves the room.

Face serious, Mia turns to me. "Look," she whispers, pulling back the lilac blanket.

And I do.

I look.

Staring down at a tiny scrunched up face that turns out to have nothing in common with a pecan nut, I take in all the tiny details. A head covered in thick, black hair, dark eyelashes that stroke pale, velvety cheeks, and the tiniest pursed lips I've ever seen. I feel the strangest sensation build in my gut and rise to my throat. I'm mute. Couldn't say a word to save my life.

Mia's eyes track over me. She can probably see the fast rise and fall of my chest, feel me trembling. She shifts her weight, pressing her arm against mine. "Here, take her."

I make a strangled sound and shake my head. "No—"

"Take her," Mia insists as she dumps the tightly swaddled bundle in my lap.

My arm curls automatically around the baby and lifts it to my chest. Before I can stop myself, my hand tucks the blanket under the tiny pointed chin so I can see better. Christ. Look at it. It's so small. So fragile.

Heart thumping, I stare at the tiny fingers. Now, *they* can't be real. I stroke them just to check, finding them warm and soft. Never have I felt anything like it.

The miniature fingers wriggle. "Shit," I say as the baby clasps my thumb. Mia laughs, and I look at her in wonder.

"She's strong, huh?" she says.

Strong? What does that word mean? I don't know. I've forgotten the meaning of every word, every *thing* as I sit there dumbfounded, my bones dissolving.

A warm energy buzzes through me, soft like the blue sky outside, then it shifts to a mildly nauseating burn. Slowly, I blow out the breath I've been holding and let the feeling settle into a gentle frequency. Perfect sunshine. All major chords and jangling notes. A golden song getting louder.

"So, what do you think?" Mia asks.

"Huh? I… uh…" I shake my head, trying to clear it. "I don't know. Just… *wow.* Wait until Abbie sees her. Nate said she's arriving tonight."

Mia's chin digs into my shoulder, her fingers stroking through strands of my hair. "Well, is she as scary as you imagined she'd be?"

I huff out a laugh. "No. I guess she's not too scary." Taking a big breath, I look deep into Mia's beautiful eyes, "I think she's pretty cool."

She smiles.

I smile.

Then, finally understanding what an idiot I've been, I kiss her. Each soft press of my lips, every single sigh is an apology, a plea for forgiveness. My head spins, my brain fragments, and my heart softens like syrup, opening and growing bigger in my chest as I give thanks to the powers that be that I'm here, that she's letting me hold her close.

And the baby—I give thanks for her too.

Fading sunlight streams through the window, turning the baby's skin gold. I won't call her Sanne.

I think Sunny suits her much better.

55

MIA

Donuts?

I watch South pace around the hospital room, his biker boots clomping against the floor. He's quite a sight, muscles and tats encased in a gray t-shirt and black jeans, his tawny hair and blazing blue eyes offset by the neon-colored flowers piled everywhere.

In truth, his stride is more of a rolling prowl, like what he does on stage. He moves one way, then turns sharply, angling off toward a different corner in time to some urgent inner beat.

Now that he's facing me, I can see his lips move against the baby's dark hair. His eyes are glazed and dreamy. Where has he voyaged to? Because, currently, only about ten percent of him is present with me in the room. When he passes close to the bed, I hear the song he's singing. A hypnotic lullaby. And one I've never heard before.

Biting my lip, I smile at him, and his lips quirk back as he sings louder. The melody coils around me, the song's frequency warm and golden and reassuring.

The baby likes it, too.

My breast milk still isn't in, and no amount of colostrum or cuddling from me has been able to settle Sanne. But South can do it. Of course.

The door opens and in walks Claudette pushing the lunch trolley, haughty expression fixed on South. The song stops.

"Oh, I see you've decided to grace us with your presence again today. Decided we're not so bad, have you?"

Heat flushes my face. I should never have told Claudette about South's lack of interest in becoming a father. The nurse seems certain that he timed his appendicitis attack to avoid the birth.

Well, I disagree with her because as soon he escaped his hospital bed Thursday, he rushed straight over to see us. And he hung around all yesterday looking charmed with Sanne as he laughed at his diaper folding attempts, calling himself a *diaper-master-in-training.*

Today is Saturday, and he's here again for the third day in a row, so I can't help but feel optimistic.

South tucks the swaddled bundle under his chin, and watches Claudette sneer at him. She fumbles her foot around for the trolley brake, her sensible, black shoe missing its mark. Her arms swing wildly and she overbalances, crashing down onto her butt. Luckily, it's fairly well padded.

"Help her!" I say to South, but it's too late, he's gone hysterical. I stretch my arms out. "Give me the baby."

Laughing so hard, he makes no sound as he folds at the waist, clutching his belly with one hand and weaving toward the bed.

Muttering, Claudette fumbles onto all fours.

"South, don't just laugh! Do something to help her. Give me Sanne first."

Shaking his head helplessly, his laugh gets louder. Other than talking cats, nothing makes him lose it more than witnessing a fall.

Undisturbed, Sanne sleeps on.

Claudette gets to her feet and brushes off her blue uniform.

"I'm sorry." South winces. "Shit, that really hurts my stomach."

Claudette opens her mouth but before she can scold, Doctor Oh No lopes into the room.

"Mia!" He skids to a stop, eyes widening as they land on South who stares back, looking confused.

Claudette places the tray on my table, sniffs loudly, and then bustles out of the room.

"Ah ha!" the doctor booms. "So *this* must be the donut maker."

Oh, shit. The trouble with lies is that they always come back to bite you when you least expect it.

Hand stuck out, Doctor Oh No heads for South.

Wearing his adorable confused frown, South moves the baby over to the other arm and shakes the doctor's hand.

Smirking, Doctor Oh No says, "So, tell me, how goes the donut trade?"

South cocks his head. "Huh?"

I swallow and quake silently.

"Your bakery. How's business?"

South glances at me, then back to the doctor. "Uh, I don't... I'm not a—"

"No, you're not, are you? Word around here is that you're actually some kind of rock star." The doctor inspects South, scrutinizing the full package, all that tallness and the muscles, the whole messed-up, golden-haired beauty. "I suppose that makes more sense."

He turns slowly toward the bed. "And how's the new mother going? Got anything you'd like to say to me?"

Wow. I'm pretty sure doctors aren't meant to be quite so familiar with their patients. It's why I like him so much—his directness is usually so refreshing. But right now it's absolutely terrifying.

Stuff it. I'd better fess up. Face burning hot, I say, "I'm so sorry, Doctor Campbell."

He smiles patiently while South's eyebrows dive into a scowl. He steps closer to the bed, uneasy gaze bouncing between me and the doctor.

"I... I may have made up the donut maker under pressure, on the spot because... at the time I couldn't tell South about the... the baby."

South's boots scuff over the floor beside me.

The doctor gives a paternal nod. "I understand. You weren't together at that point."

"Like hell we weren't!" South explodes, making Sanne snuffle. "Sh shhh. Shit, sorry, baby girl." Swaying from side to side, he rocks her in his arms.

"South, maybe try not to swear," I chide. "She's a baby, not a band member."

The doctor beams at South. "You'd better get used to that dance. You're likely to be doing it for a few years. All night long." He rests his hip against the bed frame. "So this one here is your boyfriend, then?"

"Well, not officially—" I start to say.

"*Yes.* What are you, nuts? Of course I am." South glowers.

"Hm, that sounds complicated." Doctor Oh No scratches his head. "But he's the father no doubt."

"Yes, I am," says South, still glaring at me as if he fears I'm going to deny the fact.

Little fists flailing, Sanne's cries get louder. I hold my arms out, and South huddles next to me and passes the tiny parcel over.

Smiling at South, the doctor says, "Well, congratulations. I *think*. You've two great girls there. Probably a good idea to hang on to them."

While I wrestle out a breast, South says, "I plan to."

He plans to. *He plans to.* Maybe that means he *is* officially mine again. I just wish he'd confirm it with more words. Ones about fatherhood. And happiness. And forever.

Nine days he's been back home, and I've spent the entire time confused but leaving him be, applying no pressure. I suppose I hoped that when he saw his child, clarity would hit him like a thunderbolt.

He has two choices. He can either run screaming from the nightmare of his own childhood or surrender to fatherhood, giving himself the chance to heal. My heart squeezes at the image of him wishing Sanne and I a good life as he boards a tour bus and leaves us forever.

All I want is for him to try out being a dad and give our new little family a chance.

Our eyes meet and he smiles. He seems dazed but happy. Like he's been struck by lightning and has already made the right choice.

While I attach the baby to my sore nipple the doctor ticks at his clipboard. "Feeding going okay?"

"No, she's starving. We both can't *wait* for my milk to come in."

South shuffles closer. Smiling down at my boob, his face filled with wonder, he pulls the swaddling away from his daughter's cheek so he can watch her feed. Or at least attempt to get some sustenance.

"Looks like you're managing them both well there, Mia." Doctor Campbell nods at South leaning into the action, totally absorbed. "I think you'll all be fine. I'll come back at the end of my rounds and do a proper checkup, leave you three to enjoy this in peace. See you in half an hour."

"He seems nice," South says dreamily as the door clicks shut. "Looks a bit like—"

"Sean Connery, I know. Frank calls him Doctor Oh No and he…" Whoops. What have I done?

The cobalt eyes widen, his face only two inches away, I can see fire spark in the gold sun-bursts around his pupils.

"Oh, you mean your other boyfriend. Frank the donut-guy?"

"South, I never—"

"Don't lie to me again, Mia."

Sanne pauses in her effort to drain me dry, an all too familiar frown of anguish scrunched over her forehead. My heart bleeds with love as I quickly get the baby back on track and sucking like a gummy baby-vamp.

"Ow, holy crap, that hurts."

"Language." He smirks, long fingers stroking my cheek. "Sorry, I distracted her. Next time I'll yell at you more quiet-ly." Focusing on the action again, he laughs. "Aw, look at that. She's kneading your tit."

"Yep, it's like getting blood from a stone, though, little one. And, South, must you use the word *tit*? I already feel like a bloated cow sitting in a field without you chiming in with comments like that."

"You look pretty good to me."

"You'll say just about anything to get in my pants."

He sucks the corner of his lip and nods in agreement. "Okay, so sure, you do look tired. But still very fuc—"

I push his shoulder, and he laughs at me, completely shameless.

"You're so bad. You'll have to ignore half of what comes out of his mouth, Sanne."

"So, exactly how long do you have to wait?"

I don't need to ask what he means. "Four to six weeks."

His jaw drops. "Right. So, four weeks, then. I'll be in Memphis I think, but on a plane back home straight after the show. Obviously."

"Just so you're fully informed, women don't actually feel like sex when they're breastfeeding all night long and soothing crying babies every second of the day."

He gives a confident smirk. "We'll see about that."

I frown. "Apparently, it's a major triumph if you can manage to grab a shower in the day. It's very hard, you know?"

"Uh-huh. I reckon I will be."

He's incorrigible. "Well you can have your fantasies, but the reality is that you'll be woken up every couple of hours to change a screaming baby's diaper while I nag at you. Em's filled me in on all the gory details. It's not pretty."

"Em?"

"Marco's wife, silly. Remember her?"

"Yeah, well, she had twins. Of course *that* was difficult. I'm amazed she lets Marco near her even six years later."

Oh, boy, he has no idea what's coming, or rather *not* coming, if he decides he's in for the long haul.

"Anyway, no pressure, Mia. I'll just change the diapers and then drool on your tits if that's all that I'm allowed to do." Noticing my disapproval, his eyebrows cross. "Oh, sorry. Boobs? Breasts? Bosom—*ow*—don't hurt me—I'm fragile at the moment."

Smiling, I smooth the skin I'd pinched on his arm, then stroke his hair and run a palm along his stubbly jaw. Then his lips are on mine, his warm hands bracketing my face. Whole body heating, I'm beginning to think this boy could turn me on even if my heart stopped beating.

All too soon he pulls back. "I made a mistake, Mia. *Again*. I was an idiot to push you away. When I found you at Abbie's, I should have tried to understand. Listened to you."

"Yep. You should have. But we were both wrong. I was a coward not telling you in the first place because I didn't want to lose you, and then the Rita thing... How could I not have had faith in you?"

Hands tightening into fists, he looks out the window. "I've been thinking it was my turn to save you but now I don't know... maybe all along I just needed to man up and save myself. Forget about my past."

I rub his compass tattoo and he turns slowly, his face serious and his eyes clear and steady. "I'm gonna finish the U.S. leg of the tour, slay some dragons, and then I'm coming back for you. For both of you. I want this, Mia, and you'll see... I'm gonna be the guy you always told me I was. The one who'll be there for you and our baby no matter what. So, do you think you'll be okay with that?"

I nod. There's no other choice. No other guy for me. For Sanne.

Tension leaving his shoulders, his smile stretches wide as he draws me close. "I fucking love you," he whispers against my ear.

As far as declarations go, it's hardly poetic, but to me, his words are a magical spell, binding and perfect.

"And Sanne, too. I love her, Mia. I didn't know I would... that it would feel like this. Like my heart has to live outside my body in the shape of some wrinkly little sucking machine. But you're mine, both of you. Forever."

"I love you so much," I say as I stroke his cheek.

He nods, his grin huge.

Arching an eyebrow at him, I can't help but tease. "But you want just the two of us? What about Frank the baker?

"Yeah, about him… you've sure got some explaining to do. Pass me the kid and start talking."

While he waits for me to detach Sanne, he pulls the bedside table over and lifts the lid off my lunch tray. "Mm, what's this? It smells good." His lips twist as he peers down at gooey macaroni cheese. "*Hey*, how come they don't give *you* sour yogurt? I think I'll be checking into this hospital the next time I need one."

I laugh. "That might be difficult. In case you haven't noticed, you'll need to be pregnant to do that."

56

SOUTH

Reward

"Suth, get off Lane's computer, will ya? We need to get cooking down at the bar." Gripping my shoulder, Ben leans down and peers into the screen. "Oh, hey, Mia. Hey, little Sunnywunny."

I shrug Ben off. "Don't talk to her like that. She's a baby, not a rabbit."

Scoffing, Ben smacks my head. "How goes it back home?" he asks Mia, who bounces our gurgling baby on her lap, platinum plaits and big smile heating my blood.

She laughs while I scowl at Ben, flicking hair out of my eyes.

"I heard you broke your bass on stage tonight, Ben. Good

effort! All's great here. Sanne's got South's lung power, though, so I could really do with some more sleep."

"Two more weeks, babe, and I'll be there to—"

"Hassle you for sex," Lane shouts from the bed. Our manager is always thrilled to have an Up Void member or two in his hotel room. Gives him easy targets to bitch at.

"I was gonna say *help*, but I wouldn't mind some sex."

"Marco's been counseling him," Ben says as he wraps his arm around my chest. "To not expect any. But South is pretty desperate, Mia, so you might want to take pity on him."

I shove Ben off. "Stop trying to cuddle up. It's annoying." Face close to the screen, I say, "There won't be any pity sex going on, will there, Mia?"

She moves her eyes over me in that molten way of hers, and my temperature goes up several degrees. "No. I'm looking forward to giving you a very enthusiastic welcome home."

Fuck.

Yes.

My smile grows wider, and Ben smacks my head again. "Keep it clean, Romeo. In case you've forgotten, Lane and I are still here."

Oh, yeah. I stop rubbing my thigh.

"Come on, man, let's go. You got everything?" Ben asks.

I pat over my pockets. "Wait on. Let me check... yep. Got it. I have to go, Mia. I love you. I'll call you in the morning."

"Okay! Love you lots."

Smiling at her, I end the FaceTime call, clicking randomly over the mouse pad.

Lane leaps off the bed. "Leave my computer alone!" He takes over the keyboard and scrutinizes the screen. "What have you done? Ah, *shit*, South. You'll never get a job in I.T."

"Good."

"Or any kind of desk job."

"Okay, fine." I get to my feet and stretch.

"No need to look so pleased with your incompetence."

"Sure." I start walking.

Lane throws the room service menu at my back. "Get the fuck out of here!"

"We're gone already." Ben laughs and shuts the door on Lane's sour face.

"Would you stop that?" I say, watching Ben rub his hands together as we head for the elevator. "You look like Vince."

"But it's exciting." Black eyes shining, Ben grins. "Aren't you pumped?"

I push him into the elevator. "I'm buzzing with it." That's an understatement. I whack the ground floor button and we zip down.

As the elevator doors open onto the African-safari-themed hotel bar, I search through an excess of zebra print for Nate. *Bam.* Just as planned, he and Zave are huddled around a booth drinking with *Rita*, the space next to her vacant.

Whistling an old gunslinger movie theme, I stalk forward with Ben chuckling at my side.

We arrive at the table and I take a moment to enjoy the setup. "Hey," I boom, sliding into the booth seat and moving close to Rita.

In surprise, she looks down at my thigh pressed against

hers. I grin and lay my arm along the back of the seat, just above her shoulders, snuggling up to her.

With a hint of a sly smile playing around her lips, she clears her throat and sips her wine.

Nate holds his fingers up at me. *Three.* Perfect. This is her third drink, so she'll be in just the right state, not sober enough to be suspicious and not too sloppy.

"You took your time. Been talking to your *girlfriend* again?" Nate asks.

Summoning my limited acting chops, I roll my eyes. "Not sure if you can call the baby squealing like a stuck pig and Mia moaning and complaining *talking* but, yeah, I guess I was. Jesus. I really can't handle that shit after a show, you know? I'm trashed. I just need to kick back." I smile at Rita's chest, her lips, and then, finally, into her eyes.

She smiles back.

"What you *need*," says Zave, pushing his empty beer bottle back and forth over the table, "is some action. If you know what I mean."

"Damn straight. Ah'm hornier than a three-balled tom cat."

Nate coughs loudly. Okay, so maybe sounding like some in-bred in a horror film is overplaying it a little. I raise an eyebrow at Rita and badly want to laugh at the shocked look on her face.

"You should just do it, man," Nate says. "None of us would tell Mia. Would we, Rita?"

She shakes her head. "No. No, I wouldn't tell her. A guy's got his needs, right? And it wouldn't necessarily mean anything if South slept with someone else out on tour. Most musos do."

"Trouble is, you fuck a groupie there's always the chance that it could get out to the press," said Zave. "Then you'd be *literally* screwed. You need an insider. Shame that guys don't do it for ya, South, because Ben would sleep with anyone. He'd never tell on you. And as a bonus, he's probably got some mad skills, too."

Looking proud rather than offended, Ben grins like the village idiot.

Nate runs his fingers over the leopard print table lamp. "What about you, Rita? Would you be up for a little harmless fun with South?"

Her mouth drops open. Obviously unsure of the right answer, she studies my face, no doubt remembering her attempt to fuck me on the bus. That failed effort might make her hesitate.

Giving her what I hope will pass for a hot look, I ignore my bandmates' stares and lean into her personal airspace, the silence turning heavy around us. When my mouth is an inch from hers, I whisper, "Want me to fuck you?"

As her breathing ramps up, I pull back and stare at her lips, stroking over them with my thumb. "What do you say?"

Eyes closing like a cat's in a warm lap, she nods.

"Right, your room, then. Let's move it."

She goes limp, so I help her out of the booth while the guys smirk, wishing us a long, hot night. I tow her along to the elevators.

On the journey to the tenth floor, I keep my arm slung

around her shoulders, her bony body pulled close, and stare ahead, feeling her tremble. I shake a little myself, and it's not because I'm turned on.

The elevator doors whoosh open. We stroll up the hallway, my steps slow and in sync with the deep breaths I take, in no hurry to arrive at her room. The carpet and walls blur at the sides of my vision, creating a tunnel of green and gold. It feels like I'm tripping on acid.

While Rita fumbles with her hotel door, there's an annoying buzzing noise that I eventually realize is her voice.

"Sorry, what did you say?"

"I said that I can't believe you're finally giving in to this thing that's been sizzling between us after all this time. You're a very patient guy, South. I can't wait."

"Huh. Same," I lie.

She closes the door and makes for the bed, stripping off her skin-tight, black top as she goes, then her ankle boots and ripped black jeans. "Do you have any idea how hot you sound when your accent goes way down south like that?"

Making no comment, I only stare at her. How many times might Mia have said something similar to me if Rita hadn't flapped her forked tongue around?

Wearing only underwear and a wild look in her eyes, she steps close and pulls my head down. I let her kiss me, parting my lips to give her access, to make it feel real. My heart pounds its disgust.

One.

Two.

Three.

Four. And then I push her away, struggling not to wipe my mouth.

"I've gotta use the bathroom." I give her a slow smile. What I really want to give her is a kick in the skinny ass. "You'd better be ready for me when I come back."

Breathing loudly, she trails her creepy eyes over me as I turn and walk away.

In the bathroom, I lean over the sink, my shaking getting worse. Part of me wants to walk out now because I feel like an asshole. Then I remind myself she deserves this.

If Rita hadn't lied and kept *on* lying, Mia would have told me about the pregnancy as she'd planned to a long, long time ago, I'm sure of it. And, yeah, I probably would've gone ape-shit and AWOL for a while, but then, hopefully, come around to the idea of a baby during Mia's pregnancy.

Thanks to Rita, I never got the chance to take care of Mia through those long months of having to grow our daughter by herself—the whole time feeling unloved, unwanted. I know what feeling loveless is like when you're vulnerable and it ain't fucking good. It kills me to know she went through that.

I splash water on my face and dry off with a towel. "Here goes nothing," I tell my reflection, then open the door.

Rita lies spread-eagled on her back, buck naked. Leaning up on her elbows she smiles manically. "Hurry up and ditch those clothes. I want to see that hard body of yours."

Sure, I'll be happy to show her something hard in a minute.

When I reach the edge of the bed, she gets up on her

knees, shuffling close. Biting her lip, she looks up at me and undoes the button on my jeans. I hang my head close and stare into her eyes, my chest pumping.

"Want me to suck you first?"

"Nope."

A crease appears between her eyebrows. Not easily deterred, she puts her palm over me and rubs firmly. I sneer down at my traitorous, hardening dick. That's okay. Starved for action, it would probably get excited if someone ate a hot dog in front of me or blew energetically on Scottish bagpipes.

"Lay down," I command

She smiles coyly. "Are you finally gonna give it to me, South?"

"Yeah. I am."

Body draped against the covers, her fingers circle over her stomach. Guess she imagines that looks enticing. I take the folded envelope from my back pocket and drop it on her chest.

She sits up. "What the hell's this?"

"It's your fuck you, Rita. You're officially sacked."

"But, South—"

"Don't ask Lane for a reference. Don't speak to any of us again. If you try to contact me or Mia, you'll get a restraining order slapped on you so fast it'll knock the eyeballs from your mad skull. What you did, lying about me to my girl? It was not only insane, but vicious. You're fucking up lives with that kinda shit."

"But I don't understand. Why now?"

I give her an unpleasant smile. "This whole tour, every

single person knew what an evil bitch you'd been. Lane just kept you on the payroll so you wouldn't tell me about Sanne and fuck things up even more. He was *using* you."

Mouth opening and closing, she snatches her top off the bed, covering her chest with it. Yeah, like that's gonna reinstate any dignity.

"I wouldn't touch a head case like you for anything. Do yourself a favor and get on some meds. Have a nice life." I exit fast, slamming the door behind me.

Fuck.

I want to sag against the wall while I get control of my breathing, but I don't. Instead, I get my feet pounding over the carpet and speed in the direction of the bar, away from the psycho.

Head light and body buzzing, I stretch my arms out like wings and fly along. Finally, after months of suppression, I've let Rita see the rage burning in my eyes, let her feel it radiate from my skin. And it was fan-fucking-tastic.

On the phone tomorrow, Mia will tell me it's time to forgive. To let go of grudges. She's way too nice, but annoyingly right. And I figure I probably will let myself forgive Rita —one day—when I'm a little older and wiser.

So, that's dragon number one slayed. Dragon number two —look out—because I'm on my way.

In two weeks I'll be back in Tennessee, on my home turf, and facing up to the craziest witch of all. I'm not scared.

Liar. I'm fucking petrified.

Standing in the elevator, I text Nate. *It's done. I'm on my way down. Row up the shots.*

What a night. I badly need a drink or six. And a laugh. My cell pings.

Nate: *Mia's sent me a special video from the Great Dane wedding she took you to before you guys were an item. It's a compilation of guests' footage, the highlight being that beast of a groom slamming you into a boulder. Wait until you see it. It's fucking hilarious.*

Cool. That sounds like my kinda fun.

57

SOUTH

The Dragon

"Are you sure your mom still lives there?" Mia asks, her voice coming through the rental car's speakers in an ethereal waft.

It's a perfect fall day. Better than perfect for the season, really, because it's warm.

"Yeah," I reply. "Abbie's got some people around town who keep tabs on her. She's there alright, living the life. You know, going to the dollar store in her pajamas, scratching people's eyes out in a battle for the last packet of Twinkies on the shelf."

The motor is too darn silent as I idle at the lights, gripping the steering wheel tightly and squinting into the morning sun. I prefer a car with a little more grunt, an older one that tells its stories in moans and snarls. Anyway, this one will get me where I need to go. Back to hell and out again.

"So how do you feel? Are you scared?"

"Damn right I'm scared. I haven't seen her in like… must be getting on to eight years. If the wicked old witch actually opens the door I might pass out." The lights turn green, and I ease my foot down on the pedal. "Or cry."

"You sure you should be doing this on your own?"

"Just like I told Nate last night, it's for the best, believe me. If things get too hairy, all I have to do is think of tonight. It's Memphis, babe. The last show finally. It's been a long three weeks, but tomorrow I'm on a plane back to you. Nothing can touch me now."

"I can't help but worry. It seems wrong that you're on your own with this, South. Where are you at the moment?"

"I've just had breakfast in Nashville, and I'm cruising out of town. I reckon I'll be there in about an hour and a half. I'm not planning on staying long. Then I've got maybe a five-hour drive to the gig and that's it. I'm done. If I focus on the fact that I'll be lying in the blue room blissing out with you and Sanne tomorrow, I can do it, Mia."

"You might not be blissing out when you hear her cry."

"Ah cain't wait to hear it."

She laughs. "Aw, listen to you sounding all hick-boy."

I feign outrage. "Are you insulting me at a time like this?"

"When have I ever dared to do that?"

"When? Shit, I ain't got enough fingers and toes to count all the times."

"Is it because you're back down south, hearing everyone around you talk like that?"

"Probably. And maybe because of nerves. I feel a bit light headed."

"Speaking of fingers and toes, I've decided it can be your job to cut Sanne's nails. You won't believe what a harrowing experience it is!"

"Sure. I'm a pretty skilled nail technician, so that'll be a cinch."

Just as I hoped she would, she laughs at my unjustified bragging.

"I should go and let you concentrate on driving. Call me as soon as you leave your mom's. And no matter what she says, remember that you're a really *really* great guy. Not many people could get through a childhood like yours and still be such a good person, kind and funny. After your start in life, the fact that you even have a sense of humor, let alone a brilliant one, amazes me. I love you. I'll be thinking of you."

"Love you, too. I'll call ya soon. Kiss Sunny for me."

"I like it when you call her that," she says, and hangs up.

I sail through the last set of traffic lights before hitting the open road and turning the radio up loud. Now I'm alone and about as ready as I ever will be to face the dragon.

Nearly two hours later, I park on a sad looking street and squint at peeling green weatherboards glimpsed through a wire fence and a weed-filled garden. Garden is too generous a description, really. The cottage, the whole scene, looks pretty depressing.

Well, I guess it's now or never.

Now or never.

I can drive off. Or I can man up.

What's the worst thing that can happen?

Fuck it. I'm going in.

Taking three big breaths, I climb out of the car, push open the iron gate that swings from a piece of rotting wood by one hinge, and move in a daze toward the porch.

As I lift my hand to the door, my vision blurs. *Shit.* I knock and wait. Nothing happens. I rap harder. Faster. Again nothing.

And then a voice straight out of my nightmares screams, "Fuck off, Sammy!"

Holy shit. It's definitely her. "Mom, it's me, South." Hell, my voice shakes like I'm a chickenshit kid. I pull out my phone, stare at the photo of Mia and Sunny on the lock screen. Then I clear my throat. "Come on! I haven't got all day. Open up."

Silence. Then footsteps. The door swings open and there she is, smaller, older, and meaner looking than I remember. Blond hair long and lank and thin. Eyes wide but with the *crazy* signs flashing neon-bright in them.

Mom.

Fuck.

In her track pants and Pearl Jam t-shirt that might not have been washed since the mid-nineties, she looks fifteen years older than her forty. Easy.

Her mouth keeps opening and shutting.

I want to stick two fingers down her throat and jab hard. Instead I breathe real slow through my nose, like how I used to when Up Void first started gigging, before I learned not to give a shit about what people thought. When my kicking pulse settles a little, I say, "So, are you gonna let me in?"

She steps back, I figure more out of shock than in any gesture of welcome.

The door opens directly onto a living room crammed with two sad looking couches, a TV, and a huge fucking mess. At the other end of the rectangle a compact kitchen is stacked against the far wall, dishes and filth covering every surface.

On her way to the beige laminated table, she grabs a bottle of gin from a side bench, and then pulls up a chair. The smells and sounds and general horrors of childhood envelope me.

Unable to move or even speak, for a full minute I watch her fill her coffee mug and sit there sipping at it, like I'm not in the room.

"Want some?" she finally grates, still not looking at me.

A skinny, black cat stretches out along the windowsill, adjusting its position at the sound of her voice. The plastic outdoor chair scrapes as I drag it along the floor and sit opposite her. "No thanks."

Cigarette flapping between her lips, she pats her pockets. "Too high and mighty now to have a drink with your ma, are ya?"

I slide a box of matches over a pile of junk mail toward her. "Eleven o'clock is a little early for me to get a buzz on. I'm heading to Memphis after here and it's a long drive."

"Got a show, I 'spose."

"Yeah. Then I'm heading back east."

"You live out that way?"

"Yeah." I meet her denim-colored eyes dead on. "I've got a girl there." I'll keep it singular for now. The less she knows about my life the better.

Her eyebrows shoot up. "Gotta go to the cities to get a good tramp these days, do ya?"

Eyes narrowing to slits, I say, "You're drunk."

Giggling like a ding-a-ling, she points at me and nods. "Darn straight, and I'm a lot higher than Clingmans Dome."

"Yep. Nothing's changed then."

"Well, *you* sure as hell have changed. You're a whole lot bigger'n last time ah seen ya. What was ya again? Fifteen?"

"Seventeen. Remember that time you showed up at Abbie's? *I'll* never forget it, that's for sure."

"Abbie! That self-righteous, too-big-for-her-britches, egg-suckin' child stealer." She cackles, the sound cutting out abruptly as she casts a critical eye over me. "So, you're a man now."

"I suppose I am. No thanks to you."

Half a cup of gin splashes over my face and hair, dripping onto my blue t-shirt. *Great.* Now I'll need a shower before I catch up with Nate or he'll freak out, presuming I've fallen back on old habits. Rather than use any cloth in this fetid excuse for a home, I wipe myself off with my top.

She starts with the usual screaming. "You were always a selfish little ingrate and you—"

"Fine," I interrupt, getting to my feet. "You don't want to know what I came here for? No problem. I'm going."

"Wait, South… Cain't ya sit down for five minutes? Tell me what's brought you here and got your knickers all knotted up?" She twists her lips at me, an attempt at a smile, and pours another drink.

Fuck, she's about as crazy as a soup sandwich. Sitting there smiling one second and frowning and swaying the next, she looks certifiable. I feel sorry for her and hardly angry at all. Certainly not scared. Only numb and sad.

A deep ache pounds in my chest, and I think of Abbie. Warm Abbie. Safe Abbie. Abbie who always loved me. *Thank you, Abbie, for saving me from this shitful life.*

I clear my throat and sit again. "Victor still gone?"

"Yeah. Your asshole of a father has done another runner—"

"Hey. Woah. He's not my *father*. Don't say—"

"That's right. You're that demon's spawn, ain't ya? I wanna know if you do it to girls like that, South. Ya like hurting them and makin' them scream? Like father, like son, is it?"

Brain spinning, I lean close. "Shut. Up." Huh. That feels a whole lot better. I flop back into the chair and toss a large envelope on the table. "Here. This is for you."

She eyes it like it's a sack of shit stinking to high heaven. "What is it?"

I lick my lips. "It's paperwork for a bank account. It's got money in it. A lot of it."

Her eyes gleam, probably thinking about all the drugs she can buy with the dough.

"All you've gotta do is go down to the bank in Nashville and sign some stuff. You'll need to take in proof that you've made it through a detox clinic, the details of which are in there." I point at the envelope. "And proof that you've signed up for some psychiatric help, then it's all yours." I shrug. "And then you can, you know, have a good life. I hope."

"I don't want your filthy money."

Interesting how it only became dirty once I reeled off the conditions. "Why's it filthy?"

"Earning it by selling that face of yours. Like a whore."

A laugh explodes out of me. "That's ridiculous."

Even she laughs then.

I take a big breath. Then another. "You don't... so you don't like my music?"

"As sure as I was born, I *love* it," she yells as though she's a kid at a party and has been asked how she likes the cake.

My lips quirk in surprise, and her smile disappears.

She frowns at her hands, wringing them together. Slowly, she raises her head, pins me with a sober gaze that bores straight down into my gut and says, "I do. I love it. You're better than Elvis. Better than Kurt Cobain. I can't believe that I made something so beautiful."

Well, fuck. I hadn't expected that.

I try to speak, to say thank you, to say anything at all, but no sound comes out.

"What are you gonna do if that crazy bastard who made you comes looking for a hand-out some day? If he's still alive, which I doubt."

"My real father?" I laugh grimly. "Huh. How would he know I even exist? I'm sure rapists don't usually keep track of their progeny."

"All it'll take is one look at that fine mug of yours and I

reckon he'll know you're his. Keep splashing it all over every goddamn place like you're doing now and you'll soon find out if he's alive or not."

"Well, I ain't the one splashing it. That's other people, record companies and stuff, not me. Everywhere I go someone takes my photo whether I want them to or not. And if that guy is stupid enough to get in touch, I'll make sure his ass gets a pit-stop to a real basic room with bars on the door on his way to hell. I'd love nothing more than to see him go down for what he did to you."

Hand shaking, she picks up the cup and gulps away at it. Tears running down her face, she says, "And you think I ain't been a proper ma to you and, still, you've come here?"

"I don't care about that. Well, that's a lie. Of course I care. And there's no doubt you're a shit mother. But the money's there if you need it. I hope one day you'll realize you need to fucking *do* something about yourself. When that epiphany hits, call me. If you're prepared to get treatment, get some sanity, I can help."

"So you reckon you're a big shot now, South, because you got money? Someone who fixes things? *You'd* better realize that all that stuff you've got now is only because you look like that."

"That's bullshit. I don't believe that anymore. Like you said before, I can write songs. I've got people—friends and family—who care about me, and they're still gonna care about me in thirty years because it's real. We make each other feel good, and we share stories. Stories that connect us.

Stories that'll matter when we're old and no one gives a fuck about taking our photos anymore."

Rolling the bottle against her cheek, she hoots, fist thumping the table. Man, it's like some twisted ad for gin. Or maybe more like a cautionary A.A. ad.

I get up and stroll to the door, taking my time. After I open it, I reach above my head and grip the frame, digging my fingers into the lintel.

"And you know what? I think you do love me. It's your sickness that makes you think you don't, but I reckon you do. I've got a kid now, so I know how it is."

Rotten wood crumbling under my nails, I watch shock spread over her face, her papery skin pulling tight over gaunt features. "No matter how stupid you are, you get one look at that tiny person you helped make and you're gone. Forever. So you love me. I know it now. And I feel the same about you even after everything that you've said and done and not fucking done."

Now her mouth gapes like a black hole, her skeletal body folding in on itself.

It might be the last time I ever see her so, as a warning, I try to imprint the image on my brain. No matter how sad it will be to carry it with me always, I need to remember what closing myself off from love gets me. Nothing good.

"Make a start to get better and we can talk. Who knows, if you act like a human being again, I might even bring my daughter to meet you. Her name's Sanne, and she's a month old today."

Not waiting to see her reaction, I swing my hands down

and they smack into my sides, the sound making the cat arch its neck and blink at me in disgust. I pivot to face the sun. It shines on the path, making lacy patterns over the tunnel of trees in front of me.

I've always hated trees, anything that reminded me of the place where Mom was beaten and raped, where—like a scene from a horror movie—I was conceived in a lonely, dark forest, fathered by a lunatic. But after today, I reckon I'll be okay because the path ahead looks pretty bright.

Taking one last look over my shoulder at the woman huddled in the shadows, I decide I'll say it just one time. Maybe it will help her, because hearing those words has sure changed my life.

Short and sharp, I say, "I love you," and then walk into the light, the darkness disintegrating behind me.

My boots crunch over the dirt as I stomp through the messy garden to the car. I creak open the white sedan's door and fall into the seat, a stuffy heat enveloping me. That heat rushes out the sun roof as I push it up.

Then there's just the inner heat to deal with, waves of it rolling through my body. Years of screwed down emotion unraveling, coiling free and whipping around inside me.

A few minutes pass before I can lift my face out of my hands and stare through the windshield, seeing nothing but the wave on my tattoo.

The wave.

At last I know what it is. I drag my t-shirt sleeve up, revealing the white curling talons on my bicep, the stripy-blue water in the tube. It's love. The wave is love. First Mia and now Sanne.

It's love that I feared all along. Love that fascinated and terrified me.

I close my eyes and see a dark sea rise around me, silver and black, and I cover my ears as that massive wave comes for me. Like a lucid dream, I feel the rush of being lifted, then tossed, dumped and tumbled in icy water. I'm pummeled, helpless as a baby in the turbulence, my limbs ripping apart.

Throughout this strange hallucination, my brain works overtime. Thinking. Realizing. I'm such an idiot, because when I first met Mia and she knocked me into the sea, I should have known what to do. Years of surfing taught me you don't fight the wave, you don't thrash around swallowing water, trying to work out which way is up. That's death. To survive, you have to let go. Completely surrender.

But I battled my feelings, forgetting that the only choice is to relax and count, like keeping beats in a new song. The sooner you give in, the sooner the ocean spits you out.

A dog barks across the street, and I open my eyes. It's okay, because now I understand.

Finally, I get it.

What made me crazy was the very thing I'd wanted more than anything.

To love and be loved.

Well, now I've got both of those things and, as far as I can tell, I'm happier and saner than I've ever been. My mother, my father—they're hate and fear. And they're nothing to do with me. All I have to do is relax and keep going with the good stuff. Ride the wave. Forget the past.

It's easy.

I grab my phone off the dash and press buttons. She answers immediately. "Mia, I freaking did it!" I laugh. "It was easy. So fucking easy."

She laughs too. "Oh, South, that's so great! It went well then?"

"Yep. Instead of slaying the dragon, I tried to help her be happier. Shit! Never thought I'd do that, but it feels amazing."

"See how clever you are? Hate is never the answer. Are you coming home to us now?"

"Straight after the gig, I'll be on my way."

"Okay, I can't wait—"

"Mia?"

"Yeah?"

"Thank you for loving me and for giving me Sunny."

"Loving you is easy, South. Now hurry up and get home fast so I can show you just how well I can do it."

"Yes, ma'am." I fire up the car and step on the gas.

I'm going home.

EPILOGUE

SANNE

Sunbeam

Today, she is five. She's awake before the sun because she wants the guitar. The one that shines all yellow and gold just like him. Gold like his hair, his laugh, and his cuddle. So warm.

She screams, squeals loud and long, knowing he will come.

He always does.

For a few heartbeats she waits, watching the stars twirl in the mobile above her bed. She stretches out a chubby palm, wriggling her fingers. Today, because she is big, she'll touch one.

The door creaks open. The stars disappear, and he is all she can see.

"Hey, baby," he says, reaching for her. And there's the voice she loves. It's gold, too, like gooey honey.

She squeals at the sight of him. "Look at me! I'm big, aren't I?"

Laughing, he kisses her and lifts her up high.

"Wow, Sunny-bun you are *huge* today. What happened? Wait until Mom sees you. She's gonna pitch a fit. Probably won't even know who you are! Shall we see if we can trick her?"

Nodding, she pats his cheek, and then puts her fingers over his prince's smile.

He is hers.

"Happy Birthday!' he yells, and then blurts her belly, making her gasp for breath as she giggles.

"Love you. Love you. Love you," he says between kisses, and then holds her away again. "Hey, exactly how old are you today? About nine?"

"No, Daddy!"

"Are you *sure*? You look pretty big to me."

"You're silly!" She screams as he throws her under his arm and heads for the blue room.

Sanne is still hollering when he pushes the door open.

Her mom sits on the bed, looking funny because she's upside down. There's blue the same color as water and sky all around her, and her arms are stretched wide, waiting for a hug.

"Mia, look what I found in Sunny's bed. Do you have any idea what the heck it is?"

Upside down Mom drops her arms. Sanne is swung right way up and plonked onto the bed.

Mom's eyebrows lower. "Gee, I don't know. Hmm… Whatever it is, it's certainly big."

"Huh. I know. It can't be Sanne. It looks like a nine-year-old girl or maybe even a ten-year-old."

"Mommy, it's me! I'm five. And I *am* big."

All quiet, her Mom tilts her head to the side. "Oh! It *is* you, Sunny. You look so different! I thought maybe the fairies had swapped you out. Stolen you away from us. I'm so glad they didn't. Come here and let me squeeze you. Happy Birthday, baby girl! I love you so much."

Dad makes the bed bounce when he flops next to them, and then Sunny is wrapped tight. Their arms around her and around each other, make a circle.

They're laughing. They like to laugh a lot.

For a moment she lies unmoving between them and then wriggles so she looks up at them.

Smiling at each other, their faces are close. Mom kisses him, and he sighs real big. The belly-baby is in the way but Sanne stays still, cuddled up in warmth.

Dad puts a hand on Mom's face and the other one on her big stomach, still smiling and kissing her. It goes on too long and, even though the sight of them makes her insides glow warm, Sanne gets restless and looks around the room.

Over by the window rests a shiny, purple thing. There's a big bow on it, and it's shaped like his guitar case but smaller.

She pushes up between them. "Mine?" she asks, pointing at it.

"*Yeah,*" he says, and trips as he lurches off the bed and takes big steps toward the package. He puts it on the red covers and he and Mom sit forward, holding hands, and watch Sanne tear at the paper.

"Let me help you there, Miss Fumblefingers." He pulls the wrapping away.

"Sunny," she says, tracing the bright-yellow letters of her name on the purple case. "Gold!" she yells, and they laugh.

"Yep, gold." His phone buzzes. "Damn. Who's that?"

Mom leans and looks. "Lane."

"Man, at this time of the morning? He can wait."

He takes the guitar out of the case and places it gently in Sanne's lap. She smiles at it and puts her hands all over the wood. It's smooth. And it's all hers.

"Do you like it?" he asks.

"Yes!"

Mom laughs. "What do you say, then?"

Sanne says thank you and slops kisses on their cheeks. Then she sits back and makes a bad sound over the strings. Twang. She covers her ears. Then does it again, fast this time. Twang. Twang. Twang. Then faster.

"Your turn, Dad." She holds it out to him, so he'll make it talk to her, and he takes it.

His fingers move quick. She watches. Soon he'll teach her how to do it the same as he can.

A jangly, happy sound fills the room, and her insides tingle. He starts to sing and it's her song.

Sunbeam.

Sunbeam.

Sunbeam.

They sing it together, all three of them.

Sanne sings loudly because she wants to be sure the baby will hear it. He likes this one a lot. She's sure of it.

When her song is finished, Dad takes a breath and the sound changes. The notes go up and down like a wave. She watches them smile at each other and tries to imagine what this song will be called. It's gonna be a good one.

She hears a word in her head and it keeps ringing like a bell. Over and over.

She needs to tell him the word, so he can start the story that goes with the baby's song. Her brother will have his own birthday soon. But he'll only be zero. Then one day old. Then two. It will be a long time until he gets a guitar of his own, but while he waits, Sanne will teach him on hers.

When she touches Dad's arm, he looks at her, and she whispers, "Silver. Silver. Silver."

He smiles. "Yes, Sunny. You're right."

And South starts singing.

TEMPTING IVY PREVIEW

Nico

To celebrate her sixteenth birthday, my mom visited a Roma fortune-teller who lived in the ruins of a decaying castle, a day's train ride from her Hungarian village.

With her heart beating wildly, Mom listened to a prophecy about a stubborn guy who didn't believe in love and his fated mate.

Many years later when I was twenty-four, and it was almost too late, she handed me a piece of paper and made me read it, and I found out that pigheaded idiot was me.

My mother had transcribed the Romani woman's exact words to her, and this is what they said...

Listen closely sweetheart, for what I tell you shall come to pass. You are young, but you must never forget.

I see three important men in your destiny, but only one who truly matters.

The dark farmer's love is steady and strong, but you will not want his goodness.

The blond voyager's beauty is blinding, and you will follow him far from home. This stealer of joy will crush you, but he will not take your heart. You will keep it safe for the third man. And for him, you must wait a long time.

Your only child is the one you see clearly, and you'll name him after your grandfather, Nicholai.

Your boy has a difficult path, for he refuses to acknowledge the truth. He believes only in beats of wild music and discards tender pulses of the heart, locking his soul up tight.

The woman with the key to opening it is older. Yes. So very much older than he.

One day your son will surrender. One day he will understand—only love has the purest pulse and a beat that is ever true. Far truer than any song. Hers are the lyrics he must follow, for the cup of her happiness is his to drink.

Her happiness is his. You understand?

That day, he will need your honesty, and you must tell him the truth about his father.

Because your son is the man who matters.

Your son, Zsofia, is the one.

If only I'd been ready to hear those words sooner, long before I met Ivy, then I might have been smarter and not acted like a jackass and fucked it up. But that's what I do best —fuck things up. And I can write some kickass songs, too.

Yeah, I'm pretty good at that.

Chapter 1

Ivy

"So, do you want a tequila sunrise?" I yell over the thump and crash of the band. I gaze around at the sweaty crowd packed into our favorite dive bar, Silva's, then glance back at my friend Mia. She looks a little blurry.

"No, thanks!" she says. "I plan to stay sober."

Beams of light flash purple and white over the enraptured faces pointed at the stage. The hypnotic beat makes my stomach churn, and everything appears in soft focus, like a weird dream. Or a nightmare.

I stand swaying gently in the center of the audience, bass pounding through my chest, the bodies pressed tight against me keeping me upright.

"Shit," I yell in Mia's ear. "I don't know how this has happened, but I think I'm very, very drunk."

Scowling, Mia shakes her head at me. Long, platinum pigtails bounce around her cute pixie face. "Hmm. I wonder if it might have something to do with the five cocktails you've guzzled?" she grouches. "That's why I'm staying sober tonight. Someone has to look after you."

"I'm fine," I lie, making a mental note to keep the slurring to a minimum.

"Listen, Ivy, I've known you almost three years now, and I've never once seen you wasted before. This is disturbing. And, please, what's with the tequila sunrises? You don't even like orange juice."

"That's true. It has been known to make me... um... make me..." I'd better not finish that sentence. If I do, she might not want to stand next to me.

Mia's frown grows as she latches onto my crimson velvet tunic, pulling me close so she can yell in my ear. "Make you what, Ivy?"

Not telling. Not telling.

I point at the band rocking out on stage. "Wow these guys are great." I may be trying to divert her attention, but I'm not lying.

The four-piece garage rock outfit is killing it up there with their heavy, melodic riffs, an intoxicating beat, and about the sexiest looking guy I've ever seen growling out emotional vocals. His longish messy hair, dark-angel scowl, and bulging tattooed biceps are doing exciting things to my insides.

I'd love a closer look at him. And also for my vision to be working a little better. I hate alcohol.

Not falling for my distraction, Mia shakes me hard. "Orange juice makes you what?"

"Vomit."

"Wrong answer." She reaches for my glass. "Gimme that."

Pouting, I bat her hand away. "No. I haven't finished it yet. What's happened to you tonight? You're meant to be the fun one."

"Ivy, you're having enough fun for both of us. If I had any idea that you'd start to sound like a toddler, I'd never have suggested alcohol might help you feel better. This is freaking me out. You're normally so sensible."

She's right. Getting smashed really isn't my scene. My

mom—who is a total embarrassment—boozed her way through my childhood, snoozing during ballet performances and school plays. Any event a normal parent would be wide awake for and snapping thousands of photos, she was there snoring loudly in the back row. Or trying to sleep with my male teachers. Even the married ones.

As a result, I'm deeply scarred and spend too much time worrying about what people think of me. It's an old habit. And growing up with a drunk for a mother, I tend to steer clear of alcohol. No matter how bad things get. But at work today, I cracked.

I'm an artist, and I do mixed media portraits of people with tragic backstories—paintings with all sorts of weird things stuck on them. In two months, I'm having my first exhibition at the art gallery where I work.

Honestly, I love Mad Wolf Gallery and adore hanging out with all the other artists employed there. It's the owner, Kendra, who increases my blood pressure and leads me to drink. Today, she looked at my exhibition folio, wrinkled her elegant nose and informed me that I had a lot of work to do if I didn't want to get laughed out of town. Nice one boss. Impressive way to mentor and nurture your artists.

Oh, who cares about Kendra? Another tequila sunrise and I'll forget she even exists.

I'm all set to complain to Mia that I'm the mature one here tonight, tell her she should loosen up, act her youthful age and have some fun when the music disappears, replaced by a screech of feedback.

The sizzling-hot singer yells through the mic, "We're

Granddad. And you guys are awesome. Be bad and have a great night."

I wouldn't mind being bad with him.

Disappointment settles in my chest as the band leaves the stage. I was hoping to stare at that guy a lot longer and continue my discreet drooling.

As I swing around to push my way to the bar, orange juice swishes in my belly.

"I need some air," I say, clutching Mia's arm. "I'll be right back."

"I'll come with you, so you don't get lost and stumble all the way down to the foreshore and drown. I can't have that on my conscience, can I?"

"Stay there. Honestly, I don't feel sick at all, just a little fuzzy. I'm only going out into the alley to star gaze for a minute. I'll be back before you know it. Promise."

Her mouth opens, a protest working its way out. "Ivy—"

"Oh look, is that Up Void getting ready on stage?" I yell, cutting her off.

To say she's obsessed with the next band's singer is like stating that dogs quite like being patted, or cats are okay with having their ears scratched—the understatement of the century.

Desperate for a glimpse of her crush, she scrutinizes the roadies fiddling with leads and amps.

With Mia suitably distracted, I tug the hem of my dress lower and push politely through the squeeze.

A classic White Stripes' tune distorts through the speakers, battling to be heard over all the excited chatter and laughter. I feel jealous of the hyped-up crowd and wish I was madly anticipating the next band, too. But I'm not.

I'd rather be tucked up in bed with my Kindle like the semi-old person I am. When did I become so boring?

Heaving a big sigh, I push open the back door. I'll get a big dose of fresh air, then head home. I think I've had all the excitement I can handle for one night.

Which, believe me, isn't much.

Chapter 2

Nico

I have no idea why I'm thinking about the dumb prophecy my mom's been going on about for years while I stand on stage after the gig packing up gear. The one concerning my alleged fated mate. It's ridiculous. Whenever she brings it up, I just laugh my head off and go about my business, because I'll never do something stupid like fall for a girl.

Ever.

I know for a fact there's no such thing as true love. Heartbreak and disappointment—that's about all there is.

Why else has Mom cried for my shit-for-brains father every night since he ran out on us when I was a baby?

She's had a hard life, a Hungarian village girl bringing up her bratty kid all alone in America, working three jobs to keep us alive. The last thing I want to do is make her unhappy, but as I help roadies push amps around and unplug leads, lyrics rattle around my brain about lying deadbeat losers and broken-hearted single mothers.

I'm turning Mom's pain into a song. And I can't help wondering, does that make me an asshole?

"Hey, asshole. Get a move on. Up Void's roadies are busting my balls to get our shit off the stage."

Okay, so maybe our guitarist Linc thinks I'm an ass. But he hates everyone, so I'm not too worried. And I reckon there'd be at least a few girls who agree with him. I'm not known for being a sweetheart to chicks. If I'm too nice, they get ideas and try to insert themselves into my life. And who wants to be saddled with a girlfriend? Not me right now. And probably not ever.

"Your balls can relax, man," I say as I drop wound-up guitar leads into a bag while scanning the crowd for the hot redhead I had my eye on during the show. I've got a thing for lanky brunettes, so I was amazed to find myself seeking out the curvy girl again and again during our set. Seems like she's missing in action now though. I fucking hope she hasn't already left.

"I'm done, Linc. Just gotta drop this last load in the van. Line up a whiskey for me at the bar."

His cynical gaze tracks over the buzzing crowd. "This is gonna be one of the last times Up Void play a fuckhole joint like this. They're already too big for it."

"It's good we got the support again. The crowd went apeshit for us."

"Yeah, well it sure helps that you're tight with South. Keep on sucking up to their singer, won't you?" Linc flicks spikes of black hair out of his face and jumps off the low stage into the crowd.

After zipping up four duffel bags crammed with gear, I fist bump an Up Void roadie and plunge down into the sea of drunk folk.

I make slow progress because people want to talk, so by the time I reach the rear exit, my arms are heavy with exhaustion. Finally, I push open the metal door that leads to the alleyway, a blast of cool air waking me up.

Rain splatters my face as I open the van door and throw the bags on a messy mountain of band equipment. There's a loud crash and a yelp behind me. I whip my head around and see a girl bent over, giggling as she picks up a trash can she's obviously collided with. Very nice ass.

When she notices me, she straightens up, covering her mouth with one hand and waving at me with the other.

Awesome. It's the chick I've been staring at all night. "Oh, it's you," I say as I head straight for her.

She stiffens and looks behind her. "Who?"

"You. The hot redhead."

She covers her mouth again and laughs, patting her mane of flaming locks like she's checking it's still attached to her head. "You seem very flamil... flamiliar... whoops." She snorts loudly. "Shit. I can't talk properly. I meant to say familiar. Do I know you?" Her voice is low, a little husky, and a lot sexy.

"No. But you should," I say. Yeah. I'd definitely like to get to know her a little—find out just how soft her skin is. And being a redhead, is she covered in freckles? I'm close enough to touch her now and, fuck, she looks even hotter than she did from the stage.

She sways against the brick wall, dark-red dress inching up her creamy thighs. She tugs it down. I watch her fingers smooth over her skin.

"What exactly do you mean by know you? As in the biblical sense?" She slaps her palms over her mouth like she can't believe what came out of it.

I laugh. "Sure. Yeah. What a good idea."

She has a heart-shaped face and sweet, doll-like features. The deep bow in her upper lip gives her a permanent pout. It does something to my gut. And my dick.

"I don't know why I said that. I'm not normally so—"

"Drunk?"

She nods enthusiastically. Like she's impressed by how observant I am. It's not that hard to tell she's three sheets to the wind. Or maybe a whole laundry basket full.

Her big eyes get even rounder. I can't tell what color they are out here, but I'm thinking something light. Maybe blue or green like mine are.

The back of her hand slaps my chest hard. "Oh, yeah! I do know you. You're that singer from inside. The cool band guy."

Shit. She is a bit drunk. But still very cute. And exactly what I need in my bed tonight.

"Yeah. That's right. I sing and play rhythm guitar."

"I really liked Granddad. You're great." She lists dangerously to the left, then rights herself. "What was I saying? Oh… Granddad. Yep. Fantastic."

I glance at the back door of the club, expecting to see some old dude doddering out. "So, whose granddad is great?"

"Your band. You've got really good… um… songs."

"Thanks. But what about the granddad?"

A frown crinkles her forehead. "Your band, silly."

I lean closer, get a whiff of her scent. Something sweet like oranges. "What about my band?"

"Aren't you called Granddad?"

I try not to crack up, but fuck that's funny. My laugh echoes loudly around the alley. "We're called Burntbad, not Granddad. Man, I really should learn to speak more clearly through that mic, huh? So I'm guessing you came to see Up Void tonight, not us."

"That is unfortunately true. You see, my friend is madly in love with their singer," she says, looking guilty. "That what's-his-name. You know that blond guy?"

"South. Yeah. Figures. Who isn't into him?"

She presses her palm back on my chest and leans in. "Sorry. We had no idea who the support band would be tonight. But, don't worry, I'm sure there are lots of people who're in love with you too."

I bite back a grin as her eyes widen comically. "You're very pretty in a mean bad-boy kind of way."

Shit. That's the first time anyone's used the word pretty to describe me. Hot. Bad. Prick. They're the kind of words I'm used to hearing from girls. And I've definitely heard mean a time or two before.

Glancing down at her hand clutching my t-shirt, I step forward. She steps back until she's pressed against the wall.

The brick right next to her head feels rough as I press my palm into it and dip my head close.

"So, I'm pretty, huh? And also mean? Sounds a bit like you're trying to insult me."

"Well, there's hardly any light out here, but I'm fairly sure you're gorgeous. Also, you look sort of grumpy. In a hot way, of course."

Huh. Good answer.

"Why can't I quit talking?" she asks.

"I don't know. Want me to try and help you stop?"

"Please. If you've got any ideas, I'd love to hear them."

"I'll have to show you. Just let me know if it's not helping and I'll stop right away."

As her frown deepens, my mouth takes hers, and I breathe in her confusion, drink down her shocked gasp and ragged sigh as she melts against me.

The traffic noises disappear. I no longer feel the rain falling on my skin. Instead, internal sounds rage, rocking and rolling and hammering at my skull. My gut tightens, a heavy bassline pounding through it. Music moves my breath in and out of my lungs.

Words flash. Urgent. Crazy ones.

Images flicker of flames and burning pyres. Hot skin flecked with sweat. Red hair curling. Sweet lips smiling. And over the Friday night street sounds, horns blaring, the sound-check inside the club, three words pulse through my blood.

Need.

And take.

And more.

Fuck, I'm hard as granite.

I taste alcohol.

Sharp.

Something fruity.

Sweet.

And her.

More sweetness.

Her fingers dig into my arm. I cradle her jaw, angle her face, and press deeper. This is insane. I fuck enough girls to not react like a school kid ready to detonate at first base. So why are my hands shaking? Why do I want inside this girl so badly?

Somewhere back on planet earth the hinges of a metal door screech. Someone laughs. A guy. It's deep, gravelly, loud. And it's fucking Linc.

"Oh, hey! Sorry, man," he says. "Didn't realize you were engaged in important business out here."

Shooting him daggers, I say, "And now you do. So why the fuck are you still standing there flapping your mouth?"

He laughs again, probably because I'm huffing words out like I've just sprinted around the block five times. And then he salutes me and kindly does as requested and fucks off.

Now. Back to those juicy lips.

"Who was that?" hot-redhead whispers.

"No one. Just our lead guitarist. Linc."

"Oh. He seems nice. Kiss me again?"

"Sure." The rain pelts down harder, drenching my hair as I stare at her lopsided smile. "I like the way you think." Shit my voice is raspy as fuck. Must be all the yelling I did onstage. "But do you realize we're getting soaked out here?"

I wonder if she's wet where it really counts, beneath her clothes. Because I am ready to rock, and it's taking super-human control not to slide her velvety dress up and find out.

"We should go inside," I say. Because if we don't, any second now, I'm gonna try and fuck her right here in the alleyway. And even though it's not a good idea, I can't seem to get the thought of doing it out of my head.

Sure I've fucked girls rough against dirty walls before, but this one's drunk, and I'm mostly sober. I'm not a big enough of an asshole to take advantage of the situation. No matter what Linc thinks.

A cat yowls and we watch it scramble past, chased by an even scrawnier looking dog. We smile at each other for way too long, but for some reason, I don't want to stop.

"Come inside with me," I say, breaking the spell. "The band's got a tab at the bar. I'll get you a drink." Maybe that's a bad idea, too, because I think she's had more than enough. But, then again, who am I to judge?

Usually, I don't mind getting wasted. Just not tonight. A support with Up Void is a serious opportunity. Those guys are going places fast. There's no way I'd risk fucking it up.

"The rain isn't bothering me at all." She drags my head down. "So, I'd like more kissing, please. You have such nice lips. So soft."

I groan, my breathing instantly turning ragged. This girl makes my blood wildfire-hot.

My tongue strokes slowly as I kiss her, trying to keep the

pace easy. But, man, I want to do the exact opposite. Forget my conscience. Be the asshole I was born to be—my father's son—and kiss her hard. Fuck her hard. Right here. Right now. But, instead of charging ahead, I pull back and start talking.

"What's your name?" I ask, my fingers playing through her silky hair.

"Ivy."

"Ivy, huh? It's nice. Old fashioned." I consider her sulky lips, the dip in her pointed chin. "But, I don't know, Ivy has an edge. It sounds dangerous, and you don't feel that way. Maybe Ruby would suit you better—with all this red hair." I curl a flaming strand of it around my fingers.

"How would you know whether I'm edgy or not?" Scowling, she untangles my fingers and shoves my hand away. "For all you know, I could be just as dangerous to get close to as the plant. Maybe that's exactly why my mom called me Ivy, Mister Cocky Britches. Because I'm poisonous."

I choke on a laugh. "Did you just call my pants cocky?" I sense some parental-issues rising, so I'm pretty keen to change the subject. "In case you're interested, my name's Nico. You live around here?"

"Not far. I work at Mad Wolf Gallery, a few blocks away next to the warehouse apartments. Mia and I come here sometimes after work because it's so close."

"Oh, you mean the gallery near the beach?"

She nods.

"My friend Angelo lives in that posh warehouse complex in the same street. I used to have some other friends who lived there too. But they're out on a farm now, busy being do-gooders. But you've probably seen Angelo around. Good looking rasta dude?"

Ivy scrunches up her face. "I think I've seen him. My boss, Kendra, probably knows him. She's the reason I'm in this pathetic state tonight."

"A little buzzed? Why, what did she do to you?"

"She was her usual intimidating, patronizing self. And she told me my work would never be ready for the exhibition I've got coming up in a couple of months. Called my paintings juvenile. And try hard."

"She sounds like a bitch. So, you're an artist?"

"Uh-huh. I do mixed media. Collages. That kind of thing."

"I don't really know what that is, but I'd like to hear about it. Hey, I've got an apartment out past the old brewery, where the scenery gets a little seedier. It's cool though. You should come and check it out."

She gives me a narrowed side-look, so I rub her hip softly, staring at her lips, and say, "We can finish what we started here. How about we catch a cab to my place right now?"

With her gaze roving over my face, she chews on her thumbnail. My chest tightens while I wait for her to decide.

Say yes. Say yes.

"Okay, but you'll have to meet my friend Mia first. She'll probably want to photograph you and put your number in her contacts. Maybe even take a video of you answering a few personal questions."

I laugh and lean closer, brush my lips over hers.

For a few outstanding seconds, she kisses me, and then breaks away. "I'm serious, Mister Rock Star."

"Fine." I pull back so she can see my eyes, to show her that I mean no harm. I only want to make her feel good. "I'm okay with that. But I need to get closer to you, Ivy. I'm writing songs right here, right now from just touching you. What's gonna happen when I'm inside you? I'm thinking full-blown symphonies. Angels and trumpets."

She huffs a laugh. "Boy. No wonder you musicians have legions of girls following you around everywhere."

"Yeah? Well, tonight, the only person I want to follow me is you."

She gets a funny look on her face, like she's trying to figure out a problem—me—I guess.

"Okay. Let's go for it, then. I hardly ever do anything spontaneous. I'm usually all about the planning. Tonight I'm gonna change that up."

She tugs her dress down again, grabs my hand, and tows me toward the club.

All signs of post-gig fatigue have disappeared.

Ivy's got me firing on all cylinders.

End of Tempting Ivy excerpt.

ALSO BY AMY J. HEART

Books in the Damaged Souls Golden Hearts series:

Finding E, a heartbreaking prequel to L and Eden's story.

A street boy who doesn't know what love is. One night, one girl changes everything.

Loving L, the full-length end to L and Eden's story. Can be read as a standalone.

Ex-street boy turned male model, L, has never touched a girl before. Then in one crazy hour, sweet Eden blows his mind. Blackmail. Murder. And love.

Tempting Ivy, Ivy and Nico's story.

A sexy rocker. An older woman. Fated love was never meant to be easy.

And if you like enemies to lovers stories about cursed fae princes falling for feisty mortal girls, check out my paranormal romance series, the Black Blood Fae.

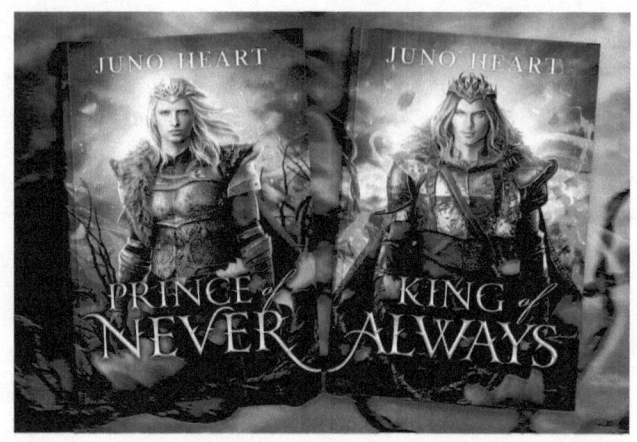

For general release news and deal alerts, visit my website and sign up to my newsletter.

ABOUT THE AUTHOR

Thank you for reading Saving South! If you enjoyed it, please read on for information about other books in the series.

A massive thank you to my grammar guru/slayer, Joanne, for spending all that time with South and Mia! You're amazing. Those red comments of yours made me laugh so hard—and then make things *so* much better... thank you for everything!

Huge thanks to Anna, Ken, Lorna, and Terry for spending time reading it and giving such mind-blowing feedback. It was soooo helpful. Thank you!

Gigantic hugs to Aubrey for the gorgeous cover!

I write about broken, golden-hearted guys and gals who, no matter the odds, manage to find redemption together.

When I'm not obsessing over damaged heroes, I'm listening to indie music, drinking nuclear-strength coffee, talking to my overly adventurous cat, extremely naughty dog, or very happy chooks.

And sometimes even my family!

When all of the above won't speak to me, I stomp off and write broken-hero contemporary romances or enemies-to-lovers paranormal romances, starring cursed fae princes and their human fated mates under a fun pen name.

If you'd like to stay in touch:
Sign up to my Newsletter
amyjheart.com
amyheartromance@gmail.com

www.ingramcontent.com/pod-product-compliance
Lightning Source LLC
Chambersburg PA
CBHW022018110726
47901CB00006B/1572